MW01485466

FIGHT TO FLY

By

Jerry Houston

PublishAmerica
Baltimore

ISBN: 1-4137-8851-3
PUBLISHED BY PUBLISHAMERICA, LLLP
www.publishamerica.com
Baltimore

Printed in the United States of America

For United States Navy Commander Carl "Ensign" Jensen

(1934-2002)

A beacon, an authority, a learned friend

Acknowledgments

This project gave new meaning to hit-and-miss. Dale Marshall toiled throughout the journey—including detours. Writers' heaven would be filled with Dale Marshalls. J.B. Souder, Rick Webb, Jack Finley, Richard Bradford, and my most esteemed aviation sage, Carl Jensen, snapped my garters when they discovered sentences—or paragraphs, or even chapters—where I'd obviously dozed. Sarah Hall, Shelly McCormack, Cindy Houston, and my life-long partner and wife, Shirley, read these snail-bred pages till their eyes hurt. With hand over heart, I extol their generosity, because a first novel attempt reeks of egomaniac selfishness. Guilty as charged, your honor, yet the aforementioned hung in. Such debts remain lifelong. Jason Dial, Dave Palmer, and J.T. McMahon lent encouragement when the clouds hung darkest. Even so, *Fight to Fly* would never have flown without Kathryn Fanning. Her professionalism provided the required lift.

Author's Note

All characters in this novel, other than the well-known historical figures mentioned, are fictional. Many people served in the United States Navy during the Korean *police action* and the Vietnam *conflict*. Any resemblance to any other person, either living or dead, is entirely coincidental. As for the flying incidents depicted . . . well, the oceans and the skies have been around a while. So I suppose that they could've happened, somewhere, sometime, to somebody.

Table of Contents

Chapter 1—SNOWBIRD

Around midnight 24 February 1966, an arctic front moaned across southeastern Nebraska's nighttime plain. On a grass landing strip the next morning, frozen mud and pencil-stiff straw crunched beneath Paxton Langford's flight boots. Pax swung his arms back and forth in front of himself, stretched while facing where the sun should have been, shivered, and watched his exhalations crystallize. The U.S. Navy lieutenant's wispy breaths and midmorning thoughts marched lockstep: *Nebraska...winters... bedamned!*

His glance at the low, fast-moving, broken-stratus layer found no blue sky, but he caught glimpses of higher clouds through the lower scud. Visibility between layers appeared good. Meteorology predicted snow—lots of it.

And trying to file a flight plan by telephone from the grass strip near Doane College wasn't working. After thirty minutes of grinding his teeth, listening to busy signals while trying to reach the Lincoln duty desk, Pax hastened to get airborne.

Yep, no good deed goes unpunished, he mused. *I shouldn't have stayed yesterday to fly that last applicant.*

"Shit!" he said and shook his head.

I'll take off, get above that stratus layer, call Lincoln on the radio, and file a flight plan . . . if I can still find a hole to climb through.

As he lowered himself into the front cockpit of the blue and gold navy trainer, a black Chevrolet coupe skidded to a stop directly in front of his propeller. "What the hell?" he said.

A curly-headed brunette waved, ran around the left wing, and climbed up beside the cockpit. Her words tumbled out: "I hope I'm not too late; tell me I'm not too late."

"For what?"

"They said you're flying to Olathe today." She rested a hand on her bosom. "And I have to go with you."

Pax shook his head, but his mind raced.

Can she be that gorgeous? Chalk-white teeth, satin skin, and . . . and she smells like . . . like cinnamon?

"Sorry. Not possible. You're civilian; this is a navy plane." He felt the freshening wind riffle his straight, black hair.

"But you flew civilian students from the college yesterday." She put her hand on his arm. "I have a family emergency in Olathe. Isn't there a form, a liability release, I can sign to make it right? I'm begging you. I'll do anything; I mean anything." She crossed two fingers by each of her cheeks, squinted crystalline-green eyes at the frowning lieutenant, blinked rapidly, and flashed a smile.

"Even if I could stretch the rules, with you signing a release form, I can't wait. I'm leaving right now; weather's closing in. Sorry."

"No problem; I'm ready. Let's go."

"What about your car?"

"My roommate will pick it up later. I'll move it over by the fence and be right back." She stepped away, but hesitated and looked again at Pax. "I'm Sally Banks, Lieutenant; I love you for it." Sally leaned over, brushed his cheek with her lips, and scrambled off the wing.

Pax continued shaking his head. "Nice question about the car, idiot."

I'm screwed . . . well, maybe . . . with a little luck. Anyway, how'd I get in this mess?

After moving the car, Sally jogged to the airplane carrying a small nylon tote as she pulled on an additional sweater—a green one, matching her slacks. Pax, in an orange flight suit and standing stone-faced on the wing, thrust a paper at her. "Sign this at the 'X'; I'll complete it in the air. You'll have to hold that little bag in your lap. Get in, and I'll fasten your straps."

He buckled and snugged her parachute straps, tightened her seat belt and shoulder harness, and pointed out a barf-bag in the map compartment. "But you won't need it. Keep your stuff away from the control stick when I take off and land."

Pax felt a familiar stimulation before he'd secured the rear cockpit. Her pert smile, the contrast of nylon rubbing against cashmere, and the cinnamon smell flooded his consciousness with gymnastic possibilities.

But it'd be hard to do in a cockpit . . . and the way this day's runnin' she can probably read my mind.

"As a bare minimum, Miss, this will cost you a dinner."

"Done," she said and thrust out her right hand. He shook it, slid the rear canopy forward, locked it shut, and forced his attention to the more immediate problem: the low stratus layer had become a solid overcast.

I'll have to chase north, maybe as far as Lincoln, finding a hole.

Pax talked himself through the engine start and taxied to the north end of the strip. He passed a thumbs-up to—*what was her name? Sally?*—in one of his rearview mirrors. She raised a thumb right back and gave him a wink. Surprised at her savvy, he shoved the throttle forward.

Cloud bottoms stopped Pax's climb at eight hundred feet, but halfway to Lincoln he found a small hole, climbed through it, turned to the southeast, and thumbed the transmit button: "Lincoln Metro, Lincoln Metro, Navy Four Zero One, over. . . ." No response. Pax pushed the throttle-grip button harder and repeated—much louder this time—"Lincoln Metro, Lincoln Metro, Navy Four Zero One, over. . . ." Nothing.

Maybe higher altitude will help.

He climbed through a second stratus layer and leveled at seven thousand feet. Clouds above and clouds below, both solid layers now, squeezed in on the plane and darkened the sky. Pax turned on the external lights and cranked up the instrument panel rheostat.

A southeast heading's my best guesstimate to Navy Olathe.

Pax rechecked the radio frequency; he'd set it correctly. "Lincoln Metro, Navy Four Zero One. . . ."

Dammit! Come on, turkeys. The weather guessers are probably drinking coffee and telling jokes in the gedunk.

He turned the airplane a few degrees and climbed toward a lighter area—*almost a hole*—that he popped through, to find yet another darkening layer close above. He reset his radio's frequency. "Lincoln Tower, Lincoln Tower, Navy Four Zero One, over. . . ." Nothing. "Lincoln Tower, Four Zero One, over. . . ." Nothing.

Murphy's Law: what can go wrong will go wrong.

With a full-blown sigh, from disgust and a growing apprehension, he dialed the emergency frequency. "Lincoln Tower, Lincoln Tower, Navy Four Zero One, on Guard, over. . . . Lincoln Tower, Navy Four Zero One on Guard frequency. How do you read? Over. . . ."

I can hear my own transmissions; they sound normal, but nobody's answering.

He knew many reasons for one radio station's not responding, but when the second one remained mute—even to a Guard transmission—a coppery taste skittered across his tongue.

He rechecked the OMNI. It still had Lincoln OMNI station's frequency set. Nothing there. He could hear no Morse code identifiers, nor did the searching pointer interrupt its lazy, clockwise swing.

Maybe Lincoln's had an electrical failure . . . but I know better. So much for Lincoln.

He removed his headphone and lip-mike and stuffed them into a map pocket.

Now what? If my radio and nav-gear have shot craps, what's next?

Between two solid layers at nine thousand feet, thick snow reduced visibility. Pax couldn't see beyond the wingtips; between-layer space became history. He concentrated on maintaining his altitude, 130-knots, and a constant magnetic heading of one-four-zero degrees, that—*flight gods willing*—should take them to Olathe. He glanced up at a mirror on his canopy's forward edge.

"How're we doing?" she yelled.

"Fine," he lied and returned her unsuspecting smile.

I've stepped in over my head this time, and with an illegal passenger. Not bad enough to jeopardize myself, the airplane, and any unfortunates on the ground, I had to gather up a beauty queen.

Pax's thumb measurements across a sectional map added to one hundred and seventy miles.

Seventy-five minutes from takeoff should put us near Navy Olathe, depending on the frigging wind. The single consolation: we're in uncontrolled airspace; odds are no other idiot will be lurching along in-the-blind, crossing our flight path. So for better or worse—because I can't think of a better plan—we'll continue toward the navy airport at Olathe with no radio, no nav-gear, and no idea of destination weather. And most dangerous, we aren't legal to be in, much less descend through, this solid cloud mass.

"Do we have a heater?" she yelled.

Her voice startled him. He looked in the mirror and could see her breath. He also noted ice crystals forming inside the Plexiglas canopy.

"Sorry," he said and adjusted the cockpit heater. He also checked the Pitot tube heat, noted the engine temperature, and pulled the CARB-HT handle.

What the hell do I remember about carburetor heat from ten years ago in Pensacola?

"It's snowing hard," she yelled. "How's the Olathe weather?"

He looked up at her in the mirror. "I don't know yet. We'll find out when we get closer."

After running a gloved finger along their path on the chart, Pax picked an

OMNI station and dialed in its frequency. But his bad luck held; as with the Lincoln station, he got nothing.

What'll I do at Olathe? Worst case: I'll get there in the clouds, without a radio and without nav-gear. For starters, I can't stay at nine thousand feet; I'll have to start down early enough to be below the clouds when I get there. What I need to know is where "there" is and at what altitude the cloud bottoms are . . . if there are any bottoms.

He sucked a deep breath and fought rising bile.

What are the odds we'll be near Olathe at my estimated time of arrival, since I know neither the wind's speed nor direction, nor do I have a piss-whiskered guess at where—or if—we got on track?

Turbulence buffeted the airplane. Its engine's whine varied pitch with each rise or fall—a deeper, straining thrum with more Gs; with fewer, a higher, faster-sounding howl. Snow became thicker and an ice "bumper" grew along the wings' leading edges.

She smiled at him in the mirror; he smiled back.

As if she has a clue. Okay, what's an acceptable degree of error in my figures? If I descend to a reasonable altitude—whatever that might be—by the time I anticipate being at Olathe, how close to the air station might I expect to be? Five miles? Ten? Fifteen? Who knows? I'll settle on ten miles, not a comforting thought, but a starting point.

Between spaced scans of the flight instruments, Pax stole glances at his Navy Olathe approach schematic. The little map depicted obstruction-tops within twenty-five miles of the airfield. There weren't many, and they were relatively low, lower than he wanted to descend without seeing the ground.

After forty-five minutes of bouncing through thick snow and dreading telling gorgeous in the back seat that she'd hitched a ride with an idiot, a flicker caught his eye.

What moved?

It took two quick circuits of the instruments before he realized the OMNI needle had stopped swinging. He jammed his headset on, held his breath, let out a long sigh, and smiled at the three-letter identifier. Despite being in Morse code, it sounded like angels' singing to Pax.

The quivering OMNI needle pointed to a station north of Kansas City, fifteen degrees left of the airplane's nose.

About where it should be. It's not Olathe, but it's something. At least I know our bearing from that particular station. The needle's moving farther left, back toward the wing. We're close to the station. When it points directly at the wingtip, I'll veer right and descend toward what I hope is Olathe.

Pax dialed in the Navy Olathe homing beacon on his radio and, once again, held his breath. Nothing. He dialed in Olathe control tower's frequency, pushed a headphone tight against an ear, and transmitted: "Olathe Tower, Olathe Tower, Marine One One One, radio check, over. . . . Olathe Tower, Olathe Tower, Marine One One One, radio check, over. . . ." Nothing.

Dammit! What's wrong with this radio? Anyway, so much for deception. I'll keep monitoring their frequency. Besides, I'd rather not contact the field until I know what their weather is; if it's below landing minimums, I'll have a problem.

He laughed aloud at his bassackwards thinking and the convoluted situation he'd gotten himself and gorgeous into—*gallows humor at its finest.*

She talked at him in the mirror. He removed the headset. "What's so funny?" she asked.

"I'll tell you when we get on the ground. We're about to start down."

"How's the weather?"

"They couldn't tell me."

She wrinkled her brow. "You wouldn't hurt me, would you?"

"Not on purpose."

And God knows I mean it.

Pax looked away from the mirror and put his headset back on.

Good luck on your first no radio, no nav-gear, and no weather knowledge instrument approach, you fuckin' idiot.

The pressured plea slipped past his lips: "Off your ass, Saint Jude; I need help."

He reduced throttle a couple of inches and trimmed the nose down a few degrees. The unwinding altimeter reminded Pax that his last barometer setting came from Lincoln, three days before. For convenience he'd been dialing in sea-level for airstrip altitude near Doane College.

Turbulence increased as they descended through thickening clouds and blinding snow. He couldn't swallow.

Now I know what cottonmouth means.

Sweat soaked through his leather flight gloves, but his hands felt cold and clammy.

Yea, though we walk through the valley. . . . We're free-falling into God knows what.

Have I done the best I can? Carb-heat's on, canopy defrost's at full-heat, we're well west of Kansas City's airport and its instrument approach

14

corridors. I'm descending north of Olathe until I break free of the clouds. If I have legal landing minimums, I'll try to find Navy Olathe and land.

But if I don't break out, I'll climb south and see if I can get above the clouds. If not, I'll try to get clear of clouds anywhere and fly those radio-failure, one-minute-leg triangles that might alert some radar observer.

Perspiration streamed down Pax's face. He slid the wet headset off and swiped at his forehead and eyes with an arm. The already sweat-soaked sleeve didn't help.

As the suspect altimeter approached one thousand feet, he slowed his rate of descent to two hundred feet a minute—an iffy adjustment with turbulence bouncing the vertical-speed needle. Trying to average its erratic bouncing, when he needed precision, hardened the growing knot in his gut.

At an indicated five hundred feet, he added mongoose-quick peeks over alternate sides of the canopy rail to his already frantic instrument scan. Snow and clouds. Clouds and snow—no clear sky, nothing to see. At two hundred feet, it became harder to force the T-34 lower. The airplane and his right arm conspired against him.

Maybe they know something I don't.

His shallow breaths came quicker. By the time Pax willed his right hand to force the airplane down to indicated ground-level, his stomach clinched and he fought trembling chills. But they remained in the clouds; he saw snow and more snow.

It could be worse; I could have already hit the ground. Obviously, the altimeter's wrong. But now what?

He took two deep breaths and quivered his head and the control stick.

Okay. Wake up, everybody!

He shook his arms, his legs, his hands, and flexed his ankles.

I didn't know clouds got this thick. One more check around the cockpit—max canopy heat; max propeller rpm; airspeed trimmed at 100 kts. Good.

He tried again.

The altimeter showed six hundred feet below ground level when Pax dropped clear of solid clouds and some of the turbulence. Snow continued, however, as he skimmed above another solid-looking cloud blanket. But a small, dark break in the lower layer passed under his left wing tip. He jerked ninety degrees left-wing-down and pulled the plane's nose back toward the hole; G-loading increased in the tight turn. He heard a moan from the back seat.

"If you're trying to make me sick," she cried out, "it's working!"

"Hang on!"

The darkened gap barely made a mouth in the clouds, with scant altitude between the lowest bottoms and the ground, but miracle-of-miracles, dead center in the maw glimmered the rainbow's pot: an east-west river with a north-south bridge. The combination skewered their position. Tom Cain had shown Pax that unique landmark during his Olathe area orientation flight.

Sweet Jesus! We're six miles north of the airport.

He stamped bottom-rudder; the nose fell toward the opening. They spiraled down; G-forces mashed them down in their seats. Sweat burned his eyes.

I need to roll wings level, headed south . . . barely below the bottoms.

Her scream lanced his concentration: "Cut it out, asshole! This isn't funny!"

He rolled out and leveled off, heading south—his canopy top scraping the cloud bottoms. Even lower cloud patches dragged through treetops.

Not much ground cover though . . . too much wind for accumulation. Maybe we're a hundred feet over the ground . . . maybe not. I don't have legal landing minimums.

Snow continued blowing. Rough air slapped the airplane through bucks and yaws; Pax floated against his shoulder harness and slammed back into his seat. He slowed his airspeed and glanced in the mirror.

Gorgeous showed tight, straight lips where smiles used to play.

Okay, what now, genius? What's your plan?

As the consequences of an illegal landing at the navy field flooded him—*they'll put my brain under a microscope*—he remembered a small, grass airstrip west of Navy Olathe.

It's worth a look-see. How ironic is that, choosing a grass field over the navy facility to avoid a hassle?

At the east-west highway, a couple of miles north of the air station, Pax banked right and arced to the west. He lowered his wheels and flaps and began searching to the left of the airplane's nose. He picked out the Quonset hut hangar and made a measured turn to a crosswind landing at the grass field. They plunked down with a solid thud, and two-inch-deep snow patches shortened their landing roll.

This nightmare might continue, depending on gorgeous, but the danger— thank God!—is over.

They taxied to tie-down rings near the hangar before shutting down. He got out on the wing, slid her canopy open, stepped to the ground, and secured the airplane.

Inside an office nook in the Quonset hut hangar, the airfield manager stared at Pax like he belonged in a zoo, but he did let him use the telephone. A frowning gorgeous stalked in with her tote. Pax looked away from her.

"Hello, Tom. This is Pax; I won't be flying back until tomorrow."

"Don't I know it." his friend said. "You can't believe how cruddy our weather is. Good thing you got the word. Do you have a phone number where I can reach you?"

"Yeah. Listen to me. Don't say a word, and don't change your expression. Understand?"

"Uh-huh."

"You know the little private grass strip west of the base?"

"Uh-huh."

"That's where I am; I'll fly the plane to the base tomorrow. Would you come and take me to the BOQ now . . . or real soon?"

"Really?"

"Really."

"Right away."

Gorgeous stood inside the door. "I apologize for yelling at you," she said. "I didn't appreciate that macho flying crap you were throwing at me."

"Complain at the ticket window; you might get your money back."

Her eyes closed to slits as her face flushed. "You must have been told this before," she said, while nodding her head in rhythm with the words, "but you're an arrogant bastard."

He moved closer to her and whispered. "Maybe. But you have a filthy mouth, and what you don't know is that we're both lucky to be alive. Weather at the air station is below landing minimums."

Her eyes snapped open. "Why did you try to land there?"

"I didn't. At least I didn't after I knew how bad the weather was."

"Didn't the field tell you about the lousy weather?"

"They would have, if we'd had a radio."

Our airborne situation was, and is, beyond her comprehension.

He sighed, pulled the signed liability waiver from his pocket, and tore it into small pieces. "You lived, so the navy doesn't need this. Please forget that flight; I shouldn't have brought you. You might've paid a heavy price for my stupidity. If word got out, I'd be in serious trouble."

She didn't answer, but walked to a battered vinyl chair by the window and stared at the blowing snow.

A few minutes later the fair-haired and red-faced Lieutenant Tom Cain, in his service dress blue uniform, came in the door stamping snow from his feet and shaking his head. "Hey, Pax, could you stand a drink?"

"Might be good," Pax said. "Tom, this young lady is looking for a lift into town. Can she ride with us?"

"Sure, if she doesn't mind sitting on your lap. The backseat in my Volkswagen's full of junk."

"That'll be fine," she said. "Tom, my name is Sally."

Pax retrieved his bag from the airplane, patted the engine cowling, and brushed the propeller spinner with a light kiss of thanks.

Pitiful little gratitude for saving our lives, but short of crawling under the wing and curling up snug against one of your main mounts, I guess it'll have to do. Maybe I'll wax your whole fuselage.

After they dropped the young woman at a house in town, Pax told Tom about the flight, but without mentioning that she had been with him. It didn't get any easier with the telling. Tom repeatedly rolled his blue eyes and finally groaned in disbelief, "You are one lucky son of a bitch. Remind me never to gamble with you."

The following day, in brilliant sunshine, Pax flew a quick and uneventful flight to the navy airfield. The T34-B's radio and OMNI both worked to perfection; maintenance personnel could find nothing wrong with either of them. Pax shrugged and walked away from the maintenance chief's desk.

What the hell? Reckon my kiss fixed 'em? If so, it had been more potent than gorgeous's cheek-peck kiss. Besides, my thoughts about her melted with the snow.

From behind the BOQ counter, the black petty officer waved to get Pax's attention. "Hold on, ma'am," Petty Officer Smith said. "Lieutenant Langford walked in."

Pax wrinkled his brow.

Did he say ma'am. . .? Ma'am?

Pax mouthed a silent thank you at Smith and took the phone. "Lieutenant Langford."

"Lieutenant, this is old filthy mouth, and even if you've forgotten our bargain, I haven't. Do you have dinner plans for this evening?"

Even the call—much less her bouncy voice—caught him off guard. He'd blown her off as a thorny day's work, yet he smiled and weighed an answer.

"Hello! Earth to Langford. Did you hear me?"

"Yeah, I heard, but you're off the hook. Consider your debt paid in full, and I hope your emergency worked out."

"That's what we need to talk about. If we didn't, I'd send a pizza and call us slick. If you already have dinner plans, I can meet you at the BOQ earlier."

"Miss, we don't need to talk, and save your pizza; I don't like pizza. To tell the truth, I don't care to be involved in any more of your problems. . . ."

Jesus! I can't believe I said that. Her calling me an asshole must have pissed me off more than I thought.

"The name is Sally Banks, Lieutenant, and you've got your own problem—in fact, several problems. For starters, a talk's no longer good enough. We're having the dinner I owe you. I'll pick you up at the BOQ at six o'clock."

"Don't waste your time; I won't be here." He would have hung up, except her laughter stopped him.

"Sure you will, Lieutenant. Because if you're not there, Monday morning a lawyer will be at the front gate with paperwork for a horrendous lawsuit against you and the navy for my back injury. Don't dress, casual's fine; you'll enjoy it. Hello! Did you hear me that time?"

And she'd looked so sweet.

"I'll call the main gate and leave your name; they'll give you a visitor's pass."

"Not necessary, Lieutenant. My dad works on base; we have a decal. See you at six o'clock. Ta-ta." The line clicked dead, but a full minute passed before Pax eased the receiver into its cradle.

This could be serious; she said lawyer.

Chapter 2—DINNER

Pax washed and waxed his white Corvette, freshened his shave, and chose tan corduroys and a heavy fisherman's knit sweater for his first-ever, blackmailed dinner.

She said I'd enjoy it. Fat chance. Anyway, I'm not gonna worry about something I can't control.

At straight-up six o'clock, she entered the BOQ front door wearing a smile that belied her earlier telephone-voice testiness. A knee-length plaid skirt and dark sweater enhanced, if possible, Pax's memory-image of his stunning passenger. He put the unread newspaper he'd been holding aside, advanced a few steps to meet her, and swept an arm toward a sofa. "Miss Banks, won't you have a seat?"

"If you don't mind, I'd rather walk while we talk. Let's stroll around the block, before we eat. I need to tell you something, and I'd appreciate it if you let me finish before you comment."

How can eyes shine like that?

He pushed the door open for her. "Your nickel."

"First, a confession: I flat-out lied about the family emergency. We finished our last class at nine-thirty yesterday, and three of us teacher assistants inhaled a couple of hot buttered rums apiece . . . getting ready for the snowstorm—"

"That explains the cinnamon smell."

She raised a palm toward him. "—and one thing led to another. For two days, my roommates kept describing this good-looking naval aviator, who," she shrugged and looked sideways up into his face, "ended up being you. Anyway, I bet them I could hitch a ride—"

"You lied to me," Pax said.

She raised both hands toward him, as if to ward off a blow, while nodding and walking straight ahead. "—to Olathe with you. I hate doing rotten things, but I do them.

20

"Next, I didn't know you were having problems with the radio. I guess the rum started working on me, but I didn't want to vomit. So when I yelled at you, I was yelling at myself, too. And although I know most of the words, I tend to watch my language.

"Finally, I'll never tell anyone about our flight. I've already called my friends and sworn them to secrecy. I needed to get this mess straight; otherwise I wouldn't have threatened you. But as a favor, I'd like you to forget that flight, too." She stuck out her hand. "Deal?"

He tilted his head and rubbed his chin. "Any more surprises?"

"Maybe a small one," she said and hefted her hand up and down, as if jangling change, "but do we have a deal?"

At least she'd come clean.

He pursed his lips. "Sure, why not?" He smiled and shook her hand. "Now, what other small surprise?"

"You dropped me at my aunt's house yesterday."

"Tom followed your directions." He stopped walking and faced her. "Don't your folks even live in Olathe?"

Sally squinted her sparkling-green eyes at him and made two small head-shrugs toward a large brick home at her back. "Please call me Sally. My parents don't invite my friends for dinner if we're not on a first name basis. And by the way, yesterday a friend from school drove me to my aunt's house." She smiled, grabbed his hand, and almost had to pull him up the walk. He glimpsed the name plaque near the front door, before she had him through a large living room and dining room, headed toward a solid swinging door.

"Hello! We're here!" she called.

A near-mirror-image of Sally pushed open the kitchen door, wiping her hands on a small apron. Pax backpedaled, making room.

"Mom, Lieutenant Paxton Langford. Pax, my mom."

Mrs. Banks extended her hand. "Welcome to our home, Lieutenant. You prefer Paxton or Pax?"

I like that firm handshake.

"Pax, ma'am, and thanks for the invitation."

"Ma'am?" Mrs. Banks repeated and raised her eyebrows. "I'm sure it's Texas, but what part, Pax?"

"Fort Worth. Is it that obvious?"

"Uh-huh, but it takes one to know one; I like it. Call me Barbara. Do you have brothers or sisters?"

Pax shook his head. "No, not blood brothers. I was raised in Fort Worth's

Masonic Home . . . never knew my folks."

Barbara Banks reached toward Pax's shoulder, but stopped short of touching him. "I'm sorry. That must have been rough."

"If it was, I never knew it; we got by."

Mrs. Banks turned to Sally. "Dad will be home in a few minutes; he's running late. If you'll pour the drinks—white wine for me—I'll join you in a few minutes."

When Sally handed Pax the requested bourbon over ice, he raised his eyebrows and pointed at her. "Your dad is Captain Banks, the air station commanding officer?"

"Not my fault."

"At least your mom seems a genuine, aboveboard lady; you owe her your looks. But without even knowing the man, I wouldn't want to play poker with your dad."

"I guess I deserve that. While we're alone, I need to know if you're married."

He hesitated for an instant. "No, I'm not married."

"Divorced?"

Pax looked at his drink, swirled it, and glanced away before staring into her eyes. "I'm not married, Sally. May we leave it like that, for this evening?"

"Good enough, but be warned, Dad's pretty nosy."

"Now I know. Thanks."

Sally's mother joined them, without the apron. Her gray wool slacks and matching sweater presented a twin to her daughter's excellent figure. An amber bead choker dressed the package. Pax stood; she waved him down. "Please don't bother. I'll be up-and-about this evening; you'd wear yourself out."

"I don't blow smoke, ma'am, but you two could be sisters—almost twins."

"That's smoke—real smoke. But thank you, anyway." She stood and walked to the large picture window. "Here's Dad, Sally. I thought I heard the old clunker."

What Pax heard, and curiosity, forced him to the window. The blue-uniformed captain parked a new-looking model A Ford in the driveway. "Wow! Ma'am, has Captain Banks had that long?"

"Too long, Pax. Way too long."

The front door swooshed open; Captain Banks strode through the gap. "Hey, honey, I'm home. Oh, here you are." The 6-foot officer with a sandy crew cut walked straight to his wife and kissed her lips, before extending a

22

hand to Pax. Their eye-to-eye probes were level; the captain's pale-blues dug hard. "Hello, Lieutenant. Is it . . . Langford?" Pax nodded. "Good. . . . That's easy to remember. My best friend's named Langford. Any older brother navy pilots? Hmm, I guess not. You don't look like him. I'll shuck out of the blue bag and be right back." He hugged Sally. "Hey, Beans. How're you doing?"

"Aw, Dad." Sally inspected the ceiling while color climbed her neck.

Mrs. Banks frowned. "Turner, you shouldn't tease your daughter in front of company."

Pax turned to Sally and grinned. "Beans?"

"Yeah, Beans," the captain said. "She's always been full of beans. Her twin brother will be cranking F-8s around for a living, but she's sure she could do it better." He pecked a kiss on Sally's head and hugged her again. When the captain breezed up the central staircase, Pax sensed a vacuum. It increased when Mrs. Banks excused herself back to the kitchen.

"You have a twin brother flying navy fighters?"

"He will be. Didn't I mention that?"

Not even a hint of a smile. None. I won't play poker with her, either.

"No. You know you didn't. You're a regular Britannica of unmentioned stuff."

At Captain Bank's suggestion, they ate dinner from TV trays in the den. A few pine logs, mixed amongst the oak, popped and snapped, slinging fiery embers against a black mesh screen. Occasional sparking slivers shot through the mesh, to die on the hearth. "Got to have some pine," Banks said. "Even paying to get the chimney cleaned every year, it's worth it."

"You'll think worth it, when you burn the house down," his wife said.

Banks rolled his eyes. "Sally mentioned that you're a recruiter, Pax."

"Yes, sir, I'm helping out. My orders keep me in Olathe for three months. After that—"

"Where did you come from? You a hotshot back from Vietnam?"

"No, sir. Sixteen junior officers back from Vietnam deployments got ninety day temporary orders to recruiting districts. I'm in that program, but I'm headed the other way."

"To Vietnam?"

"Eventually. I have orders to VF-39 at Miramar."

"You're kidding! VF-39? Great. Sally's brother, Bud, will be in your sister squadron, VF-37. How's that for a small world? You'll find the Crusader a quantum leap from the T-34."

"I know; I did a tour in F-8s."

Banks did a double take. "Which coast? I'm an F-8 jock."

"Which squadron?" Pax asked.

"Cobras, VF-16, in Forrestal, 1961 to 1962. How about you?"

Is this real or am I dreaming?

"Me, too, two years ahead of you. Of course, I was a peon; you were probably a department head."

"I'll be damned. Babs, did you hear? Can you believe it? Talk about coincidence."

"Food's getting cold, Turner," Mrs. Banks said. "Let Pax eat. He doesn't shovel it in and keep talking like you do. Are you sure you won't have a beer or some wine, Pax?"

"No, thanks, ma'am," Pax got up, holding his empty glass. "But I would like some more water. These enchiladas remind me of Fort Worth."

"Give me your glass and sit, Pax. Please. I don't like aviators in my kitchen."

"Babs, please bring me another beer while you're out there. How about you, Beans?"

"No thanks, Dad, and the name is Sally."

A crackling log spit red coals at the screen. "A lot of fireworks in the den tonight," Banks said and winked at Pax. "You married?"

"No, sir, I'm not."

Sally brushed the red embers well back into the hearth with a small fire-tool broom and replaced the screen with a lot more vigor than the task required.

"Divorced?"

"Dad, don't you think you're kind of nosy?"

"I'm interested, Beans. I thought maybe Bud could round up a gal for Pax in San Diego."

"Baloney. Lieutenant Langford," she stalked toward the kitchen, "doesn't need help finding dates. And I will have another beer."

"Captain, I'm not divorced, either. Didn't I see a Silver Star on your blouse?"

"Yeah. Three MiGs during the Korean flap."

"What MiGs? I don't remember any navy MiG kills in Korea."

"MiG-15s. You wouldn't know about them; few people do. It happened during the truce negotiations, so there was little publicity." Banks pulled the screen back, fed two more logs to the dwindling blaze, and headed for the kitchen. "Sure you won't have a beer or anything?"

"No thanks, but I'll come with you and get some more water—if Mrs. Banks won't mind. What were you flying?"

"An F9F-5 Panther in VF-781. We were in Oriskany. Flu had kept me in sick bay for two days before the flight. I couldn't even believe I was on the schedule; my gut was queasy, my knees shaky. Hey, gals, you coming back to the fire?"

"In a minute, Dad; we've heard the story." Her smile didn't hide the eye-darts.

Mrs. Banks shook her head. "Oh, Pax! I forgot your water; Sally and I started talking. Here you are."

Back in the den, Banks leaned against the fireplace mantle and stared into the flames. "In 1952—November 18th, to be exact—we were steaming north in the Sea of Japan, about 40-degrees north latitude. Blowing snow during the launch, shitty weather, expected to get worse.

"After takeoff, CIC called with a flight of high-altitude bogies coming down from—and get this—Vladivostok."

"Russians?"

"Damn straight. The combat information center vectored us outbound and told us to climb, but our flight leader's plane had a fuel-control problem. He and his wingman returned overhead the ship; I continued the vector with my wingman. After topping the snow and clouds, around twelve thousand feet, I tallyhoed and reported seven high contrails inbound. We soon identified the bogies as silver-colored MiG-15s. They became our targets."

"Targets?" Pax said. "Had CIC cleared you to fire?"

"Maybe not at first . . . but the ship damn well wanted them intercepted quick as we could get on them. But the MiGs headed back north and pulled away from us. As we climbed through twenty-six thousand feet, they split into two groups. Four reversed right; three reversed left, and all seven dropped below contrail level. We lost sight; Oriskany lost radar contact, so CIC vectored us back toward the task force.

"I called for a gun-check and squeezed off a few rounds, before I spotted them again: four in a close trail formation, descending from my ten o'clock. I figured they were playing chicken, but when their leader approached firing range I saw muzzle flashes under their intakes. The entire division—four planes—fired at the same time. Could you even believe that? Anyway, that cinched it. I broke hard into them. That's when the CIC controller screamed: 'Do not engage! Repeat, do not engage!' Christ. I felt like I was having a nightmare. Anyway, I shouted back at them, 'We're already engaged! The bastards shot at me!' At least somebody in CIC had some balls. His immediate response: 'Roger. Go get 'em!'

"Their tail-end-Charlie overshot level, so I reversed hard and hammered him good . . . from up close. That MiG started burning, but my wingman followed him clear down to the cloud deck . . . trying to get his own guns to work. That left the other six salivating over me. You spend a career huntin' them, and—bang—you're ass-deep in 'em. MiGs pounced from every direction."

Pax stood and moved to one side of the mantle, facing the captain. "How about your flight leader? What was he doing?"

"I didn't have any idea, but his section was circling the ship at fifteen thousand feet. He said later his radio was intermittent. Who knows?

"I do know one against six sucks. I couldn't break into anyone without waving my ass at someone else. Ask me what fear-sweat smells like. . . . Anyway, I hit one more guy—damned hard. I had to roll under him to avoid parts coming off his plane.

"Sometime in the fight I told the ship I could use a little help. They vectored the leader's wingman . . . but I didn't know about it. The fight kept me damned busy. Another MiG flashed in front of me—he'd lost sight, I imagine—so I clamped on and hosed him down, too. But my day turned sour. Something exploded behind me. I lost hydraulics, and my rudder pedals went stupid—no response.

"In the left mirror, I could see a MiG slinging tracers at me, but they were missing. I had elevator control left, so I pumped hell out of the stick. Another Panther closed behind the shooting MiG, but it didn't scare him much. After what seemed like an eternity, I got down to the clouds—not a damned minute too soon. My rudder cables were shot away; the elevator hung together by bits and pieces. Thank God for the Grumman Ironworks.

"I had manual ailerons—no hydraulic boost—and part of the elevator. Oriskany's CO turned the ship a few degrees to help me make final bearing."

"How bad was your plane damaged?" Pax asked.

"My plane captain counted more than two hundred holes, but they came from a single 37 mm hit in the engine compartment. After salvaging some stuff, we deep-sixed that Panther over the side.

"Anyway, I guess the ship thought I might have been in a lot of trouble with Washington, so they spread the wealth around: I got credit for one kill and one probable; my wingman, though his guns never fired, one damaged;

the leader's wingman, who took a high-deflection and long-range shot at what might have been my third flamer, one kill.

"My gun camera film probably told the complete story, but much of it got discarded by the processing kid. Nobody asked me how I felt about the way they split the pie up. No, that's not right. Two days later, my CO asked me what I thought about our intelligence officer's report. I told him I wasn't paid to think, but to fight. He looked at me kind of funny and walked off.

"After a few days, Oriskany returned to Yokosuka, Japan, where I debriefed Admiral Briscoe. While the ship was in port, the three of us credited with kills were flown to Korea and introduced to President-elect Eisenhower in Seoul.

"The navy farted around about a week deciding whether to award us medals or courts-martial. If the Russians had bitched, it would've probably been the latter. I guess embarrassment kept 'em quiet. Admiral 'Jocko' Clark pinned the medals on us. End of sea story."

"Did three of you get Silver Stars?"

"No, the leader's wingman and I did. My wingman got a DFC, and I think he damned well earned one for trying to distract that MiG on my tail."

"Captain, I'd give everything I've got or ever will have for a chance like that. I always loved to fight the F-8, but I left the navy because we didn't have a war—or any prospect of getting one. I screwed up—big time."

"Be careful what you wish for, Pax. It might come true."

"I should be so lucky. My worst fear is that Vietnam will end before I get a chance like you had."

Mrs. Banks brought coffee into the den. "Pax, I have pecan pie, vanilla ice cream, or you can have both."

"Black coffee, please, since you already have it made, and thank you."

Sally brought a can of Coors and sat next to Pax on the sofa. "Are you past the navy's dilemma yet: courts-martial or medals?"

"I told Pax about my court-martial."

Mrs. Banks jerked around. "You weren't court-martialed."

"I can't get the story exact every time."

"Right, Dad." Sally put her hand on Pax's leg. "After two years, I could recite Dad's MiG story verbatim."

"I'm afraid she's right, Pax," Mrs. Banks said. "Sally and Bud used to take turns telling Turner's MiG story to each other. They even had the gestures and pauses down pat; they kept me in stitches."

"Damned little respect around here for the breadwinner," Banks said and chuckled.

Pax stood. "Your story deserves respect, and I appreciated hearing it. I also enjoyed the meal, Mrs. Banks, and your hospitality. I hope to see you again while I'm here."

"Come back anytime, Pax," Mrs. Banks said. "You can see we're kind of informal."

Sally moved to Pax's side and took his hand. "I'll be back early."

The captain stood and extended a hand. "Glad to know you, Pax. Maybe you can take me for a ride in your T-34 someday, on a test flight or something."

Sally squeezed Pax's hand.

"I'll keep it in mind," Pax said.

Pax and Sally turned along the curbside walk, when Banks's voice stopped them. "Sally, may I see you a minute, please?"

She soon hurried back down the steps and reached for Pax's hand.

"Problem?" he asked.

"No. Dad apologized for calling me Beans."

"Are you sure you didn't mention our flight to your dad?"

"No, I certainly did not. His request for a flight sounded like I did, but I didn't." She crossed her heart. "Honest."

"Well, you have great folks, and I enjoyed the meal. Paid your debt in full. Believe me, we're even. You don't even have to walk me back to the BOQ."

She let go of his hand. "I don't have to do anything, Pax. Ever! Why can't you relax. . .? I'm sorry. Look, it's Saturday night; I'm a cheap date, two beers max. Do you like to dance?"

"Some, not much; I'm not very fancy."

"Don't worry. I'm talking beer joint, jukebox, and sawdust on the floor. Have a car?"

"The White Knight," he said and pointed. Pax opened the Corvette's passenger door.

"A fifty-six, right?" she said. "May I drive?"

"Yes, and not even. Maybe when I know you better."

A half-dozen couples shared the dance floor. Trini Lopez, Al Hirt, and Ray Charles earned their money—made the jukebox proud. Pax's self-conscious maneuvering finally eased into comfortable swaying against Sally's pliant pressure.

I can stand about a month of this.

28

Sally's two beers turned into three. "I'll get this one," she said. He refused the offer, but continued to match her: Pepsi for beer.

"You don't like beer?"

"Some. I'm not much of a drinker."

"That'll make history in a fighter squadron."

"You're a good dancer. I like this music, and I like this place."

"Good. And you're getting looser; or I'm getting loaded, or both. Are you a good fighter pilot? Wait! Let me rephrase. Are you a," scowling, her chin tucked in, she pointed both thumbs straight up and wiggled her fists, "shithot fighter pilot?"

"Being a daughter hard in your family?"

"Nope. Being a daughter is a piece-a-cake. Dad loves me more than anything . . . always has . . . without a doubt. But my brother loves my dad the same way, and he always busts his butt trying to live up to whatever he thinks Dad expects of him. Football, Annapolis, and now this fighter pilot crap. I know my brother; he'll be stretched thin in a fighter squadron."

"He told you this?"

"You kidding? He'd cut his tongue out first."

"Maybe your brother—what's his name?—can fly better than you think."

"Turner. Turner Maximilian Banks, Junior. Call sign: Black Max. That's his name; pleasing Dad's his game. He wants to take up where Dad got derailed, and I'm scared to death for him." She shivered and let out a long sigh. "One more dance before we go?"

Ray Charles convinced the dancers "It Makes No Difference Now." Sally's forehead nestled against Pax's neck, her body—though molded to his own—seemed weightless.

How can she do that?

The song ended too soon, but he held her an extra couple of heartbeats. He knew that for a fact, because her heart thumped against his chest.

The sentry saluted them back through the main gate. "Your dad got derailed? What did you mean?"

"He didn't tell you? Four years ago, Dad had a supersonic ejection off Cuba—on the gunnery range. No one expected him to live. But he fought; God knows how he fought. He started walking six months ago. He hoped and prayed they'd let him back into fighters. When they wouldn't—too much restricted motion—and he was promoted to captain, they gave him Olathe. We've been here four months."

"I read about that ejection. He must be rawhide tough."

"Yes, but that didn't keep him from screaming, crying out in agony trying to stretch those atrophied muscles. Bud cried with him, saw a challenge, and picked up the family-dropped baton; Hail Caesar and the Banks family name. Sorry, I didn't mean to unload on you."

"No sweat, I asked the question. Thanks for the dances. I hope I didn't hurt your feet."

"Oh! Our house already. My feet are fine, Pax."

"How will you get back to school?"

"My aunt's a peach. She drives me back tomorrow . . . on the sly. Spring break's in a month. If you think you'll be here, I'd like to see you again. Don't get out." She leaned over, brushed his lips with her own, and hurried up the sidewalk to her porch.

"Good. She's home," Mrs. Banks said.

"Yeah. Big damned improvement over those long-haired hippies she's been bringing home to piss me off."

"She does no such thing."

"Bullshit."

"I take it you approve of Lieutenant Langford?"

"I told Sally he was too damned old; she should stay away from him."

"Why would you do that, Turner?"

The captain smiled in the darkness. "Because I damned well know our daughter." He buried a laugh in his pillow.

"You ought to; she thinks like you do."

Chapter 3—SAINT PATRICK'S DAY

"Hello, Pax. Barbara Banks here. Am I interrupting anything?"

"No, ma'am. Nice to hear your voice again." Pax switched the receiver to his left ear and fished a pencil from a shirt pocket. "How may I help you?"

"Turner's birthday is Thursday. Bud and Sally are coming in to surprise him. Bud wants to meet you; we told him you flew F-8s in Turner's old squadron. I hoped you could join us for dinner. No presents, nothing fancy, casual like before."

"Thursday. . . . Mrs. Banks, I fly to Columbia, Missouri, this afternoon on a recruiting trip. We're never sure what kind of response we'll get. If I can possibly get back, I'd like to come. May I leave it like that?"

"Certainly, around six o'clock. Have a good trip; we'll hope to see you."

For the following three days, Tom Cain tested potential aviation candidates at the University of Missouri, and Pax flew the qualifiers. But having completed the testing, Tom—in one of the navy's white Chrysler recruiting convertibles, with its 3-foot "Wings of Gold" on each door—stood ready to head for Olathe. On a wing beside Pax's cockpit, and over the idling engine noise, he shouted, "Six more candidates need flights!" Tom sprayed him with spit as he yelled, while Pax shielded his face by finger-combing his hair. "The Beechcraft mechs quit at seventeen hundred; I'll have to take off tomorrow before they get to work. I need the plane at Olathe for fueling by sixteen hundred."

"No sweat," Pax said. "I'll leave by fourteen-thirty. See you there."

Tom stepped from the wing, and Pax fished a handkerchief from a pocket and wiped his face.

Scattered stratus didn't diminish the twenty-five mile visibility, and flights ran on schedule. Pax snuffed lungfuls of crisp air, enjoying the wide-eyed looks and even wider smiles from the pilot wannabes. After flying the last candidate, he refueled, checked the weather, filed a flight plan, and returned to the airplane at 1425.

Forty yards behind the T-34, beyond a chain-link fence, a blue Thunderbird slid to a halt, scattering gravel in a chalky-white blur. A dark-haired young man jogged from the car and vaulted the 4-foot fence. As he neared, Pax recognized him as a candidate who had waited until dark the preceding day—without getting a flight, as it turned out.

I'd forgotten about him. Damn!

The young man bent over, bracing his hands on his knees, and took a couple of deep breaths. "Whew! Man, I'm glad I caught you . . . figured you'd be gone."

"I almost am," Pax said and glanced at his watch. "What's the problem?"

"My flight. You haven't flown me yet. I waited the whole afternoon yesterday. Remember? I've had classes today; I got out ten minutes ago."

Pax grinned and nodded. "Yeah, I remember. . . . Do you still have that release form?"

The young man fished the folded form from a Levi's pocket with a move that would have made most quick draw gunslingers blush. "Yes, sir, right here." He tried to smooth its folds before handing it to Pax.

"Okay, Mister Larry Jackson," Pax read from the paper. "Tell you what. I'm running late. When we land, I'll taxi over here by your car. You jump out, slide the canopy closed—make sure it's latched—so I can take off again in a hurry. Can you do that?"

Jackson shot him a thumbs-up. "You got it, Lieutenant."

Pax talked Aviation Candidate Jackson through the normal demonstration flight, while sneaking peeks into the rearview mirror, checking the youngster's reaction to G-forces. Jackson's grin said it best; he loved it.

After twenty minutes, they landed, taxied in, and stopped near Jackson's car. He jumped out, slid the canopy shut, and shook a double-thumbs-up at Pax, who goosed the throttle and taxied back to the runway. As Pax broke ground, Jackson waved from his car. Pax rocked the wings and turned toward Olathe.

He raced the setting sun westward. A night landing posed no problem, but catching the fueling crew did. Pax eased the throttle forward, and like a barn-bound horse, the trainer sped for its hangar.

The top half of a red-orange sun perched on the darkening horizon as Pax nudged the elevator trim forward. His descent from four thousand feet increased the speed past 165-knots. A glance at the cockpit clock showed

1635.

"Navy Olathe Tower, Navy Four Zero One, VFR from Columbia, Missouri, ten miles east," Pax reported.

"Roger, Four Zero One . . . runway one eight . . . altimeter setting three zero one zero . . . no reported traffic. You're cleared number one in the break."

A nose-low, left turn aligned him for the south runway. "Navy Olathe, Four Zero One approaching the break."

"Four Zero One is in sight . . . cleared to break."

Pax snapped the little trainer 90-degrees left wing down and pulled the stick back near his stomach. After 180-degrees of level turn, he remained much closer than normal to the runway—about one-fourth the normal distance abeam.

Talk about turning on a dime. A damned-near-overhead abeam position gives you a different perspective, but like they say: "A red-hot fighter pilot can salvage anything."

Pax slapped the gear- and flap-handles down, pushed over left aileron, and offset it with as much right rudder as he dared. The resultant sideslip fought to lose height, without gaining airspeed. "Olathe Tower," he called, "Four Zero One abeam . . . gear down and locked . . . final landing."

"Roger, Four Zero One . . . you're cleared to land."

Pax shoved the control stick full forward.

Anything to get nearer the ground. What better way to lose altitude than pointing straight down? And—without stalling—I'll snatch the nose back up.

But after two inches of backward movement, the control stick stopped. Stuck. Time slogged in molasses. Seconds progressed by hundredths, and each hundredth plodded by individually.

The unexpected danger, however, prompted eloquence. As that particular—and by rights, his final—sunset progressed, Pax bellowed: "A-a-a-r-r-r-g-g-g-h-h-h!"

And having his airplane's nose pointed straight down—at five hundred feet above the ground, and having that airplane's control stick frozen rock-solid—produced an acrobatic pilot. Pax put both feet on the instrument panel and savaged the stick back with both hands, using fear-laced strength from generations past, present, and future. Nothing!

It won't budge.

A particular patch of frozen Kansas turf became an ever-increasing input to Pax's short-circuiting brain. He'd soon smash his nose flat on it. That vision paid off.

I yanked back and got nothing. Fuck it! Do something else.

He shoved the stick full forward and right back. It came, and his adrenaline-spiked brain kept Pax from pulling into a stall. A throttle balls-to-the-wall, moderately-buffeting pullout, skimmed the landing gear over the runway lip.

I made it! Jesus!

The airplane accelerated well down the runway before he thought to retard the throttle. Pax's entire body tingled, and chills sped through his bones. God-awful bile flooded his mouth.

C'mon! Don't puke.

But he knew he'd stared into the abyss.

The engine ticked over as if whispering. Pax checked the instruments to see if it was running.

How can it sound so damned normal?

As Pax parked the airplane, the purpling sky made the field seem deserted. But it wasn't. A puffing Tom Cain clambered onto the wing.

"For chrissakes!" Tom pointed toward the approach end of the runway. "What the hell kinda deal was that?"

Pax tried counting to ten; he didn't make it. "Screw you, Tom! The damned stick froze. The frigging airplane is hard-down; nobody's flying it till we know what happened. The sonofabitch coulda killed me."

"Well, Jesus! You wouldn't believe how that looked. I thought you'd busted your butt."

"Shoulda seen it from my end."

"I'll call the Beech reps; see you inside." Tom stepped from the wing, shook his head—while mumbling to himself—and stalked to the line-shack.

Pax sat a while longer, slowing his breathing, hoping to get past the queasiness before securing the aircraft. He raised both hands chest-high, spread the fingers, and checked for shaking.

Not too bad.

He pulled himself erect and swung clear of the cockpit. A cool breeze shot through the sweat-soaked flight suit and made him shiver.

Am I shaking from the cold? Sure. I'd have to be cold in a wet flight suit.

He slid the rear canopy open, and the mystery dissolved. Pax grasped the canopy sill and felt his knees quaver. He swallowed hard. And again. He sucked a couple of deep breaths with his eyes closed

The parachute, a gray-green backpack, lay askew across the seat-pan. At the center of its top, a three-inch vee indentation told the tale.

I cashed a big chip with some patron saint, or this particular tale might've been buried—and me along with it.

Pax stared at an evening star and pressed both temples between his palms.

How many pilots have died from this identical mistake? That young kid, Jackson, jumped out of the cockpit like I told him to and slammed the canopy shut. He didn't secure the parachute or the seat straps, because I didn't tell him to.

Pax dropped his chin to his chest.

Once again, I've been one lucky sonofabitch, regardless of how dumb.

Tom returned with the fueling crew. "I couldn't catch the Beech guys; I'll call them at home."

Pax beckoned Tom to join him on the wing. "No need. See the top of the parachute? That came within a gnat's ass of canceling my ticket. I popped the stick forward to lose some altitude, the chute rose from the seat, and it wedged between the stick and the seatback when I tried to pull the nose up. Another dumb-shit on my part."

"You didn't secure the rear cockpit?"

Pax shifted his gaze sideways, from the parachute to Tom's look of disbelief, and shook his head. "Nope."

"At least we know the airplane's okay." Tom scratched his head. "Did this scare you as much as it should have?"

Pax hesitated a moment, chewing at his lower lip, before he turned to Tom. "Have you ever had a large icicle jammed through your heart?"

Tom nodded twice. "Gotcha, pal," he said and stepped off the wing.

Pax stood under the shower's hot spray for five minutes after he was already squeaky-clean. That he remembered Barbara Banks's dinner invitation before he was late amazed him.

Another stroke of luck. How could I forget that? Too busy trying to bust my ass, I guess. That might explain it.

Khaki trousers, a white shirt, and cordovan loafers felt about right. He pulled a red sweater over his head and ran a comb through his hair as he jogged from the BOQ.

Sally's black Chevy in the driveway confirmed her arrival. Pax grinned and sniffed the air for cinnamon. Smelling none, he chuckled and rang the doorbell.

Am I really this eager to see her? Must be.

Sally opened the door; they both laughed. Her sleeveless red sweater-vest broke the set. Otherwise, her khaki slacks, white blouse, and cordovans matched perfectly. He took her offered hand and bussed her cheek. Her fresh—even if cinnamonless—scent, which he couldn't name, stirred dancing-close memories. Sally held his hand and led him into the living room.

"Pax, this is my brother, Bud."

"Hello, Lieutenant," the younger man said. "Dad tells me we'll be in the same air wing, and you've already had a tour in F-8s." Bud's grip suited Pax—firm, but not macho—and his eye contact never wavered.

"Right, Bud, maybe we can look out for one another."

Pax noted that Bud's crew-cut matched his dad's, but its dark brown color matched his mother's. His brown eyes matched neither his dad's blue nor his mom and sister's green.

An auburn-haired woman, about Sally's age, wearing black slacks and a white sweater, came down the stairway. Sally said, "Becky, this is Pax Langford. Pax, my good friend from school, Becky Johnston."

"Hi, Becky. What did Sally do, make you drive her down here while she slept?" Pax asked.

"Not the whole trip, Pax, but I can tell you know her well."

Captain Banks came in carrying a magnum of champagne in a large ice-bucket, followed by Barbara with a tray of crystal flutes.

"Let's get the toasts to old age out of the way," the captain said, "before we relax.

"Hi, Pax, good to see you again." They shook hands, and Pax puckered a near-kiss at Barbara's offered cheek. Bud twisted the cork from the bottle, which popped loud enough for everyone's satisfaction, and Sally caught some overflow in her hands, which she licked. Bud filled their glasses. The Banks' happiness completely washed over and included Becky and Pax.

Bud cleared his throat, subdued a grin, and faced his dad. "A toast," he said and raised his glass, "to Bobby Layne's favorite receiver at Texas University, to a Korean *police action* MiG-killer, and to the first man to live after stepping from a supersonic jet to check for a flat tire. I give you Navy Olathe's bull-of-the-woods on his forty-third birthday—United States Navy Captain Turner Banks, my old man."

"Hear, hear," the listeners chanted.

The captain's ruddy neck throbbed almost purple, and his eyes welled. But he fished out a handkerchief and wiped away the evidence. He nodded a tight smile and raised a glass toward his son. "Such praise, coming from a more recent favorite receiver at the Naval Academy, and a soon-to-be combat-tested, navy fighter pilot is much appreciated. I'm honored to be your old man.

"Forty-three years don't make a man old, unless most gamblers sold him out at thirty-nine. You three pulled me past the odds; your love beat the bookies. Pax, you and Becky don't know how Babs and Beans—"

"Dad," Sally said and groaned.

"Excuse me. Babs and Sally took turns watching at my Bethesda bed, juggling school schedules for almost two years. They brought me back from a black hole. At the same time, they finished school. Hell! As much as they were doing, I'd have been embarrassed to die. During school breaks, Bud beat up on me if I wasn't training hard enough. They're a hard driving bunch, this family; I'm proud to be a member."

Pax raised his glass and swept his arm from son to father. "Well said by you both."

Will family moments always hurt? God, I hope not. But when'll it stop?

The captain raised the large bottle in front of Pax. "How about a freshener? Can't walk on one leg."

Pax eased his empty glass out of range. "No, thanks, I'm fine. Your family exudes warmth, Captain. I'm glad things worked out."

"Thanks, Pax. We've been lucky. . . . Did you land about sunset?"

The ladies headed for the kitchen. "No, it's okay, gentlemen. We gals don't need any help," Barbara said.

Pax nodded toward Banks. "Yes, sir, about an hour ago."

"Bud and I were playing catch in the front yard; we watched your approach. What the hell happened?"

Pax told them.

Bud's expression never changed, but his dad bowed his head, shook it, raised his eyes to his son, and winked. Banks stepped closer to Pax, gripped his shoulders and made a big production of looking into each of his ears.

"What?" Pax asked.

"I can't understand it," said the straight-faced Banks.

"What?" Pax repeated.

"Most people that lucky have rabbit feet for ears."

Pax laughed the loudest.

"How did you have the guts to go full throttle when your nose was pointing straight down?" Banks asked.

"Dad, let's change the subject," Bud said.

"It's okay, Bud. Captain, I don't remember adding full power; I don't remember adding any power."

"Bud and I watched it happen, but I'll never know how you kept from pulling into a stall."

"Dad, I think we ought to drop it."

"Thanks, Bud, but I don't mind. And I don't blame your dad for being curious. I saw a student get low and slow in a Panther at Pensacola. He panicked, jerked the nose up, stalled, and crashed. Killed him. Even with adrenaline spurting from my ears, I remembered that.

"Truth is I never imagined I could make the runway. My hope—a fervent prayer, I guess—was to minimize damage. Anything less than perpendicular impact looked impossible for several raggedy-assed heartbeats. I'm sorry you had to watch it."

Banks raised his glass to Pax. "Had that been me, I'd be shit-faced drunk by now. Thank God for miracles. But Bud's right, topic closed."

Becky waxed comical at dinner; her school stories kept everyone laughing. Pax realized that he was nodding a silent approval.

If Sally wanted to provide Bud good company for the weekend, she's done it.

Bud's attentive eyes and gentle zingers toward Becky confirmed Sally's success. After dinner, the two younger couples confessed an urge to see the local beer-joint. The elder Bankses decided not to accompany them—to everyone's satisfaction. But as they walked toward Sally's car, Banks called Pax back to the front porch. He spoke louder than a whisper, but not much. "I talked to one of our old squadron mates yesterday, Smokey Harper. When I mentioned meeting you, he said you and Brandy had been their favorite couple." The voice stopped, but his piercing, icy-blue eyes screamed several questions from under arched eyebrows.

I knew it had to happen. If not now, later.

"That's right, Captain, Smokey and Irene were good friends. Our first dinner, when you were satisfying your curiosity about me, you ran out of questions before I ran out of answers. If you had asked me if I had been in a car wreck after a graduation party, and if my wife, Brandy, and if my two-year-old son, Paxton, had been killed . . . and if you had asked me if I'd been drinking . . . well, I would have answered yes three times."

Banks stared at Pax's face for a couple of beats, bowed his head, and looked at his own feet. He pushed something aside with a shoe and took a deep breath. "I'm sorry, Pax. Sorry it happened, and I wish I could have waited until you decided to tell us. I haven't said anything to anyone else." He shook Pax's hand. "Go have a good time."

"It's been a full day already; I doubt we'll be too late. Good night, Captain."

The beer-joint crowd packed around a too-short bar, almost hidden in cigarette smoke. A live band, indistinguishable above the din, appeared to be playing something. Pax felt, more than heard, the bass drum beat and smelled stale sweat and cigarettes. "What do you think?" he shouted at the others.

"I'll have a Coors," Sally yelled between cupped hands. Bud and Becky nodded they'd take the same. Pax pointed Bud toward an empty table before elbowing his way into the melee at the bar. The Saint Patrick's night special was draft beer dyed green, and gallons of it were getting spilled.

When he returned with the drinks, two leather-clad bikers and their women sat where he'd pointed Bud. It took Pax several glances into the darkest corners before he spotted Bud standing and waving at him.

"I couldn't see you," Pax said and handed them their beers. "I was looking for your red sweater, Sally; when did you change?"

"I'll never understand why people think fighter pilots have such great eyes," Sally said. "I changed before we left home. We looked too much like brother and sister," she leaned toward him and spoke behind her hand into his ear, "and I don't feel like your sister."

"That's good news," he said.

"We could have kept the other table," Bud said, "but it meant kicking the crap out of those bikers. Becky had her fists doubled-up and was raring to go, but Sis voted no."

Becky shook her head. "Not close to the truth. One of the animals yelled at Bud, 'Hey, dick-head, that's our table.' To which your Sally replied, 'Hey, dick-head, there's no sign on it.' But we decided that particular table was too close to the loudspeakers and beat feet back here."

"Good choice," Pax said and faked a punch at Sally's arm.

Bud and Becky left for the dance floor. Sally was halfway out of her seat, but Pax held her arm. "Wait. Please. I need to tell you something."

Chapter 4—RENDEZVOUS

"What? *Not* another lecture about my filthy mouth . . . is it?"

He shook his head and held one of her hands in both of his. "Sally, I *was* married."

She withdrew her hand. "But you told Dad—"

"I told your dad I wasn't married and I hadn't been divorced."

Sally arched her eyebrows and shook her head. "I don't understand."

Cigarette smoke and stench swamped the underpowered filtration system, and Pax's ears ached from the loudspeakers' blare. He put a hand over one of Sally's where she gripped the table's edge. "My wife and two-year-old son were killed in an automobile accident four and a half years ago. I was driving, and I'd been drinking."

"Why didn't you say so?"

"When? The first night I met your folks? It didn't seem appropriate dinner conversation. Besides, it's personal; I doubt I've told more than three people since it happened."

The band took a break; Bud and Becky returned. Bud drained his beer and spun a pointed finger in a circle over their bottles. "Again? You drinking Pepsi, Pax?"

They nodded. Pax squeezed Sally's hand and pointed toward the dance floor.

"Why not?" she said and led the way to the jukebox. Their Ray Charles selections filled the floor, and Sally filled his arms as well as he remembered.

Have I screwed this up? I sure hope not.

"At least now I know you don't like boys," she said.

"No, but I like you, and I love what I do."

Sally moved away a bit and looked into his eyes. "Which is?"

"I fight airplanes."

"You and Dad. Are you also *the world's greatest fighter pilot?*"

"I used to be; it's been a while."

"Everything considered, don't you think you overdid the holier-than-thou act about *my* little secrets?"

"Hmm, maybe."

"Maybe. . .? Did you say *maybe*?"

"Your questions interrupt my counting. One, two, three. I may step on your feet. One and two."

She put her head on his shoulder and moved closer.

Pax turned off the shower and listened. Another ring made him reach for a towel.

Who the hell's that? Three people know I'm in Colorado Springs; nobody knows where I'm staying. Nobody. A wrong number? In a motel?

He swore at two additional rings, while he tucked the towel around his waist and wet-footed to a bedside table. He snatched the receiver to a damp ear. "Langford."

"Whoa! What did I interrupt?" Sally asked.

He looked at the receiver and shook his head. "You're amazing. I checked in ten minutes ago, and nobody knew I'd be *here*. How'd you get this number?"

"You're *easy*, Langford, but you still haven't told me why you barked at the phone."

"If you know so much, you should realize I'm dripping wet out of the shower."

"I knew that."

Her perky voice reminded him—*as if I need reminding*—how those green eyes could sparkle. "Uh-huh, now where are *you*?"

"I'm at school, and as I remember, your schedule puts you in Fort Collins in a couple days. Right?"

"Yeah. Day after tomorrow, for three days. Why?"

"Well, that might work. Our debating team drives there tomorrow, but their coach got sick. The English department wants me to go along, more as a chaperon than a teacher. Would I get in your way?"

"Tell me where you'll stay; I'll avoid it."

Reckon I can find a snow-covered chalet with a fireplace?

As he listened to her throaty chuckle, the hair on his arms stood.

"I don't know," she said. "Team members get dorm rooms; teachers get invited into a faculty home. Got a pencil?"

"Wait one; yeah, go ahead."

She gave him the Colorado State University's Student Union number and

41

asked what time he would get in.

"I'll land mid-afternoon."

"Okay, call me at that number, day after tomorrow at six o'clock. Maybe we can get a cup of coffee or something."

"Dinner sounds better, but I'll call at six. *Now*, how did you find me?"

"Like I said, Pax, you're easy. Ta-ta." The phone clicked dead.

A short phone call means nothing. Does it? I'd be wrong to read anything into it. Wouldn't I?. . . . I didn't go looking for a replacement, babe. Honest.

Night came, but sleep didn't. He finished a paperback. He drank water. The bedding got twisted. He straightened it out. And when fatigue sealed his eyes, Sally joined the riot of tumble-down nightmares. He shot down a MiG and saw Brandy in the parachute. Or was it Sally? He crashed the T-34, time and again, and from the gore he heard little Paxton, Brandy, and Sally laughing . . . like maniacs.

Lurching upright—wide-awake, heart pounding—in the dream-tossed bed left him exhausted, but reluctant to sleep again. What was worse, the horrific nights slowed the clock—no matter how often he tapped or shook his wristwatch.

That second hand wouldn't overtake a palsied snail.

Yet, two long days later, when Pax flew from Colorado Springs toward Fort Collins, he'd found no answers, solved no problems.

These Colorado snowflakes have a solid future compared to mine. Vietnam looms large between me and any plans . . . even should Sally and I meld our plans.

And what makes me think we have a future? Why am I so eager to see her, in—he checked his watch—*three hours and ten minutes? Too many questions—not enough answers. I could make a list, but she'd probably laugh at me. Hell, I should laugh at myself.*

Looking out, Pax estimated the visibility at twelve to fifteen miles, but radio weather advisories reported "beyond gale-force" westerly surface winds at Fort Collins, with gusts to 95-mph.

Tom said we'd use a small macadam airstrip west of town. If the wind's not right, I can always divert to Boulder.

At Fort Collins, Pax discovered that the narrow runway ran north and south, while the hurricane-strength wind whipped down from the west through a pine-covered valley and over a long, river-bed reservoir before plummeting from a high, earthen dam, two miles upwind of the runway.

No plane can land in that much crosswind.

Even flying down the strip, looking for potholes, proved nigh impossible—it required 75-degrees of crab. While at the south end of the strip, Tom Cain leaned into the wind, crossing his arms back-and-forth over his head—the "wave-off" signal.

"*Maybe,* maybe not," Pax said.

What would I do if I had to land? Right now! He smiled. *Why not? Let's at least have a look-see.*

Pax circled at eight hundred feet until his nose pointed west, straight into the wind and perpendicular to the runway. When overhead the runway, he lowered the landing gear and flaps. The airplane began backing up, away from the runway.

Look at that? Winds blowin' faster than landing speed.

"Humph! Now what?"

He tried it again, but without flaps.

I'm not backing up, but you'd need a calendar to measure forward progress.

He cycled the gear up-and-down. Gear up, he moved forward; gear down, he inched ahead. Hard as the wind blew, though, its velocity varied as much as 40-kts, with anvil-lick gusts slamming into the plane. The g-meter pegged-out in both directions.

Wind spilling over that damned dam must cause the turbulence. The only advantages I've got over a bronc rider are my seat belt and shoulder harness. Can the airplane take it?

After a couple of tries, he wallowed exactly over the runway's center.

Now, can I stay here?

The engine noise changed with the sharp up-and-down wind gusts and alternating wing-drops.

Kinda like balancing a baseball on a vertical yardstick.

Pax found he could keep it in one small piece of sky.

He took a deep breath, reduced a tad of throttle, and eased the nose down a few degrees. At four hundred feet, he leveled and further convinced himself he could maintain a semblance of stationary flight. So it went. At fifty feet, corrections became larger and more rapid.

I can do this; I can plop this baby in the center of that runway.

But after being ignored, Tom jumped into the Chrysler and drove—flashing its lights—part way down the runway. Out of the car again, he jumped up and down giving Pax frantic wave-off signals. Pax ignored him and continued playing helicopter. With patience and pains, he eased his blue and gold version of an Otis elevator onto the widest strip of blacktop runway in the United States—albeit the shortest.

At touchdown, with no forward movement, his airspeed indicator bounced between 75- and 85-knots. So despite achieving his goal, touching down in the center of the runway, the plane was—for practical purposes—flying. It shook and bounced. Pax needed throttle to stay in the middle of the runway.

If I shut the engine down, I'll be blown backwards off the macadam. And I can't turn and taxi down the runway without getting blown sideways or flipped over on a wing. This ad-lib landing, although successful, might prove a hollow victory.

Tom leaned backwards into the gale and gave Pax a head shake and shoulder shrug, neither of which camouflaged his "dumb-shit" evaluation. Pax motioned him back to the end of the runway and began experimenting. After a few minor glitches, he discovered a way to maneuver sideways down the runway. He added enough throttle to get airborne, while balancing left aileron against right rudder. After a small sideways hop, he retarded enough throttle to touch back down.

It doesn't look too professional—hopping down the runway sideways, like a kangaroo with vertigo--but it does the job. I can already hear my next happy hour line: "Any drunk frog could've done it."

And once he saw Pax's scheme working, Tom caught the spirit and stationed himself west of some tie-down rings past the south end of the runway. Pax continued his sidewinder advance until Tom signaled the plane was lined up and Pax should retard some throttle. The almost-flying airplane backed over the tie-down rings. Tom crossed his forearms (the emergency braking signal) and ducked under a wing. Pax added sufficient throttle to stop his backward movement and soon felt the plane being snugged to the ground.

Wind howled, and the wings flexed against Tom's tie-down ropes, but Pax's flight was over. His unconventional bucking bronc was back in the chute. Tom appeared from under a wing and passed the edge of a flat hand across his throat. Pax gladly killed the engine.

Once outside the protective cockpit, and without engine noise, Pax marveled at the wind's ferocity. He couldn't walk without leaning low into it—low enough to touch his fingers to the ground. And its shrieking put his teeth on edge.

It might rip that convertible's top off. No wonder he tried to send me somewhere else.

Tom maneuvered the car with his piercing blue-eyed stare varying neither left nor right. "You act like a damned idiot. Yet, you lucked out again. Why do these things?"

"How many times in your life, Tom, have you seen an 85-knot, perpendicular crosswind?"

"I never have, before today."

"Me neither. When it gets high enough, we always change runways, or else we don't fly. But we're talking normal situations; today *ain't* normal. The wind exceeded our landing speed. Think about it. If we always had a wind this strong, landing areas could just be 40-foot squares."

"Okay, smart-ass, what would've happened if the wind had come to a sudden stop? I'll tell you what would've happened: you'd've busted your butt. Right?"

"You're right, no argument. You win. . . . But *it* didn't, and I didn't."

"And what if I hadn't been there to tie the plane down? What then?"

"But you were, and you did. Did I forget to thank you?"

"Don't grin at me, Pax; I'm serious." Tom's rapier-like glances slashed at Pax. "That landing was dumb! You can't keep getting away with that crap."

Pax put his hand on Tom's shoulder. "Partner, I didn't mean to upset you. We're our own bosses out here; we have lots of leeway. We didn't come in here pell-mell and flop the bird down crossways on the old runway. There was a possibility; I tested it; it worked. Now we both know what can work in a similar situation. It wasn't anything you couldn't have done." Pax curled his toes and bit his tongue to keep from grinning.

Tom turned toward him. "Maybe, . . . maybe so. I might've done the same thing, but I doubt it."

Overhead signal lights swung pendulum-like at the Fort Collins intersections. Refuse blew from and through alleys, across wide streets, and lay pinned against the buildings, fences, and shrubs. Their motel's large sign had been ripped from its pole. Four men labored, dragging it from the center of the parking lot when Tom stopped in front of the office.

"Tom, I have a friend in town who has invited me for dinner. Do you need the car?"

"Aha! *That* might explain your hardheadedness. Got a hot date?" Tom asked and tossed him the keys.

Pax smiled and hurried down the passageway to his room.

One more hour and I'll hear her voice.

But he was off by five minutes—and more than five hundred miles.

Becky Johnston answered the call for Sally. "I'm sorry, Pax, but Sally's in Olathe. Her dad collapsed yesterday morning on a handball court and is in the hospital. I took her place with the debating team. She asked me to have you call her."

After one ring, Sally answered: "Hello."

"How's your dad, Sally?"

"Hi. He seems okay; they're running lots of tests. The doctors tried to be encouraging. They said there was at least one excellent sign: Dad's cranky as hell. They'll be glad to get rid of him."

"How's your mom?"

"Okay; I'll tell her you asked. She's at the hospital. This scared her. Bud's on the way to San Diego, doesn't know, and we probably won't worry him."

Pax didn't know what to say, but after a silent beat or two offered, "I hope your dad's tests are full of good news. Does he play much handball?"

"He used to; this was his first game in a long time. I guess he overdid it. Are fighter pilots terminally stupid?"

Pax said nothing.

Her voice trembled. "Sorry, I didn't mean that. I'm just relieved he seems all right. And I'm sorry we missed dinner. Why don't you ask Becky?"

"Thanks, but no thanks."

"That's a pretty good response for a fighter pilot."

"Everything tends to work out for the best. How long will you stay in Olathe?"

"Depends on Dad. I may stretch it through Saturday and drive back Sunday."

"I won't get back till Sunday; give your folks my best."

"I will. Thanks for calling; you're sweet. Goodbye, Pax."

"So long, Beans." Pax grinned and hung up.

The next morning a candle could have burned without a flicker on either end of the macadam runway, and a steady stream of flight candidates awaited their turns to defy gravity with the navy lieutenant in the orange flight suit.

A Saturday telegram, directing Pax's return to Olathe, hung from his key-hook when he returned to the motel.

"Horseshit," he said.

After eleven flights today, I'll wait till morning.

Sunday's crack-of-dawn takeoff had Pax pointing the T-34's propeller spinner toward a whitish-yellow sunrise. The engine thrummed its reliable tune, while Pax hummed a mindless accompaniment. Twenty minutes after leveling off, each wing's leading edge began erasing from view large swaths of near-featureless, near-endless Kansas plains. He stretched his neck and twisted his upper torso to its limit in each direction and cranked the T-34 through a quick aileron roll.

"Man, *this* is flying; having somebody else in your airplane . . . that's called *being airborne.*"

Chapter 5—GOODBYES and HELLOS

Two official navy messages at the BOQ office modified Pax's orders. His reporting date to VF-124, the San Diego F-8 replacement training squadron, had been moved up. "Not later than 4 May 1966," Pax read aloud. "In three days? More than two weeks early, but I guess they're serious."

"Sir?" Petty Officer Smith's wide-eyed query broke Pax's concentration. "Sir?" he repeated.

"Oh, nothing. Looks like this is my last night. I'll check out in the morning."

"Yes, sir, Mister Langford. Enjoyed having you."

A quick call, answered by Barbara Banks, confirmed Sally had already left for school and the captain was home from the hospital—well enough, but ordered to rest for a couple of days.

"Would it be okay if I come by for a few minutes, to say goodbye?" Pax asked. "My orders have been changed; I leave in the morning."

"Oh, Pax, I hate to hear that, but certainly, come ahead."

Captain Banks, wearing wash khakis and a faded sweatshirt, met him at the door. "Bud called from San Diego last night. Your new squadron had a midair Friday morning. They lost both pilots, and both were second tour F-8 drivers."

"I guess that explains it," Pax said. "Anyway, I wanted to stop by to check on you and thank you both for your hospitality."

"Our pleasure, Pax," Barbara said, "but Sally will be disappointed. Maybe you can call her and say goodbye."

"I will. Captain, did the quacks give you a clean bill?"

"Sorta, but you know quacks. I'd bet on outliving the two who worked on me. I'm glad you'll be in Bud's air wing. He likes you, and I think he'll listen

48

to you—more so than to me. If you happen to write Sally, you might tell her how Bud's doing. He thinks it's illegal to write letters."

"I'll be glad to. I hope Sally and I'll be writing."

The men shook hands; Pax kissed Barbara's cheek.

"You and Bud be careful out there, Pax," she said and pumped her thumb over her shoulder toward her husband. "Real men get the job done and come on home. Wannabe heroes are dime a dozen. They end up dead." Captain Banks nodded agreement, so Pax raised a thumbs-up, nodded, and left. Walking back to the BOQ, he tried to visualize another airplane through an F-8 gun sight. Six years hadn't dimmed the image.

When he called Sally, her vehement reaction to his orders surprised him.

"Dammit! Something told me not to leave. I had a powerful urge to stay, but I thought it concerned Dad."

"I saw them this afternoon; your dad looks great. Maybe Bud and I can steal a couple of F-8s for a weekend in Olathe. Or you guys might even get out to San Diego; who knows? Anyway, we had fun."

"Yes, we did. You take care." The words dried up for them both, so they exchanged addresses and hung up.

Okay, I wanted this war; now I'm on my way. But I have to hurry, and the war's gotta last till I get there.

Two suitcases, two laid-flat, hang-up bags, two parachute bags full of flight-gear, and a beat-up briefcase filled every cranny in the Corvette.

I won't have to worry about picking up any hitchhikers.

Two and a-half days later, Pax changed into a short-sleeved khaki uniform in his NAS Miramar BOQ room and reported to his new squadron. The VF-124 junior officer of the day, a crew-cut, black-haired lieutenant junior grade, looked at Pax's orders and sniffed. "They expected you earlier this morning; the welcome aboard speeches are over."

"Damn!" Pax deadpanned. "Reckon anyone taped them?"

"I doubt it. The operations officer, Lieutenant Commander Grayson, is in the ready room if you want to let him know you're here."

"Hacksaw Grayson?"

"Himself. Are you friends?"

"I'll go find out and let you know."

The JOOD picked up a clipboard and ran a finger down the day's schedule. "He briefs in a few minutes."

"Thanks, Lieutenant," Pax squinted at the duty officer's name tag, "Nelson. See you around."

He ambled along the second story passageway's gleaming, gray tile deck and looked down through waist-high windows, opposite the offices and ready room, at twelve gray and white F-8s undergoing maintenance on the hangar deck. Through open hangar doors, to the south, Pax counted fifteen more F-8s parked in slanted rows on the flight line.

I'm back. Anyone'll play hell prying me out of fighters again. No way. That Meridian, Mississippi, purgatory tour—my payback for leaving the navy—is in the rearview mirror, a debt damned-well paid.

The balding Hacksaw Grayson, in an orange flight suit, leaned over the ready room squawk box. "C'mon, Chief," Hacksaw sweet-talked the box, "how much longer for that fourth aircraft?"

Static spewed from the speaker, but jumbled oaths and clatter gave way to a response, of sorts. "You can have it now, sir, if you don't want it fueled or preflighted. Otherwise, it'll be forty-five minutes, . . . sir. Did the schedule change, . . . sir?"

"No change, Chief. Thanks." Hacksaw looked up from the box and spotted Pax, at the same instant Pax recognized Bud Banks on a second-row, leather sofa, looking through a thick notebook.

"Pax Langford, you prodigal son, where the hell you been?" Hacksaw grinned, took Pax's extended hand, and pulled him into a bear hug. "God, son, we done got the California Highway Patrol looking for your young ass. You get lost? What the hell kind of boondoggle put you in Olathe, Kansas?"

Pax winked at Bud over Hacksaw's shoulder. "Temporary orders, Cecil."

Lounging pilots perked up, looked at Hacksaw, and at each other. "Cecil?" one asked another.

"Yeah," answered the second pilot, "he called Commander Grayson—the famous Hacksaw—Cecil."

"Aw hell, Pax," Grayson rumbled, not moving his lips any more than a well-practiced ventriloquist, "how'd you remember Cecil?"

"Wasn't too hard. If you remember, I tagged you Hacksaw."

"Oh, yeah. I'd forgotten, but we won't go into that. Is Brandy with you?"

"No."

"You didn't let that foxy little wife get away, did you?"

Pax noticed Bud's head come up from the folder.

He hadn't been told.

"Brandy died in a car accident."

Grayson grimaced and sucked air through his teeth. "Sorry, pardner, I didn't know. Gotta go brief my flight, but I'm sure glad you're here. Be in the club later?"

"Maybe. I have to unload some more gear at the BOQ and get something to eat."

Grayson shot Pax a thumbs-up and left the ready room. Pax walked over and shook Bud's hand. "Your dad said you'd called about the midair. What happened? Tactics?"

Bud nodded. "Lost sight of each other, looks-like . . . explosion . . . no ejections. Our skipper said BUPERS moved your orders up, along with another lieutenant I believe you know. Camp Brogan?"

"Camp Brogan? Afraid so."

"He sure as heck knows you. Several other instructors know you, too, or about you. You forgot to mention your reputation. Have you ever lost a dogfight?"

Pax glanced around the ready room and leaned close to Bud. "I don't think dogfights or reputations count for much unless you're firing real bullets. You living in the BOQ?"

Bud shook his head. "Four of us have a snake-ranch in La Jolla. From what I've seen, I'd recommend town over the BOQ. Pax, I wasn't eavesdropping, but I heard you and Hacksaw. I'm sorry about your wife."

"Yeah, thanks. Sally and your dad knew." Pax felt, rather than saw, relief flood Bud's face. "I guess they didn't get a chance to mention it to you. Did I miss anything important today?"

Bud picked a book bag up from the floor and extracted a schedule. "This says we start through the instrument squadron Monday. That takes a week. We get settled, update our flight gear, get a medical up-chit, and read this pass-down folder. It hangs there by the squadron duty officer's desk."

Pax stood, stretched, and headed for the door. "See you Monday, if not before."

From the ready room, Pax descended some stairs to the hangar deck and weaved between the F-8s. He smiled at, touched, courted—fell in love again—with the sleek Crusaders. He'd forgotten how big they were: over fifty-four feet long, sixteen feet to the top of the tail, and a wingspan of thirty-six feet. The office, his cockpit, placed him nine feet behind an F-8's pointed nose. Forty-five feet of fuselage behind him held guns, missiles, fuel, electronics, an in-flight refueling probe, and an afterburner equipped Pratt and Whitney engine with the power to stick his own nose anywhere he'd want to put it.

And while neither Pax, nor his friends, thought of their work in erotic terms, he'd smiled at civilians who thought the language of flying fighters sounded sexy. Engines were rated in pounds of thrust. Entering clouds constituted a penetration. Maneuvering into a kill position against an opponent meant settling into his rearward hemisphere, within weapons' range, where you'd either speed a missile up his butt or hose him down with twenty-millimeter cannon shells. And no adversary willingly backed into those weapons. A kill, or even a simulated kill, reeked of indescribably violent rape.

Pax had met and become friends with a psychologist at Texas A&M who—in a rare state of lucidity—had described fighter pilots flying in afterburner as omnipotent hard-ons, at least in their own subconsciousness. And like Hacksaw Grayson—when confronted escorting less than attractive women—most F-8 drivers responded, "Hey, a kill's a kill."

Pax's musings evaporated as a tall, dark-haired, first class petty officer appeared at his elbow.

"Mister Langford?"

Pax faced him. "Yes?"

"It is Lieutenant Langford, isn't it?"

"Well I'll be damned, Silky Chandler," Pax said. "The navy must be bare-boned for first class parachute riggers."

"And crazy fighter jocks," Chandler said, showing a toothy grin as he shook Pax's outstretched hand. "I had the duty the other night and saw your orders. I couldn't believe it; we thought you went civilian."

"I did, but it didn't work out. Seems like an interesting time to be coming back, though. Maybe we can prove these F-8s can do what we always bragged they could."

"Guess what?" Chandler's ear-to-ear grin erased the six years since Pax had served with the lanky enlisted man on the East Coast.

Pax shut one eye and rubbed his chin. "Well, you're grinning like it's good news. What did you do, quit drinking and learn to shine your shoes?"

"Nope. But we're going to VF-39 together. And guess who else."

Pax grabbed his head with both hands. "Aw, man, I thought you had good news. Crud! Next thing I know, you'll be telling me Lieutenant Brogan's been ordered in."

"You already heard; ain't that a kick? I wouldn't be a tin-bender in VF-39 for full commander's pay. We already got bets laid on who'll pull a wing off first."

"Good to see you again, Petty Officer Chandler." Pax grabbed the rigger's hand. "Congratulations on both promotions. But being in the same squadron, I doubt Lieutenant Brogan and I will be fighting each other too much."

"Right, Lieutenant, pigs can fly and shrimp can whistle."

As he walked away from Chandler's chortle, Pax remembered some of his first commanding officer's advice.

"Don't waste time trying to bullshit the men; it can't be done."

Pax stowed the rest of his gear in his BOQ room, washed road grime from the Corvette and from himself. Slacks, a knit golf shirt, and loafers felt about right, with a long-sleeved sweater for later. He walked through the Miramar Officers Club front door at 1800 and gravitated toward a raucous din. As expected, Wednesday's happy hour crowd reflected an hour and a-half head start.

Short-skirted waitresses carrying laden trays weaved between crowded tables and standing circles of boisterous aviators. Most clusters centered around young men with flying hands, reenacting dogfights. More experienced hands even flew holding full glasses, seldom spilling a drop. Virtuosos flew two full glasses and waxed philosophic with a cigarette dangling from down-turned mouths. They squinted hard against the curling smoke—which further emphasized their deepening crow's-feet: fighter pilots' badges, earned from hours searching for targets near the sun. And as moths to the flame, wall-to-wall gorgeous, young, well-tanned women displayed fetching glimpses of breasts and legs.

I've been gone too long; getting back—knee-deep-in-it back—sounds, smells, and looks like a prisoner's dream.

It filled his lungs and swelled his heart.

Hacksaw drank from a full pitcher; he waved an empty one at a passing waitress. His blond fringe of hair and short-sleeved khaki uniform shirt were drenched. Moisture dripped from both shaggy eyebrows. "Hey, Pax, where've you been?"

"What happened, Cecil?"

"Aw, nothing much. Little redheaded waitress—a new one—got pissed 'cause I patted her ass. She poured a pitcher of beer on me. Ain't that the shits?"

"I guess. You haven't changed much."

Hacksaw's grin narrowed his eyes to slits. The Mississippian's bulbous cheeks glowed pink as he tried to wrap Pax in a soggy embrace. "You sumbitch, Pax. It's good to see you again."

"Hey, squadronmate," the grating, unmistakable voice put Pax's teeth on edge, "don't let a quack see you two embracing like that." The firm grip on both of Pax's shoulders—from behind—annoyed Pax even worse than the voice.

I ought to elbow the sonofabitch in the gut!

Holding beer-soaked Hacksaw at arms length, Pax turned around, breaking the shoulder grip. Camp's blue-gray eyes sparked level at Pax. The blond crew cut and accustomed sneer hadn't changed. A tailored uniform shirt emphasized his well-maintained and powerful vee.

"Thought you had another year at Meridian, Langford," Brogan said, "learning to fly again. Whose ass you been kissing now?"

Pax's face froze in a death mask smile. "Hey, Camp," he whispered, which made Brogan lean closer—a quizzical look taking hold—"I won't tell anyone we're headed for the same squadron if you won't." Pax knew his own eyes were flashing; he predicted Camp's reaction.

"Screw you, Langford!" Brogan spun away and lurched toward the bar, trailing a jostled wake of disgruntled drinkers.

Hacksaw dripped afresh. "Seems she's adamant against havin' her ass patted." Even in the close confines of a happy hour crowd, the beer-soaked Lothario earned his own circular space. Pax nodded and figured nobody liked standing on soggy carpet or absorbing a waitress's ricochets. Nor did he. And he didn't want to share confined air with Brogan.

"I'm outta here, Hacksaw. Where's a good place to eat?"

"Try Gordo's on La Jolla Boulevard, buddy. Great bar, great prime rib, acres and acres of prime pussy. If you can't get laid in Gordo's, you better start dancing backwards."

Pax figured that convertibles were invented with San Diego in mind. The Corvette's throaty exhaust rumbled back at him from ice plant-covered embankments. The terraced hills supported white stucco and tan adobe houses with red-tiled roofs. Winding down the road toward the Pacific Ocean and its salty smells should have been more enjoyable.

You'd've loved this, Brandy. We should have shared it.

The red traffic signal caught him daydreaming. He stopped in the painted crosswalk, before backing up. A black-and-white cruiser, its officer waggling a finger toward Pax, crossed through the intersection.

Forget her, Pax, she's gone. How many times have I told myself that?

He pushed past standing would-be customers in Gordo's entry to glimpse the interior bedlam. A long, polished bar withstood the four-customer-deep throng's push. Table chairs sagged under lap-sitting loads, and booth benches groaned from three-customer squeezes. Hacksaw's description lacked depth. Gordo's bacchanalian flavor galloped beyond the loosest pale.

A pair of Spanish guitarists strummed, picked, and thumped from a platform behind the bar, while two flamenco dancers stamped their love at each other. But few patrons watched or listened. Flush-faced drinkers grinned and laughed, and bodies were squeezed together. Gordo's Wednesday night business tolerated music, booze, and food, but Gordo's reeked of wanton sex.

Pax shook his head—*I don't think so*—and started to leave.

"Whoa, fella!" blurted the nearest of three women standing together at the head of the long line. She put her hand on his sweatered arm. "Are you alone?"

"What?" Pax asked and cupped a hand behind his near ear. "What did you say?"

"I said—"

"Make sure he's not in the navy," one of the other two women said.

"—we need a fourth to get a table. It's a Wednesday night rule. We'll buy you a drink to sit with us until we order. Okay? Please?"

"Table for four!" a sweating waiter called out. A foursome behind the three women and Pax started edging past.

"Hold on, folks, we got our fourth," the woman said and grabbed his arm.

Well, I've seen uglier women. Much uglier.

He let himself be towed along behind the waiter. The group pushed and rubbed their way to a back table, nonchalant about crossing several bridges of physical intimacy en route.

They ordered four glasses of burgundy. Introductions were short: Pax met Jan, who had snagged him as he tried to leave; Robin, by far the prettiest, but who had a slight discoloration around one eye and seemed allergic to the navy; and Paula. All wore wedding rings.

"I came to eat; it looked too crowded," Pax said.

"Wednesdays and Fridays are feeding frenzies at Gordo's," Jan said, "but I'm not talking about the prime ribs."

"If you aren't in the navy, you're welcome to eat with us," Robin said. "If you are in the navy, you're welcome to finish your drink and leave. Sorry, but that's the way it is." Her easy smile belied the direct challenge in her eyes.

Neither of her companions objected to the pronouncement, however, so Pax raised his fishbowl-sized glass, "Ladies, I propose a toast to the United States Navy, which seems to have blessed me with good company for the evening." They drank to his toast.

"So what do you do, Pax?" Jan asked. "Where do you work?"

The three women are attractive, but especially that navy-allergic, dark-haired Robin in her peek-a-boo peasant's blouse. I'd probably enjoy spending the evening with them, but I'll be damned if I'll renounce the navy to do it.

Robin, who sat to his right, favored him with a teasing smile, leaned closer to the table, and actuated the full peek-a-boo.

"I'm a doctor," he said.

"What kind?" Robin asked.

"O.B.," he said. "I'm from Kansas. What do you ladies do?"

"We're navy wives," Robin said, "and our husbands are gone, so we avoid navy people. Don't want to sully the navy's image, do we?"

"Seems reasonable. Do you recommend the prime ribs?"

"Later we do," Jan said. "We try to have a couple of glasses of wine first. Speaking of which," she raised her empty glass at a passing waiter, "anyone else ready yet?" Both her companions nodded concurrence.

Pax addressed the waiter, "Make mine a Pepsi."

"Now I believe you're a doctor," Robin said. "Give me your hand; I'll tell your fortune."

Across the table, Paula handed Jan some money and stood. "See you tomorrow, Robin," she said and walked away. Robin traced her fingernail along Pax's palm and mumbled a few words. She looked up, frowning. "You've been married twice and have three kids. What happened?"

"Show me where it says that." he said and looked in disbelief at the hand she held.

"Right there," she said, pointing. "Plain as day, but something happened. What?"

New drinks came; Jan poured half of the extra into Robin's glass and the rest into her own. She handed Robin some folded bills, whispered something in her ear, and left.

"Was it something I said?" he asked. "Are we abandoned?"

"Do you care?" she asked, at full peek-a-boo.

"Nope."

"You see, I'm in town visiting from Fresno," she said. "This could be your lucky night."

After the ribs and a short hand-holding walk around the block through a thickening fog, Robin let go his hand and faced him. "Doctor Pax, do you perform examinations . . . after hours?"

"In emergencies, for friends or charming dinner companions, or both, as a special favor. But I don't yet have a local clinic. Are you asking for yourself?"

She took his hands and held them against her breasts, leaned her head back. "Hmm, I'm a bit light-headed. Does my heartbeat feel normal? What do you think?"

"It's an emergency, no doubt about it. You should be lying down, sooner the better. Maybe we can find someplace."

"Someone's watching over us," she said. "My motel's right across the street and down a block." Still holding his hand, she led him along the sidewalk.

Pax leaned his mouth close to her ear. "Are you, uh, on the pill? If not, we need to stop by my car."

"Forget your car, Pax; this is an emergency, but the answer is yes. Thanks for asking; doctors are nice people. Let's hurry."

After their second groping, Robin arched her sweat-glistened body hard against him and sucked in a gigantic breath before collapsing into rag-doll limpness. Pax couldn't even hear her breathing. He scrambled from the bed, wetted a wash cloth, and folded it across her forehead. She licked her lips, opened her eyes, saw him, and smiled. "Wow. What happened?"

Light from the bathroom revealed additional discolored areas matching Robin's one dark eye.

I'll bet she doesn't have an easy life. She's getting her licks in tonight against somebody—playing catch up.

Without knowing when it started, maybe after a short nap—but whenever—as things sped up again, Robin raised a hand trying to muffle her laughter when the headboard began banging against the wall. Pax felt torn between reclaiming a pillow from the floor and ignoring the tattletale thumping. But the laughing had to stop, so he snatched up the pillow and jammed it behind the offending headboard. He hoped the thumping hadn't earned a call to the office.

Funny, I didn't hear the banging earlier . . . either time.

Anyway, her headboard-banging giggles and his exhaustion pretty well wrapped up the marathon for Pax. Completely sated, sore—in self-defense—he came clean: "Robin, you're a healthy specimen, and I'd like to examine you again . . . in about a month—no sooner. But I gotta tell you, I'm no doctor; I'm a navy pilot."

She raised on an elbow; disgust hardened her face. A pointing finger beat rhythm for her words. "I don't like liars." She glared at him for a couple of seconds and rolled to face the wall. She pulled the sheet up tight around her neck.

"Me neither," Pax said.

But pussy-baited traps always catch me—they'll make me lie, cheat, or steal. I'll apologize for the lie in the morning.

Exhausted, he burrowed his head into the motel-hard pillow.

A maid's knocking stirred him; he was alone. Robin had left the nest bare, not even a hairpin remained. Curious, Pax checked the front desk. "I'm here to pick up a lady in room 112; I can't remember her name."

"Sorry," the clerk said, "I checked Mrs. Smith out at six o'clock this morning. Was she expecting you . . . ? Seems odd."

Pax shrugged his shoulders. "We talked about it last night; maybe I misunderstood. Thanks."

Driving back to the air station, Pax tried to frame a question regarding Robin's life, but he had no idea where to start.

What the hell? I'll never see her again.

Entering NAS Miramar's back gate wiped her from his slate.

After a quick shave and shower, Pax took his flight gear to the squadron riggers and left it for any required checks or modifications. He stopped by the dispensary after lunch to get the required medical up-chit. A tall, somber-looking flight surgeon informed him three inoculations had lapsed. "No shots, no up-chit, Lieutenant."

Pax felt his shirt turning damp. "Okay, but I don't do well with shots. How about one today, one tomorrow, and the third during my annual physical next month? I'd appreciate it if we could spread them out."

A slight smirk accompanied the head shake. "I remain amazed at our warriors' psyche. Fully half you fighter pilots would rather make a night-trap than get a shot. But I'll go along; you can get your up-chit after tomorrow's shot."

The agreement didn't make it any easier. When he walked from sick bay, Pax's uniform looked like he'd finished running a mile. He rested his head against the Corvette's steering wheel for several minutes, till the wooziness passed. He drove to the squadron, expecting to read the big, black notebook. But Camp Brogan had it.

"Damn, Pax, is it raining?" Brogan asked.

"Nope."

"You don't look so hot. Have you read this yet?"

"Nope, but I'll get it tomorrow. See you."

Chapter 6—TRAINING

Pax, Camp Brogan, and Bud Banks checked into VF-126, the instrument training squadron, on Monday morning. Coffee cup in hand, Bud concentrated on the welcoming spiel. Camp feigned acute boredom; an after-breakfast toothpick dangled from his lips. Pax sat with his arms crossed.

How often does the CO have to give these same opening remarks?

Through the morning lectures, Pax evaluated the staff instructors and his student peers. He questioned the three instructors on two small—what could have seemed insignificant—points, while Camp looked toward the ceiling and groaned. Bud watched the two lieutenants.

Camp's nonchalance is pure bullshit. I don't buy it—not for a minute. I've seen that facade before. Camp competes like a whirlwind. He'll chew you up and spit you out, with what he'd like you to think is minimal effort. These nine instrument flights are round-1 in what happens between us, and Bud has no idea that the gauntlet's been flung. But he'll learn, maybe.

The first TF-9J "Cougar" familiarization flights should have been sightseeing jaunts for everyone; Bud enjoyed his. Pax, however, once out of sight of the others started asking his instructor questions. And he requested no-attitude-gyro and no-compass approaches—anything to impress the instructor with an extraordinary interest in, and dedication to, that essential kingdom of instrument gauges.

This guy'll arrive at the Officers Club bar with renewed enthusiasm for his work.

So went the week. Any comments between Camp and Pax were complaints against impossible instrument approaches and the much-too-demanding instructors.

"Camp, I think I'm losing my touch," Pax said. "These approaches are damned hard."

"Yeah, maybe," Camp said. "My problem is flying the Cougar worth a crap; that kicking yaw-damper drives me nuts."

Bud listened to the disinformation, but said little. Pax's conscience almost kicked in enough to tell Bud what was going on. Almost, but not quite.

So when the instrument syllabus grades arrived back at the F-8 squadron, ranking Pax first and Bud a distant third, Pax was confident that Bud figured the grades must have been conferred by seniority.

"Don't sweat petty larceny grades," Camp told Bud.

But Camp's eyes smoldered when Pax said, "I don't understand those grades; *I* wasn't satisfied with my work."

Survival school at Warner Springs came next. A week of escape and evasion training, including three days in a simulated prisoner-of-war camp, described the course content. Horror stories abounded, however, of gross physical abuse during the last three and a-half days in the dry southern California hills. And most tales, the worst ones in particular, proved true.

After being captured at Warner Springs—and as soon as they'd entered the simulated prisoner compound—the three F-8 pilots watched in disbelief as the senior officer in their thirty man class received a gut smash with a rifle butt and, after falling to his knees, was knocked flat and pinned to the sunbaked ground. A second guard drove both his knees into the prone "prisoner's" stomach, grasped him by the flight suit collar, and bounced the gasping officer's head off the ground until the gasping stopped. Course rules forbade student interference: first-time violators were required to repeat the entire course; second-time offenders were removed from their squadrons and not allowed to deploy.

Emotions varied during the prisoner experience. "I knew about pain before this week," Pax wrote on his course critique. "A third class petty officer slapping the shit out of me taught me little, maybe some emotional restraint. Maybe."

Camp stood in the critique, and—at his sneering best—told them, "The two or three lessons learned this squandered week could have been covered in a thirty minute lecture. The entire course reeks of some pansy's wet dream. Absolute horseshit."

Bud told Pax what he'd written: "Great course. Recommend President Johnson and Robert McNamara attend—as simulated prisoners."

Two Monday mornings later, thirty minutes before sunrise, the three pilots and their chase instructors hurried through F-8 preflight inspections. Pax's gut churned in anticipation.

So I've been six years out of the bird . . . should my gloves be this sweat-soaked? I don't remember being this keyed up my first F-8 flight, eight years ago . . . as an ensign.

Starting procedures flowed, however, recalling familiar feelings and sounds. Pax enjoyed taxiing from the line first, followed by Camp, and the three instructors. Bud remained in the line, completing his checks as the first four planes taxied to the runway.

The Pratt and Whitney J-57's gentle rumble and the F-8's excellent nose-gear steering reassured Pax. The aircraft's instruments read normal, and once-familiar thumps and whines settled into his memory voids like old friends. As their planes pivoted to a canted line abreast in the warm up area—short of the runway—for their engine run-ups, Pax remembered how much the Crusader, with its two-position wing raised, resembled a bird of prey prior to pounce.

By the time he called the tower for takeoff clearance and, with his right hand, rammed the canopy locking handle forward, his movements and thoughts flowed automatically. Pinpricks of excitement climbed his back, as he confided to his oxygen mask, "Yessir, by God, I'm home."

At the tower's clearance, Pax pushed the throttle to its forward limit and watched the engine instruments wind and settle. Satisfied, he released the toe-brakes and accelerated down the runway. He lifted off, raised the landing gear, and lowered and locked the two-position wing without thought—back on a bicycle. He didn't fly the Crusader; he simply willed it hither and yon. Control and throttle movements must have happened, but they did so unsummoned, part of a natural flow. He skimmed over flat clouds and spiraled down around vertical ones, grunting with effort, as if he, himself, powered the plane as he'd soared in his dreams—without benefit of an airplane—for as long as he could remember.

Practice touch-and-go landings back at NAS Miramar completed the familiarization flights. Pax and Camp adjusted their landing patterns to touch down at the desired spot on the runway, at the desired airspeed. Bud, as a normal "nugget," searched for landmarks finding the proper landing pattern. He didn't find and refine them that first flight, but few nuggets did.

Later that afternoon, when Bud walked into the Officers Club bar, his face retained the mile-wide grin he'd worn throughout his flight and debrief. He sat beside Pax and rested his hand on the lieutenant's back. "Did it feel like you remembered?"

"Pretty much. I'd missed it, and now you know why."

"God, I guess. Jesus! I felt like a ham-fisted cretin or something, the way you taxied out of the line before I was halfway through my checklists." Bud nodded at the bartender. "I'll have a draft, and . . . Pax?" Pax nodded. "Make it two drafts. And," Bud looked sideways at Pax, "I talked to Dad, called to tell him about the flight. Beans was there; she'll be *here* next week . . . interviewing with Pacific Coastal Airlines."

Pax's ears buzzed as he shifted to face Bud. "As a stew?"

"Seems so. I guess she's tired of school, or Nebraska, or both." The two officers smiled at each other and lifted their frosty mugs, but a heavy hand on each of their shoulders broke the moment.

"Hey, shipmates," Brogan said, "where's my beer?"

"Wherever you left it, Camp," Pax said. "Can't you remember?"

"Ha-ha, hotshot," Brogan said and sat the other side of Bud.

"You pussies ready to roll dice, or do you want to go ahead and pay— save time?"

"Bud handles my light work," Pax said. "Take it easy on him, Bud, he's not into math. I have to make a phone call." Pax winked, slid his full beer over to Bud, and left.

Sally lifted the receiver after one ring. Her voice took him back to the dance floor; he hadn't forgotten that voice.

"Hello," she repeated. "Anyone there?"

"I thought you didn't like flying," he said.

"Bob? Jack? Ted? Bill, is that you?"

"*Some* of those captains may take offense if you call them assholes."

"Who is this?"

"When do you get to San Diego?" he asked and realized the wide-stretched grin hurt his jaw. Her feel and smell and taste flooded his brain.

"Is this Lieutenant Langford? I'd forgotten what you sounded like; I'm sorry."

That little skit had some zing; she knows how to lay it on. I'm flattered.

"Don't be sorry," he said. "Everyone can't be a teacher. Besides, seeing a pretty face in southern California will be refreshing. You can't believe how ugly these girls are."

"I've heard; Bud's been complaining. Seems he can't sleep worrying about the problem. Dad's grinning like it was him who flew an F-8 for the first time. What *is* it with you guys and Crusaders?"

I can see that teasing smile; hell, I even smell cinnamon.

"Oh, it's no big deal . . . about like heroin addiction, I imagine. So when did you get the stewardess bug?"

"I'm tired of snow, and I thought I'd work on a tan next winter. Rumor has it smarts aren't essential in aviation; my experience backs that up. Dad approves; Mom thinks it's hormones. What do you think?"

"If your mom's right, maybe I can help. Will you call me when you get here?"

"Yes."

He gave Sally his number and wished her folks well.

"Ta-ta, Orville," she said. "Give my best to Wilbur."

Her laughing lilt before hanging up grabbed his heart. He could've talked for hours—or at least listened—the buzzing dial-tone mocked his loss. He considered smashing the receiver against the wall. "A week," he said. "One short week."

Two flights a day helped eat some clock, but nighttime—nightmare time—dug in its claws, fought for every second, and the weekend stretched at least a month. But Thursday afternoon, Pax saw the yellow telephone-message slip in his BOQ box. LT Langford: Interviewing p.m. Back by six-thirty. Please call 222-6280, Room 317. Sally.

Pax knocked on her Point Loma Lodge door at eight o'clock.

"Who is it?" she asked.

He hesitated, struggling for an appropriate answer, when she flung the door open. Her face was flushed.

"Hey, dummy, your name's Langford."

"So it is. God, you look good."

They embraced, kissed, and she pushed back, looked up, and pecked another quick kiss on his chin. "Are you going to feed me, or do I have to call my brother?"

"If we hurry, we may make our reservation."

She threw a light, white sweater over her shoulders and slipped her arm through his. He tried to meet the other guests' and lobby employees' envious leers with Cheshire cat smugness, but pride and pleasure forced a wider smile.

"Beans, I've got some bad news for you. Those ugly pills you've been taking . . . well, they ain't working. Did you wear this dress to the interview?"

"No, but I wish you had been my interviewer. These are healthy women out here. Damn! I felt like a boy." But her light-beige, spaghetti-strapped sundress, with small black and white polka dots, belied the claim. "Interviews wear me out," she said.

"Did you get the job?"

"Who knows? We'll be *notified* of their decision. Where did you get the coat and tie, Orville? You spruce up pretty good."

Stepping from the elevator into the restaurant's penthouse splendor dazzled them both. The darkened, glass-walled lounge displayed most of downtown San Diego's sparkling lights, as well as Coronado's, beyond the harbor. At their eye-level, less than two blocks away, an airliner descended with its healthy whine—despite noise abatement procedures—and flared into harborside Lindbergh Field. Their corner table provided the best view in two directions.

"Pretty fancy, Orville; this rivals Slovak's Hot Dog Emporium back in Crete."

"It comes recommended. If you get work, I can watch you land from here."

A tall, buxom, deeply-tanned apparition in diaphanous white gauze took their drink orders, flashed a four thousand dollar smile, and disappeared. "You and Bud *must* be suffering out here. This could be the boob capital of civilization."

Pax shook his head, pursed his lips, and raised both eyebrows. "The problem with working so hard . . . well, we never notice these things."

"I'd *better* get out here. I'll bet you're a horrible influence on Bud." Their glances locked; he reached for her hand and felt charges of energy coursing through his body from her touch.

"I've missed you," he said.

She smiled, and her eyes reflected shimmering pinpoints from the table's candle. "I'll bet."

After ordering dinner they tried to dance, but Sally became flustered by Pax's instant and persistent state of arousal.

"For pity's sake, dummy; take me back to the table. Thank goodness it's dark in here."

At the table, Pax shrugged his shoulders. "What can I say? I guess I'm sorry."

"Dad says your goal in life—your number one priority—is shooting down enemy airplanes. Of course, he thinks that's super. But is *that* your main ambition?"

Cold water—by whatever name—and it's working.

"I'd like to get to Vietnam before the war ends. It's hard to rationalize being what I am, doing what I do, without straining at the leash. So your dad's right."

Sally drained her wine glass. "Do you hate the Vietnamese?"

"Not yet."

"Do you hate the Russians?"

"I don't think so."

"But given a legal opportunity, you'd kill any other person in another fighter plane."

"An enemy. And he wouldn't *have* to be in a fighter."

"I was raised in your kind of zoo. I'll bet *High Noon* was your favorite movie, or maybe *The Bridges at Toko-Ri.*"

Food and more wine for Sally slowed her verbal assault against Pax's earlier romantic manifestations, but the growing ideological schism cast a pall—however small—on the evening. They danced, but without flame, and the evening ended at Sally's door. Two additional days, which included Bud, never quite repaired the damage.

Standing in the terminal, perplexed, Pax stared after her departing airplane.

Where'd the time go? What happened to the things we could have—should have—talked about?

Pax inched his Corvette through gravy-thick fog to the hangar.

For a bombing lecture? This must be a joke.

But the starch-creased instructor wasn't smiling. "I'm sure that you'll like bombing in the F-8," he said.

"Since when?" Pax said.

"What's the matter, hotshot?" Camp asked. "You afraid of ground fire?"

"Don't know, Camp; I've never seen ground fire. But I know a few bomber pilots. I'd rather fight airplanes than haul bombs; that's why I chose fighters."

Camp looked around the room, winked at the others. "Wars often impose on prima donnas, Pax. You'll live."

So they bombed. They carried small, blue, Mark-76 practice bombs which were equipped with smoke spotting charges to raked-dirt targets near El Centro. Larger, sand-filled practice bombs they dropped against simulated targets—wrecked vehicles—on the Gila Bend range, and they dropped live-bombs (500-, 1,000-, and 2,000-pounders) against newer wrecked vehicles on the Chocolate Mountain range, north of Yuma, Arizona.

Pax spent a lot of time shaking his head.

How can they take a beautiful, clean-lined fighter and hang so much garbage under the wing? They fly like . . . what they've become—dump trucks.

Thursday afternoon, after their last bombing flight, Brogan poked Pax's shoulder. "I pegged you right, hotshot, you don't like getting near the ground, do you? You haven't hit jack-shit this week."

"Camp, I'd sooner have my ass sandpapered than drop bombs."

The instructor entered the debriefing room behind Pax, but either didn't hear or ignored the statement.

"Everyone qualified," the instructor said. "Even you, Pax. Those last two drops saved your bacon."

"Guess I lucked out," Pax said.

Brogan twisted around and flipped a toothpick stub at Pax. "You'll need more than luck next week, hotshot. Think you can remember how to *fight* the airplane?"

Pax lowered his head, shut his eyes, and massaged his eyelids. His face remained impassive.

Yes, you loudmouthed peckerwood, I remember enough to kick you out of the sky. And believe me; I'm looking forward to it.

Rather than voice his thoughts, he looked up and said, "I'm sorry, Camp, what did you say?"

"Hah! You heard me, Langford. You've been away too long. Whipping your butt won't even be a thrill," he snuffed a huge breath and stretched, "but I'm going to do it anyway, just to get your mind right."

Bud listened to the exchange, raised his eyebrows anticipating a retort, but Pax said nothing else. Bud tarried when the others left, but spoke before Pax reached the door. "Are you setting him up? Were those bomb scores bogus?"

"Bud, some days I have no idea what I'm doing. The instructor failed to mention that I hand-delivered those last two bombs. In fact, I spent ten minutes checking my plane over close for shrapnel damage, because I busted the release altitude something fierce. Getting that low, gunners could have had a field day hosing me down.

"What do you hear from Beans?"

Bud hadn't quite been facing Pax, before the question, but he jerked around, looking surprised. "Didn't you know? She came back two days ago."

Chapter 7—LEGERDEMAIN

Friday morning's tactics lecture could not have been better scheduled. Pea soup fog, darkened by overlaying cloud cover, gripped San Diego. Condensation dripped from airplanes on the flight line and from automobiles parked near the hangars. Civilian and navy meteorologists predicted no improvement for the entire day—little chance for flying.

But by ten o'clock the sun burned through, and a half-canceled, half-slid flight schedule renewed the squadron's primary activity. Pax watched aviators zipping G-suits and cinching torso-harnesses in the passageway abutting the lecture room. An hour after lunch, LCDR Hacksaw Grayson's syrupy Mississippi drawl won the unfair fight. Camp Brogan's eyes drooped shut; his chin slipped from a two-handed bridge and dropped a couple of inches before jerking up. His F-8 Handbook slammed to the deck. Pax rubbed his own eyes and tried to hide a yawn. Bud chuckled, but more in sympathy than mockery.

Grayson stepped from behind the lectern, hooked both thumbs in his webbed khaki belt, and arched his eyebrows at the handbook retrieving—should've been listening—officer. "Are you bored with my tactics lecture, Lieutenant Brogan?"

"No, sir, uh-uh." Camp said, stood, and stretched his arms toward the ceiling. "Too much lunch . . . how about a coffee break?"

Grayson resumed his post behind the lectern and flipped through his notebook. "I want ten more minutes; if you need to, keep standing."

Pax jumped up also, moved to the wall opposite Brogan and leaned against it. Hacksaw glared from one stander to the other, his mouth curling into a near-sneer. But his twinkling eyes betrayed the façade, and his face reddened as its smile returned. "I know *you* two think you have this mastered. The lecture's aimed at Lieutenant Banks."

Bud sprang to his feet, stretched, and yawned behind the back of a hand. He blinked his eyes—hard. "And I'm listening, Commander."

Grayson slammed his notes shut. "Forget it. Any questions? No? Good! Monday morning brief's at 0530. Get some rest; maybe you won't fall asleep during the fights. I'll see you at happy hour."

Bud turned to Pax. "I don't remember if I mentioned it or not, but my housemates are already in VF-37. We're having some air wing people over this evening, about eight o'clock, nothing fancy. Some of them will be from your squadron; you're invited as well."

Pax started to accept, when Brogan butted in, "Yeah, come on, Pax, you haven't even met the skipper yet, have you?"

Pax altered his acceptance nod to a neck stretching exercise. "Sorry, Bud, I've made other plans, but thanks." He shook his head at Brogan. "No, I haven't met Commander Dodd, but I'll make it by the squadron next week."

"I recommend it, hotshot. They may get to thinking you don't like your orders. I've been over there three times. Looks like I'll be the admin officer. You're penciled in as senior watch officer and assistant maintenance . . . if you're interested."

"I'm *always* interested in things *you* say, Camp, but right now I'm looking forward to all that happy hour beer you're about to buy me. In fact, I doubt I'll even bring my wallet."

And he almost didn't need to. Pax nursed his first freebie through three subsequent dice rolls, gave beers to Bud and Hacksaw—anybody but Brogan. As Camp financed the party, his neck got redder and redder. Hacksaw chuckled and nudged Camp. "Mister Brogan, I got hogs back home know more about dice than you do."

Camp glared at Hacksaw and started to respond. Instead, he looked beyond Pax, smiled, and stood. "Hi, Sally," Camp said and extended a hand above Pax's shoulder, "will you please bring me some luck?"

Pax's gut clinched and his ears buzzed, but—sure enough—when Sally came into view, she took Camp's hand, sat on the knee he patted, and blew into the offered dice cup. She mimed a kiss to Bud and wriggled her fingers at Pax. "Who's winning?" she asked.

Hacksaw scrambled to his feet. "Everyone but Camp, pretty lady; please don't change that. I'm Hacksaw Grayson."

Bud stood. "Commander, this is my twin sister, Sally."

"I can tell . . . ," Hacksaw said and nodded his head, "but it looks a hell of a lot better on her."

Pax pinched his wrist, but it wasn't a bad dream.

There she sits . . . in Brogan's lap, or on his knee, or wherever. Rat's ass!

Pax lost the round, laid some bills on the table, and pushed his chair back. "Lady Luck got fickle," he said. "Sally, have you flown yet?"

"It'll be another week," she said.

"Do well," he said, stood, and made a sweeping salute. "I'll see the rest of you Monday." Temptation fought him hard, but he refused to look back and see whether Sally remained on Brogan's knee or took his vacated chair.

How in the screaming hell did she meet Camp? Or get around to perching on his frapping knee?

Every intuition he had said don't look back, so he didn't. And the weekend dragged out for a month or two.

The three afterburner, section-takeoffs shattered Monday's daybreak. The F-8s' wings were slick. Under-the-wing pylons and bomb-racks had been stacked deep in the hangar—with Pax's sincerest blessing. Each two-plane section adopted a combat-spread formation—level, abeam, a mile to a mile and a-half between aircraft—passing the coastline south of Del Mar Racetrack. Accelerating to climb-schedule airspeed, Pax gloried in the early morning freedom. When he pulled the F-8's nose up, his altimeter needles spun clockwise. He checked his oxygen system at ten thousand feet, and each section headed for its own assigned piece of sky-pie, south of San Clemente Island, for simulated combat training.

Each section operated on a separate radio frequency, but Pax knew their commentary hadn't changed much since World War II: "Okay, Hacksaw Two," Grayson said, "split away forty-five degrees for one minute . . . and the fight's on."

Here comes the tingling. The old adrenaline pumps must be working.

He squinted hard, keeping Hacksaw in sight, and fought for a missile firing position, without dipping below the assigned safety deck, at ten thousand feet. He knew most nuggets busted the safety altitude on the first tactics flight, when afterburner was not allowed.

Hacksaw Grayson's evaluation came after a turn and a-half: "Nice move, Hacksaw Two. I'll make it a little tougher this time."

But nice moves got better, and tough enough never came.

When Pax and Bud left the afternoon tactics flight debrief, Bud was shaking his head. He remained grim in the replacement pilots' locker room. Camp, however, flush from success, winked as he waggled an extended thumb up-and-down after whispering his instructor's name.

Hacksaw stuck his head into the door. "Tomorrow I fly with you, Camp, same brief time in the morning."

When Grayson left, Camp nudged Pax. "How was he?"

"Pretty good. He wore me out. Of course, I'm pretty rusty."

"Langford, you're a piece of work. You'd walk a mile out of your way to lie to me."

Pax stopped tying his shoes, held both hands out from his sides. "You know how to hurt my feelings. Please ask me that question again."

Camp shook his head at Bud and glanced at the ceiling. "What I wanted to know, Pax, is how does Hacksaw fight the airplane?"

"Oh," Pax nodded and rubbed his chin. "Pretty well. He wore me out. Of course, I'm pretty rusty."

Brogan threw his helmet into a locker and slammed its metal door. "Screw you, Pax! Screw you!"

Pax shrugged; Bud grinned; Brogan stalked out.

Pax eyed Bud. "Since you're not jumping up and down, I guess those first two flights didn't suit you."

Bud turned away, shook his head. "Nope. I couldn't do anything."

"What happened?"

"I kept losing sight. When I did see him and pulled into him I almost stalled. My nose got low. Every single fight I busted ten thousand feet. I stunk!"

"Probably not as bad as you think. You weren't supposed to win. Believe me; it wasn't a fair fight."

Bud straightened and crossed his arms. "What do you mean . . . wasn't fair?"

Pax raised his hands, simulating two airplanes flying abeam. "Remember how the fights started? Both planes turned 45-degrees away from each other for a minute. How did you know when to turn back into the fight?"

"The second hand on my clock."

Pax said nothing but continued to stare at Bud.

"What? I didn't cheat! I came back at him after one minute."

"Hey, I believe you. When did you lose sight of him?"

"Right away, heading back at him." Bud's face turned serious. "Did he cheat, get a head start?"

"I doubt it."

Bud shrugged his shoulders. "What? I don't get your point."

"If a fight's going to start in one minute, both pilots don't have to watch

71

their clocks. You did, off-and-on, for the whole minute, even harder toward the end. While your instructor kept *his* eyes focused on your airplane. When you needed them most, your eyes had become focused close range—on your clock. And getting first visual contact in any engagement makes a huge difference. Today it wasn't vital, because you knew *about* where he was—but it mattered. During this morning's flight, when we weren't using afterburner, smoothness counted for more than aggressiveness. Letting your nose get buried below the horizon almost guaranteed busting the ten thousand foot soft deck, for sure if the instructor kept you turning."

"Makes sense; wish I'd known it before the fights."

Pax stared at the shoe he was tying. "It might not have meant as much then. Making mistakes ruffles your feathers, bruises your ego. So what! We're here to learn what we need to know. Period. If I can help, I will."

Bud sighed, walked to the door, and leaned on the jamb. "Thanks. Too bad I don't know what I don't know, so I could ask earlier.

"Pax, I hope I'm not talking out of school—it might not even matter to you—but Sally didn't want you thinking Camp was a close friend of hers. He's not, but you left too soon Friday for it to shake out."

"It matters; thanks for telling me. What do you hear from Olathe? Have you thought about asking for a plane to fly back there?"

"I owe them a letter . . . or three, but I haven't asked for a plane. You want to fly back with me?"

"No. I'd enjoy seeing your folks, and I hope you can get a plane. But Sally moving to San Diego kind of dropped Olathe off my map. Does she have a telephone yet?"

Bud shook his head. "She and three other new gals are sharing an apartment till they get past the six-week probation period. Their phone should be in Wednesday."

"Good enough. I'll see you in the morning."

Pax wasn't ready for his BOQ room's solitude, but he didn't feel like the O-club, either. So he drove through the west gate toward the coast. From a walkway above La Jolla Cove, he inhaled the eucalyptus trees' gas-like aroma and watched the haze-dimmed sun dip below the horizon.

The two good tactics flights had polished his memories: embers long since banked by time and lack of opportunity. Yet . . . it was like he'd never been away. And Sally cared what he thought. . . . She cared.

By week's end, two things came clear to VF-124's tactics instructors: (1) Bud Banks measured equal to the best nugget pilots they'd had, and (2) Camp and Pax could outfight the instructor pilots; neither had lost a single engagement during the entire tactics syllabus. Happy hour speculation between instructor pilots broke about even, depending on which of the two had beaten them the quickest. But to a man, the instructors agreed a one-on-one fight between the future squadron mates would be worth watching.

Bud strained his ears to glean any gems from the O-club bar beer-talk, but instructors clammed up around replacement pilots. Egos teetered at risk, and the majority of instructors could beat most replacement pilots. So curiosity drove him to the source. Over an O-club lunch, with only them at the table, Bud posed a question: "Pax, what's your first move in a fight?"

Pax folded his napkin, matched corner to corner, edge to edge. "You asked a general question. My *general* answer would be to avoid losing. With more specific parameters, I might be able to narrow the choices. But there's no such thing as a foolproof formula. You're fighting another man's brain; its options, while not limitless, are vast and ever changing."

"C'mon, Pax, I've read the theory. It's hard to believe you can start each fight from scratch and win with such apparent ease. Are you so much smarter, so much stronger? What gives you such an edge? I'd like to know, if you'll tell me."

"I would if I could, believe me, but the telling is not so easy. Most of us know the theory. Everyone knows to trade airspeed energy for altitude when things get iffy, and we all know not to overshoot an enemy who's cranking into us. Do you agree so far?"

Bud's expression remained blank. He searched Pax's eyes for devilment. "Yes."

"Good, because that's it; there are no secrets. Now you know what I know. The main difference between us rests in the black ink of our logbooks. I've got two thousand more flight hours than you have, much of which has been devoted to recognizing changes in relative motion. Early recognition wins the fight, and even beyond early recognition comes reasonable prediction . . . which relies even more on experience. Hang tough; it'll come. Everyone says you're doing great."

Bud's serious demeanor almost made Pax smile. "Okay," Bud said, nodding, "I've checked the logbooks. Hacksaw has a thousand more hours than you do. So does Commander Wright. That didn't help *them* when they fought you."

"No it didn't, and I'm not trying to put you off, nor am I being modest. But I can't speak for anyone else, nor rank what's important to them. You can't know what another person might have on his mind while he's fighting an airplane. But if you're able to completely concentrate on another airplane and that airplane's pilot during an engagement . . . well, you enjoy a large advantage. That might be an edge, if indeed I have one."

"Does Brogan concentrate like that?"

"I don't know. Probably, ask him."

Bud snorted a short laugh; a waitress snapped her head around to see what caused it. "I did. At least I asked him if he had a plan of attack before a fight."

"And?"

"He wised off and said as long as everyone kept backing up in front of him, he didn't need much planning."

As they walked from the club's swinging doors, Pax squinted skyward, adjusted his khaki fore-and-aft cap, and removed his sunglasses from a shirt pocket. "I told you the truth. You can be sure that Camp concentrates harder than hell, despite the casual attitude. He fights the bird about as well as it can be fought."

Bud nodded. "I'm sure he does. By the way, if you ask for it, I'm supposed to give you this." He handed Pax a small folded card with a phone number on it.

"Thanks a bunch. I'll see you back at the hangar."

She answered before the second ring. "Hello, this is Sally."

"Hello yourself, Sally. This is Paxton Langford. My class leaves for Yuma in the morning for a week of gunnery. Would you like to go to dinner tonight?"

"Yes, I'd like to, but I can't. I have a training flight to San Francisco; we were walking out the door. Please call me when you get back. I've got to run, sorry."

Chapter 8—GUNNERY

At nine o'clock on Saturday morning, Hacksaw Grayson's four Crusaders descended in a left turn toward Yuma, Arizona's Marine Corps Air Station. Bud Banks fought the desert's thermal turbulence and kept a tight left wing position on Hacksaw. Pax nodded, in silent approval, from the number four-slot on Brogan's right wing, and despite their taking staccato up-and-down jolts, Pax knew Brogan nailed down a solid number three-slot off Hacksaw's right wing.

I'd be hard pressed to match his touch. Maybe I could; maybe I couldn't. Right now I've got as much as I can handle in this four-slot.

The left turn, with Hacksaw's throttle near idle, forced Bud, on the inside of the turn—and already at idle—to flick his speed brake out and right back in to maintain position. But doing it he was, and damned well.

I wish Captain Banks and Sally could see how Bud's flying has progressed. It would make the captain even prouder of his son, and perhaps ease Sally's worries about whether or not Bud's in over his head.

Pax's right arm and shoulder muscles damped most of the thermal gusts' uneven demands. Anticipation and finesse shortened the required control movements, but strength helped. Such focused tension—pride-driven tension—washed near-exquisite pain over Pax. The desert's heat slam-banged the four aircraft the same amount, but each shift—however small—from Pax's prescribed position jabbed his ego, for reputations abuilding shouldn't be tarnished.

I hope to hell Camp and Bud are having to fight this hard to maintain their positions. Christ! This "finger-four" parade formation is working our butts off.

Sweat burned Pax's eyes; he tried blinking back each salty, stinging drop to no avail. And the damnable hard-rubber oxygen mask bit hard into the bridge of his nose. Two situations required his wearing the mask: flying in close formation or fighting the plane, and those times were to accommodate instant communications. Most of the time, he let the mask, which he considered an ill-designed rubber vise, lie in his lap with the oxygen turned off. When necessary, he held it—with a feather-touch—against his face for radio transmissions.

Hacksaw raised his right fist against the canopy top, signaling Bud to cross under into the vacant space between Hacksaw and Camp Brogan. Halfway through Bud's repositioning, Hacksaw rolled his F-8's wings level and reported their position. "Yuma Tower, Gunfighter Four One Six, flight of four, six-miles north for landing."

Pax squinted against the sun after Bud's cross-under, checked the near-straight line of flight helmets, and deemed their formation flying passable—given the turbulence.

I'll have to compliment Camp for not passing along Bud's airplane's little jiggles.

Pax touched down before Hacksaw cleared the runway.

Not bad landing intervals—a good ending to a challenging flight.

But as he rolled clear of the runway, deposited the sweat-dripping oxygen mask in his lap and raised the canopy, hell's furnace scorched his face.

God-almighty-damn, and it's not even ten o'clock. Wow! June 25th in Yuma, Arizona—how lucky can we get?

The ready room's weak air-conditioner fought a losing battle. Hacksaw held a sweating Pepsi can to his brow. "Those thermals jacked us around pretty bad during the letdown, but you guys seemed to be handling it. Pax, how'd it look from the tail-end Charlie slot?"

Pax stretched and yawned. "I don't know; I fell asleep sometime during the descent . . . didn't wake up till touchdown."

Bud's head jerked in Pax's direction. "Hah! Fat chance. I apologize to both you guys. I bounced over hell's half acre out there; some of those jolts slammed me up and down damned hard."

"I never noticed," Camp lied and winked at Pax. "Seemed smooth to me."

Pax looked past Bud's questioning stare toward the grinning Hacksaw. Bud shook his head and glanced back at the now somber Hacksaw, who said, "We'll check into the BOQ, have lunch, and get back for the fourteen hundred Course Rules brief. As far as I'm concerned, flight suits are the uniform of choice while we're here."

The second four-plane division taxied onto the parking ramp as Hacksaw and his pilots left the hangar for the BOQ. Both Hacksaw and Pax had their cars driven to Yuma earlier by a couple of student pilot watch-standers who were waiting for their class syllabus to start.

In Pax's Corvette, Bud continued the probe. "I don't see how *you* kept from being thrown into Mexico; as rough as I was in the number two-slot, you had to be catching hell."

"Uh-uh. Brogan ignored you. He stayed welded solid in the three-slot; you jiggled some, but in your own little box. Camp made it easy on me; he can *fly* the airplane. And you weren't bad either. Heat turbulence can knock your socks off."

"Listening to you two, I thought I must have been in a different flight. When we landed, I felt double-dog pooped; you had me going in the debrief."

Over evening Margaritas, Pax returned to Bud's formation flying. "You used your speed brake well this morning; Hacksaw didn't leave you much throttle to play with."

"Thanks. Honestly, between needing the speed brake and the turbulence, there were a couple of times I felt sure I'd have to leave the formation. That's the hardest I ever worked in my life."

"I believe that, *and,*" Pax raised a finger and beat a cadence with the next words, "remember, we landed at ten o'clock in the morning. These desert thermals can kill you. A lot of hotshots, trying to impress someone by screaming into the break on a hot afternoon, have left their asses and pieces of airplane scattered halfway to the Mexican border."

After four Yuma gunnery flights, the pecking order—based on hits in the towed target banners—had Camp Brogan beaming. "No sense *having* guns if you can't use 'em," he said.

Pax knew Brogan spoke the truth, which galled him even more than Brogan's gunnery scores. And both Bud's and Hacksaw's hit totals more than doubled his own.

There was no mystery; gun-camera film didn't lie. The inexplicable truth—at least to Pax—was that his gun sight pipper hadn't settled on and tracked the target banner. Hacksaw stopped the film and moved it, frame by frame, to convince Pax of the problem. Pax could do nothing but nod agreement. Yet, hits wouldn't come for Pax, and his gun-camera film continued to tattle—no steady banner tracking.

After four days and eight mediocre flights, Pax began pushing his runs, popping over the banner at the last possible instant, firing at minimum range—and closer—trying anything to up his "bean-count."

The fifth evening Hacksaw pulled him aside. "I don't like what you're doing in the pattern, Pax. It's dangerous, of course, but worse—it's dumb. And it's not helping. Smooth up your tracking. It's simple; you aren't keeping the pipper on the banner. Period."

Pax sucked in a deep breath and pursed his lips in a tight, straight line. "I buy everything you say, but that doesn't make it simple. We *both* know a good sight-picture when we see one; I don't fire without one. And no one is more shocked than I am when we play that film back."

Hacksaw's scowl stayed in place a long time; Pax wondered if his friend had even heard him. But a widening smile brought back some sunshine. Hacksaw draped an arm around Pax's shoulders. "Quit trying so damned hard, buddy. Relax. . . . You're pressing too much."

Pax and Bud sat drinking after-breakfast coffee the next morning in the BOQ dining room, when Hacksaw stuck his head in the door. "Pax, can you spare about fifteen minutes, please?"

"Sure, we're finished," Pax said and pushed back from the table. He gave Bud a mock salute. "I needed an excuse to avoid some letter writing."

"While we've got a couple of hours," Hacksaw said, "I thought I'd run into town and fire in my son's new target rifle for him, get the sights right. We could do it later on the base range, but the gunnery sergeant says it's too hot out there. Anyway, we'll be flying. I'd rather not go in by myself. You mind tagging along?"

"Glad to. Anything to keep from writing letters."

There were no other customers. And after balking, before accepting Hacksaw's folded ten-dollar bill, the attendant agreed that a .22-caliber rifle wasn't much different than a .22-caliber pistol. The two naval officers owned the air-conditioned pistol range. Hacksaw fired five-round magazines at 25-, 50-, and 75-feet, sitting in a chair, using a small sandbag rest on the counter between himself and the firing alley. His tight clusters on the three inch bull's-eyes proved the factory sight settings needed no adjustment.

Pax patted his friend on the shoulder. "No wonder you're pounding the crap out of those banners."

"You want to try a few?" Hacksaw asked. "The sight's pretty good at 75-feet."

"Sure, but don't think you're getting a bet out of me . . . after watching you shoot."

Hacksaw drew a perfect sight-picture on the back of an old target for Pax to look at, but Pax got no clusters, tight or otherwise. After several five-round magazines, he had a single hole in the black. Other holes were scattered with no discernible pattern—equal opportunity misses—a total of nineteen hits from twenty-five rounds.

"This is kinda what I figured, ole buddy," Hacksaw said. "You're too good a pilot; you fly the bird too well to be getting goose-eggs on the banners."

"You think it's my eyes?" The air-conditioning didn't keep beads of perspiration from forming on Pax's forehead, and his sport shirt felt clammy. Question marks began dancing across a hazy horizon, the sands of which had once formed a predictable future. He wiped damp palms on the offending target as he wadded it into a tight ball.

At least I hit the wastebasket.

Hacksaw shrugged. "Who knows? Could explain what's been going on. How have you done on your physicals? Strong eyes?"

Pax sat on a metal chair and rubbed his forehead with the back of a hand. "Marginal, I guess, but legal—at least till now. My annual physical is due when we get back to Miramar."

Hacksaw squeezed his shoulder. "C'mon, let's get out of here."

Driving back to the base, Hacksaw shook his head and sucked his teeth. "I'm not trying to tell you how to run your business, Pax, but I'd be damned careful about how I got my eyes checked. Your wings might depend on it."

Pax nodded but said nothing.

The next to last shooting day in Yuma, Pax peppered both target banners hard. Hacksaw squinted a tight stare at Pax when their hits were called in over the ready room squawk-box. Camp Brogan ordered the squadron duty officer to have the airplanes' bullet colors and the number of target hits in each color confirmed.

"Why the commotion, Camp?" Pax asked. "I sprinkle a few hits in the banner, and you want to audit the bean counters. Jesus! Gimme a break."

Camp turned to respond, but after two gulps of air, words didn't come. He flipped his knee-board in the air, caught it, and walked to the window overlooking the hot concrete parking ramp. The gunnery officer and his sweaty crew bent close to the banner there, recounting the different colored bullet holes.

The tally remained the same. No surprise to Pax. He knew how hard the ordnance crews worked to get their gun systems up to speed. He'd even seen crews place occasional wagers on individual pilot's—or even a particular aircraft's—firing results. Overbearing or arguing pilots made banner scoring an odious chore, so Hacksaw refused pilots access to banners until scoring was complete. The ordnancemen loved him for it.

Camp had averaged twenty-five hits per banner from four hundred rounds carried each flight, which was hitting the banner at a 6.25% rate if the four guns fired every round. But that seldom happened, because guns jammed, metal-link belts broke, or pilots wouldn't have enough good runs to fire their rounds. Therefore, Camp's real average netted him 11%, three points above Hacksaw and five over Bud.

The last two banners, however, showed forty-two and fifty-six hits from Pax's guns. And to Camp's obvious dismay, the ordnance crew reported that only three of Pax's four 20-MM cannons fired the first flight and fifty rounds remained in the belts after the second flight. This meant Pax fired 14% and 16% on the last two flights.

"Good shooting," Bud said.

Pax rubbed his chin. "Thank you, it's a start."

Camp returned from recounting the banners, himself, after the ordnance crew's second effort. "A couple of holes could've gone to different shooters," he said, "but overall the count was fair. Since tomorrow's our last banner, are you pussies up for a wager? I'll give Bud ten holes, Hacksaw five, and you, Pax, whatever you think you need for a dollar a hole."

Hacksaw's grin widened as his eyes narrowed. "I'm in," he said.

"Why not?" Bud said.

"Today proved flukes can happen," Pax said, "but even so, I guess I'll donate. You and I'll bet even, but we should draw for aircraft assignment prior to manning up. Do you agree, Hacksaw?"

The grinning lieutenant commander slapped his cupped hands together in a loud explosion. "You're damned right! Now let's go rescue some of those poor grub worms from those tequila bottles."

Cigarette smoke mixed with a strong smell of urine, but flickering candlelight missed most of the squalor. San Luis cabarets benefited from darkness. Hacksaw mumbled, "You know what keeps these aboveground cesspools on Yuma detachments' last-night itineraries?" Nobody ventured a guess. The super-relaxed Mississippian answered his own query, "Ten pounds of tradition and ninety pounds of undying optimism."

Camp's clapping with raised arms and bumbled stamping accompanied some ferocious, dance-related belly-bumping against an over-rouged, fifty-year-old *senorita*. From across a splintery table, Bud evaluated the dance floor performance.

Hacksaw's sparse blond hairs lay matted askew across his shining pate, while his big teeth dispatched the evening's second tequila-drowned grub. He squeezed Pax's shoulder, leaned close, and whispered, "You ole sumbitch, I don't *even* want to know how you hit those banners. But your physical back at Miramar keeps nibblin' at me."

Pax, the designated driver, leaned his head close to Hacksaw. "One dragon at a time, pardner, one dragon at a time. Speaking of which . . . it's time we dragged-ass outta this joint."

So they did, but under strong protest from Camp. "Why is it," he demanded to know, "every goddamned time I finally fall in love, you Baptist deacon bastards wanna haul ass?"

Pax and Bud enjoyed a quiet breakfast. Hacksaw joined them in time for a quick cup of coffee. They banged on Camp's door as they left for the hangar and tried not to laugh when the open-mouthed, head-holding wreck jerked his door open.

Gotta give Camp credit; he's made the brief, even though we can't look at him. His eyeballs need Band-Aids, and his breath can peel paint.

Hacksaw canted his head and double-clicked his teeth—those same, vicious, worm-dispatching masticators from the night before. "Maybe you shouldn't fly this morning, Camp."

"I'm fine. Don't be trying to weasel out of our bet."

And to his further credit, they agreed, Camp flew *and* put thirty holes in the banner—which matched Hacksaw and beat Bud by six. However, Brogan lost thirty-five dollars to Pax's sixty-five hits (out of 325-rounds fired, or 20%).

Camp said nothing, but counted out forty-four dollars, dropped them on the duty officer's desk, and strode from the ready room.

After three minutes, the second watch officer came in and reported, "Some poor slob's in the head about to puke his liver up. I don't know who; I don't want to know who." The young replacement pilot shuddered. "You cannot *believe* the smell."

Hacksaw winked at Pax. "Ain't that awful . . . the way some people treat their bodies. Damn!"

Pax picked up the money and beckoned the disgusted junior officer to him. "Please take this money down to the line shack and tell the Chief that Lieutenant Brogan wants to put this toward a keg of beer for the men." He glanced at Bud and Hacksaw. "Okay?"

Both nodding officers flashed him a thumbs-up.

Chapter 9—FIELD CARRIER LANDINGS

The returning gunnery detachment found San Diego and Naval Air Station Miramar basking under cloudless skies with unlimited visibility. Pax landed, cleared the runway at the end, and began the automatic ritual: he unlocked the canopy, hooked a yellow nylon restraining strap to the locking lug under the canopy's right sill, and allowed the strap to play out until it became taut.

I remember when the canopy straps became standard equipment. Some early Crusaders had lost a couple of canopies to winds over the flight deck, when designed snubber limits were exceeded. Rumor had it that the chief petty officer, who suggested the nylon strap fix, spit tobacco juice between the Chance-Vought factory rep's shoes and said, "So much for fancy engineering."

Eighty degree air—thirty degrees cooler than at Yuma—blew across Pax's sweaty flight suit, raising goose bumps on his forearms. For after sweltering in Yuma's desert heat, even San Diego's unseasonably warm Santa Ana winds felt like air-conditioning. He extended his arms from the cockpit, wiggled his fingers, and shuddered. The cooler, refreshing air might as well have been pure adrenaline. He sucked in two belly-deep breaths. "God! No wonder people love San Diego."

The flight taxied to the fueling pits, refueled their aircraft, and continued to the parking ramp. They wrote up airplane discrepancies on maintenance "yellow-sheets," debriefed the flight—"Any questions?" "No."—and arrived at the O-club seven minutes before the gong announced happy hour.

Hacksaw, Bud, and Camp rolled dice for two pitchers of beer before Pax joined them. "Where you been, hotshot," Camp asked, "looking for more pigeons to pluck?"

When he answered, Pax spoke to Hacksaw, "I stopped by sick bay to schedule my physical; I'm a month overdue today. Didn't want to aggravate the quacks."

Hacksaw waggled four fingers at a passing waitress and slid the dice cup toward Bud. "Losers bring 'em out, kid; you and Camp are throwin' a hell of a party, and Hacksaw's thirsty."

Four sixes on his first roll made Pax a winner. He ordered the drinks and excused himself. From a pay phone outside the men's room, he called Sally. A roommate told him Sally would be back soon.

"Okay," he said, "please tell her Pax called, and I want to take her to dinner. I'll call back at six."

The roommate said she would.

Pax paused back at the table long enough to slide his Camp-bought beer to Bud, and said, "Sorry, gents, I left something at sick bay. I'll see you Monday morning." He strode from the club, drove to the package store, and bought two bottles: a fifth of Johnny Walker, another of Jack Daniels, both Black Labels.

When he walked into the dispensary, carrying the bottles in a tan paper sack, two corpsmen stood talking at the front desk. They looked at Pax before one left, saying he was going to the chow hall. Pax approached the remaining petty officer second class. "Good evening, are you busy?"

"No, sir, not now . . . we have been. Can I help you?"

"I'm not sure. If you had to pick your slowest evening—the least busy—which would you choose?"

The corpsman shrugged. "I don't know. Friday maybe, they stay about like this. Why?"

Twenty minutes later, minus the sour mash, Pax went to his BOQ room and called Sally.

"Good thing you called earlier," she said, "or I'd've been finishing dessert by now. Where are we eating?"

"I heard about a place on the harbor. Steak and wine any good?"

"Yummy! Hurry," she said.

And hurry he did; he knocked on her Pacific Beach bungalow door eighteen minutes later. Sally opened the door and glanced over her bare shoulder—which flared a pale green sun dress. She kissed his cheek and held his arm. "I'd invite you in, but there's no one to meet, and there's nothing to see. I'm the last gal out, and I missed lunch. Like I said before, this working girl has an appetite."

Pax leaned away—to arm's length—looked her up and down, and whistled his appreciation. "I like the dress, but *what* a tan. I thought you had a job, but you're browner than any beach bum."

Her green eyes sparkled a shade darker than the dress, but lighter than the trees they were passing. She watched him as he drove. The gentle, Santa Ana-warmed evening breeze caressed them, while Al Hirt's sultry horn notes pulsed from the radio. The Corvette's effortless, throaty rumble echoed from the road. Words, even a single word, might break the spell. But she did it. "How did you and Bud shoot?"

"How do you like your job?"

"I asked you first."

"Bud shoots better than most first tour pilots. In fact, he's doing well across the board. Stop worrying; he's a good aviator."

"And how about you? Did you *sleep* with the scored target banners in Yuma?"

He glanced at her . . . and once again.

The corners of her mouth aren't right—mocking maybe?

"Where did you hear that?"

"It's true?"

"Sally, there are many truths. After drinking a snootful of ten-cent rum drinks one night, I woke up in the BOQ at Guantanamo Bay wrapped up in a target banner. God knows how it got in my bed. Where did *you* hear about that?"

"Hey, it surprised me, too. A first officer on my second flight said he'd been a Crusader pilot on the east coast, so I asked if he knew you. Said he did; *good* friends, he said. And he raved about Brandy, said to say hello. So . . . hello."

How can she be so engaging one minute and so . . . something different the next?

He eased into a parking spot, killed the car and the radio. She waited till he opened her door before saying, "Pax, I'm sorry I brought it up. It's what you do for a living, and Bill Strange, he was the first officer, said you do it better than most. I guess I can't get used to anyone liking it so much. I always thought Dad was some kind of eccentric—a war-loving oddball. Now I'm afraid Bud will become one. Forgive me?"

He nodded.

She might have a point.

"No problem, and I'll bet I'm as hungry as you are."

The hostess told Pax there would be a fifteen minute wait, that she'd call them, and escorted them to the bar. They opted for a terrace table, ordered drinks and faced their chairs toward the water and Coronado. Yachts and near-yachts—a string of white dashes—passed them right-to-left, inbound from wherever they'd been.

Sally swept a hand toward the water. "Looks almost like a parade. Do you sail?"

"No, but if I did and owned one of those beauties, I imagine I'd be anxious to get it berthed before dark. I guess everyone dreams about owning a boat, maybe even living on one—it's a good fantasy. Why? Are you into boats? Is that how you got so tan?"

She shook her head, but her eyes danced with mischief. "Don't look around," she said, "but one of my roommates sat down two tables away— she didn't see me—and she's with the captain from our morning flight. I didn't know they had anything going on."

Pax scooted his chair back toward their table. "Is there a problem? Is he married?"

"Doesn't matter. Coastal says assume every captain is married—first officers, too. And never believe *pending-divorce* assertions."

The hostess appeared and led them into what, for a moment, seemed like a dark dungeon of a dining room. Blinds had been tilted against the setting sun, and scurrying waiters went table to table lighting candles. Their table sat alongside what would become a window again, when the blinds were reopened, and three tables away from a hefty, heavily-bearded piano player. The Floyd Cramer medley showcased his skill.

Sally reached across the table and placed her fingers on the back of Pax's hand. "This is nice; I'm glad you invited me. What were you about to ask me when the hostess grabbed us?"

"How do captains and first officers feel about PCA waving those red-flags at the stewardesses, concerning the pilots?"

"I have no idea, nor do I care. Doesn't look like the flags work, but San Diego's a great place to live. I plan to keep my job."

From a roll-around cart, they selected raw sirloin strips, which would be grilled and served with baked potatoes, a large spinach salad, and—at their waiter's suggestion—a bottle of Beaujolais. The waiter and wine came right back. When the serious young man pulled the cork and offered Pax a small dollop for tasting, Pax passed the glass to Sally. "I defer to your judgment," he said.

"I'm no expert," she said, but took a sip and handed the glass back to the waiter. "Kind sir, please pour your wine."

When the fat man fell into a magical rendition of *Camelot*, he had the keyboard dancing and his brow glistening with tiny sweat-beads. The tune ended to enthusiastic applause. Pax raised his glass to Sally. "Here's to good music and better company."

They touched glasses. "And to mysteries, large and small," she said. "One of which, I'd like to broach. Call me nosy if you like, or tell me to buzz off. . . but I'm curious. On the terrace, I drank wine; you drank water. If recent history rules, you'll have one glass of wine. Period. Well and good, but I wonder why. Is it a rule? It must be related to the accident, but how? Why one drink? Why any drink? I'm curious; am I out of line?"

He looked into her eyes, but without focus.

Damn! A fair question, but one with no short answer. Even so, I can't ignore it.

She waited; he looked beyond her, above her head, opened his mouth, and took a deep, deep breath. He started to speak, but as he looked at her face, his eyes welled.

"No," she said and reached for his hand. "I . . . I don't want to know; forget I asked."

He placed his free hand over hers. "Please forgive me, but I *must* get past this. Maybe you've helped. I'll try to explain.

"Brandy and I went to another couple's home for a graduation party. We left little Pax at a sitter's house. Two hours later, we picked him up and started back toward our apartment—three blocks away. I'd had three or four beers. Three, I think, but it could have been four, no more. At a stop light, one block from home, a pickup truck with four plastered students ran their red light. They plowed right into Brandy's door. She had little Pax in her lap." Pax stopped talking; he stared through Sally and gnawed at his bottom lip. After a few heartbeats, he blinked away the past and was back. "The car in front of us crept through the intersection; I followed it—almost bumper-to-bumper. When I realized we'd be hit, there was no place to go. It happened too damned fast. I came to—for a minute or two—in the ambulance, but no one told me anything till the next morning."

Sally squeezed his hand. "You couldn't have prevented it."

"I don't think so, but without those beers . . . maybe; it's impossible to know. Anyway, guilt rides a strong horse. I couldn't look in a mirror for a year; I hated myself." Pax hesitated and looked away; his eyes filled again, but he continued. "One night I came to a compromise. I couldn't undo the past, but I could damned-well prevent a repeat performance. You guessed right. I decided one drink's enough; it gives me peace of mind. I've not told anyone else this."

Sally nodded once, and time got away from them. They were holding hands and looking into each other's eyes, without another word, when their dinner arrived and the blinds were opened. North Island's sparkling lights shimmered toward them from across the water, while the fat man bent some more Floyd Cramer-like slip-notes into *The Sound of Music*.

The single fudge sundae they shared for dessert tasted almost as sweet as Sally's single goodnight kiss.

At 1400 on July fifth, from the top of Mount Soledad in La Jolla, California, a hiker glanced inland—east-northeast—and saw the Miramar Naval Air Station. He watched as four F-8s began Field Carrier Landing Practice approaches. From the hiker's seven-mile-distant observation spot, the minuscule airplanes appeared to be inching around a counterclockwise pattern. Each plane, in its turn, would plop down amidst a gray puff, and bounce into the air again for another circuit. A tranquil and relaxing observation—from Mount Soledad.

Not so, however, beside the runway abeam the touchdown point where two committed observers cringed from Pratt and Whitney J-57s' thunderous roars. VF-124's skinny, redheaded Landing Signal Officer, Lieutenant "Stoney" (for stone deaf) Pebbles, waited six seconds for the climbing airplane's noise to subside while he glared up the glide slope at the next F-8—which was overshooting the runway center-line. Stoney relayed to his writer comments for the previous pilot's approach. The oncoming F-8 dipped its left wing and stopped the drift, as Stoney depressed a transmit button on the black telephone in his left hand. "Catch the overshoot sooner next time, now get your attitude set."

Bud Bank's voice blared from the speaker by Stoney's feet, "Gunfighter Four One Four, Crusader, Ball, four-point-five."

"Roger, ball, Four One Four," Stoney answered. "Steady your nose. Now line it up." As the airplane continued down the glide slope, getting closer to touchdown, Stoney began to raise his right hand, which held the wave-off lights pickle-switch. Depressing the pickle would actuate bright red wave-off lights, telling the pilot nearest touchdown to add full power and climb around for another approach. A wave-off signal, by voice on the radio or by the red lights: a mandatory signal. Automatic! No questions; add power and go around for another try.

Within seconds, Bud and his Crusader were too close for Stoney to improve the approach; last second instructions would be more hindrance than help. Bud's F-8, side number 414, slammed down beside Stoney and his assistant with a tad less than forty-five hundred pounds of J-P5 jet fuel aboard and with its engine screaming leapt back into the warm, following crosswind.

Stoney's eyes locked onto the next F-8 while he shouted additional grading remarks on Bud's approach to his fast-writing assistant. The four pilots would fly six or seven approaches each, two times a day for four days, to follow with two periods a night for ten nights. Stoney would observe, grade, and debrief every single practice carrier landing during the upcoming periods, but he didn't mind. Because after the practice, he would—from USS *Gettysburg*'s LSO platform—exhibit his handiwork: well-prepared pilots, making both day and night carrier landings, with he alone being responsible for bringing them safely aboard.

Before landing on *Gettysburg*, however, Stoney Pebbles would be living in their heads, orchestrating their moves, with their F-8s responding to his will. If not, he'd leave them ashore . . . deemed unsafe for carrier qualification landings—his evaluation final: a prudent system for a demanding and unpredictable environment.

Stoney worked as hard as the pilots who cursed and fought the overshooting crosswind. Because winds might blow from inconvenient directions, and bad weather might cancel scheduled flights. But nothing could slow the parade of days marching from the calendar. USS *Gettysburg* (CVA-35) would put to sea in twenty-two days, and remain at sea no more than four days and three nights. West Coast naval aviators believed ready, by their LSOs, would attempt to get ten day and six night arrested landings—becoming carrier qualified and current—during that four-day period. Period. An available flight deck provided no slack time; be there and be ready . . . or be damned.

Stoney finished a solemn debrief as Hacksaw opened the door. "How'd it go, Stoney?"

The gaunt LSO, expressionless as a doorknob, glanced at each pilot, going from face to face. "First days never go well; they're even worse with following crosswinds."

Hacksaw looked up and down the passageway, and tiptoed into the room, easing the door shut. "I'm sorry I asked," he said.

Tired chuckles escaped from everyone but Stoney. The ticking clock belonged to him—and he to it—for the next three weeks. As the pilots headed for their locker room, Hacksaw motioned for Pax to lag behind. "When's your physical?"

"Next Tuesday, the twelfth," Pax said looking sideways at his friend, "and I could sure use your help Friday . . . at happy hour."

Chapter 10—SAN CLEMENTE

Pax and Bud entered the replacement pilots' locker room together and headed for their individual lockers. "Hey, Bud, what's the story on this Doug Garvey? How come he's joining us now—without going to Yuma?"

"Our maintenance officer transferred to the Aeronautical Engineering Duty Officer program, so he won't deploy with us. VC-7's Lieutenant Commander Garvey received hot-off-the-press orders directing that he qualify aboard USS Gettysburg and report to VF-37. He has more than five hundred hours in F-8s, but he hates the idea of coming back to sea duty six months early."

Pax zipped up his flight suit. "Hacksaw says Doug never quits frowning."

Bud checked over both shoulders and lowered his voice. "I don't know about that, but you ought to see him knock back the booze. Last week, he slept over a couple of nights at our ranch—passed out. He must have a brick for a liver. Anyway, I can't imagine chug-a-lug Doug as maintenance officer."

The conversation's subject walked in and began disrobing. He looked neither right nor left; he might as well have been alone. When he came into the briefing room, he sat in back—three desk-chairs away from his nearest neighbor.

I'd swear Doug's eyes look focused well beyond Stoney Pebbles. But on what? Would I want him as my maintenance officer?

Stoney stood back from the blackboard and surveyed his chalky diagram of a landing area that resembled the angled deck on an aircraft carrier. "Gentlemen," he said and cleared his throat, "you fly your last scheduled day periods this afternoon. Right now, not *one* of you is ready to bounce at night. Nobody arrives abeam the platform on altitude, on airspeed, and with the proper distance from the runway." He walked to the blackboard and marked a large "X" at the diagramed angle deck's abeam position. "If you don't get *here* within proper parameters, you make the rest of the approach much harder. And don't kid yourselves into thinking crosswinds have been the problem. I'm looking for improvement." Stoney's glare encompassed each of them. "Work at it!"

"Individual thoughts for the day," Stoney said, pointing at the appropriate pilot. "Bud, get your nose attitude set as you roll into the groove; Pax, quit jacking your throttle around—make smaller corrections sooner; Camp, watch the ball till touchdown—you're settling in close; Doug, try to keep from overshooting the groove—otherwise you'll be ess-turning most of the way down the glide slope. And for incentive: whoever flies the worst pass buys the first round at happy hour. See you on the runway."

As soon as Stony left the briefing room, Pax turned to Bud and in a serious but louder than necessary voice said, "Not getting your nose attitude set early always guarantees having the worst approach."

"Baloney," Camp said to Pax. "Jacking the throttle around, sending those smoke signals out your tailpipe will earn you the worst pass prize."

Doug missed his cue, but Bud picked up the beat. "Ess-turning down the groove goes against human nature and makes a double-ugly pass."

But by the time Bud had said "human nature," granite-faced Doug had picked his way through the chairs and out the door, gone like fog before the sun. Camp shook his head. "Always laughing so much . . . it makes a man fleet of foot."

Pax knew their intervals were better, and the ball-calls sounded crisper than during their earlier flights. For one thing, the Santa Ana condition no longer vexed their pattern, so wind came straight down the runway, slowing their closure to touchdown and easing their transition into the groove. Stoney's transmissions held a little less bite.

"Not bad, Four Two Three," Stoney told Bud, "but keep working the ball clear to touchdown. Don't get lazy."

"Roger, paddles," Bud called.

Pax heard the smile in Bud's transmission and knew the feeling. Finding the gouges around the pattern, hitting the check points, sliding down an invisible rail to a perfect touchdown point—where the yellow-orange "ball" disappeared, aligned with the green datum lights—reflected an exceptional degree of hand/eye coordination. His East Coast LSO had described it best: Landing on centerline, on heading, on glide slope, and on airspeed . . . to a moving, and often pitching, flight deck is akin to juggling six balls. It seldom happens; for sure, no one masters it.

But Bud's success, while nice to note, meant little to Pax. His own goal for the afternoon: no comments from Stoney, couldn't happen without total concentration. He fought the slightest lapse, screamed at himself. And listened, listened for Stoney's first comment directed at Camp—with thirsty ears, through four approaches.

Camp and Pax flew opposite each other in the pattern: Camp touched down as Pax arrived at the abeam position and vice versa. Both pilots made their "ball" calls, and Stoney's "Roger ball" responses were followed by lengthy silences. Not so with Bud, nor with Douglas Garvey.

Half the second period passed as before, but after Camp's fourth touchdown Stoney keyed his mike. The radios roared, relaying Camp's full-power liftoff, then went silent.

Pax jerked his gaze toward the landing area.

What the hell happened there? Never mind, keep rowing your own boat.

So he did, and both he and Camp kept earning Stoney's benign neglect . . . until Pax's final approach. Pax knew the approach couldn't be better; getting the ball to disappear left into the datum lights would polish off two near-perfect bounce periods. His concentration and touch on the controls approached an otherworldly trance, well beyond understanding—much less explaining.

But an instant prior to Pax's touching down, Stoney flashed the red wave-off lights—much too late to prevent the landing. "Now what?" Pax yelled to himself.

What in the hell's Stoney's problem?

Pax stood by a window, fuming, when Camp stormed into the debriefing room and threw his helmet bag at a leather sofa. "Stoney's a fuckin' chickenshit!" Camp blurted. "Gave me a goddamned wave-off at touchdown. Jesus!"

Pax looked down, covered his face, and tried not to grin. Bud and Doug came in with Stoney, both listening with expressionless faces and lots of head nods to the LSO.

"I've debriefed Bud and Doug," Stoney said, eyeing Pax and Camp. "You two owe us drinks for not responding to wave-offs."

Camp threw both arms up. "Bullshit! You can't keep from touching down on that late a signal."

"You're right," Stoney replied and smiled, "but you can damned-well jam your throttle forward—which neither of you did. Just because things are going well out there, don't go to sleep on me."

Camp turned to Pax. "He fucked you, too?"

Pax nodded. Camp looked at the ceiling, expelled a sharp, lip-flapping breath, and shook his head. "Okay, let's head for the club. The first dumb-shit round's on me; I hope nobody chokes on it . . . honest, Stoney."

Hacksaw had a good head start on happy hour, but Pax needed him, explained why, and watched while his double-fisted-drinking friend connected the dots. The picture came together in stages for the Mississippian, but the process paralleled his widening grin. "You sneaky sumbitch," he said and they left the club.

At the dispensary, the same corpsman appraised a familiar looking paper sack under Pax's arm. "Good evening, gentlemen, how can I help you?"

"I don't know if you can or not," Pax said. "Commander Grayson, here, thinks he's got the best damned eyes at Miramar. I think he's wrong; we've put a few coins on it. How 'bout showing us an eye chart?"

The corpsman shook his head. "I don't think so, Lieutenant. We're not supposed to let you practice on those charts."

Hacksaw moved close to the counter and spoke in a hoarse whisper, "Hell, we ain't gonna *practice*. What's happening is I'm looking to lighten his wallet a tad. Ten seconds after seeing the chart, I'll be foldin' some of this boy's serious green. We don't wanna get you in trouble, though. If anybody comes in, tell 'em I got something in my eye. Okay?"

The straight-faced petty officer agreed, letting Pax put the sack under his counter before they walked back to the eye examination room. The wall chart contest ended as a tie, but Pax beat Hacksaw on the tiny chart in the little lighted box. He accepted four twenty-dollar bills from Hacksaw as the three of them walked back down the passageway to the corpsman's post.

"Thank you very much," Pax told the corpsman.

Hacksaw blew out a Bronx cheer. "I damned sure don't thank you very much."

The corpsman smiled at Pax, and the two officers headed back to the club. In the car, Pax returned Hacksaw's money and patted his friends back. "You're a real pal; I appreciate your help."

"And you're plumb past sneaky, fella. I better watch you."

Inside the club and back at their table, Pax couldn't avoid a beer roll before getting away to call Sally. He asked Bud, "Who's been buying so far?"

"This is the first roll. We drank your round, Camp's round, and Doug's round. Doug won the worst pass prize, and now we're into skill dice. Our jolly LSO drank his freebies and hit the road."

Camp slammed the dice cup down by Doug Garvey, which made him jump. "You bought the last round, Doug; bring 'em out."

Pax watched the leaning officer go through the motions. Doug listed even farther to his left, stared at a spot in the middle of the table while blowing into the cup, and rolled out five aces. *"Drinks for the house!"* boomed Camp. An instant hush, and scrambling bodies and excited cheers closed around the table, each face straining to see who'd pissed off Lady Luck. The dice remained frozen, as did Doug's open-mouthed gaze at them. Even his table-mates sneaked sideways peeks at him: their taboo-breaking party financier.

Hacksaw scraped the dice into the cup. "Camp, you turkey, you're supposed to give a guy the option of buying for his table the rest of the night. Damn!"

"You're right; I screwed up. Sorry, Doug," Camp said, sounding almost sincere.

Pax couldn't watch anymore. Doug reminded him of a puppy being scolded for something beyond its comprehension. Besides, Pax's hand itched for a telephone.

Sally answered after half-a-ring. "If you're not in a straitjacket, the answer is yes; if you are, it's maybe."

He had to laugh. "That deserves a good response. Give me ten minutes, and I'll call you back."

"No you won't, because in ten minutes you'll be halfway here, I hope. But before I forget, is Bud there?"

"Uh-huh."

"Tell him to call me tomorrow. I've got some news he may like. Becky Johnston gets here tomorrow; she'll interview with PCA Monday."

"Should I say anything, or do you want to tell him now?"

"No and no. There's a barefoot bar right around the corner—very casual. Interested?"

"I'm on the way," he said and got halfway across the parking lot before remembering the message. Pax grinned and shook his head all the way back to the table, where he leaned close to Bud. "Call Sally tomorrow."

Bud nodded and raised the dice cup over his head with both hands and shook it hard. "Don't Garvey me, dice; don't Garvey me."

Doug had one eye shut, the other he cocked at Bud—in recognition of sound and motion. The brush with notoriety passed his notice. Pax looked around the table, found no one too concerned about the leaning, one-eyed LCDR, so he left.

A quick shower and Pax trotted from the BOQ. And stopped dead. The granddaddy of pea soup fogs obscured everything beyond five-yards. Pax retreated to the front desk, called meteorology first and Sally next. "Have you looked outside?" he asked.

"Yes. Where are you?"

"The BOQ. Our weather guys say this stuff is here to stay, maybe forever, but at least through tomorrow afternoon."

"I'm glad you didn't get caught halfway. Me, I'm going to bed; I hide from bad weather."

"You're making me yawn," he said. "Last one asleep's a rotten egg." So they exchanged goodnights.

Stoney Pebbles stood behind the lectern, displaying his no-nonsense countenance. "Tonight," he said, "you'll make two approaches to touchdown at San Clemente. I'll be there, on the runway, before you start down. You've each flown sixteen night periods, a lot of them here, a couple at El Centro. Believe me, San Clemente feels like a ship; winds blow harder out there and it'll be blacker than the inside of a cow. Stay on your gauges, respond to those controllers; they know what they're doing."

"Where's the wind from?" Camp asked.

"It could change, but an hour ago they had an easterly wind. You'll be using runway five and have a left-hand pattern, one landing from the teardrop approach, another from the bolter or wave-off pattern. I can't stress it enough: stay on the gauges, don't get tied up trying to pick up your interval on the downwind leg. Miramar expects to remain visual through midnight, but I'll get fifteen minute reports and pass on any changes. Questions?"

The four aviators sitting in front of the lectern looked at each other and back at Stoney, shaking their heads.

"Fine. Plan on the first plane pushing over from marshal at 2200. We'll debrief tomorrow at 1000."

When Stoney left, Bud stood and stretched. "Tell me again why we want to fly to a little island and land . . . at night."

Camp drop-kicked an imaginary football. "I figure they're tryin' to scare the shit out of us."

"Works for me," Pax said.

"Lucky" Doug Garvey, new nickname attached-for-life, left the room without comment and, at 2130, blasted off the Miramar runway in afterburner. Pax followed Doug, Bud next and Camp last. As each moved toward San Clemente's northern tip, he eliminated excess fuel according to his nature. One F-8 climbed through thirty thousand feet in afterburner, another dumped fuel from its wingtips while corkscrewing through rolls in a lazy arc, two dumped fuel in level flight.

Pax checked into marshal first, received an approach time, got a time check, and dumped more fuel. They had been briefed to touch down on initial landing with maximum allowable fuel aboard. The pilots adjusted their holding patterns to push over from overhead as second hands on instrument panel clocks ticked through the twelves. Playing transfer switch against dump switch added spice to the equations, kept minds from noticing deep purple glimmerings disappearing to the west.

Looking good . . . fuel's right . . . penetration checklist complete . . . 5-4-3-2-1.

Retarding the throttle and extending the speed brake, Pax reported, "San Clemente Approach, Gunfighter Four One Four, departing marshal, leaving eighteen thousand feet."

Radio transmissions flowed in automatic sequences, directed turns achieved desired results, and Pax concentrated on his instruments. The headwind proved strong, because closure took longer; however, at three quarters of a mile, the amber meatball beamed at him from dead-center between the horizontal green datum lights. In close, he might have settled a tad, but not bad. The second landing went the same. He cleaned the airplane up—raised its landing gear and lowered its wing—and climbed for his most economical fuel-burn altitude back to Miramar.

The high-pitched transmission cut through the black night like a tracer: "This is San Clemente on guard frequency; we have an F-8 in the water. Stay clear." The same transmission came again while Pax jerked his plane around for a backward glance, a futile gesture, so he headed east again and soon descended into Miramar.

Taxiing toward the fueling pit, Pax radioed the ready room and asked what they knew. "Nothing yet," the SDO said. "Is anyone with you?"

"No, I'm the first one back. Out," Pax said and switched to the tower frequency and waited, listening for flight members to check in. An F-8 entered the break and landed with Pax hearing nothing. He rechecked his radio frequency.

Who flew in the water? Why? How were they stacked up behind me? How many approaches completed after I left?

He couldn't sort it out. A voice . . . Camp's voice, called at the break. At the same time, the silent plane neared the fueling pit and swung around. Pax recognized Bud's helmet.

Thank God.

Bud pointed to his helmet, and signaled thumbs down.

Oh, a radio failure.

A small circle of pilots, including Hacksaw in civvies, closed around Camp, who leaned against the corner of a gray maintenance desk. No eyes blinked. "I didn't know until right now," Camp said, looking at Bud, "whether it was you or Doug in the water. San Clemente tower called a plane turning downwind to level out and to climb. I had already cleaned up and headed for home. When the tower said they had an F-8 in the water, on Guard frequency, I turned back, made one circle at five thousand feet, saw a helicopter airborne, and decided to come on back."

Bud shrugged. "I never heard anything. My radio started getting scratchy during the second approach, but I didn't know it had failed until I tried to call the ball. Maybe I saw the crash, but I didn't know what it was—a small flash somewhere off to the left of my nose. Without a radio, I came on home."

The squawk box on the gray desk came alive. "Is Commander Grayson down there? Stoney's on the duty officer's phone and wants to talk at him."

A maintenance chief spoke to the box. "On his way."

The three sweaty aviators followed Hacksaw to the duty office and listened to a stream of "Uh-huhs."

Hacksaw thanked Stoney, hung up, and sucked his teeth. "The tower directed their helicopter damned near straight to some wreckage; two rescue boats are on scene now, but nobody's optimistic."

Pax touched Hacksaw's shoulder and whispered, "Is Doug married?"

"No, but he has two ex-wives and two children living in town. I've got to call the skipper."

Camp eased closer to Bud and Pax, squinted his eyes, and said, "Please, please don't ever call me . . . 'Lucky.'"

Chapter 11—*USS GETTYSBURG*

Stoney glanced at the wall clock, 0955, and stared through the sweating, briefing room window into a gray, misty wall of blindness. Dense fog enveloped Miramar a few minutes after sunup; planes remained parked in their spots, covered with dew and an equally heavy pall of quietness. His three coffee-mug-carrying replacement pilots entered the room behind him and took their seats.

As Stoney walked to the lectern, Pax judged the lanky LSO even skinnier than usual. Stoney pointed at Bud. "Hacksaw told me about your radio failure. Between your not calling the ball and the tower's unanswered Guard Frequency transmissions, I thought . . . I didn't know what to think."

"Stoney, did *you* notice Doug's losing altitude?" Camp asked. "Could you see him?"

The LSO's lips clamped into a straight line as he shook his head. "He lifted off okay; I turned to pick up the next plane while I talked to the writer. When Bud didn't call . . . I locked-in on him. The tower made the Guard calls, but I didn't see Doug again. Neither did my writer. Two tower observers thought Doug's lights went out as he lost altitude. Who knows what happened? The pieces they recovered weren't two miles from shore, but I didn't see him go in."

"No chance of ejection?" Pax asked.

Again, Stoney shook his head. "The San Clemente operations officer called at nine o'clock this morning and said they'd found evidence that confirmed Doug crashed with the plane."

Camp stood. "Any debrief, Stoney?"

"Not for you, Camp; both passes were good."

"Okay, I'm off to dental," Camp said and left.

Stoney turned to Bud. "Your one pass looked acceptable, a little settle in the middle, too much power, a little over the top . . . maybe a 4-wire."

Bud nodded. "Did you see me rock my wings on the wave-off? I tried to let you know my radio was out."

"*I* didn't," Stoney said. "My writer thought you did, but I was looking for Doug's plane."

Stoney pulled a chair around to face Pax and drummed his fingers on Pax's desk-top. "You quit working in close. Why do you fly the ball so well down the glide-path, but let it sag close to touchdown? Same-o, same-o for the last three or four periods. You'll end up catching too many 1-wires at the ship. I don't like that. Keep the ball in the middle; it *belongs* in the middle— clear to touchdown."

"Gotcha," Pax said. "What time did you get back this morning?"

"About 0200. Slept on a sofa in the ready room. The fog's coming so early made me look smart. We'll have two bounce periods Monday evening and hit the ship Tuesday. With much more practice, people start getting bored and lazy." Stoney raised his eyebrows at Pax. "Some quicker than others."

The ready room's front chalkboard message:
GARVEY MEMORIAL SERVICE
BASE CHAPEL SAT/23 JUL/1000
TROPICAL WHITES
. . . which didn't lift any spirits—or disperse the fog.

Bud and Pax alternated between looking out the window for any hints of improvement, and studying the memorial service notice. "I flew with the man twice a day for three weeks," Pax said, "but other than radio transmissions, I can't remember his saying a word. Am I screwed up or what?"

"Same here," Bud said. "Once, in response to a direct question, I heard him answer, 'Ice.' He didn't talk a lot."

"We've been flying so steady, I'm out of touch. How did Becky's interview go? Or have they hired her by now?"

Bud shrugged his shoulders. "Don't know. Sis hadn't heard from her two days ago. Becky didn't think her interview went well." Bud removed his wristwatch, adjusted it to match the wall clock, and yawned. "Night flying plays hell with a fella's social life."

"That and fog," Pax said. "If I skippered this outfit, I'd secure the squadron right now, and let everyone crawl back home during daylight—before happy hour for damned sure."

Hacksaw stuck his head in the door. "Duty Officer, we're shutin' down. Monday's rough flight schedule's posted in operations. Pass the word."

Bud gave Pax a sideways fisheye. "I'll be damned; you knew. I don't know how, but you knew."

"I told you what I'd do. Let's get out of here."

Pax called her from the Officers Club right after lunch, as blue patches started showing through the dissipating fog. "Fair Sally, would you rather go to dinner tonight or Ensenada for the weekend?" he asked. Her delayed response made him grit his teeth.

I wish to hell I could jerk that question back.

"I must be talking to one of the three *lucky* pilots from San Clemente," she said.

Oh Christ!

He shuddered more at her tone than at her words.

"Not to worry, though," she continued, "I'd hung up from telling Dad I hadn't heard about the crash, when Bud called asking about Becky. He told me that *you* hadn't crashed either; I guess he thought you wouldn't mind."

Pax didn't answer; he couldn't think of anything to say.

"Anyway, I called Dad back," she said. "He worries. . . . You there?"

"Uh-huh."

"Becky's here; she got back yesterday. I wouldn't feel right leaving her."

I know penance when I hear it, but. . . .

"I guess you're right, Sally; I'll call when we're back from the ship. Bye." And he hung up. Back in his room, listening to country songs on the radio, Pax laid out a white, short-sleeved uniform for the next day's memorial service. He frowned, ran a finger along the bottom of the lonely, red and yellow National Defense ribbon beneath his Wings of Gold. "With a little luck," he murmured, "I'll find you some company before long."

If they keep fighting, so I'll get a chance. But will they?

Pax arrived for the service at 0945, but so few parked cars made him check his watch. When he entered the close to vacant chapel, four other scattered officers sat on the left side of the center aisle. He recognized no one and figured they were from VC-7.

But what do I know? They might have been Doug's best friends.

He moved to the front row, left side, and sat midway down the bench.

Why not? We flew together night before last.

Two minutes before the hour, a small hard-core group of mourners, accompanied by two navy captains and Hacksaw Grayson, baby-stepped their way down the center aisle and into the right side, front two rows of seats. In the middle of the front row sat two women with two children between them, a boy and a girl, maybe eight- and six-years-old. The daughter's mother wore black; the son's wore beige. Hacksaw shared the front row, next to the aisle; he nodded at Pax.

An organist keyed the Navy Hymn's first notes as Pax's second hand drug across the twelve, which also coincided with the chaplain's taking his seat.

Navy protocol might not fill a chapel, but it can damned-well read a clock.

Pax tried hard not to think of the children, but he failed.

Can their loss equal my hurt over little Pax? No, they have their mothers.

And each mother had an arm around her mirrored reflection of the recently departed, tight-lipped aviator: Lieutenant Commander Douglas Garvey.

The chaplain's canned words droned, and why not? Naval aviators had been tenuous bets—at best—since the navy's first aviation fatality.

Brandy likened me and my pilot friends to children teasing a rattlesnake.

So chaplains needed no originality. A mantra from Orville and Wilbur's aspirations, sprinkled with lots of sea spray, earned solemn head nods from the captains, which begat following nods from lesser lights. And in what seemed a single heartbeat, the chaplain stood in front of the children, handing them each an American flag that had been folded and tucked into the obligatory triangle.

Hacksaw's low-pitched compliment filled the near-empty chapel: "Your daddy's mighty proud of you children today, and so am I." And that, the most sincere offering of the day, unhinged the most recent wife in black. Hacksaw moved to her side and helped lead the stricken handful from a standard, Mark I, navy memorial service.

In the normal peel-back-from-the-front chapel evacuation, Pax followed behind the captains, who followed behind the family. He noted, if not a crowd, at least several additional attendees waiting to join the flow. Beyond Camp, who somehow had slipped into the row behind him, he saw Bud, Sally, and Becky Johnston. Funny, nobody mentioned coming, yet there they were. He felt good about being there. From their expressions, they must have felt the same way. He waited, squinting under the bright sunlight, until they emerged.

"Hi, Becky," Pax said. "Welcome to San Diego." Sweeping an arm to include the four, he said, "I'd like to invite you to the club for lunch."

Sally shook her head. "Wish I could, but I have a flight. Bud and Becky are dropping me at the airport." She arched her eyebrows and deadpanned,

"I thought you'd be in Ensenada."

"No problem," Camp said. "I'm going to town anyway. Let me drop you at the airport; they can have lunch."

Sally looked at Pax and smiled. "Camp, are you sure it's no trouble?"

Camp convinced everyone but Pax that he had been on the way to town.

"Could you wait two minutes at my place—it's on the way—while I throw on my uniform?" Sally asked.

Camp flashed a surreptitious wink at Pax. "It would be my pleasure, pretty lady."

"Have a nice flight, Sally," Pax said and looked at Bud. "I'll meet you and Becky at the club."

Driving to the club, Pax's mind churned full tilt.

Some days a fella can't even enjoy a plain vanilla memorial service without some Canoe-U crapper trying to snake his gal. My gal? Why did Sally's little telephone snit gall my butt so bad? I'll have to think about that . . . someday . . . maybe. It might not matter.

Tuesday broke clear with unlimited visibility. The three aviators arrived at the hangar well in advance of the 0930 brief, despite having flown twice the previous night. Their anticipation spiked the air like lightning-charged ozone.

Hacksaw poked his mock-serious face into the briefing room. "You lucky turkeys, I can't believe we taxpayers give you guys money for landing on the ship. You oughta be ashamed."

"Come go with us," Bud said.

Hacksaw looked from Bud to Pax, and—in a softer voice—said, "Soon enough, Lieutenant . . . soon enough." Hacksaw glanced at Camp, who had moved to the lectern, "Your 1130 Charlie time looks good. How early did Stoney want you overhead?"

"He didn't say," Camp answered, "but I'd planned on checking in at eleven fifteen, which will give us time to dump down. I want us airborne by ten thirty."

Hacksaw tapped his forehead with an abbreviated salute. "Keep the ball in the middle, guys, and have fun."

Camp kept the briefing brief. "Individual takeoffs, switch to tactical frequency going feet wet, rendezvous two-five-zero at fifty miles off Miramar, angels twenty-two. We're Cobra flight; Bud's number two. I'll see you when I see you. Questions?"

In answer, Pax and Bud stood, shook their heads. As they donned their G-suits and survival vests, Pax nudged Bud. "I know Stoney covered this; I know you'll be guarding against it, but I'll still bet a beer you get hung in the arresting gear after a landing today."

"You talking about a beer bet each landing, or one beer for the whole day?" Bud asked.

"One beer all day."

Bud shrugged and nodded. "You're on."

Camp cackled loudly, "You've been had, Bud. Pax, I'd be ashamed." Camp put his arm around Bud's shoulders. "You *will* get hung up, the Air Boss *will* blast you over the flight deck loudspeakers, and whoever's following you in the pattern *will* get waved off. And you'll feel like hell about it, nevertheless, it *will* happen."

Pax sped through the preflight checks. He started, taxied, and got airborne well ahead of the others.

Too much ahead? Did I forget anything?

Getting back on a ship after even a short port visit always got his blood up.

After six years, this is downright honeymoonish.

When they rendezvoused in a loose vee, Camp followed his TACAN needle to *Gettysburg*'s overhead holding pattern and checked in. "Trojan, Gunfighter Four One Six, overhead, angels eighteen, flight of three, low state eight-point-five, over."

USS *Gettysburg* (CVA-35), call sign "Trojan," a 27-Charley class aircraft carrier, sliced through the calm sea more than three miles below. A static crackle became a solid transmission link: "Roger, Gunfighters with a flight of three, take angels one-six, expected Charlie-Time one-one-three-zero, altimeter—three-zero-one-six. Request side numbers, pilots' names, and individual fuel states, over."

Camp passed the information, while Pax strained for glimpses of the ship. Getting two thousand feet closer hadn't made it grow much; *Forrestal* had been bigger.

Am I looking at the right ship? Christ!

His shudder came unbidden and seemed to activate the napping radio waves.

"Gunfighter leader, air boss says . . . Gunfighters expect two touch-and-goes each prior to arrested landings. Gunfighters first in the pattern: Charlie-

Ten. Foxtrot Corpen— three-zero-zero. Acknowledge Charley-Ten, over."

Camp eased his airplane's nose over, reduced power, and maintained the wide left turn. Pax worked the figures backwards.

Camp'll want to be alongside, at eight hundred feet, four minutes before Charley-time. With the ship turning into the wind, expecting to steady up on course three-zero-zero, Camp has to coordinate our descent and turning rate to where the turning ship will be in six minutes.

In a descending left turn, Camp raised his right fist at Bud, signaling for Bud to move from left to right wing position—between Camp and Pax. The carrier steadied on course as the three-plane, right echelon of F-8s flew down her starboard side and started their individual breaks, turning downwind. Pax sneaked a quick look at his clock: four seconds early.

I'll mention that to Camp . . . jerk his chain.

Twelve seconds after Bud, Pax dropped his left wing and commenced a level turn, lowered his landing gear at 215-knots, unlocked and raised the two-position wing lever at 180-knots, and continued slowing and descending until he reached six hundred feet and optimum angle-of-attack at the 180-degree abeam position. His right hand touched the hook handle before he remembered the touch-and-goes.

I'd better wake up.

Fuel state good . . . dump-switch secured . . . gear down . . . wing up . . . hook up. Pax called abeam the LSO platform and again in the groove as he picked up the ball.

"Roger, Crusader, ball," Stoney answered. "We have an axial wind at thirty-knots."

Gettysburg's smoke trailed straight aft, and she pushed a large bow wave, making her own wind. The sea's glassy surface confirmed it.

No wonder Bud got so many line-up calls; I should have picked up the clues.

Each pilot got his touch and goes and six arrested landings before being launched to the beach. As Pax saluted the catapult officer for his last launch, VF-37 and VF-39, squadrons from his future air wing, had F-8s feeding into the pattern. *Gettysburg* was their ship; she would be his ship, too, and soon.

Hacksaw met them at the top of the hangar stairs. "How many did you get?" he asked. "Any problems? Planes okay?" Before anyone could answer he continued, "Stoney called from the ship, said you looked good. Expect two day traps tomorrow afternoon and as many as four night traps. Come in at noon tomorrow; I'll be here." Without a backward look, the LCDR hurried down the stairs and out of sight.

Camp's gaze trailed Hacksaw. "His house must be on fire."

Bud tapped Pax's shoulder. "Owe you a beer; I hung up after my first trap—even after your warning me."

"I noticed," Pax said. "For a few seconds I thought I'd get a wave-off, but you hustled across the foul-line."

"Were you guys having trouble with line-up?" Bud asked.

"Nuh-uh," Camp grunted, "but I guess we forgot to tell you to aim at the crotch."

"Pardon?" Bud said and turned to Pax, who nodded.

"Look," Camp said, "when the ship is making her own wind, you tend to drift left. When you get on centerline, point your nose at the right edge of the far end of the angled deck: the *crotch*. It gives you a proper crab into the slight, right crosswind. As you get in closer, ease the nose back toward the centerline."

Bud looked sideways at Pax and raised his eyebrows. Pax nodded. "I guess Stoney didn't brief that, and I didn't think to mention it. But it works," Pax said.

The three aviators completed their qualification landings on the second night, and Stoney flew in from the ship Friday morning for their debrief. Before saying a word, however, Stoney wrote a summary on the chalkboard for each pilot. Hacksaw watched from the back of the briefing room.

As usual, Stoney briefed from behind the lectern, talking directly to one pilot at a time. "Bud," Stoney started, "you had two wave-offs and three bolters—one might have been a hook-skip, but on the other two you touched down well beyond the wires. In all five cases you got low in the middle of the approach. Work on keeping the ball in the middle; don't let it sag.

"Camp, two bolters, but good steady work on the glide slope. If everyone worked as hard as you do on the glide path, an LSO's job would be a piece of cake.

"Pax, you're the reason LSOs drink too much, smoke too much, and can't sleep at night. I'm glad you're not in my squadron. You caught fourteen 2-wires, two 1-wires, and you knew you were doing it. You snagged both 1-wires, the first day, when you were obviously deck-spotting. Don't be so damned lazy. Fly the friggin' ball to touchdown. If you bolter, so what?"

Pax said nothing.

"And before I forget it," Stoney continued, "the Catapult Officer said you were wearing glasses last night." Camp and Bud both looked at Pax, their brows furrowed. "I said I'd check on it."

"I did," Pax said. "Have you seen those Highway Patrol glasses advertised . . . the ones that reduce glare at night? I couldn't tell much difference . . . maybe a little."

"Do you have them here?" Stoney asked.

Pax nodded.

"May I see them?" Stoney asked.

"Sure," Pax said and left the room. He returned and handed the yellow-tinted glasses to the frowning LSO. Camp and Bud watched with high interest. Hacksaw moved a few seats closer to the group. Stoney looked through the glasses at his briefing notes, at the chalkboard, and out the window. He rotated the frames while looking through the lenses.

"There's no correction in these?" Stoney asked.

Pax shook his head. "No, they're supposed to reduce glare from lights at night. I sat by a traffic light one night for several minutes to see if they altered the green, red, or amber, and they didn't. So I tried them. Like I said, I couldn't tell much difference."

"Okay," Stoney said. "Work on keeping that ball in the center . . . all the way to touchdown."

Pax remained in his seat after Stoney and the other two pilots left. The Mississippi drawl oozed over his shoulder: "You're one sneaky sumbitch, Paxton Langford. I'd better keep my eye on you, and it looks like I'll be in a position to do it."

It took a microsecond, but when Pax spun around, Hacksaw's grin matched his head nod. "Found out yesterday," he said. "Camp's gonna replace Doug in Bud's squadron. I'll be comin' to yours next month as ops officer. Not right now, but someday over a few beers . . . I'll tell you why these orders are extra special for me."

Their handshake and grins said it best, and they agreed to toast the situation at happy hour.

Hacksaw squinted at Pax. "Now that you can see so damn well, what's your fascination with the 2-wire?"

Pax glanced over his shoulder at the door and back at his friend. "Look, I don't preach this, Hacksaw, but you know damned good and well the only difference between a 2-wire and a 3-wire is who feels better: me or the LSO. If I'm dead-on in close and the ball sags a little—and I mean no more than half-a-ball—well *big deal*. I get a hook-skip, there's an extra chance to snag a wire. I don't *go-for-it*, and 1-wires suck, but I don't buy Stoney's *If you bolter, so what?* crap, either. Boltering crowds bombing on my things-to-avoid list, especially at night. As for the two 1-wires, I'd forgotten how much burble there is in the groove when a carrier's making her own wind. It took me two traps to get calibrated."

Hacksaw canted his head. "Why not use the first two passes, the touch-and-goes, to get calibrated?"

"I used those passes to fly the ball . . . clear to touchdown."

"Don't tell me anymore, Pax; you make my head hurt."

Chapter 12—VF-39 "LANCERS"

"Pax, why don't I save you a trip?" Sally said. "Bud picks Becky up at five-thirty; I'll come to the club with them. Okay?"

She sounds different . . . almost enthusiastic.

"Sure, I'll see you when I see you. You sound cheerful; are you off probation?"

"No, but you have a good ear, sir, and I'm ready to celebrate. From what Becky said, Bud's satisfied the free world's safe now, since he's ready to go to sea. I wish I'd heard him tell Dad about it."

"Me, too; maybe we'll get a rehash tonight. See you at the club." He hefted the receiver a couple of times before setting it in its cradle.

Maybe not calling for a week paid off. Women! I'll never figure 'em out. Can they figure themselves out?

But her logistical logic gave him an extra hour; he spent it washing and waxing the White Knight. He shaved, showered, and considered stretching out on the bed—for a minute or two, no more—to rest his eyes, but prudence kicked in. Instead, he stroked his cordovan loafers a couple of licks with a shine rag. When he figured his friends were due, he started walking to the club. Sure enough, Bud and the girls drove into the parking lot before Pax reached the club's front door. He veered toward them. Sally wore the sea-green dress that matched her eyes. Pax shook his head. "How brown you gonna get? Each time I see you, you're twice as dark. I can't believe it."

Bud let out a laugh. "Believe me; she's not even halfway there. Give her another two weeks."

"And *she's* lucky," Becky said. "The best some of us can do is freckle, burn, peel, and start over again."

Pax kissed Sally on the cheek and rested his fingers at the small of her back when they entered the club. "To tell the truth, I've forgotten what color your skin is," he said and grinned. "Show me your tan-line?"

Her eyes sparkled as she laughed at him. "What tan-line?"

The happy hour cauldron appeared ready to boil, and coveys of nubile women matched laughter with khaki-clad aviators. Pax held Sally's hand and stood motionless at the turmoil's edge; Becky stood beside them. Sally pulled Pax's hand down and stretched to speak in his ear, "Shall we find seats, or would you rather stand here and drool on the carpet?"

At least the glint's back in her eyes.

Bud returned from a dark corner. "Hacksaw's saving us seats back there," he said and began threading Becky through the throng, followed by Sally and Pax. The hustling waitresses—some carrying four full pitchers of sloshing beer—snaked through the crowded drinkers. Bud progressed by baby-steps.

"'Bout time!" Hacksaw bellowed, as he and Camp slid chairs out for the girls. "Damned near gave up on you. Rollin' dice against Camp makes me sleepy."

Camp jerked a thumb toward Hacksaw. "And he falls into more lucky rolls than any peckerwood I ever saw. Maybe *you* guys cheat less; I'm bringin' 'em out." He slammed the leather dice cup down and jerked it clear. Even as Pax read the dice, Hacksaw covered them. "Camp," Hacksaw whispered, "you laid five 1-eggs. What's it gonna be, drinks for the house or *our* drinks for the night? Your choice."

Camp stood and bowed to the girls. "Ladies, your gracious presence restrains my response, so I shall go outside and howl at the moon. Pax, I no longer trust Commander Grayson; he may be from the dark world. I leave this small token in your care." He put a folded hundred dollar bill in Pax's hand and weaved his way through the khaki swarm.

"Last fellow who rolled five aces paid a steep tab," Bud said. The guys nodded.

A tall, sandy-haired commander appeared at their table, leaned toward Pax, and stuck out his right hand. "Lieutenant Langford, I'm Coleman Dodd from VF-39. May I have a word?"

Pax stood, shook Dodd's hand, made introductions around, and followed the commander away from their table. Farther from the din, Dodd turned and put his hand on Pax's shoulder. "I apologize for intruding, Pax, but Ann and I are having a get-together at home tomorrow night; we'd like you to come. Bring a date if you want. Hacksaw and Wilma will be there. Casual, like you are is perfect. Eight o'clock." Dodd's gray-green eyes never wavered.

Pax accepted the invitation, thanked him, and listened to directions to his future skipper's house. Hacksaw looked up and snapped his fingers when Pax returned to the table. "I promised him I'd tell you about the party, but I forgot. About twenty minutes ago, Ann Dodd asked me if you were coming."

"No sweat," Pax said and looked at Sally. "Would you like to meet some people in my new squadron tomorrow night? We've been invited to CDR Dodd's house."

"*We've* been invited?" Sally said.

"He said bring a date; you qualify. Wanna go?"

She squeezed his hand. "I fly tomorrow, and we won't get back until six. Could we make it?"

Pax nodded. "They—" Camp Brogan put his hands on both of their shoulders. "Pardon me, Sally, I need to borrow Pax for a minute."

Pax excused himself and followed Camp past two tables to a quieter spot. "What's the problem, Camp?"

When Camp turned back to answer, his flushed face surprised Pax. "Did Commander Dodd tell you my orders got changed?"

"No, he invited me to his house. What do you mean *changed*?"

"I take Doug's spot as Maintenance Officer in VF-37; I like the job better . . . and I already know the skipper."

"Well, good luck," Pax said and they shook hands.

"Speaking of luck," Camp said, "I'll bet you a hundred bucks I bag a MiG before you."

Pax shook his head. "I've got a better idea; follow me."

At the table, Pax touched Hacksaw and Bud's arms. "Our lucky dice roller here suggested we pledge some money toward the first MiG kill. Interested?"

"How much?" Bud asked.

"Each pilot puts a hundred dollars in the pot," Camp said. "First MiG gets it."

"Count me in," Bud said.

Sally held her empty glass upside down over the table. "I'd rather have another drink than a MiG."

Becky joined her friend in the inverted, empty-glass order. "Me, too."

Hacksaw signaled a waitress for another round and scratched his chin. "Your MiG bets," he said, "almost make me want to go to sea; believe I'll call my assignment officer."

Everyone laughed except Hacksaw and Pax. Camp leaned across the table toward Pax and said, "I didn't hear you getting in the pot, hotshot."

"You and I have a bet, Camp," Pax said, "but the big pot bet needs some adjustments. I want to think about it."

"Whatever you decide, your money belongs to me," Camp said and disappeared into the crowd.

Before Hacksaw left, he turned to Sally. "Wilma and I will see you tomorrow night; she looks forward to meeting you." He talked louder to the men. "You two refuel from an A-3 on Wednesday and check out; both your skippers want you yesterday." Hacksaw winked at Pax and left.

They surrendered the bar to a diminishing, but louder, crowd and moved into the dining room. When they ordered lobster specials, the waitress told them that their order included two free bottles of champagne for the table. Pax squeezed Sally's hand and asked Bud, "What did you tell your dad about landing on the ship?"

Bud blushed, stared at his bubbling goblet, and shook his head. When he looked into Pax's eyes, words still didn't come.

"Did you understand the question?" Sally asked.

Bud nodded. "He sounded excited, wanted to know if the night traps scared me. I lied to him and said no. He said, 'Bullshit.' We both laughed. I told him you didn't wave-off *or* bolter."

"What's a bolter?" Becky asked.

"When you land beyond the wires and have to takeoff again," Sally said.

"But sometimes you land in the wires, and your hook misses anyway," Bud said. "That sucks."

"Enough shop talk, please," Pax said and stood. "A toast to the ladies."

Bud rose for the toast and smiled at Becky as their dinner arrived. Thereafter, conversation lagged appetites until four empty plates applauded the chef. Sally interrupted dessert speculation by standing. "Pax, I'm sorry, but you need to take me home." She shook her head and looked at Becky. "I apologize . . . too much champagne. Sorry."

Sally shaded her face with a hand. "Come in. It kills me to look into that sun. What a day."

Pax struggled at keeping a straight face. "You *look* pretty good; at least you had a good night's sleep."

She spun back to face him, and a scarlet blush overpowered whatever tan she'd achieved. "I'm going to ask this once, and I want the truth," she said and sat on the edge of the sofa. "How did I get to bed, and how did my dress get hung up?"

Pax did not want to talk down to her, so he sat beside her. "You kind of went to sleep coming home, and you kind of dove for this sofa when I got you in here. I like your green dress and didn't want it sleeping on the floor.

The picture of your folks told me which bedroom you use, so we—you helped a little—hung up your dress and put you to bed. I left a light on in the bathroom and wrote you a note. On top of other drinks, champagne destroys samurai warriors—don't worry about it."

She kept her hands in her lap and stared at the opposite wall. "Okay. Thank you. I may never drink another glass of champagne. This whole day felt inside out. My brain and tongue stayed fuzzy, no matter what I tried. It's a wonder I didn't throw up on a passenger." She stood and faced him. "Do you *want* me to go with you tonight? I'd understand if you say no."

Pax stood, pulled her to him, and kissed her forehead. "Of course I do."

The view from Mount Soledad's southern slope, across Pacific Beach and Mission Bay, improved beyond belief as the road curved upward toward the crest. The sole response available was to shake their heads. In the darkening evening, myriad lights to the south sparkled alive, seeming to gain strength from the western horizon's disappearing purple hue.

A petite brunette opened the rough-hewn door and said, "Hi, I'm Ann Dodd. Don't tell me; you're Pax Langford and Sally Banks, right?"

Pax nodded. "You're good; that takes practice. Thanks for inviting us."

"Wasn't hard," the small woman said. "I knew everyone else. Besides, Wilma Grayson's been filling me in on you two. Coleman thinks he flew with your dad, Sally, in Korea . . . but he'll ask you about it."

"Ann, how did you find this house?" Sally asked.

Ann Dodd's smile could have been a child's at Christmas. "Isn't the view fantastic?" she said. "We get no credit. Coleman's grandfather built it *himself* twenty years ago. He died year before last and left it to Coleman."

Coleman Dodd came up behind his wife. "Hi, Pax. Hi, Sally. Glad you could make it; follow me. House rules: I make your first drinks, after that it's self-help."

The long southern edge of a 45- by 15-foot deck perched atop railroad crosstie beams and eight, deeply-buried, telephone-pole piers. However, its sturdy guardrail bestowed confidence, a meaningful barrier to the 40-foot drop from the deck's edge. But beyond that three and a-half foot guardrail spread one of La Jolla's prime nighttime views. Floor-to-ceiling glass fed the panorama indoors. In response to their gasps, CDR Dodd said, "The glass and deck cost more than the house and lot, but we thought it needed doing."

Wilma Grayson ran into Pax's arms, gave him a big kiss, and a blink later put an arm around Sally. "I've already met your brother, and if you couldn't tell, Pax stole my heart years ago."

Before Sally could respond, Ann Dodd introduced them both to Betty and Commander Clancy Connor, the Executive Officer. Pax admired Sally's ease in the rush.

Her being a navy junior must make this social stuff second nature. I don't know which pleases me more: getting back into a squadron, or watching Sally—having the bachelors, and even the husbands, eyeballing her with such open admiration. But why not? God, she's beautiful . . . and she's sticking to me like lint.

At last, Pax maneuvered Sally near the deck's guardrail, eased his arm around her shoulders, and whispered, "Does it burn your skin or anything when this many guys are eyeballing you so hard?"

"Who me?" she asked and smiled. "I didn't think you noticed."

"I noticed, but I don't blame them. Had you come with somebody else tonight, I'd be sneaking looks at you."

She turned and stared toward the shimmering lights. "Can you imagine waking up looking at this every morning?"

"Oh, I could get used to you."

She laughed. "Not me, dummy." Sally swept an arm toward the southern horizon. "Out there."

"Out there, too."

Hacksaw and Wilma Grayson joined them on the deck. "Buddy," Hacksaw said, "the junior officers don't know *you* yet, but they agree you'll be an asset if you keep bringing Sally to the parties."

Wilma waggled her finger at Sally. "He's telling the truth."

"CAG Dengler's inside," Hacksaw said. "Have you met him?"

Pax shook his head.

Hacksaw moved closer and lowered his voice. "He's an attack puke from Leemore, and he can't even spell Crusader. He will drop bombs with it, but he won't fight it—no way. He's on the fast track, though . . . been promoted early at least twice. Here they come."

Coleman and Ann Dodd brought the Air Wing Commander and his wife onto the deck and repeated its construction details. As they neared, CDR Dodd said, "CAG, you've met Hacksaw and Wilma Grayson," They nodded and exchanged pleasantries. "but I don't believe you've met Sally Banks or Pax Langford, who's joining the squadron."

The six-foot, slender officer bowed toward Sally. "Sally, I'm Andy

114

Dengler." He shook Pax's hand. "Pax, welcome aboard. I'd like you both to meet my wife, Robin."

Mrs. Dengler's face emerged from shadows as she and Sally shook hands, and Pax stopped breathing. A sudden and deep chill froze his marrow.

Chapter 13—AIR WING THIRTEEN (CVW-13)

Pax and Sally left the party right behind the Graysons, who'd pleaded early baby-sitter problems. Pax's internal cold front followed them down the hill.

"Had you met CAG's wife before?" Sally asked.

"What was her name? I didn't hear her name."

"Not hearing her name didn't make you squeeze my hand that hard; I wanted to jerk away. Robin! Her name's Robin."

"I'm sorry. Hacksaw told me CAG didn't like fighters, and he came on like Prince Valiant to you. I might have clinched my fists to keep from sneering; I didn't mean to hurt your hand."

"Why don't you buy a house with a view like the Dodds have and rent it to me and Becky while you're gone?"

"Why don't you and Becky buy a view-house and rent *me* a room while I'm here?"

At Sally's house, Bud and Becky sat captured by a TV movie, so Pax and Sally took a walk. And after some price and payment speculation, they agreed a large enough view-house to accommodate four uncommitted adults would be too expensive—out of reach.

"Ditto for two committed couples," Sally said. "What we need are some rich grandfathers . . . in failing health."

"How's your car running?" Pax asked.

"Why?"

He grimaced. "I need a home for White Knight, or else I have to store it. Does Becky have a car?"

"I'll keep your car," she leaned around to look up into his face, "if I can drive it."

"You've got a month to think about it, and I have to check on a few things. Having you along tonight helped me a lot. I hate being a solo new guy in a large group. Thanks for going."

They kissed at her front door, while Pax damned TV movies and people who watched them. His mind raced as he drove back to the base, and a mile inside the back gate frustration boiled over. He shook his head and expelled a long breath.

What in the screaming hell were the odds? Christ!

Commander Air Wing Thirteen, Commander Andrew E. Dengler, replaced the pointer in its chalkboard tray, stepped away from the wall-mounted maps, and studied his pilots' faces. He chopped one rigid hand into his other palm. "Timing . . . timing . . . timing. Target coordination, proper roll-in headings, and jinking off targets save lives. I'll not settle for less. *Any* questions?" No one rose to the dare. "Good. Time on target will be met, gentlemen."

Pax stood with the other pilots as "CAG" Dengler strode from the briefing room. CDR Dodd leaned toward Pax and whispered, "Believe me now?"

Pax shook his bowed head. "No way. I heard it, but I don't believe it. Did CAG attend Air Wing-21's post-deployment brief? If he did, he *knows* VF-211 shot down three MiGs, and none of Air Wing-21's aircraft losses were to MiGs."

CDR Dodd arched his eyebrows and nodded with a half-smirk. It matched his half-hooded eyes. He moved behind Pax to a window and scanned the clouds. "CAG says Air Wing-13 bombs targets. Period. He wants fighters glued to the strike group's rear, so MiGs have to fly through us to get the bombers."

"Great," Pax said and fished a half-roll of Rolaids from a flight suit pocket.

The twenty plane, simulated strike against the southernmost tip of San Clemente Island progressed as briefed. Pax flew a little over a mile outboard of CDR Dodd, so he could scan through his leader toward the bombers. He compared the strike (his third flight in VF-39) to his first basic tactics flight—more than eight years before.

If this portends normal deployment operations . . . well, surely it doesn't. I'd almost as soon bomb. Almost.

CAG Dengler started his strike critique with a question. "Fighter sections have any comments?" They didn't; he dismissed them. Pax watched his skipper's neck redden as they left the debriefing and retraced a two-hangar walk back to their squadron spaces. CDR Dodd's strides gobbled the distance.

"Ever do any heel-and-toe racing?" Pax asked, trying to keep up without jogging.

Dodd didn't respond nor slacken the pace; he bounded up their hangar steps and never looked back. "No debrief, Pax," he said, turned through an outer office, stalked into his own, and slammed the door.

The skipper's yeoman, Petty Officer First Class Ceicelski, glanced up wide-eyed from his typewriter and shrugged at Pax, who returned the gesture. The squawk box at Ceicelski's elbow came alive: "Ski, I need to see Commander Connor, and get Lieutenant Commander Grayson at VF-124 on the horn."

Ceicelski stabbed the box, "Aye, aye, Captain."

Pax hadn't walked past two doors before the XO emerged from the ready room, a man on a mission.

"Afternoon, Commander," Pax said.

The furrow-browed XO barely nodded at him. When Pax glanced into the ready room, LCDRs Tom Weaver and Ollie Anderson, seated on a front row, leather sofa beckoned him in. "How'd the strike go?" Weaver, the blond, hatchet-faced maintenance officer asked.

"No official word," Pax said. "We were booted out of the strike debrief; the skipper said none for us, either."

The two LCDRs eyed each other and shook their heads. "The skipper's gonna kill CAG," Weaver said, "or get relieved from command . . . maybe both."

Anderson, the peachy-cheeked, brown-haired Admin Officer, shut his eyes and nodded. "CAG's run us out of two other debriefs this week. He doesn't give a rat's ass about fighters, or a rat's ass who knows it. Hell, he acts like he *wants* everyone to know."

"Why?" Pax asked.

"Good question," Weaver said and raked his fingers through thinning, straight, fair hair, "but we don't have the answer."

A gangly, freckled, redheaded ensign handed Pax a coffee mug. "Lieutenant, I'm Fred Newman, mess treasurer. One's hanging by the pot; this is a spare. I get your call sign right?"

Pax hefted the mug and inspected both its sides. On the back was an overhead, black silhouette of an F-8; the "Lancers" decal (a black, silhouetted, mounted knight) graced its front, underneath his "AHAB" call sign.

"Looks good, Fred. What do I owe you?"

"Five-fifty each; I'll add it to your mess bill," Newman said and rushed back to the duty desk's ringing telephone.

"Ahab?" Anderson questioned and stood to stretch.

Pax nodded. "Yeah. Melville's guy."

Anderson pursed his lips, pushed out his chin. "Good sound, but as I recall, Ahab's obsession destroyed himself . . . and everyone around him—save one."

"You superstitious?" Pax asked. "I wanted two short syllables; these came early in the dictionary, so I stopped looking. I expect I'm more lazy than obsessed."

"Ahab . . . Ahab . . . *Ahab*," Tom Weaver repeated. "Shit hot. I like it and don't think I've heard it used before."

The XO stuck his head in the doorway: "Fred, put the skipper in my slot on this afternoon's strike; I'll be over at VF-124."

"Yessir, Commander," Fred's long arms flailed at the front-wall chalkboard as he made the flight schedule change.

Tom Weaver stared at the new version, pulled at his narrow chin, and said, "Humph. Methinks something rotten in Denmark lurks."

"Ah, yes, without a doubt," said Ollie. "The old man going back-to-back into the breach, skullduggery's afoot . . . for sure."

Pax looked from Tom to Ollie and back to Tom. "Does the whole squadron talk like y'all, or have you two regressed a few centuries?"

Tom Weaver scanned the entire ready room with his pale-blue eyes, faced away from the duty desk, and put a slender finger to his lips. "Coleman Dodd wouldn't fly two hops in one day with Andy Dengler to save his own life. We don't know the particulars, but their rift smells wide, deep, and longstanding. So something's up; believe me."

Pax decided against calling Hacksaw to find out what was going on, but he planned on listening to the skipper's fighter brief for the afternoon strike. However, CDR Dodd briefed in his office, and the other three pilots wouldn't talk afterward.

I guess Tom Weaver had it pegged right: something does smell rotten . . . or damned interesting.

Being the new guy in the squadron, Pax said nothing. But after CDR Dodd's four-plane division taxied from the line, most of the remaining pilots drifted into the ready room. The XO, CDR Clancy Connor, sat on a corner of the duty officer's desk, swinging one cordovan-shoed foot back and forth. He stared at the wall-mounted Ultra High Frequency tactical radio, and—as if subject to his interest—a sudden flurry of speaker static turned into familiar control tower litany: "Roger, Saddle Bag Two Zero Six, your flight of twelve cleared for takeoff in order."

When CDR Connor swiveled his head away from the radio, his smiling gaze stared through Pax without a hint of recognition. And as the roaring airplanes lifted from nearby runway Two-Four, the XO nodded a few times and directed Newman to switch the radio frequency to air wing tactical.

Tom Weaver, wearing a khaki windbreaker with a "Head Wrench" patch—a gift, he said, from the maintenance gang—moved closer to the speaker. Ollie Anderson entered the ready room, cradling a few manila folders in the crook of an arm, glanced at the flight schedule on the chalkboard, and eased toward the group. He raised his chin toward the XO. "What's going on?"

CDR Connor deadpanned for a moment, before smiling. "We're listening to the strike."

Ollie glanced again at the flight schedule, rubbed a knuckle over an eyebrow, and frowned at the XO. "I thought *you* were leading the fighters on this strike."

The ready room radio again crackled to life. "Saddle Bag flight, check-in."

Pax recognized the CAG call sign, even though he couldn't yet recognize Dengler's pinched, oxygen-masked voice.

The flight check-in proceeded: "Two . . . Three . . . Four . . . Five . . . Six . . . Seven . . . Eight . . . Fighters up."

"The *four* fighters are up?"

Even from twenty-five miles, the sarcasm stunned Pax. Connor grimaced; Tom Weaver and Ollie Anderson exchanged big-eyed glances.

"The four fighters *are* up." CDR Dodd's lilting response elicited nervous chuckles around the desk, except from the XO.

CDR Connor checked his watch, stood, and reached across the duty desk, placing his hand on ENS Newman's shoulder. "I'm going to the head. Don't change this frequency; I'll be right back."

"Aye, aye, Commander."

From Newman's questioning demeanor, Pax figured the ensign knew nothing about what was happening on the strike.

And that makes two of us.

Weaver motioned for Pax to follow him. After a few steps, he stopped—his back again to the duty desk—and asked, "Did you follow that radio check-in?"

Pax nodded.

"CAG insists on training command procedures, no matter how cumbersome. The skipper doesn't buy it, and the check-in flap's one small example."

Pax bit his bottom lip and tilted his head. "Does CAG know how we check-in? *I'd* never heard a 2-, 1-, 2-, 1-click check-in before getting here."

"I doubt it. Hell, CAG dials in his radio frequencies; presets didn't work once—so he says. He's a real piece of work. We're already switched, clicked aboard, and thinking about MiGs before he ever bumbles onto a new freq."

The XO hurried through the door, shrugging his shoulders. "Anything yet?"

Newman shook his red head, and, belatedly, said, "No, sir."

A different sound came from the radio, with more static, Pax thought. "*Rat-tat-tat-tat,*" came a loud transmission. It was repeated. "*Rat-tat-tat!*"

Three seconds later, CDR Dodd's voice boomed from the speaker. "Saddle Bags, Saddle Bags, bogies at six o'clock high and low. Break! Break! Break!"

Again, the different sound: "*Rat-tat-tat!*"

The XO said, "Okay, the fat's in the fire; switch back to squadron tactical. Carry on, people."

Pax managed to be talking to the crew-cut, gray-haired Maintenance Chief, CPO Kelly, when CDR Dodd walked in from the flight line to fill out a postflight gripe-sheet. With as innocent a smile as he could summon, Pax asked, "How'd the flight go, Skipper?"

CDR Dodd continued writing, finished listing the needed aircraft work, then, expressionless, glanced at Pax. "Not too bad . . . not too bad." And turning back toward the rest of his division—two of whom continued with gripe write-ups. "You can call it a day; I'll catch CAG's debrief and see you tomorrow."

CDR Dodd and the other three pilots abandoned the maintenance counter without another look or comment in Pax's direction. So much for detective work. Chief Kelly's friendly query snapped through, "Anything else for me, Lieutenant?"

"No, Chief, but thanks a lot. I'll see you tomorrow."

Pax sat working at a beat up desk, removed from the normal hubbub of night-shift wrench-work, and thumbed through the maintenance chief petty officers' personnel folders. Getting up to speed and acquainted meant absorbing their track records. He'd learned that dropping bits of information about people's backgrounds, in conversations with them, speeded the acceptance process—they knew he cared enough to check. Trust and respect, coin of the *navy realm*, had to be earned ASAP, because meeting navy flight schedules with maintenance people, always placed time at a premium.

CDR Coleman Dodd trailed scarlet-necked CAG Andrew E. Dengler— as had been requested—into CAG's office. Dengler flipped on the light, held the door open, and slammed it behind Dodd. "Where the hell were the rest of your pilots, Skipper?"

"In the bar, I hope." Dodd remained standing at parade rest.

Dengler's eyes flashed and his voice boomed. "Commander, are you tired of being a CO?"

"Andy, . . . are we going to yell at each other, like plebe year, or get something done?"

CAG took a deep breath and straightened while his jaw muscles flexed. His eyes closed to slits, and he exhaled. "Have a seat, Coleman, please." CAG dropped into a second leather-covered chair in front of the desk. "Okay, Coleman, shoot."

"CAG, you flipped my guys off twice already this week, dismissing them from the debriefs . . . like they weren't worth your time. Truth be known, the way you're using us, we *aren't* worth beans to anyone in the strike group . . . including ourselves."

CAG feigned a stiff-arm. "Spare me another fighter-sweep brief, Coleman. But now, with your fighter pilot's eyes, did you recognize those four F-8s, or not? They interfered with a scheduled strike in an official exercise area, and I plan on having their ass."

Dodd stretched both arms over his head and twisted from side to side. "They were RAG F8s, VF-124, but they hit us before we got to the strike area."

"I don't agree," CAG said and reached to the squawk box. "Chief Scott, find out if Commander Rankin, at VF-124, will be in his office in about . . . oh, say twenty minutes."

"Aye, aye, Captain," crackled the tinny response.

Coleman Dodd studied his flight boots, and doubled both fists. "Andy, I'm telling you this as a four-year roommate. You go huffing and puffing into Ted Rankin's office, he'll knock you on your butt before he even says hello. I mean it. When you told his instructors you didn't have time for tactics flights in the Crusader, you pissed in his punch bowl . . . big time."

"So what," said CAG. "I decide what I need. He's a support activity—*service to the fleet*—or haven't you heard?"

"Okay, Andy. But remember, I've known you forever . . . and how much *you* wanted fighters. Don't stay pissed off forever. You need us; you're not using us, and more's the pity for it."

The squawk box interrupted: "CAG, Skipper Rankin says he has to leave in twenty-minutes, but to come on over."

Dengler opened the door. "Thanks, Chief." He nearly closed the door again. "I know you mean well, Coleman. Start bringing your guys back to the debriefings; they'll be welcomed. I need to beat feet." He opened the door wide, moved back a step, and motioned the fighter squadron commander through.

Dodd paused at the door. "CAG, I'd like to come along. Rankin won't doubt my identification of his planes; it might help."

Dengler smiled and punched Dodd's shoulder. "Okay, let's go."

Pax couldn't believe an hour and a half had passed. Same old song, though. Personnel records always drew him deep into other people's worlds. He checked the ready room before securing; ENS Newman remained, manning the duty desk. Pax moved his status board peg from "ABOARD" to "ASHORE," flipping a casual salute toward the lanky redhead.

I'll swing by the club, see Hacksaw, and get the skinny on the strike.

But the bartender thumbed at an empty barstool, as if everybody knew the corner one belonged to Hacksaw. "He ain't been in yet; I was *about* to check the local hospitals."

"Maybe he's flying," Pax said. "Thanks anyway."

None of the other three pilots from Skipper Dodd's flight was in the bar either. Pax checked his watch, 1830, and called VF-124's duty officer. "This is Pax Langford from VF-39. Is Hacksaw Grayson still around?"

"Yessir, but he's in with the CO, CAG Dengler, and your skipper. They've been at it a good while and called for coffee a few minutes ago; there's no telling when Commander Grayson will get free. Is there a number he can call?"

"No. I'll see him tomorrow; thanks."

And that's for damned sure.

Chapter 14—DOWNHILL RUN, NO BRAKES

The Mississippian entered the dining room with a grin like a railroad engine's light on a dark night. Pax expected him to explode into laughter before he got to the table.

"Wanna know what happened, don't you?" Hacksaw said.

"Since you mention it, what did happen—both airborne and *afterwards* . . . in your skipper's office?"

Hacksaw checked over both shoulders, and whispered, "Between us, Pax, okay? Word gets out, my ass is toast."

Pax nodded and pursed his lips. "Don't tell me if you'd worry about it."

Hacksaw grimaced and squeezed his eyes shut. "Bullshit! I gotta tell somebody; it's too good to sit on."

The redheaded waitress, ignoring Hacksaw, spoke to Pax. "Would you gentlemen like anything from the bar with your lunch?"

"No, darlin'," Hacksaw said, "but if you're at happy hour tomorrow I'll give you some business."

She smiled at Pax and walked away, avoiding eye contact with her nemesis: the ass-patter.

"Stays pissed a long time, don't she? Anyway, pardner, your skipper asked me if I could jump CAG Dengler's strike group with four of our RAG F-8s. I told him I'd have to ask Commander Rankin, so he sent Commander Connor over to explain the situation and to give us Dengler's probable strike plan. The idea tickled my boss to death; he wanted to lead our fighters himself, but thought better of it."

"How'd you hit 'em?" Pax asked.

"Fast as a bastard, one section high, the other low, came straight over and under both escort sections. We smoked in at one-point-two, had three hundred knots overtake. A-4s broke in every direction. Your skipper said CAG Dengler

went shit-house on the radio, and also tore him a new ass at the debrief."
Hacksaw checked over his shoulders again and leaned low over the table. "If
my skipper hadn't been there, Dengler would've had my ass. You should've
heard Rankin: 'Goddammit, CAG, there aren't any safe areas out of Miramar.
This is a fighter base; fighters jump your ass. It's what we *do*; it's what *MiGs*
will do. You want sanctuary, take your fucking wing back to Leemore.'"
Hacksaw pushed his chair back and sucked his teeth. "Pardner, I thought
they'd fight; I heard *this* shit clear from Rankin's outer office—with the door
shut."

Pax sat slack-jawed, eyes wide open. He mouthed the words: "No shit?"

Hacksaw nodded and leaned forward again. "I kid you not. CAG said
we'd jumped him in the restricted area. Rankin said he doubted it, but they'd
damned well soon know. Anyway, he called for me and we went through the
whole thing: how I thought the wing must have been out for photos, the way
they were bunched up; how I'd double-checked with a wingman to see if our
TACANs matched—ensuring we weren't in the restricted area; how the
fighters were damned near locked in a cruise position on the bombers; and
how I'd called my shots on guard channel . . . so they'd know we saw them."

A waitress handed them menus, but Hacksaw—after checking his watch—
said, "No time to eat, pardner; but I wanted to keep you in the loop. Don't
breathe a word of this. You bringin' Sally to the Connors' party Saturday?"

Pax snapped his fingers. "Maybe. She's been at Olathe. Thanks for
reminding me."

Entering the squadron ready room, Pax found his worst nightmare: lined
up pilots walking by two shot-giving corpsmen. He spun to leave, but CDR
Connor spotted him. "Whoa, Ahab! Get up here by me, so I can watch these
gentlemen harpoon you."

The corpsmen offered two flavors—yellow fever or tetanus. Pax needed
but the yellow fever *treat.*

The XO faked a cruel streak: "I'd be ashamed, Ahab. Settling for a single
shot."

What a deal! Like being bitten by a one-fanged rattler.

Pax looked down at the hangared F-8s from the second-story passageway
window, taking deep breaths while his sweat-soaked shirt dried. By the time
he knew he wouldn't faint, a corpsman stood at his elbow. "Lieutenant
Langford, remember me? I let you and the commander use the eye charts."

"Sure," Pax said, eyeing the corpsman's nametag, "Petty Officer Crawford. Sorry I didn't notice you; I don't like to watch the shots, but I'm okay now. Things going well for you?"

The corpsman fidgeted, looked from side-to-side while shifting his weight. "Lieutenant, I didn't mention your name, but the other day I did let slip to my chief about you and the commander having that who-could-see-best contest. He's convinced you conned me, like maybe one of you needed some help reading those charts. He said it'd be a damned shame if anyone crashed on the ship and killed a lot of folks. Anyway, I've been worrying about it ever since."

Pax straightened as tall as he could and looked into the corpsman's eyes. "Petty Officer Crawford, I'm sure that no officer would ask you to do something you knew was against the rules. So I don't think you need to worry. Besides, anyone foolish enough to try and get by those eye charts would be inclined to fly wearing glasses . . . might even keep an extra pair in his flight suit. Hell, someday glasses might be legal. Okay?"

"Yes, sir, I'm okay. But please be careful."

Pax winked at the corpsman and headed for the hangar deck.

Same old song: don't try to shit the men; it can't be done.

Ollie Anderson, carrying more folders, stopped Pax at the ready room door. "I talked to Hacksaw Grayson about his roommate on the ship. One lieutenant commander will have a lieutenant roommate, and Hacksaw said he'd take you if you have no objections."

"Sounds good." Pax tried to read the roster on top of Ollie's stack.

"You've got a new squadron roster in your mail slot, and a mess bill, and a squadron duty officer watch bill. As senior lieutenant, you're the Senior Watch Officer, responsible for the monthly watch bill—starting next month. For which, you don't stand watches. There's also a combat tactical organization chart; Commander Dodd picked you as his section leader." The admin officer started away, but spun back. "Are you bringing your pretty girlfriend to the Connors' party?"

"I hope so; thanks for reminding me."

Pax's mail slot held everything Ollie had promised. He removed the squadron roster and the tactical organization chart. He scanned the pilot roster, which—starting with CDR Coleman Dodd—listed each officer's call sign, billet, school, and home town. The tactical organization chart assigned each pilot—by his call sign—to a four-plane division, each of which included two, two-plane sections. The chart confirmed Ollie Anderson's comments:

CDR Dodd had the first division with Fred Newman on his wing; Pax led the second section with Allen Bates on his wing.

Who's Bates?

He ran a finger down the first roster. Bates was the safety officer and next senior lieutenant below himself.

I don't think I've met him.

He looked at the officers' status board. Bates was pegged "ashore." Beside the peg, under "remarks," a grease penciled message: leave . . . 8/11.

Pax headed for the operations office where he located the pilot logbooks. Bates' logbook revealed two thousand total flight hours, with eleven hundred in F-8s, two or three deployments, and plenty of arrested landings. Pax's smile broadened as he nodded.

Replacing his wingman's logbook, Pax noticed the three-book-fat logbook with "CO" on the cover. Reaching for it caused an involuntary look over his shoulder toward the passageway door. He wasn't surprised at the numbers: more than 4500 flight hours and 895 arrested landings. Pax nodded in satisfaction at what should be a dynamite division. Fred Newman ought to learn a lot. Pax flipped through the earlier pages of his CO's logbook, looking for evidence that Skipper Dodd and Turner Banks might have flown together in Korea.

He felt the hand on his shoulder and heard CDR Dodd's whispered query at the same time. "You trying to find out how old I am, Ahab?"

Pax didn't jump, but he knew his face was flushing. "No, Skipper, I was checking to see when you and Captain Banks flew together in Korea."

"We were in *Oriskany*. I flew Banshees; Turner flew Panthers, so we never actually *flew* together. But we played a hell of a lot of poker together. Did you know he shot down *at least* one MiG?"

Pax replaced the logbook. "Bud might have mentioned it, and he flies like it's in his blood."

"Bud told me *you* were the natural; that's why I picked you for my section leader." CDR Dodd's mouth didn't grin, but his eyes reflected a degree of merriment. "Two naturals in the same section ought to keep you both on your toes."

Pax felt a tinge of empathy for a raw steak . . . hanging before a drooling wolf.

Did Dodd mean section, or did he mean division? Would the wolf be Dodd or Bates?

"Skipper, I look forward to flying in your division, but now I gotta go brief a night hop."

"Have a good one. I'm so far behind my wife's prior-to-sortie honey-do list that we might as well deploy tomorrow. Along about now, calendar pages get steep and icy, no way to slow down. You bringing Turner's daughter on Saturday?"

Pax tried not to chuckle. "I better call and find out; she's been in Olathe . . . supposed to get back today."

CDR Dodd shot Pax a quick thumbs up and left him in the operations office. Who in the hell else could possibly ask him about Sally? He reached for the phone.

Becky Johnston answered. "She's in the shower, Pax; Bud and I met her plane."

No, he didn't want Becky to get her out of the shower. He left a message about the Saturday party, told Becky he had to fly, and that he would call Sally the next day.

By the time Pax landed and debriefed the night intercept flight, his bed beckoned. But by a dim bedlamp he studied the new squadron rosters, trying to match names to faces, names to call signs, and call signs to faces. Yet questions bedeviled him, even knowing they couldn't be answered on the ground.

Soon—very soon—I'll rank my own worth-a-shit-in-the-air list. Like squadron pilots do . . . and always have done.

FIGHTER SQUADRON THIRTY-NINE (VF-39) "LANCERS" PILOT ROSTER

Officer	Call Sign	Billet	School	Home Town
CDR Coleman Dodd	"Lancer"	Commanding Officer	USNA	Oklahoma City
CDR Clancy F. Connor	"Clover"	Executive Officer	Notre Dame	Dallas
LCDR Cecil F. Grayson	"Hacksaw"	Operations Officer	NavCad	Jackson, MS
LCDR Thomas D. Weaver	"Needle"	Maintenance Officer	Purdue	Indianapolis
LCDR Ollie H. Anderson	"Viking"	Administration Officer	Minnesota	Duluth
LT Paxton (N) Langford	"Ahab"	Asst. Maint. / S.W.O.	Texas A&M	Fort Worth
LT Allen H. Bates	"Motel"	Safety Officer	NavCad	Jacksonville, FL
LT Guy T. Lawrence	"Gypsy"	Landing Signal Officer	Virginia	Norfolk, VA
LT Chris J. Nixon	"St Nick"	Avionics/Supply	Notre Dame	Columbus, OH
LT Buck N. Walker	"Buckshot"	Airframes/Paraloft	Texas Tech	Albuquerque
LTJG Mack O. Burgess	"Truck"	Communications	USNA	El Paso
LTJG Abe H. Lincoln	"Raham"	Legal/Classified Mat.	Kentucky	Paducah
LTJG Trevor D. Blaine	"Irish"	Armament/LSO in Trng.	USNA	Boston
ENS Tony L. Valentine	"Vino"	Personnel Officer	USNA	Philadelphia
ENS Fred A. Newman	"Windmill"	Line Officer/Mess Tr.	San Diego St.	San Diego

FIGHTER SQUADRON THIRTY-NINE (VF-39) "LANCERS," TACTICAL ORGANIZATION

LANCER Division	CLOVER Division
(2) WINDMILL Newman	(2) VINO Valentine
(1) CDR Dodd	(1) CDR Connor
(3) AHAB Langford	(3) VIKING Anderson
(4) MOTEL Bates	(4) GYPSY Lawrence
HACKSAW Division	GATOR Division
(2) IRISH Blaine	(2) TRUCK Burgess
(1) HACKSAW Grayson	(1) GATOR Broussard (CVW-13 LSO)
(3) NEEDLE Weaver	(3) BUCKSHOT Walker
(4) ST NICK Nixon	(4) RAHAM Lincoln

Sally answered Pax's after-breakfast call. "We're leaving now for a flight," she said, "but Saturday night sounds good."

"Super, I've missed you; how about dinner tonight?"

"Me, too. Around seven? Uh-uh . . . make it seven-thirty. Got to run. Bye."

I'll give her one thing: she doesn't gab much on the phone. And every time I think about her—more than a little bit, of late—I find myself smiling.

CDR Connor finished frowning over the ready room message board, initialed its cover sheet, and extended it toward Pax. Pax thought better of telling him he'd already read the thing, so he took it and said, "Commander, I see that Gator Broussard, the CAG LSO, leads our fourth division. Is that normal, for staff officers to lead squadron divisions?"

Connor ran both hands through his sandy-blond, curly hair. "No, and I asked the skipper the same question. He asked me how many airplanes we had. I told him twelve. He smiled at me and said if we ever got sixteen we'd change the chart. Politics, I'd say. Gator's on CAG's staff; he flies with us and one of the A-4 squadrons. CAG may fly with VF-37 . . . occasionally . . . in the daytime, but he never flies with us. Never. Maybe it'll make Gator feel more at home, and we *had* to put our three other pilots somewhere. Putting them in a Gator-led division looked neater than showing them as fill-ins."

CDR Dodd hurried into the ready room, rubbing his hands together, eyes agleam. "Get your flight gear on, Ahab; we're going flying. The Stallions' air force fell on its sword; they need two more planes. Skipper Milano wondered if we could pick up the slack. Chop! Chop! Brief's in fifteen minutes."

As fast as he moved, Pax was trailing the maintenance officer, Tom Weaver, out the door, and the duty officer's rapid squawk box directives to maintenance faded before Pax reached the locker room. A whirlwind change between slamming locker door bangs and Pax, trailing untied bootlaces, jogged back toward the ready room. The frowning skipper stood shaking his head. "What took so long?" CDR Dodd's relentless stride ate the two-hangar-stretch fast enough to make Pax consider some additional roadwork.

Several pilots, including Camp Brogan and Bud Banks, arrived for the briefing after Dodd and Pax had slipped into front row seats. Everyone snapped to attention when CAG Dengler entered.

CAG strode to the lectern. "Be seated, gentlemen."

The simulated strike brief sounded familiar to Pax—boring at best—until toward the end when CAG first noticed Dodd. "I thought VF-37 had the fighters on today's strike, Skipper."

"Commander Milano and I decided to mix some sections today, CAG, to get both squadrons' pilots used to flying together."

CAG Dengler's slow smile reminded Pax of anything but mirth. "Good," CAG said, "get us to the target unmolested. We'll see how *your* escort tactics work out."

The six fighter pilots remained after the normal brief, four "Stallions," Pax, and Skipper Dodd. Camp raised his chin at Dodd. "Commander, how would you like us to cover the strike?"

"You stick with the bombers; keep your 'Sea Bat' call sign. Pax and I'll be higher, as 'Lobo' flight," Dodd said. "A six-bomber strike, simulating an extra-heavy bomb load—i.e., flying much slower—stinks to high heaven. CAG may have a surprise in store; be ready to get jumped by bogies."

"Concur," Camp said. "CDR Milano told me we're no longer welded into an assigned escort spot. Is that your understanding?"

Dodd nodded. "Correct, fighter sections can maneuver. Responsibilities haven't changed, but weaving behind the group lets you keep your energy higher and improves lookout. You concentrate on level-to-low threats; we'll take any high guys."

"You'll take-off first?" Camp asked.

"Right. We'll follow CAG's bombers."

Deception played little part in CAG's surprise. Dodd pointed at three A-4s with no bomb racks or external fuel tanks, taking off as CAG's bombers started taxiing. Pax raised a thumb. Dodd taxied them toward the runway behind the small bombers. Camp's four planes swung in behind; he also pointed upward and raised three fingers. Dodd and Pax both nodded.

Crossing the coast, Dodd selected afterburner, started a .9 mach climb, and with a pushing outward signal, moved Pax into a combat-spread position. They came out of afterburner and leveled at 24,000-feet. Knowledge of the slick A-4s, Pax knew, wouldn't make them any easier to spot. He raised his helmet's dark visor, exposing even darker sunglasses, which gave him the sunlight protection he needed . . . and a lot more help.

Dodd "S"-turned high behind the strike formation; the bombers leveled at their briefed altitude of 16,000-feet. Pax kept Dodd between himself and the strike bombers, so he could clear his leader's tail without losing sight of the bomb carrying A-4s. He rotated his lookout scan, first ahead and outboard, next behind Dodd, and last he'd stare momentarily at the bombers—keeping a distant focus—which captured occasional glimpses of Camp's four weaving fighters. But if the slick A-4s were close, they remained invisible.

Pax knew each mile nearer the target increased the likelihood of being attacked. His head swiveled faster, his eyes strained to see even farther and focus better.

During his lookout pattern and infrequent, rapid glimpses into the cockpit—maybe sufficient to notice a red warning light—Pax felt the bombers remained almost motionless, making slug-like progress. The better, he realized, for enhancing any attacker's overtake capability.

Dodd's voice exploded in Pax's helmet. "Saddle Bags, one bogie, five o'clock high, no problem. Sea Bats, heads up from your side."

Pax saw Dodd's afterburner ignition puff, rammed his own throttle outboard, and rolled into what he hoped would be a good supporting position on his leader. "Six is clear, Lobo," Pax reported and nearly added "no joy on the bogie," but a single A-4 flashed along Dodd's projected pursuit curve. "Tallyho the bogie!" Pax added.

"Fox away," Dodd reported his simulated Sidewinder missile firing. "Closing for guns."

Pax followed his leader close aboard, but on the opposite side of, the single A-4, deselected afterburner as Dodd did, noted their 1.1 mach, and listened while Camp's flight spotted and defeated the other two attacking A-4s . . . before they threatened the bombers, from the sound of it.

Dodd and Pax, inverted at the top of a large barrel roll, high over the bombers, listened as a high-pitched voice intruded on the moment. "Saddle Bag Lead, Gator, over."

CAG acknowledged the transmission.

"CAG, this is Gator. I'm headed back to base; I may have some fuselage panels missing. Request another Gator detach and join on me."

"Roger, Gator Lead. Gator flight return to base."

"Thanks, CAG. Gators switch to squadron tactical."

The debriefing ready room lacked the slightest flicker of camaraderie. For thirty minutes, CAG pointed out minuscule errors in trivial procedures throughout the simulated strike, but with no mention of the fighter intercepts. "On top of everything else," he continued, "one of our planes came back with some of its panels missing. This was not a good flight."

Despite CAG's obvious exasperation, CDR Dodd's face had remained impassive throughout the harangue. And this fact hadn't been lost on the CAG, who pointed at Dodd.

"From your experience, Commander, must we expect fuselage panels to get knocked off our airplanes anytime a supersonic fighter rips by us?"

Dodd stood and stretched both arms overhead, scrunched his head down into his shoulders, and blew out a huge breath. "I don't know, CAG. Supersonic F-8s fly close aboard each other going in opposite directions every single day with no more than a slight bump. *If* Gator's panels were indeed secured before takeoff, maybe speed bumps and A-4s could become a problem. It deserves watching."

"We've wasted enough time on this," CAG said and looked back to the other pilots. "Any other questions or comments?"

A few pilots shook their heads; most prepared to stand.

"Very well," CAG said and started for the door, but paused. "Commander Dodd, could you give me a few minutes, please?"

"Yes, sir," Dodd answered and turned to Pax. "Go ahead to the club."

When Pax got there, Camp Brogan, Bud Banks, two other "Stallions," and three A-4 drivers stood at the bar in short-sleeved khakis, flying beer mugs and laughing. Camp waved him in. "Hey, Ahab, how 'bout a beer?"

Pax nodded, looked at the big, dark-complected A-4 pilot standing next to Camp, read his "Gator Broussard" nametag, and smiled. "Sorry about those panels, Gator."

The CAG landing signal officer squinted down at Pax's nametag. "Ahab . . . that's what I thought Camp said. How fast were you going?"

"Beats me," Pax said. "I kept busy enough trying to miss you. The back of a slick A-4's kinda hard to track, and I didn't know for sure you were a single."

Camp held a fresh beer out to Pax and winked. "I read a Patuxent River report that said if you drag a one point four shock wave past an A-4 it'll set off its ejection seat. That dog of a plane I flew today couldn't get past one point three. Maybe tomorrow."

A tight-lipped Broussard shook his head at Camp, and leaned toward Pax. "By the time your skipper gets here, he may not think that's funny."

Pax knew he'd regret hitting Gator. No, he'd regret the consequences of hitting him, as he regretted the fact his own ears were aflame. So he smiled at Broussard and looked at Camp. "Have you noticed how much better Gator sounds on the ground? His voice isn't pitched near as shrill." Pax guffawed and walked away shaking his head, but his neck hair felt charged with current.

Will that asshole take the bait?

And—as he'd hoped—after seven steps, a hand tapped his shoulder, but when Pax spun around in a crouch, he saw a wide-eyed Bud, backing away on tiptoe. "Whoa! It's me," Bud said.

"So it is." Pax's muscles relaxed like toppling dominoes; his breaths came slower.

"You *were* pissed," Bud said. "Good thing Camp stepped in."

"Stepped in?"

"Yeah. Broussard moved after you; Camp stepped in front of him and said, 'Uh-uh! He'll kill you.'"

"*Camp* said that?"

Bud nodded. "Those exact words. You could almost hear Gator's head gears clanking . . . and smell the smoke. In the end, though, he shook his head, snorted, and went back to the bar."

Pax let his head sag forward and blew out a huge breath. "Remind me to thank Camp. Gator's one big son-of-a-bitch; I don't know how he fits in an

A-4."

"I fly Camp's wing now, and you were right: he flies the hell out of the bird."

"Good, I'm glad; you ought to learn a lot. I have to split."

"Yeah, say hi to Sis," Bud said, grinning.

And looking at Bud, Pax saw what he was positive the Korean *police action* vintage Turner Banks must have looked like.

Chapter 15—SUNSET SUCTION

For the first time, Pax sat in the Corvette's passenger seat—striving to convey a calm confidence—while Sally maneuvered through Old Town's before-dinner traffic like she alone had driven the car's 90,000-miles. As if reading his mind, she turned to him and wriggled her eyebrows. "How am I doing, coach?"

Despite his best effort at nonchalance, he abandoned her perky smile to cover the road ahead for hidden menace—whatever its shape or malicious intent. She snickered and patted his knee. "Relax; I have a valid driver's license."

"Hey, you're a great driver, but I'm not used to sitting here . . . doing nothing."

Sally's beige linen skirt had side splits to mid-thigh, and her tanned legs earned at least half of his attention—a more than adequate compensation for not driving, Pax thought. He had even started contemplating Sally's questionable tan-line, when she veered the Corvette into a parallel, curbside parking spot—a car-length beyond a fireplug. Admiring those tanned legs had led him a long way from business at hand. Pax's stomach did a back flip; he sat reared-back, staring straight ahead, and open-mouthed.

"It's an easy car to park, isn't it?" she said.

Old Town's mostly adobe, but sometimes stucco buildings, beneath their red tiled roofs, lazed beneath stately star pines and bark-shedding eucalyptus trees—redolent with their natural-gas aroma. They strolled through two blocks' worth of widely varied cooking smells, before music—not food—determined their restaurant choice. A group of mariachis, abandoning some veranda diners—but playing at full volume—preceded Pax and Sally through saloon-like swinging doors. A mustached waiter diverted them from the trumpeting parade and hustled them up a short stairwell to a secluded, candle-lit table for two which overlooked the larger, lower dining room.

Their drinks came. Sally, flushed from her expert chauffeuring exhibition, stirred a frozen margarita while they listened to the strolling musicians. Her tan emphasized the gleaming whiteness of her teeth. Pax savored the view.

I could sit here and watch her forever. And that's a good thing, 'cause the damned mariachis make conversation nigh impossible.

About mid-entree, requests and tips must have played out, because the mariachis filed out. The relative silence in their wake reminded Pax of some unexpected, cool breeze on a Texas summer sizzler.

"How are your folks?" he asked.

"Good. Healthy and inquisitive. And I was the designated messenger. I spent most of the time answering Dad's questions about Bud. Dad would've been a good prosecutor; he won't accept 'I don't know.' Bud never writes letters. Never!"

Pax reached across the table and placed a hand on hers. "Do you think he'll write to Becky?"

She removed her hand from under his and pressed her temples. "Too much ice, too quick," she said and squeezed her eyes shut. "I haven't a clue what's between them. Do you?"

He waited until she opened her eyes, and shook his head. "Bud and I see each other, but we don't talk about girls. *Gettysburg* deploys in three weeks; everyone's hustling, trying to get his personal business taken care of before the setting sun drags him over the horizon."

"Do you have much unfinished business?"

"Uh-uh, not much. They tuned the car last week; I'll have the oil changed before I leave. My insurance covers you, and the tags won't expire. Is it too early to invite you to dinner in Coronado on the twenty-ninth?"

"No, but I may not be good company; I don't like goodbyes. Is this to the air wing thing at The Mexican Village?"

He shook his head. "Not unless *you* want to go there."

"It's your last night; it ought to be your choice. We'll do whatever you want to do . . . within reason, of course." Her smile seemed teasing, and Pax fought hard to erase the wanton visions she seemed to be scanning from his forehead.

"It's been awhile since I've seen a man blush," she said. "Should I be red-faced too?"

"I don't think so, but I've never been good at hiding my feelings. You must know by now how much I'm attracted to you."

"Hah! Maybe so; maybe no." Her green eyes accelerated the flickering candle reflections into miniature lightning flashes, as she extended a pointed finger across the table and traced a short line on the back of Pax's nearest hand. "I know you're a healthy male, and you respond to a female. But I'm only one fish in the sea."

Pax swallowed. "Are you looking for a commitment?"

She closed her eyes and shook her head.

"Because if you are—"

"I'm not," she said and took his hand into both of hers. "We may have a future together, somewhere, sometime, but I'm trusting my dad on this call. He explained ad infinitum about first-time combat deployments, concentration lapses and their consequences. He likes you, but he says your plate's full . . . even if you don't know it."

"With the respect due, Sally, your dad has no idea how big my plate is. Should my business and your business become our business, it wouldn't *be* any of your dad's business."

She nodded and squeezed his hand. "Funny you'd say that; I mentioned something along those same lines. Dad asked me if I thought this would be an appropriate time for Bud to become engaged—or any otherwise—committed, at the expense of total concentration on the job at hand. A slam dunk checkmate; put away the pieces."

Pax watched her eyes well, even as she tried to smile; he looked away and cleared his throat. Her hands, squeezing his, told him what he needed to know about their future.

Driving to the hangar next morning, Pax knew the day held something in store, but he couldn't remember what. As he moved his status-board peg to the "aboard" column, it came to him. Bates's peg, the next below his own, indicated his safety officer wingman had returned from leave.

An officer Pax didn't know stood at the duty desk, flipping through the daily messages in their metal folder. His erect bearing and tailored khaki shirt confirmed a fitness buff; the polished brass, and spit-shined cordovans matched his own. Pax glimpsed a zig-zagged scar across the pate where blond hair used to be, before a pair of sparkling, pale blue eyes fixed on him, and two rows of big, white choppers flashed a smile his direction. "Hello, section leader, I'm Motel Bates."

"Ahab Langford," Pax said as they shook hands. If first impressions meant anything, Pax would bet a bundle he and Motel could carry their load . . . and then some.

Without preamble, Motel said, "When you've got half an hour I need to walk you through our weekly aircraft inspection."

"Huh?" Pax said.

"It's part of our check-in procedure. We do some things here you won't be used to, check a few extra spots on the airframe where we've found some problems." Motel's smile did little to hide the seriousness in his voice. He handed Pax a mimeographed check-in sheet; all items had been initialed except the safety officer's weekly aircraft inspection orientation.

"I've never seen this before," Pax said.

"I'm not surprised; admin doesn't like to do my work for me. I read your file last night . . . and your log book. I don't think I'll be showing you much you haven't already seen."

Motel had been too optimistic. His half hour turned into more than two hours—climbing under, over, and into one of the sun-baked Crusaders on the VF-39 line. But the safety officer's enthusiasm and F-8 maintenance knowledge shamed Pax into docile submission. He listened, learned, and clamped his jaw tight to keep from telling Motel he wanted to fly the damned thing; he had no intention of buying it.

Exasperated, Pax said, "If you fly as well as you preflight, you ought to be leading the section."

Motel's eyes crinkled at the corners. "Nobody preflights like this, but these are things we want checked on our weekly safety inspections. Problem being, nobody can ever find two hours to spare me . . . so I fudge it a little."

"Lie like hell, you mean," Pax said and started walking toward the hangar.

"We're almost through," Motel called after him.

"You're almost through," Pax said without looking back. "I am through."

Motel laughed from beside the airplane while Pax disappeared into the hangar.

LCDRs Weaver and Anderson, standing by the Duty Officer's desk at the front of the ready room, made a big production of checking their watches when Pax walked in.

"Back already?" Weaver asked. "Motel must be under the weather."

"Yeah," Anderson agreed. "New guys never escape in less than three hours."

Pax stood shaking his head at their banter when Motel walked in, his blue eyes flashing as he pulled on an earlobe. He sidled up to Pax, but stared past him—out a near window—and deadpanned, "It won't take us long to finish."

Pax's words came softer than Motel's had, "It sure as hell won't, pal. I'm done."

The following day Motel and Pax flew together in Skipper Dodd's division, and Pax confirmed immediately what he'd hoped for after scanning his wingman's log book: Motel could flat-out maneuver a Crusader. Pax's glances during their afterburner section takeoff found Motel welded in position, and even during Dodd's hardest maneuvering—which had Pax humping—Motel's responses had to have been perfect. For every time Pax glanced at where Motel should have been, there he perched—with no wing jiggles, no little zooms or dives, but locked in position. And Motel's swiveling head, as he swept the sky looking for other aircraft, earned him even more points in Pax's evaluation. He remembered Dodd's words—*two naturals in the same section*. It looked like a good call.

At debrief, CDR Dodd spent most of his words in Windmill Newman's direction. Normal stuff for an average nugget: things Pax and Motel had heard in their first squadron. "Pax, you and Motel seemed comfortable. Any problems?"

Pax looked at Motel, who shook his head. "I guess not, Skipper," Pax said.

"Good enough," Dodd said. "Last one to the club buys the first round."

The free drink challenge spurred them to the locker room where they changed from salt-stained flight gear back into their uniforms. As Pax finished tying his shoelaces and looked up, Motel motioned at him to slow down and shook his head once. As soon as Windmill Newman rushed out, Motel said, "The skipper never hurries; he *wants* to buy the first round. He won't be there for another fifteen minutes."

Pax nodded. "Nice flight. Next time you lead the section; we'll plan on alternating our lead."

Motel glanced at him sideways and raised his eyebrows. "Every flight?"

"Chances are. . . ." Pax said and closed his locker. "Let me find out how you think before I sign any blood-pact."

At happy hour, Pax learned Allen H. Bates didn't drink, nor did his drop-dead gorgeous, ash-blonde mother-of-three wife, Pat. However, she tended to join her husband during happy hours, and on Fridays they ate dinner at the club.

"Living on the base makes it pretty handy," Pat said as she held the back of Motel's hand against her cheek. "We're both anxious to meet Sally."

"According to Pat," Motel said, "the wives approve your taste. I know the bachelors applaud it."

"We'll see you tomorrow night," Pax said and picked his way out through the growing happy hour throng.

He had matched colas with Motel and Pat, hoping that Sally might show up. For two days, no one had answered her phone; he quit calling each night at nine.

I hope she remembers the Connors' Saturday party invitation.

She had; a Saturday noon call to his BOQ room confirmed it.

"I thought maybe you'd been fired and left town," he said.

"What time you picking me up?"

"How's eight sound?"

"See you at eight," she said. "Gotta run. Bye."

"Humph," he snorted, looking at the buzzing phone before dropping it in its cradle.

But eight o'clock sharp found her ready, and Sally's smile chased any doubts away. Pax stood stunned, looked her up and down, whistled, and eyed her up and down again. "Wow," he said and took both her hands while shaking his head.

She tiptoed and kissed him. "You like?"

He nodded. "Yeah, I like it a lot . . . the whole package."

From her thin leather sandals, right up those tanned legs, past some khaki culottes, to a white, short-sleeved cashmere sweater, Sally took his breath away. He knew the beaded jade necklace and matching ear studs complemented her eyes . . . as if those sparkling green eyes needed any help. Ever.

Pax thought he detected a sudden blush creep through Sally's tan as she hugged him again. "I've missed you," she said and before he could respond, added, "Let's hurry; I'm hungry."

"I tried to call you," he said and closed the car door.

"We've rushed around this whole week. Maybe it's over for a while."

When he'd started the car, she reached for his hand. "Tell me what you've been doing."

"Mainly enjoying my new wingman, Motel Bates."

"*Motel?*" she said and tried to pull her hand free. "You've got to be kidding."

"Nope, Motel's his call sign. The squadron probably hung it on him; I doubt it's one he would have picked."

The drive to Miramar's back gate passed quickly. As soon as the sentry had saluted them through, she asked, "Who tagged you with Ahab?"

"Self-inflicted wound, truth be told . . . but everyone's got to be called something."

"I suppose," she said and leaned around in front of him. "Give me a call sign. What name would you hang on me?"

"Got to think on it. Call signs are too important for hip-shots. Help me find the Connors' place: three-fourteen."

The still-arriving cars and guests helped their search. Skipper Dodd and his wife paused alongside as Pax opened Sally's door.

"Speak of the devil," the commander said. "Ann and I were trying to figure out, Sally, what a smart, industrious, gorgeous gal—like yourself—could find to talk about with this run-of-the-mill lieutenant."

Ann Dodd shook her head. "Ignore him, Pax. An old squadron buddy came by this afternoon, and they tried to catch up on the drinks they'd missed."

Sally smiled at Pax. "But the skipper's got a point."

"Hey," Pax said and wrapped his arm around Sally's waist, "no piling on; you're supposed to help me out."

They laughed their way through the Connors' open front door, and headed for the party's buzz—which came from the back patio. Betty Connor met them with a hors d'oeuvre tray, but their eyes focused beyond Betty. The back yard had been transformed into a Japanese-lantern-lit slice of *Madame Butterfly*, complete with multicolored paper lanterns, streamers, and three would-be geishas wrapped in kimonos with obis.

Commander Connor, close behind his wife, offered a tray of hot sake. "Or for pantywaists," he said and sneered, "there's a tub of iced Kirin and Asahi beer."

Sally tried the sake; Pax held out for a beer. Two elderly Japanese women fried tempura in deep fat, trying hard to keep ahead of two eager lines. And before long, hot sake had the junior officers conversing in their best guess at Japanese. Ensign Windmill Newman waxed fluent. "Ichiban. Ichiban," he said, as he placed his palms together under his chin and bowed to the tempura cooks. They smiled, dipped their heads a bit, and tittered.

Pax drained a beer trying to cool his tempura-burnt mouth and was headed for the kitchen when he saw Motel and Pat. Both were drinking diet Pepsis.

He pointed at their drinks. "Where'd you get those?"

Motel laughed. "Tempura's pretty hot, isn't it? Soft drinks are in the fridge. We brought the Pepsis; help yourself."

Pax straightened up from retrieving a cold can, shut the refrigerator door, and backed smack-dab into CAG's wife.

"Hello, Pax," she said.

"Good evening, Mrs. Dengler."

"Nice party, isn't it?" she said.

"Yes. Real nice." Pax wanted out of the kitchen—better yet, clear out of the house—that instant.

Robin Dengler started to say something else, but her husband came through the door, glared at Pax, pulled his wife's arm, and said, "We're leaving," nodded at Pax, "Lieutenant."

They were there; they were gone. Pax hadn't seen anything unusual, yet something lingered, something besides the chill from their previous encounter.

Guilty conscience? Maybe. But something else, too.

Pax heard Sally's laughter and followed it to her and the Dodds. Ann Dodd had the floor. "You should have heard them. Your dad probably thinks they're in jail by now."

"Your skipper and his friend called my dad," Sally said.

"And he remembered those poker games, Pax," Dodd said.

"Bad pennies, Sally," Ann said. "These guys keep cropping up out of the past. You can't ever get away."

Sally squeezed Pax's hand. "Tried the tempura yet?"

"I had one, but let's get another," he said and led her toward the gray-haired Japanese cooks.

"No more sake," Sally said, "but maybe one of those beers. Which is best?"

With no warning, two thick, blond-haired arms came from behind her; each rested on one of her shoulders. Both fists held an icy-cold, full beer. "Either one's damned good, pretty girl."

"Hacksaw Grayson," Sally said and laughed as she turned toward the Mississippian. "You sure know how to sweet talk a girl."

"How'd you know it was me?" The innocent, wide-eyed query made them laugh.

Wilma Grayson handed one of Hacksaw's beers to Sally and took a swallow of the other. "Sally, he doesn't even know he sounds like a hog-caller."

Hacksaw draped an arm over Pax's shoulders. "Roomie, I talked to Washington this afternoon. My orders are cut; I'll be a VF-39 'Lancer' by noon Monday."

Wilma Grayson had her fists doubled up on her hips as she faced Pax and her husband. "And you know what, Pax? You're welcome to him. He's been pacing trenches in our carpets, worrying about missing that damned boat."

Hacksaw moved to his wife's side and wrapped her in his large arms. She looked up for a kiss and got a big one. "Ain't she somethin'?" Hacksaw said.

Pax couldn't answer, for he'd glimpsed the spotlighted doe's angst before Wilma looked away. And from the squeeze of her hand, he knew Sally had seen it too.

As soon as the sentry had saluted them out through Miramar's back gate, Sally broke the silence. "I've grown up swearing to myself I would never, ever let myself be trapped into my mother's life, into Wilma Grayson's life . . . with her three little boys. How can any woman justify raising children without their father?"

Knowing the difference between a question and a challenge, and not wanting to argue, Pax sat mute.

But Sally wouldn't buy his silence. "Over?" she said. "Are you willing to shed any happy thoughts on the subject?"

"No. An opinion, maybe. Hacksaw would be worthless without Wilma and they both know it. Oh sure, he loves her, but he needs her a whole lot more. She must know it; she accepts it."

Sally stared straight ahead.

Points? No points? Pax couldn't tell, but no further conversation diluted Al Hirt's "Honey in the Horn" from the radio.

Did I do something wrong? I'll be double-damned-dipped before I'll ask.

Nor did words delay a perfunctory goodnight peck at Sally's front door. *What the hell? I wish I'd held out for a handshake.*

Chapter 16—ANCHORS AWEIGH

Monday morning's spirited grab-ass diminished as the red second hand on a navy-issue wall-clock climbed toward twelve. Officers found their places and snapped to attention at 0800 when CDR Dodd walked into the ready room. Monday mornings' officers meetings started on time, whether the CO was aboard or not. Anyway, that was the word. And it might have been true, but so far Dodd had crossed the threshold as the red hand passed top-dead-center. Wags even opined the clock set itself to the CO's entry. During Pax's short time aboard, he had yet to hear CDR Conner call the room to attention. Pax guessed it would have been redundant.

Skipper Dodd spoke as he entered. "Take your seats, gentlemen." He stopped beside the lectern and nodded at the XO. "I'm sure, Commander Connor, everyone who attended your Saturday night Japanese extravaganza joins me in saying thank you, very shit-hot, and well-done. Your and Betty's party set a high-water mark."

Loud "hear, hears" and enthusiastic clapping induced the XO's half-turn and quick nod in acknowledgment. The noise abated.

"Two weeks from tonight, gents," CDR Dodd said. "August twenty-ninth marks the turnaround training complete, and we'll be embarked in *Gettysburg* with our aircraft and men." He ambled toward the door, and back to the lectern. His furrowed brow and compressed lips didn't invite extraneous comments. As he directed a piercing stare from one face to the next—pausing about two seconds on each—the ready room became snowfall quiet. Pax didn't know if anyone else was even breathing; he sure wasn't.

CDR Dodd's sentences came unhurried. "Gentlemen, see to your men. The married ones should have allotments going to their wives. Ask if the checks or deposits have started arriving. See if they need help with anything else." He pointed at Ollie Anderson. "Commander, don't accept excuses from *anyone* up the line . . . on personnel matters. Get my help if you need it. Understood?"

"Yessir," Ollie said between head nods.

Staring a hole right between Ollie's eyes, Dodd asked, "Commander, are up-to-date wills and emergency instructions in the officers' personal folders?"

"Except for a few, Skipper," Ollie said and paled at least two skin tones. The XO's additional glare didn't lighten Ollie's load.

"I'll ask you that same question tomorrow morning," Skipper Dodd said and glanced at the XO. Dodd strode toward the door. The XO's exuberant call to attention begot pop-up targets faster than any FBI live-fire range.

"That stampeded the goats on San Clemente Island," a junior officer whispered from the back row.

Department heads had little to say, so Connor stood and with growing volume said, "Make your flights, get your shops' moves scheduled, and don't leave the squadron area during working hours without indicating on the checkout board where you'll be. We don't have time to track you down. Questions?"

A few heads shook, but most remained motionless.

"Good. And don't make Commander Anderson chase you down for those papers the skipper mentioned. In fact, 0730 tomorrow is the deadline for having them in your folder. Ollie, in my office."

The remaining officers rose as one when the XO walked out, followed by the day's too popular admin officer.

"Windmill," Tom Weaver said, "since you're the junior pilot—and single—you do realize when you bust your ass the first ten thousand dollars of your insurance go toward a squadron party, right?"

Several pilots started clapping, but Windmill silenced them with the emergency stop signal—both fists overhead with crossed wrists. "You cheap screws, I'd already left you the whole enchilada . . . but I guess I can change it."

After several attempts to find First Class Petty Officer Chandler in the airframes shop, Pax caught him there and had him backed into a corner. "Yes," Pax said, "I understand how *you* feel about air force water wings, but that wasn't the question."

Silky Chandler raked a hand through his thick shock of black hair and shook his head. "Lieutenant, you told me to check where I could get some. I did; I can't get any. I also checked on their reliability, which they ain't got."

"How come six pilots in our sister squadron have 'em; where'd they get theirs?"

"Lieutenant, this is hearsay, but some of those pilots traded their survival knives at an air force base for those water wings. As for using them . . . maybe *their* riggers are too damned scared of their pilots. You know I'd like to help you," Chandler's eyes met Pax's square-on, "but I won't—not if it means I have to pray even harder every time you fly. I *know* what your Mark-III Charlie floatation device can handle; I have confidence in *it*."

"Okay," Pax said and nodded. "I'll keep wearing that bulky, hot pain in the ass. But if *I'm* not wearing water wings, I'd better not see anyone else in this squadron wearing them."

Chandler's grin broke wide and his dark eyes sparked. "Not on my watch you won't."

After lunch, Pax poked his head into the operations office. Hacksaw Grayson sat behind a gray metal desk, his ankles crossed and propped on a pulled-out drawer. He glanced up from the paper he'd been studying. "Hey, roomie, tell me about this Blaine guy. Can he fly?"

"Irish? Must be *pretty* good, he's LSO under training. I think he's a canoogle."

"Canoogle?" Hacksaw's eyebrows pinched together. "What's that?"

"Canoe 'U' . . . Annapolis . . . one of *them*."

Hacksaw grimaced and sucked his teeth. "Oh, dear God. I'd trade two of them for a NavCad any day of the week."

"Wouldn't mention it to the skipper . . . at least for a week or two. Might hurt his United States Naval Academy feelings."

Hacksaw bowed his shaking head and skewed a look toward the door. "Hey there, Camp, you lost?"

Pax felt the unwelcome arm on his shoulder even before he could look around. Neither he nor Brogan spoke. After several seconds, Camp lifted his chin toward Hacksaw. "Thought Tom Weaver worked here."

"Did," Hacksaw said.

Camp shrugged and held both hands out.

"Down below," Hacksaw said and rotated a thumb downward. "He's head wrench now . . . like you."

"Oh, you bumped him down to maintenance," Camp said and moved as if to leave, but he spun back, reached for Pax's upper arm, and whispered, "If you ever get serious about Sally, you could get out of the navy. She tore those blackjack dealers new asses in Vegas."

Camp's eyes stopped matching his smile long before he walked away, and once more, Hacksaw concentrated on his tactical organization chart.

Did I hear that sonofabitch right? Did Hacksaw hear?

When Hacksaw looked up, any doubt vanished. "I have no idea what he was talking about," Hacksaw said and jerked his thumb at the door, "but Camp Brogan's always been a genuine horse's ass."

"Won't argue that with you," Pax said and stretched his neck through a full circle, "but I've never known him to lie. Anyway, Motel and I are gonna go yank and bank . . . try to shoot each other down. See you later."

Pax sat on the end of a bench that he'd pulled against his locker. His sweat-soaked back hunched against the locker's door; his flight suit's main zipper gapped open to his waist. He pointed both flight boots—laces loosened—straight down the bench and hugged his knees. Coming through the passageway door, Motel hesitated by Pax and moved on down to his own locker.

"Nice lead," Pax said.

Bates didn't acknowledge the comment. He hung a wet torso harness and flight suit beside a helmet bag in his locker, then backed off several yards before lobbing each flight boot through the locker's open door. As he bent forward, tying his cordovans' laces, Motel glanced down the bench a couple of times where Pax remained motionless.

"It's normal to debrief in the ready room, Pax, but maybe we're better off here. Five points: First, you rode in way too close on the section takeoff; it affected my airplane, and I didn't like it. Second, on the run-ins it seemed like you were trying to ram me, playing chicken or something. I don't like that either. Third, you ignored the safety-deck calls and kept maneuvering for position. That sucks. If you can't get it done above the soft-deck, forget it. Fourth, even after I'd acknowledged your good moves and leveled my wings, you pressed the attack right up my back. What did that prove?" Motel took a deep breath and slammed his locker. "See you tomorrow."

Pax hadn't moved or changed expression. "*Five* points, you said."

"Yeah, five," Motel said and looked at his splayed fingers. "Last, coming into the break you moved in close enough to affect my airplane, almost like you were daring me to move you back out where you belonged. Why? No, wait!" Motel raised a palm toward Pax. "I don't care why. This was not a fun flight; maybe we shouldn't fly together."

Pax cracked a small smile. "How about the fuel checks?"

"Yeah, I forgot," Bates said and nodded. "'I'm fat,' doesn't hack it; I want to know how much you've got . . . the *normal* response."

"Anything else?"

"No, that's enough."

"How about my guns tracking call on the second engagement?" Pax asked.

Bates looked up toward a shadowed, overhead corner while he thought. "Since you mention it, you were too acute."

"Yeah, I was," Pax said. "That flight wore us both out, but I think you caught everything."

Motel knit his eyebrows an instant and visibly sagged his shoulders. "That crappy flying was intentional?"

"Like I said, I want to know how you think. I also wanted to know how you'd react: so far, so good."

"Screw you very much." Bates expelled a sharp breath, but some twinkle had returned to his eyes. "Lord only knows how close I came to slugging you when I walked in here. I wanted to."

Pax laughed as loud as he ever had in his life. "You'll do, Motel; we'll make a good section."

Like an eye-magnet, Pax's BOQ room telephone kept drawing his looks—some of which became stares.

But call her? I sure as hell won't. Damned women anyway. Why'd Camp's "Vegas" crack rub me so raw? Did she go to Vegas with that sonofabitch? No way. If she had, would Camp have said anything? I don't think so.

And despite the debrief, Pax suspected his being pissed at Brogan had more than a little to do with how the flight with Motel had gone.

Dumb. Dumb. Dumb.

Pax took a frustrated step toward the phone, weighing whether or not to rip its cord from the baseboard . . . when it rang. He let the second ring stop.

"Langford here," he said.

"Did I catch you in a bad mood?" Sally asked. After a couple of silent beats, "Or were you asleep?"

"No worse mood than normal, and I wasn't asleep. How are you today?" He ground his teeth to keep from asking if she was calling from Las Vegas.

"I called to apologize about the other night. You didn't cause Wilma's scared look, and I doubt you scheduled this deployment. Anyway, I'm grilling some burgers and thought I'd offer you one."

"I accept. Can I bring anything?"

"No . . . , unless you'll want beer; I think we're out."

148

"Okay, anything else?"

"Would you rather have cheese?"

"Huh?" he asked. "How about meat? You got any hamburger?"

She laughed. Pax furrowed his brow.

"We've got everything; I'm at your front desk. Bud and Becky are out in the car. May I ride with you?"

"Gimme a minute; I'll be right down."

Sally's blue shorts, white sweatshirt, and sandals matched her relaxed manner. She didn't mention Las Vegas, nor did Pax, as they followed Bud and Becky to the girls' house. They passed idle chatter, some concerned a cranky passenger she'd worked to win over on her morning San Francisco flight. More of the same at the house. Bud hadn't changed from his khaki uniform.

Pax and Bud grilled hamburger patties; the girls assembled the fixings. Appetites drove the action, and loading the patio table drew them together.

"I hope you like Vidalia onions," Becky said, "because I sliced them pretty thick."

The men, both chewing away, nodded vigorously and flashed the *okay* sign.

Pax washed the last bite of his first burger down with the remnants of a Coors Light, while Sally put a second on his plate. Bud received similar attention from Becky, along with another beer.

Shaking Pax's empty can, Sally said, "We have diet Pepsi or Diet Coke."

"A diet Pepsi, please," Pax said, but something in Sally's look tripped an alert wire. He jerked around to glance at Bud and Becky, with their big smiles and a double-dose of whatever Sally had. At last, he noticed the ring.

"When?" he asked.

"Friday morning in Las Vegas," Bud said.

"Well, congratulations, Bud," Pax said as he stood and shook his friend's hand. "Becky, I'll bet you were a beautiful bride, and I have a kiss coming." Which he placed on her cheek.

"Some things can't be put off," Bud said, "and marrying my gal fit that category."

The newlyweds drowned in each other's eyes and smiled as if daydreaming, oblivious to Pax, to Sally, or—it seemed—even to Monday week's rending departure.

"I'll bet your folks were excited," Pax said and glanced at Sally. Her red face surprised him, but the spin-around into the kitchen surprised him even more.

"Uh . . . truth is, Pax," Bud said and cleared his throat, "we haven't told them yet. We're going to call them in the morning."

Pax looked across the small table and nodded. "I know they'll be thrilled for you both." He trailed Sally into the kitchen.

She stood at the sink, the back of her neck flushed, dabbing Kleenex at her eyes. He touched both her shoulders and whispered close to her ear, "They'll be fine . . . and so will your folks."

She turned to face him, the tears running freely. "You think so?"

One nod brought her into his arms.

God, I hope so, but what I know—what I damned-well know—is that Sally's tears, unexpected like that, were a gut-shot.

She dabbed some more at her eyes. "After I put these things in the dishwasher, would you like to go for a walk?"

He nodded, and together they made quick work of squaring the kitchen away. Sally paused at the patio door. "We're going for a walk; see you two in a little bit."

Pax heard no response, but Sally led him by the hand out the front door and down the sidewalk for half a block before she spoke. "As you can imagine, the Vegas trip for them to get married came out of the blue. Bud called and told me about it Thursday morning. I gave him a lot of grief; I couldn't understand not calling Mom and Dad."

Since she seemed to pause, Pax asked, "Well . . . was there any reason for speed?"

They stopped at a corner under a street lamp. She blew out a breath and looked up sideways at him. "I don't know. I didn't ask; I didn't *want* to know. You'd like to wish them well, but I'd also like to kill them both. Dammit! He wanted to ask you to stand up for him, be his best man, but I vetoed that. Thursday *happened to be* the morning after I'd told you about Dad's objections to predeployment commitments. Anyway, Bud said it was going to happen with or without me, and he'd take care of telling the folks. And he asked Camp Brogan to be his best man."

"They're wingmen—makes sense. Did you fly to Vegas?"

"No. Becky and I had a flight Thursday. We drove up in Bud's car after we landed. Can you believe it? We had to kill nearly two hours in a casino waiting for the first open slot in *any* wedding chapel. They got married at zero one thirty-five on the twelfth; we ate breakfast and drove back . . . in time for Bud and Camp to go to work. Becky and I made our Friday afternoon flights. Some honeymoon.

"Anyway, I imagine that contributed to my dippy attitude Saturday night. And Bud swore me to absolute secrecy, of course, and every day since— with him not calling home—I'm in the middle. Mom and Dad won't say a word to Bud, but they'll give me some world-class, tight-lipped looks."

Pax couldn't help but grin a little. "I guess Bud's plate was bigger than mine."

She faced him head-on, wriggled a foot between his feet, wrapped her arms around his waist, and snuggled her head into his chest. "My little speech on the subject comes back to haunt me about every fifteen minutes."

When she kissed him like she meant it, Pax—ever mindful of that *cold water* treatment—began easing backwards, but Sally maintained contact and pressure. So he surrendered to the moment and let his pounding heartbeats muster the troops.

"My car can make it to Vegas," he said, but his husky voice croaked on "Vegas," making them both smile.

"I'm sure it could. Believe me; I feel what you feel. But after time to think—what you said about Hacksaw and Wilma. It made sense. Let me know when you can't do without *me*. You're not there yet; maybe someday you will be."

Before aircraft carrier combat deployments, few could say what happened to the final two weeks. Nor were Pax and Sally exceptions to the rule. Bud and Becky were married—ages ago, it seemed—and, as if by magic . . . the darkest, meanest magic imaginable, Pax and Sally sat holding hands across a small round table in a seafood restaurant near Hotel Del Coronado.

He wore the short-sleeved white uniform and its black shoulder boards— each with two gold stripes—showing the world he was indeed a United States Navy lieutenant. Sally's yellow, spaghetti-strapped sun dress with its white polka dots emphasized her suntan. And her figure—God knows it emphasized her figure.

"Did you know," Pax asked, "our waiter has brought two cooks and a dishwasher from the kitchen to look at you?"

"What makes you think they aren't interested in you?" she asked and wriggled her eyebrows.

"Will you write?" he asked.

"If you do."

"You can count on it."

"Good."

He checked his watch again. Unlike the watched pot, his looking seemed to hasten its march. He'd have to ponder that—night time . . . and goodbye time . . . passing faster.

"I told Bud I'd try and get to Mex Village by eleven to say goodbye," she said.

He nodded. "Ten minutes."

When they got to the Mexican restaurant, most of the singing clusters were identifiable by squadron. Pax spotted Camp Brogan and scanned his group, but Bud and Becky weren't with them. He shook his head at Sally.

"Here they come," Sally said. "Look at them."

Pax followed Sally's gaze back toward the restrooms and watched the newlyweds' approach—two steps forward, hug and kiss; one step backward, kiss and hug. For sure, they had been drinking.

"While you're saying goodbye," Pax said, "I have to see a man about a dog. Be right back."

The hugging kissers didn't even notice him brush by, which suited him fine; he truly had a mission. Five minutes later, as he exited the men's room, a hand touched his shoulder from behind. He looked around to see a flush-faced woman. It took him a couple of beats to recognize Robin Dengler.

"He knows, Pax. I'm sorry, but he *knows*. Please be careful," she said and walked past him into the ladies' room.

An instant chill wedged between his shoulder blades and slithered up his neck, before her words got lost in the general buzz. But his ears throbbed red-hot. He glanced around, but caught no stares, nor did he see the man who had just steam-rolled into his life. Pax took a quick stride back toward Sally before he heard his name.

"Pax!" someone shouted from behind him.

He took another step.

"Pax Langford!" The second call came louder and from much closer.

He looked around, expecting he knew not what, but fearing the worst.

"Are you fighter pilots stone-deaf?" asked an approaching officer—it wasn't CAG!—whom he recognized as Lieutenant Tom Cain.

"Tom?" he said. "What are you doing here?"

The lanky officer put his arm around Pax's shoulders. "You mean you've missed me since Olathe? I belong here; I'm in VA-136. We're deploying together."

"Good deal! I'll see you on the ship, partner, but I've got to run now," Pax said, shook hands, and headed for Sally. She saw him coming, pointed at the front door, and met him there.

"Let's leave," she said. "Bud and Becky decided to park by the ship tonight. I want to catch the midnight ferry if I can."

He squeezed her hand. "Good plan. The White Knight turns into a pumpkin at zero one hundred."

Pax eased by a block-long line of idling semi-rigs that still needed unloading. Even approaching midnight, two conveyer belts continued their uphill drag to the hangar deck, stuffing the huge, pier-side USS *Gettysburg* (CVA-35). The closer they got, the larger the ship loomed. Three football fields long, with the tails of aircraft jutting out from the flight deck, some fifty-seven feet above the water.

Pax pulled as close as traffic would allow, shut off the engine, and got out. Sally met him in front of the car. "You be careful," she said, "but get your MiG killing behind you."

"Piece-a-cake," he said and realized time had evaporated—again—with too many things left unsaid, too many plans unbroached. So they kissed.

She shook her head, waved once, got in the Corvette, and drove from the pier. He stood rooted to the macadam, choking back a roiling need to scream.

Why didn't I tell her I love her? How is she supposed to know?

He bowed his head. Who did he think he was fooling? He knew. Deep in his clawed-raw gut, where denial dissolved, Pax knew. He feared another serious loss. And Sally had become precious to him, even more than precious—serious. With his entire being he wanted to marry her.

Pax stopped by ready room number three long enough to place his peg in the "Aboard" column. And having done so, heretofore unfelt pressure dissolved. He'd made it. With the sunrise, he and *Gettysburg* were headed for war. And far over the western horizon, he knew that some North Vietnamese MiG pilot had better be feeling a chill up his oriental spine.

Chapter 17—DA NANG

USS *Gettysburg* operated near Pearl Harbor for forty-eight hours, while her pilots made refresher landings and sat through lengthy briefings from two U.S. Pacific Fleet intelligence officers. Pax felt over-briefed and under-flown, but he had no doubt about what he would remember most from crossing the broad Pacific Ocean—yet another inoculation.

After leaving the dispensary, Pax trudged up three ladders and eased down a long passageway to the stateroom he shared with Hacksaw Grayson. As Pax flicked on their overhead light, the Mississippian rolled halfway out of the lower bunk and put his feet on the deck.

"Rat's ass!" Pax said. "The damned corpsman used a bicycle pump for that gamma globulin shot."

Grayson grinned his eyes down to slits and plucked at Pax's shirt. "I told you they'd get you. You been running, or is it raining?"

"You're a riot, roomie. That corpsman went away and came back three different times before he could shove that plunger to the hilt. I'll bet he left the needle in ten minutes."

"Uh huh," Hacksaw said. "Where the hell you reckon them flight surgeons dug up a syringe that big?"

Pax didn't answer, but he pushed his forehead into the side of the upper bunk's mattress cover . . . wishing he had the bottom bunk. Since he didn't, he stood by his desk and waited for the nausea to pass.

Pax eased onto chairs for a few days, but both the knot and the soreness were gone and forgotten by the morning *Gettysburg* moored pier-side at Cubi Point in the Philippine Islands' Subic Bay, sixty-five miles west of Manila.

In a squadron maintenance officers' meeting, prior to docking, the maintenance officer, LCDR Tom Weaver, pointed at Pax. "I'd like you to accept our corrosion control spaces in the detachment hangar."

Pax nodded. "Yes, sir."

Weaver queried LT "Roller" Rinc, an aviation maintenance limited duty officer, "Roller, are you senior to VF-37's beach-det maintenance officer?"

"No, sir," the slender, near-bald officer said, "Lieutenant Shaw's a mustang; he come up through the ranks like me, and VF-37's his second F-8 squadron. He's helped us a lot in the past; we speak the same language."

"Good," Weaver said. "We've talked about our cardinal rule, Roller, but make damned sure the men know it: any disciplinary problem in Olongapo, *or* on the base, gets the offender on the next plane to the ship. No exceptions. None."

"Aye, aye, Commander."

Pax didn't detect even a minuscule expression change in Roller Rinc's face, yet something happened.

Was that a flash of forbearance in Roller's dark eyes? Or did I imagine it?

With the fly-off of projected combat-loss replacement aircraft prior to arriving, and a mixed squadron off-load of maintenance personnel at Cubi Point, the ship shed her "fat." *Gettysburg*, with her best combat mix of aircraft—always a compromise between embarked aircraft capability and deck-handling ease—followed the sunset toward her destiny, whatever North Vietnam and fate would muster.

The second morning after leaving Cubi Point, at a pilots meeting in the ready room, Skipper Dodd stood beside their squadron-emblem-adorned lectern. His quiet stare deterred movement; most breathing became shallow. The overhead air-conditioning vents, however, continued their soft whirring.

"Gentlemen," Dodd said, "I'll leave the statistics to Commander Grayson, but I have a couple of things first. . . . Are we ready for this deployment? Yes, without a doubt. Will each of us make it back home?" The commander stepped away from the lectern and glanced—face-by-face—into the other officers' eyes. "We hope so," he continued, "but that depends more on each of you than it does on me." Skipper Dodd turned toward Hacksaw and swept an arm toward the lectern. "Commander Grayson."

At the front of the ready room, Hacksaw slid a green chalkboard to one side, uncovering another behind it, with a date and several columns of figures on it. He scooted the lectern out of the way against a side wall, and with a wooden pointer he tapped at a yellow-chalked date: 19 September 1966. "Gents, I thought you might like to see these numbers. In the past year—

since 19 September 1965—the navy lost 188 aircraft from carrier decks off Vietnam: 135 combat losses and fifty-three operational losses."

Hacksaw waited, giving the pilots time to scan down the figures. "You can see," he pointed to a lower line, "we lost thirty-nine F-8s: twenty-seven to combat, twelve to normal operations. Are those figures significant? I don't know. What I want *you* to know is we lost almost half as many aircraft to normal operations as we did to combat. What these figures tell *me* is we'd better not relax because we aren't over the beach. Dumb-shit mistakes kill you as dead as surface-to-air missiles. Looking at the killed-in-action and missing-in-action lists tells me something else. Some of those losses were damned good pilots. I'm not trying to scare anyone, but let's not forget: these bullets are real and gettin' dead's a lengthy commitment."

Windmill Newman's nasal voice from a back row pierced the quiet, "Skipper, this don't sound like a fair war to me."

Dodd nodded at the laughter, thanked Hacksaw, and faced his pilots again. "Before I walked in here," he said, "CAG Dengler called my room to tell me that *Constellation* and *Coral Sea* each lost another F-4 today . . . one operational, one to combat.

"We're lucky. Captain Conrad commands *Gettysburg* as well as anyone ever has, and CAG Dengler expects perfection on every flight; we know that. But that's not enough. I'm going to let you in on a little secret. On every flight you make from an aircraft carrier—*Gettysburg* or any other—there's one man specifically assigned to *ensure* that *you* bust your ass." Dodd paused and nodded at his wide-eyed, doubting pilots. "Believe me, gents; it's true. And these hit-men are sneaky; you'll never know who your guy is, because they change assignments. One day it's a plane captain who leaves a safety pin in; another day an approach controller turns you the wrong way, maybe even on the same day a tanker pilot shorts you five hundred pounds of fuel.

"Remember this: *you* have around-the-clock responsibility for your own ass."

Dodd shrugged. "Am I talkin' too fast for anyone? What's my message? There are no guardian angels on this ship. Be polite and be professional, but be ever alert for the unexpected. If it doesn't feel right, it may not be right. Question things early on; don't wait until you're in a bind.

"During this first line-period, I'm giving you a freebie. You question everything that doesn't feel right. I'll take responsibility for any of your questions. Understood?"

Pax watched the somber head nods. No one ventured a question.

USS *Gettysburg* arrived off South Vietnam's northern coast on the afternoon of 19 September 1966, a few miles north of an area referred to as Dixie Station. The PACFLT briefers had explained that prudence dictated letting newly-arrived aircraft carriers spend a couple of days and nights flying on Dixie Station with Da Nang—in northern South Vietnam—which supported several marine and air force squadrons, for a nearby divert airfield. This provided a benign environment while getting flight-deck personnel up to speed and every pilot night current—qualified for night landings, as defined by the Naval Air Training and Operating Procedures Standardization bible.

The second night on Dixie Station, after *Gettysburg* trapped her last bird, she heeled port in a gradual starboard turn. A slight tilt of ready room and stateroom decks did not go unnoticed by air wing pilots. For when she steadied on her next course, *Gettysburg*—their home—would devour the remaining miles between themselves and an ageless, beckoning siren: mortal combat.

Immediately after sunset on their first day at Yankee Station, Pax steadied his Crusader on final approach bearing. This landing, his second for the day, would qualify and be recorded as a night arrested landing, even though sufficient light remained to discern a reasonable horizon. Everyone called these landings "pinkies." A palpable adrenaline rush—normal for Pax's night carrier landings—had not yet kicked in.

Motel Bates had led the flight and was about a minute ahead of Pax in their descent toward the ship. After checking each other's tailhook and passing a thumbs-up signal, they were given different approach frequencies to prevent interference or misunderstanding between themselves and *Gettysburg*'s final approach controllers.

Pax scanned his instruments. He knew fighting the Crusader was dessert, but flying it by its flight instruments was the meat and potatoes of staying alive. Responding to a real good controller always felt like dancing to Pax . . . the rougher the weather, the sweeter the music.

The expected transmission crackled into his earphones: "Lobo Four Zero Six, twelve hundred feet, at eight and a half miles. Dirty up."

"Roger, Trojan," Pax said and moved the small wheel-shaped knob inboard and down with his left hand. "Lobo Four Zero Six going dirty."

A red warning light in the wheel-knob burst alive and three wheel-position indicators changed from "UP" to barber poles. But during the few seconds he unlocked and raised the wing, the red light went out and three miniature wheels replaced the barber poles. "Lobo Four Zero Six, gear down and locked, state five point one."

As the airplane slowed toward landing speed, Pax flicked his hands around essential points in the cockpit, touching handles and switches—the before landing checklist: arresting hook handle, down; fuel dump-switch, off; landing gear handle, down; throttle friction wheel, loosened.

At 140-knots indicated airspeed, he pushed the approach power compensator switch forward with his left index finger and said to himself, "I hope, I hope, I hope." It engaged, and at 138-knots the throttle moved forward, responding to Pax's right thumb's nose-up trim inputs.

Yes! Right-on!

He'd grown almost too fond of "auto-throttle" approaches—and he knew it—but like cruise-control on a car, once he'd become used to it. . . . Anyway, he flew approaches—night approaches, in particular—without auto-throttle under mental protest.

"Lobo Four Zero Six, Trojan final controller, do not acknowledge further transmissions. Four Zero Six, you're approaching two and a half miles, commence a normal rate of descent."

Pax thumbed in a few degrees of nose-down trim and let the vertical speed indicator settle at six hundred feet per minute rate of descent; he noted the throttle automatically retard a few percent of power. He followed the controller's minor heading changes and adjustments to his rate of descent. Both controller and Pax were striving to guide the Crusader down a near horizontal and ever diminishing sized "funnel in the sky," to arrive: three-quarters of a mile behind the ship, on altitude, on final bearing, and at optimum landing airspeed. In close, comments would switch from the radar controller to the LSO, and Pax would switch from flying instruments to watching carrier lighting for glide slope and centerline information.

But Pax had been peeking and he could already see the meatball's amber light and the centerline's lights.

God bless these glasses.

The controller passed the expected information: "Lobo Four Zero Six on final bearing and glide slope at three-quarters of a mile. Call the ball."

"Four Zero Six," Pax said, "Crusader—ball—four point eight—auto."

"Roger, auto-ball. We've got thirty knots right down the angle."

Good. He'd hoped Lawrence would be waving. "Gypsy" always let them work, without a running commentary. Like now, but there wasn't much to talk about. Pax was tracking right down the centerline, and the amber meatball's beam was dead-on, centered between the split horizontal row of green datum lights. And aft-of-the-island burble was so slight that the ball didn't even sag in close. He would've bet on a 3-wire, which is exactly what he caught.

As normal upon touchdown, Pax pushed the throttle forward. He felt the arresting cable's reassuring tug, which started pressing him forward into the shoulder straps. But the one-potato tug gave way to a sickening, half-assed acceleration forward—like tripping and falling. He crammed the throttle outboard into the afterburner detent, snatched the gear-handle up, and tried to lift the airplane back up into the darkening void with a one-handed death-grip on the control stick.

Pax's afterburner light-off illuminated *Gettysburg*'s forward port side and gave him a reflected horizon off the water. A fleeting glimpse at the instrument panel had him fifty feet underwater, so he looked back outside, keeping his wings level in relation to the dimming, reflected water surface.

Even before he knew he could save it, his earphones crackled: "Lobo Four Zero Six, your signal is bingo to Da Nang. Come left. Da Nang bears one-six-zero at one hundred and ninety-five. Trojan's airborne tanker is sour: there's no giveaway fuel. Over."

Pax said nothing until he'd nursed his airplane up through one hundred feet, but as soon as he knew he could fly, he lowered and locked the wing, raised his hook, came around toward his divert field and accelerated to climb-schedule airspeed. Then he asked, "Trojan, Four Zero Six, why the bingo? Over."

"Four Zero Six, flight deck personnel say your arresting gear hook-point broke off. Advise Trojan Strike Control on button eight when receiving Da Nang TACAN. Over."

Bad luck—nothing more, nothing less. At least that explained the partial tug. But I'll be lucky to make Da Nang . . . even with no delays.

"Roger, Trojan, Four Zero Six's state is three point three. Switching to button eight," Pax said.

He watched the altimeter wind, amazed at the light-fuel-loaded airplane's rate of climb. Lightning flashes illuminated towering thunderheads in his flight path.

Not enough fuel to climb over or go around them; I'll have to plow through.

The searching TACAN needle locked onto Da Nang a few degrees left of his nose with the range indicator at 110-nautical miles. Knowing his location helped offset the ordeal of plunging into a turbulent cloud mass.

"Trojan Strike, Lobo Four Zero Six, level two six zero. Da Nang bears one five seven at a hundred and five, state one point four. Over."

"Roger, Four Zero Six. A line of thunder-bumpers between you and Da Nang, but the field is reporting VFR. Da Nang altimeter: two niner eight three. There's a maintenance crew at Da Nang to replace your hook-point. You have a confirmed noon Charlie-time tomorrow—twelve hundred local. Over." *Gettysburg's* transmissions remained strong, but with much background hissing.

I'll bet that's from the lightning.

"Four Zero Six with a noon Charlie. Out."

Pax dialed in Da Nang Approach Control's frequency as the lightning flashes and turbulence confirmed Trojan's report.

"Da Nang Approach, Da Nang Approach, Lobo Four Zero Six. Over." After calling, Pax considered starting an idle descent prior to initial contact; he had little time and no fuel to waste. "Da Nang Approach, Da Nang Approach, Lobo Four Zero Six. Over," he repeated.

"Roger, Lobo Four Zero Six, this is Da Nang Approach Control. Go ahead."

Gaining radio contact—that initial hurdle jumped—warmed an incipient chill.

"Da Nang Approach, Four Zero Six is inbound from Trojan on an emergency bingo with minimum fuel, requesting radar vectors to a straight-in approach. Over."

How many times have I danced this jig? It always amazes me when pilots' transmissions retain such brisk, matter-of-fact tones. For not too deep—behind that professional facade—lurks a fang-bared urge to blurt out: "Oh, man! It's great to hear your voice. Now I'm no longer alone, and I'll feel a whole lot better when you hurry up and get me on the deck, because I'm low on fuel, the weather's crummy, and I'm landing at a strange field."

He'd never made such a confessional transmission, nor had he ever heard one. But he—for sure—heard this Da Nang controller's response.

"No can do, Lobo. Da Nang is under rocket attack. We are accepting no approaches at this time. This field is closed."

A revived chill, icier than ever, shinnied up-and-down Pax's spine—an Iditarod Trail round-trip in less than a heartbeat.

Pax slowed his breathing and enunciated for posterity and the approach control tape, "Da Nang Approach, Lobo Four Zero Six is approaching twenty-miles on the three five zero degree radial at angels twenty. I have enough fuel to hold at altitude for ten minutes max. After ten minutes, I want radar vectors for an approach to Da Nang Airfield. If unable, I want radar vectors to an area where you would have me eject. I'm running out of fuel. Do you understand my situation? Over."

"Wait one, Lobo."

Pax imagined an operations officer, maybe even a commanding officer, flipping an imaginary coin.

"Lobo Four Zero Six, Da Nang is under heavy rocket attack. Given that knowledge, if you desire an approach, Lobo is cleared to descend to four thousand feet. Come left to heading zero nine zero. Over." The voice was new and more confident: a real pro, Pax guessed, perhaps now back from a coffee break.

"Lobo out of twenty for four; coming left to zero nine zero." Pax retarded the throttle to idle but held off using the speed-brake until he knew for sure how they'd work him. With seven hundred pounds of fuel remaining, the red low-fuel warning light had been glowing steadily for eight minutes.

Lightning streaked between heavier cloud cells, and the instruments were alternately awash in blue-white light and a pale red glow. He'd almost gotten used to the hissing in his earphones. A bitter metallic flavor danced across his tongue, while the hard rubber mask wedged deeper into the bridge of his nose.

"Lobo Four Zero Six, come left—the long way—270-degrees to a heading of south. You'll be making an arrested landing on the starboard runway. Clear the gear as expeditiously as possible and taxi back up the runway. You'll be met by a follow-me truck that will lead you to a revetment. How do you copy? Over."

"Lobo copies, Da Nang, but I can't arrest. My tailhook fell off; that's why I'm here. Over."

"Roger, Lobo, understand. The left runway is unavailable. Can you stop without arresting on seven thousand feet of runway? Over."

Good question. I'm light; that'll help. Is the runway wet? What the hell am I thinking about? Like I have a choice.

"No sweat, Da Nang. Piece-a-cake," he said.

"Roger, Lobo. Double-check your external navigation lights off until after landing. Snipers have been shooting at landing aircraft."

"Lobo copies; lights are out. Contact—runway in sight—gear down and locked."

Pax slammed the bird down hard on the sure-enough-wet runway's end, extended the in-flight refueling probe, and held the control-stick forward, with full aileron deflection into the slight crosswind. He fought the drift with opposite rudder, trying to keep his nose tracking between the dimly-lit runway lights. As soon as the airspeed indicator dropped to a hundred knots, he began braking as hard as he dared. At sixty knots he unlocked the canopy, eased it open and inserted the canopy-strap lug, and let it spring open. His airspeed dropped, but the last runway lights rushed ever nearer.

It'll be close.

He stopped a few yards past the last runway light and released the left bayonet clip to let his nose-gouging oxygen mask hang free. He scarfed down a couple of deep, humid breaths.

Hell, I even have room to turn around, and no rockets or snipers got me.

"Yeah," he said, "piece-a-cake . . . my ass."

Chapter 18—ALONE

When Pax landed from Da Nang, Sally's first letter peeked from his ready room mail-slot. She asked if he'd gotten a MiG yet, and described the pleasure cruise she imagined him to be enjoying. Becky—who by the way was not pregnant—and she were coping quite well. A certain Corvette, however, seemed to be pining for its absent owner. Not to worry, she added, it was her pleasure to have been crowned Drag Strip Queen of the local neighborhood.

CDR Dodd's mocking voice snatched him back from a vision of Sally's smile. "Hacksaw, has your roommate come into a large inheritance?"

"Why, Commander, 'cause he's grinnin' like a dog eating stickers?" Hacksaw asked. "I'd bet on a Sally-gram."

"Small reward," Pax said, "for cringing the whole night under rocket attack."

"Some of 'em must've come pretty close," Hacksaw said. "You stink like a feedlot."

"Close enough! I felt the concussions."

"Really?" Dodd asked.

Pilots gathered to hear a firsthand account of hostilities. Even those who kept their

seats paid serious attention.

"With our hut surrounded by sand-filled barrels, I'd figured to stay in the rack,"

Pax said. "But that first blast changed my mind in a hurry. Those sand-bagged bunkers

along the roads weren't very big, but jamming into 'em didn't bother anyone—at least it

didn't bother me."

Windmill Newman wanted to know—sure enough—how close the rockets came.

"Close enough!" Pax said. "Shrapnel whistled through the bunker

163

peepholes twice; a marine corporal took a hit at the corner of our hut. Bloodstains marked where he'd been."

"Sounds like war stories, Ahab," CDR Connor said. "How many beers had you put away?"

"No money," Pax said.

Both CO and XO frowned at each other, shook their heads and walked away.

Five days later—with CDR Dodd grounded—Pax and Motel Bates were scheduled for target combat air patrol, supporting a 12-bomber strike against a North Vietnamese truck repair facility between Haiphong and Hanoi in Route Package VI Bravo. Buckshot Walker would man the Lobo spare airplane.

CAG Dengler, the strike leader, had finished briefing the bombers' run-in and egress. He addressed VF-37's CO. "Commander Milano, Sea Bats will stay with the bombers. Lobo section will orbit north of the target." Milano poked a hand into the air; CAG nodded at him.

"CAG, with the northern orbit being right between Kep and Cat Bi MiG bases, I'd recommend our four fighters take that; let the Lobo section escort the bombers."

"I think not," CAG said, shaking his head. "Any more comments?"

There was none. Pax tried to ignore CDR Milano's red-faced glance. Walking back to the ready room, Motel chuckled.

"What?" Pax said.

"I read about this worker in Hershey, Pennsylvania, who fell into a huge vat of chocolate. Problem being, no matter *how* much he loved it, he couldn't eat his way out."

"I hear you. Maybe CAG's trying to make us both aces in one flight."

Buckshot Walker nudged Motel from behind. "Hey, fella, if you're allergic to chocolate, I'd be more than happy to take this flight for you."

Motel didn't even look back. "In your dreams, *fella*."

"If you guys don't see MiGs on this flight," Dodd told them as they left the ready room, "I'm sending you both down for eye exams."

"Fair enough," Pax answered. Motel didn't reply, but Pax thought he looked like a bettor who'd drawn a fourth ace. The three fighter pilots took a couple of steps down the passageway, before CDR Dodd stuck his head out of the ready room. "Hey, Ahab, we'll be listening on strike frequency."

Pax shot a thumb in the air and kept walking.

As the "Lobo" pilots reached the flight deck and walked toward their planes, Motel leaned close to Pax. "If we even smell MiGs on this flight, Dodd will never look at another cigarette."

"I'll bet you're right." Pax remembered his surprise when the skipper told the pilots about setting his oxygen mask on fire when he lit a cigarette while airborne. Dangling his mask by a bayonet fitting and leaving his oxygen on had been two dumb-ass mistakes. Nobody dared laugh, though. Two days later the left side of Dodd's face had begun scabbing over. But that particular cigarette, which he never even got to smoke, cost him this prime opportunity to maybe see a MiG.

Dodd's wingman, Windmill Newman, had been "volunteered" to take Motel's place as Duty Officer, so Pax's section could fly the TARCAP. When Pax told Windmill he would have the duty for a few hours, the young, red-faced pilot scanned the entire ready room—checking for sure Dodd wasn't there—and shouted: "If that fucking cigarette costs me a MiG, I'm jumping overboard!"

As Pax approached his assigned F-8, Lobo 409, aft of the island superstructure on the starboard side of the flight deck, the brown-jerseyed plane captain reached out for his helmet-bag. Pax shook his head and hopped onto the extended step below the left side of the cockpit. He lobbed the green nylon bag over the canopy rail onto the seat-pan cushion. As he dropped back on the flight deck, Pax watched red-jerseyed ordnancemen secure an AIM-9D "Sidewinder" air-to-air missile on the port pylon.

"Two 'winders, full ammo," the ordnance supervisor said.

Pax acknowledged with a thumbs-up. His preflight walk-around took no more than two minutes, but when Pax glanced across the flight deck, Motel was already strapping into his cockpit.

How the hell did he do that? So much for those three-hour, nitpicking, safety inspections.

Pax started the engine. Most of the systems had been checked, when Chief Franklin, Lobo maintenance chief, jogged up and slapped the port side of Pax's fuselage. The chief raised three fingers, pointed at Motel's bird, and gave a thumbs-down signal. Next, he raised four fingers, pointed at Buckshot's bird, and gave another thumbs-down.

Dammit! Both planes down.

Pax nodded, patted the canopy sill, and thrust his left thumb to the top of his canopy. As pilots radioed their aircraft status, Pax pressed the sides of his helmet tight to his ears, listening while the Sea Bats checked in.

Good. The five Sea Bats checked good.

The Air Boss's directions from Primary Flight Control (Pri-Fly), the elevated control tower overlooking the flight deck, filled his ears: "Lobo Four Zero Nine, Trojan, over."

"Roger, Trojan, Four Zero Nine."

"Your wingmen's airplanes are both down; we'll launch the Sea Bat spare, One Zero Three, as your wingman. Do you copy?"

"Roger, Trojan. One Zero Three with Four Zero Nine. Out."

Rat's ass. MiGs galore and a stranger for a wingman. At least I'm leading the section.

Pax strained his neck trying to locate Sea Bat One Zero Three on the flight deck, but he had no luck.

At 16,000-feet, during the left-hand rendezvous pattern, a Sea Bat F-8 closed from inside the turn.

Yep, One Zero Three.

The F-8 crossed beneath him and steadied in the starboard wing slot. Pax glanced toward the new wingman and saw Bud Banks—oxygen mask dangling from one bayonet fitting—grinning up a storm. Pax nodded, raised a thumbs-up, and jerked the same thumb backward over alternating shoulders . . . loosening Bud out to a free cruise position for their inbound leg to the beach.

CDR Milano's deep voice filled Pax's headset: "Saddle Bags aboard."

CAG Dengler acknowledged: "Roger. Saddle Bag switching strike frequency."

As briefed, CAG Dengler began a gradual climb and steadied on a heading to the coast-in point, which they planned to cross at 23,000-feet. The bomb-laden A-4s would need the excess altitude. They'd trade it for a much faster, more maneuverable airspeed by dropping to their roll-in altitude after crossing the beach from over the water—going feet-dry.

Pax and Bud, already at 25,000-feet, made gentle turns and reversals to keep from getting too far ahead of the bombers. During one shallow right turn away from the A-4s, Pax saw—way out, at 10 o'clock near the horizon— a narrow, slow-climbing smoke plume continue upward until it disappeared in an abruptly-forming pinkish cloud. The surface-to-air-missile (SAM) must have been fired at another strike group. His earphones crackled: "This is Red Crown on guard. Bandits! Bandits! Bandits! Blue bandit, zero-nine-zero, Bull's-eye, twenty."

Uh-huh, a MiG-21, 20-miles east of Hanoi.

He felt thirsty. The coastline emerged through the low-lying haze; Pax estimated the bombers going feet-dry in five minutes. Two minutes later, Pax called, "Lobos detaching, switches hot."

CAG's acknowledgment got blocked. A high-pitched voice broke in, "Mayday! Mayday! Skin Game Two-Zero-One on guard. I'm hit. Skin Game Two—"

Pax twisted his radio function switch counterclockwise one notch, blocking guard frequency transmissions. Two more smoke trails streaked skyward in the west.

Screeches and clicks replaced the guard frequency transmissions, as greenish-yellow lines traced their way from the center of Pax's threat-sector-indicator mounted on his right glare-shield. He knew a line climbing to the instrument's top (12 o'clock) meant the threat-controlling radar, be it for guns or missiles, was straight ahead. A line to the right (3 o'clock) meant the threat was from his right. He thought of these threat lines as spokes; the longer the spoke, the nearer the threat.

Dropping his right wing, he double-checked the best coastline gouge he had for going feet-dry: close enough.

Whoa! Did my red SAM light flash? Maybe not; I didn't hear anything.

Bud crossed to left abeam.

Good; Bud'll be looking through me toward the probable threat. Thirty miles to target.

Descending through 18,000-feet, Pax set power at 96-percent and saw his SAM light flick on and off. He knew a SAM site's radar was painting him as a blip during its 360-degree searching sweep. He exaggerated dropping his right wing to signal Bud, and lessened the bank, but continued around toward the north. Bud dug to the inside of their arc, his expected call came when due: "Lobo, six clear."

Pax saw Bud climb back up on the inside of their arc, timing it to arrive abeam and level as they steadied out. "Roger, Lobo, *your* six is clear," Pax answered and leveled at 15,000-feet. The chirping and cheeping kept time with Pax's threat indicator spokes. Three more smoke trails climbed from the western haze. The SAM light flickered more often. Pax and Bud changed their headings a few degrees in either direction, weaving toward and away from each other, clearing each other's rear hemisphere (6 o'clock) and searching for low flyers.

Maybe five more miles to target; we'll orbit north.

A climbing SAM to the west exploded into a red and black cloud, which could have been bad news for someone. Pax squinted against the haze, trying to see through it.

We should be approaching the target. Hell, I can't even see Hai Duong, much less a truck park. Okay, Haiphong's at 3 o'clock; those SAMs were at 9 o'clock . . . maybe out of Hanoi. We're over it; gotta be. Five miles and turn.

"Did you call, Lobo?" Bud asked.

"Negative, Lobo; strangle guard."

Dammit! I should have told him sooner.

An overpowering sense of slowing engulfed Pax, but a quick gauge check showed over 500-knots.

Which way to turn?

A steady, red SAM light, now confirmed by that sickening radar-locked-on warble: Dee-Doo! Dee-Doo! Dee-Doo! with a strong vector-spoke at 3 o'clock forced the issue.

"Lobo, left ninety," Pax called.

Bud's "Lobo, six clear" call came as the SAM light went out and its intimidating warble ceased. Another smoke trail, nearly dead ahead, burst into a reddish-black cloud. Pax saw what he thought were exploding antiaircraft shells ahead, to the left of their flight path. "Lobo, right one-eighty," he called. He strained to see anything moving below them. Being twenty miles from two MiG bases was an answered prayer.

We're hunters; MiGs are prey. Right! But that doesn't keep me from being thirsty. And no roll-in calls from the bombers yet.

Pax checked his clock. Had it stopped? It must have stopped. Bud cut to the inside, drifting ahead and slightly above Pax, going for his next abeam position. "Lobo, you're clear," Pax called.

They steadied heading toward Haiphong, but Pax had no desire to restir its now wide-awake SAM sites. He tapped the instrument panel clock; he'd hold this course for fifteen seconds. The SAM light with its accompanying low warble came after five.

Close enough.

"Lobo, left one-eighty," he called and tried to locate either of the MiG bases through the low-level haze. He rechecked his airspeed.

Bud pulled to the inside of Pax's turn and passed ahead and above him. Pax called, "Lobo, six clear."

"Saddle Bags in." CAG Dengler's call sounded pinched, maybe breathless.

Good! One more circuit and we'll follow them outbound. Jesus, I'm thirsty.

A new SAM light came steady, as did the low warble, Dee-Doo! Dee-Doo! Dee-Doo! The main threat-vector spoke bloomed at two o'clock.

Probably from one of the MiG bases.

Bud steadied abeam on Pax's left.

"Lobo, left one-eighty," Pax called.

As he banked left, Pax saw three rapid, red and black explosions, dead ahead at less than a mile. He increased his bank. The SAM light and warble stopped.

Headed back toward Haiphong, Pax saw smoke rising from what must have been the Hai Duong truck park. Reaching the target smoke, Pax lowered his starboard wing and called, "Lobo, right ninety," when—near the ground— he spotted a pair of dark, camouflaged, delta-winged fighters streaking toward Haiphong.

Pax wrapped the starboard turn into an inverted roll to keep sight of the bogies and jammed the throttle into afterburner: "Lobo! Tallyho two bogies, low, going away! Hang on!"

"No joy, Lobo. Your six is clear," Bud called.

Captain Banks would be proud of Bud's calm transmission. I'll ease this roll to match the bogies' heading; that dive gave me humongous overtake. I'll fire sidewinders first—from dead 6 o'clock and slightly below—then close for guns.

"They're straight ahead, Lobo, near the horizon," Pax called and . . . and he saw the engine smoke and the drooping stabilators.

"Ah-h-h hell, Lobo, they're Phantoms; coming left," Pax called and used their 660-knot airspeed zooming back to altitude.

"Roger Phantoms, Lobo. Concur." Bud called and cut to the inside of their turn. The strike group began calling "feet-wet," by sections, as the bombers recrossed the beach.

Pax planned one wide, sweeping turn before going feet-wet. Maybe MiGs had flushed those Air Force Phantoms from a mission. He leveled at 10,000- feet, 400-knots, and was considering whether or not to reengage afterburner, when yet another ominous Dee-Doo! Dee-Doo! in his earphones was at once followed by the dreaded Deedle! Deedle! Deedle! Deedle! with its flashing-red SAM light.

Holy shit! Guidance signals; missile's in the air.

"High SAM alert," Bud called, "no joy."

"Gates! (Select afterburner)" Pax called, jammed the throttle into burner, and shot a nanosecond glance at the threat-indicator. A white smoke-puff behind Bud's bird confirmed he'd followed suit on the "gates" call, and he was closing on Pax.

"Coming left, Lobo. Hard!" Pax called and strained to see through the low haze toward Haiphong.

It has to be coming from Haiphong—has to be.

He knew staying alive demanded he displace his F-8 perpendicular to the SAM's flight path—as much as possible, as fast as possible—but timing the move was critical, a relative motion problem. He won or lost on those judgments everyday.

He saw both fiery plumes a couple seconds before the missiles took shape.

Jesus! They're heading at me.

"Going down, Lobo!" he called . . . and that he did, in sort of an inverted barrel roll. Of two considerations: saving his own bacon, or giving Bud enough slack so he could stay with him . . . well, Pax eased his pull a tad after both missiles exploded beyond them. He didn't hear the SAMs explode, nor was he aware when his SAM warning light went out.

And he left the afterburner engaged—this time—pulling into a climbing left turn, then felt a shiver of relief when Bud's F-8 pulled to the inside of the turn.

"Six clear, Lobo," Bud called.

Before Pax could respond, the flashing SAM light's Deedle! Deedle! Deedle! Deedle! chilled his spine again. He shot another glance at the threat indicator: a bicycle wheel—spokes around the clock. "Lobo, come right!" he called.

"Lobo, high SAM alert!" Bud called.

"Roger, no joy," Pax called. Deedle! Deedle! Deedle! Deedle! screeched through his ears . . . drilled into his brain. The SAM threat light looked much brighter. He saw no plumes; he saw no missiles, yet the indicator was full of spokes. Long spokes. Deedle! Deedle! came louder, but he could not spot the approaching SAMs. Kaboom! He heard it, felt it, and saw a red-orange bloom fill his mirrors.

Whew. A miss—I think.

"Deedle! Deedle! Deedle!" continued.

"Lobo, another one's coming!" Bud called.

"Roger." But Pax couldn't see anything. The flashing SAM light drove him through a series of sweeping barrel rolls that required afterburner to maintain adequate maneuvering energy, and even with the burner each barrel roll cost him 2,000-feet.

The next explosion was close aboard the inside of his rolling radius. He felt something . . . like a handful of BB shot, or gravel, pepper his wings or fuselage somewhere aft of the cockpit. He scanned the engine instruments—okay.

A continuing Deedle! Deedle! Deedle! drove its message home. Sweat poured into Pax's eyes, making the garish SAM light painful to watch. His right arm ached from maintaining the high "G"s, and his parched throat almost gagged him. He couldn't see Bud nor could he see the next SAM, but his cockpit tattletale screamed that *at least* one more was inbound.

The next two explosions weren't quite so close, but they worried him more.

Had Bud been hit?

Even below 3,000-feet the terror persisted. Deedle! Deedle! Deedle! pierced his soul. He slapped desperately at the flashing-red light, hoping it was stuck. It wasn't. Two more explosions, both jarred his F-8.

Oh, shit; this is it.

Below 1,000-feet now, Pax prayed to clear a looming ridge. By an eyelash he did, and descended into and perpendicular to a shallow valley. Even in afterburner, his airspeed had bled to 180-knots. He jerked the unlocking lever, raised the wing, and eased in forward stick—as much as he dared—trying to accelerate faster.

I need speed, altitude, and the-hell-outta-here.

"Lobo, how do you read?" Pax called. Nothing.

Some section leader I am.

Deedle! Deedle! Deedle! Deedle! The terrifying death-warble again.

I'm at 200-knots, with 1,500-feet, and my fucking wing's up. Bullshit! Where's a missile comin' from?

But he spotted them: two of the dust-blowingest, fire-trailingest, blackest SAMs in North Vietnam. They were in trail—one behind the other—and they were accelerating almost parallel to the valley floor. Their projected path might well ram his cockpit.

Time slowed to a crawl. He couldn't go lower, the other side of the valley was starting to climb in front of him, and he didn't have enough speed to turn much. But he eased a little right aileron into the missiles. The rattlesnake-ugly SAMs kept porpoising up the valley, ever faster.

How fucking big can they get? I'm gonna die to the most god-awful sound on earth.

171

Deedle! Deedle! Deedle! Deedle! savaged his ears.

The lead SAM's nose cone, now grown the size of an Atlas rocket, boresighted him.

Half a heartbeat to live. Adios.

He closed his eyes, held his breath, and felt a violent bounce, then another. Nothing more.

Did it happen?

Two rapid explosions to his immediate left shook him from death's grasp.

They missed! I'm alive! I'm fucking alive and breathing, and my plane's still flying. The bastards missed me. Hot damn!

He lowered his two-position wing, locked it, and accelerated on the deck. In a gradual right turn, he clicked the guard receiver back on . . . listening for an emergency beeper. He topped the same ridge at 500-knots, searched ahead and both sides for smoke, and accelerated clear to the coastline. He doubted any Crusader had ever gone feet-wet faster.

The engine showed no trauma. And fuel? How the hell could he have so much fuel? He tapped the clock, checked it against his watch, and realized his SAM circus had lasted less than six minutes.

Now what's happened to Bud? How the hell can I explain not knowing when—or even if—my wingman got hit? Or went down? Or had a good chute? Or got captured? I didn't see anything or hear anything. Hell, I wasn't even listening on guard frequency.

Sally's unsummoned image wore an unbelieving frown.

I won't ask Red Crown if Bud called feet-wet. Hell, we're supposed to be together. Nor will I check-in with Trojan until I get to the ship. There's a chance Bud made it and will be waiting for me overhead the ship. It'll be a miracle, but it wouldn't be the day's first.

And there he orbited—overhead the ship—right where Pax prayed he'd be. As Bud slid into position, he motioned wiping sweat from his brow, and tapped the side of his helmet and his nose . . . followed by a thumbs down. He'd had a radio failure. Pax nodded and answered with a thumbs up.

After landing, Pax walked around his F-8. The air-frames chief had a grease pencil, circling a dozen or so dime-sized perforations in the horizontal tail.

"No sweat, Lieutenant," the chief said. "It'll be back in the air on the next cycle."

The whispering buzz in Strike Operations ceased when CAG Dengler entered. Pax had squeezed through the hatch a few seconds before him, and hadn't seen a seat, so he stood at the rear of the briefing area.

Each bomber section evaluated their own runs; some leaders reported target hits by preceding sections. Estimates would be confirmed or refuted by RF-8A bomb damage assessment photography. CAG thought the strike went well—considering the visibility— but before leaving he asked, "Any aircraft damage?"

Pax raised his hand. "Lobo flight, CAG; I had a few small hits on the horizontal stabilizers."

"You were TARCAP. From what?"

"A SAM, sir."

Dengler wrinkled his face. "No SAMs fired at the *strike*. Were you out trolling for MiGs?"

"No, sir. We followed you out. The first SAM came at us from Haiphong."

"Did you say *first*?"

"Yes, sir. There were more."

CAG smiled. "Was that before or after you tried to bag the Phantoms?" Dengler spun away, harrumphed, and strode from the room. There weren't even any nervous titters.

CDR Milano beckoned at Pax, walked him to a couple of chairs in the corner, and shook his head. "Don't let him get to you. What'd the Phantoms look like?"

"Camouflaged, dark colors. They were haulin' ass toward Haiphong, right on the deck. . . . And before I forget, Bud flew a good combat wing. I'd take him anywhere."

"He's impressed us, too. How many SAMs?"

Pax's short, bark-like laugh came from nerves. "I don't know. Too fucking many. Over ten . . . less than thirty, maybe. After so many, with a lot of them close together, you lose count."

Milano threw his head back and laughed. "Good ole CAG saved me from myself. It could have been us up there."

When Milano left, Bud came and stood in front of Pax's chair, shaking his head. "I'm sorry I lost you; I thought you exploded. My radio crapped out; the thing that kept working was that high SAM screech. I ended up in the weeds by myself." Bud shrugged. "So I hauled ass."

"You did exactly what you should've done . . . what I would've done," Pax said. "You didn't miss a thing. Cross my heart."

Pax finished brushing his teeth and turned out the light over the sink. From the bottom rack, Hacksaw's soft Mississippi drawl pushed out the slow question, "Roomie, was you scared shitless?"

"Worse than that . . . and, pardner, I don't know if the devil yodels or not. But *if* he does, I'm pretty damned sure what it sounds like."

Chapter 19—EBONIST

Pax and Tom Cain sat drinking coffee in the wardroom when Hacksaw joined them. "Hey, Ahab," he said and extended his hand to Tom. "I'm Hacksaw Grayson."

"Tom Cain, Commander."

"Tom and I recruited together at Olathe," Pax said. "He's in VA-136."

"Speaking of which," Tom said and stood, "excuse me; I need to get back to work. Glad to meet you, Commander."

Hacksaw stretched and yawned. "Roomie, these damned bridge watches might be more than I bargained for. I feel like a zombie."

"I'll never know why you're doing that. I don't even understand why the skipper's *letting* you do it. Isn't combat challenge enough?"

"You may be right, but if I can get my *officer of the deck, underway* ticket punched, it might save me a shipboard tour of duty—maybe."

Pax shook his head.

Hacksaw raised his chin toward the door Tom had disappeared through. "You know about him?"

"I guess not. What?"

Hacksaw leaned closer and spoke softly, "Won't go over the beach; they're shippin' him home."

Pax frowned. "How do *you* know that?"

"His skipper, Commander Goodwin, told me. Three different flights, right to the coastline, and turned back . . . *engine* malfunctions. Maintenance folks couldn't duplicate the problems on the deck. Two days ago, Cain told the skipper he couldn't do it. Too scared, and he dropped his wings on Goodwin's desk."

Pax sucked air, and blew it out in a prolonged sigh. "I know Goodwin from way back, but we're not what you'd call friends. I noticed Tom wasn't wearing wings, but the shirt was clean . . . no holes. I figured he forgot 'em. . . . Anyway, it's not that tough to *get* scared out here."

"Yeah, I saw your bird; that'd keep me puckered a day or two." Grayson tilted his chair backwards, looked at the overhead and chuckled. "If you wanted to see a couple of pissed off fighter pilots yesterday, you shoulda seen Motel and Buckshot when they got back to the ready room after both their planes went down. We heard in Strike Ops when you called those bogies. Where the *hell* were the MiGs?"

Pax shrugged. "Who knows? But I'll tell you this: If I'd been a MiG driver yesterday with *any* idea of how damned many SAMs were about to get launched, you couldn't've got me airborne with dynamite."

The Mississippian's grin widened. "Bud was down looking at your Swiss-cheesed tail. Said 'tween the SAMs and your maneuvering, he got slung off, lost his radio, and couldn't find you . . . came out alone."

"Wasn't his fault," Pax said. "Third or fourth missile brushin' by sorta torqued me into unbalanced-corkscrew mode."

"I hear that." Hacksaw's smile vanished. "Bud said CAG got nasty in debrief. For what?"

"He must have found my aircraft recognition lacking. I thought he was going to tell me that North Vietnam didn't *have* any Phantoms."

"How about accusing you of trolling for MiGs?"

Pax stood and stretched. "You and Bud had a hell of a conversation."

Hacksaw also stood. "That didn't come from Bud. CDR Milano looked at your plane, too; he told me . . . said it was horseshit and uncalled for. He was steamed. I'm gonna mention it to the skipper."

Pax pursed his lips and shook his head. "Don't do that . . . please. Dodd's in the doghouse over that cigarette deal. There's not a lot he can do. Okay?"

Grayson cocked his head. "You sure?"

Pax nodded once.

Pax's 2400 wake-up call came ten minutes late, so chow trumped shaving. He splashed water on his face, climbed into his green flight-suit, and felt his way along the dim passageways toward the flight-suits-only "dirty-neck" wardroom.

Carrying a plate of eggs and bacon from the serving line, Pax spotted Tom Weaver and Chris Nixon already eating. Weaver waved.

"I wouldn't think the maintenance officer's flight needed a spare," Pax said.

Weaver smiled and pointed a finger at Pax. "You're right; we won't, but we do like good company for breakfast . . . at whatever hour."

"Hear about the MiGs?" Nixon asked.

Pax shook his head. "Uh-uh."

"Yesterday an *Oriskany* F-8 got a MiG-21," Nixon said. "And—you ready for this?—an *Intrepid* Skyraider driver bagged a MiG-17 north of Thanh Hoa during a ResCap."

"We must not be living right," Pax said.

A Filipino steward refilled their coffee cups, left the carafe, and removed Weaver and Nixon's empty plates.

Weaver pushed back his chair and stood. "At least MiGs are flying; we have a chance. Nature calls. See you in the ready room."

Weaver briefed the 0200 Lobo mission: a normal barrier combat air patrol. Pax yawned, but nothing seemed normal to him about flying racetrack patterns 200-miles from an aircraft carrier in the middle of an ocean in the middle of the night. The meteorologists lent little humor to their 0030 briefing: both the 1,300-foot overcast and scattered rain showers were expected to persist through their 0345 landing time.

Pax translated those sterile numbers into everyday pilots' vernacular: *It'll be pitch-black under the low overcast on final approach—no moon, no stars, and no horizon.*

And his *for-real*, scheduled follow-on flight's 0515 recovery would be no better.

The squawk-box over the duty officer's desk came to life. "Pilots for the 0200 launch man your aircraft."

The ready room SDOs acknowledged in order, "Ready One, aye; Ready Two, aye; Ready Three, aye. . . ."

The three Lobo pilots, wearing their chaps-like anti-G leggings, torso-harnesses, and survival vests, filed from the ready room carrying their helmet bags.

"Ahab, you've missed some sleep for nothing," Weaver said, "but we appreciate your manning the spare."

Pax reached to pat Weaver's back. "Yeah, you could be right, but there's something magical about looking for an airplane on a black-assed flight deck—I can't stay away."

My odds of getting airborne on this flight are about one-in-four. And that one chance will come from a legitimate mechanical gripe on either Weaver's or Nixon's aircraft, because Crusader drivers fly their flights—especially night, crappy-weather flights. Pride demands it; I like that.

The flight deck glistened with damp reflections of flashlight beams, and the refreshing salt smell braced Pax for a rapid preflight. He looked up from completing his systems' checks, when a yellow-jerseyed taxi director jogged to his plane, signaled him to hold his brakes, and had his plane captain start breaking loose the tie-down chains.

So much for predicting the odds.

Weaver and Pax, following amber-lighted signal wands, taxied past the island structure—faintly washed by low-powered and diffused red floodlights—toward the forward, starboard catapult. Weaver got positioned first. As his nose gear dropped over the catapult shuttle, a canted slab of jet blast deflector thrust up from the deck behind his F-8. And that JBD provided Pax's intake its protection from Weaver's tailpipe.

Thunderous vibrations from Weaver's full-power engine check shook Pax's aircraft, and the searing exhaust gases, as usual, overpowered Pax's air-conditioning system. His idling engine's attempt to provide "conditioned" air couldn't hack it. And even though he sucked one hundred percent oxygen, Pax's stinging eyes welled from Weaver's F-8's acrid exhaust contaminants.

Pax watched Weaver's control surfaces waggle full-throw in both directions, completing his final checks. And when Weaver's external navigation lights came on: he affirmed to the world that his Crusader was ready to fly. The catapult officer, left and forward of Weaver's wingtip, made a final check toward the bow, leaned forward into the thirty-knot wind, and touched the flight deck with his green signal wand. A two and a half potato count later, the steam catapult's ram propelled the F-8 down the shuttle track and into the air. The whole aircraft carrier shuddered when the catapult ram slammed into its water brake.

Steam from the catapult track hid the taxi director's amber wands for a few seconds. But they reappeared and coaxed Pax toward a shuttle he could not see but that his nose gear had to ease up and over. He spread and locked his wings, aligning down the catapult track and nodded acknowledgment to his plane captain's final signal that told Pax the wing-lock flags were out of sight. He recognized the wand motions that urged him forward. That particular taxi director could spot an F-8's nose gear on a dime in a typhoon—a priceless talent.

Pax's nose gear eased over the shuttle. The faint, but discernable "clunk" which followed meant the holdback fitting was taut. His director swept both amber wands into the "tension" signal, which told Pax to drop both heels to the deck (releasing his toe-brakes) and go full-throttle. The director pointed both wands forward, passing control to the catapult officer, whose green wand was extended over his head. That vertical wand began rotating like a small merry-go-round. The engine gauges spun up to expected values while Pax flexed his flight controls through full deflection with the control stick and rudder pedals. They tested good. Pax regripped the throttle, squeezing it tight against its catapult-lock and switched on his external navigation lights.

From the time the catapult officer's wand touched the flight deck, Pax knew that he had about two seconds before the catapult's forward thrust would jam him aft into his seat-back. At the end of the catapult stroke, beyond the carrier's bow, Pax would slice into an inkwell. He pressed his helmet backward, snug against the headrest, and focused his eyes on the attitude-gyro. Nose position and wing-bank-angle information—critical knowledge for staying alive—would come from that instrument. He had heard pilots confess to sweet-talking their attitude-gyros before a night cat-shot.

Potato number two had become history, when a sudden torch-like heat seared Pax's neck. Scorching hot air blew from both sides of the cockpit. A fraction of a second from a night catapult shot doesn't allow adjusting or securing offending equipment. The imminent catapult stroke held him an immobile hostage. Neck skin burned. Pax's hands were full of throttle and control stick. The adrenaline surge slowed time. Portions of a second became relative.

How long before neck skin chars black?

At last, the catapult fired; it brought no relief. The searing blasts against both sides of Pax's neck turned his gasp into something he'd never heard. But clearing the catapult's viselike grip did let him scrunch below the canopy-sill nozzles, while he raised the landing gear and lowered the wing . . . while switching hands on the control stick as he attempted to lower the temperature rheostat. No dice. He turned cockpit pressurization off. Cockpit smoke—and pain—had tears streaming down his oxygen mask. He twisted the knob at his right elbow to get the ram-air vent open. Things were going to hell fast; he needed relief. Now!

External air . . . blessed, cool, external air displaced the super-heated, acrid fumes. Pax removed a flight glove to explore his neck. In doing so, he brushed a knuckle against a parachute harness buckle that remained stove-hot. His neck felt damp and was painful to the touch. The right side hurt most.

The emergency strobe light, sewn on the left shoulder of my torso-harness, must've deflected some of the blast.

No one but Pax knew of his problem in Lobo 403, but he felt he had it under control. Even before he got comfortable in his cooling cockpit, however, something else spiked his heart. The runaway air-conditioning had charred the entire cockpit Plexiglas and windscreen. Outside of the cockpit he could see nothing. No red or green wingtip lights or anti-collision light reflected from clouds. Nothing.

As if inside a Link trainer, Pax climbed toward the rendezvous point evaluating his situation. He must see to land, either ashore or back aboard. Period. And approaching rendezvous altitude, it occurred to him that landing was not unique in that need. He held Weaver on radar, but joining in formation was not an option—at least with Weaver leading.

How hot had it been? Neck burning hot, for sure, but how bad did the canopy scorch?

Expecting a rough surface, Pax touched the canopy. A slick film smeared under his glove. Oil! Not charred, but covered with oil. For the second time in five minutes, Pax sagged with relief. He jerked a handkerchief from a zippered pocket and wiped everywhere he could reach. As he leveled off, small peepholes got larger, and stars winked at him . . . as if they'd been in on the *jokes.*

Pax skimmed over a layer of clouds at 20,000-feet. He held Weaver ten degrees right, at two miles, on radar. He closed to one mile before he saw him and joined on his wing. Headed north, to a Red Crown-controlled CAP station, Pax had Weaver switch his radio to Lobo squadron tactical frequency.

"Roger, Ahab, whatcha got?"

"My air-conditioner went full-hot. The rheostat wouldn't work—in AUTO or MANUAL—so I secured pressurization."

"Roger, Lobo switching back to Red Crown."

A few minutes short of halfway through the flight, Pax's cool cockpit had turned cold. He twisted the ram-air vent knob closed. And noticed the fuel gauge.

"Lobo, switch tactical," he called.

"Roger, Ahab, what's cookin'?"

"I've been asleep, Needle. My main fuel gauge is down to 1,500-pounds. With no pressurization, my wing fuel's trapped."

"Can't you put up with a little heat till you transfer your fuel?"

"No way! If I have to, I'll jettison the canopy before turning the pressurization on. Should we head south?"

"Have you tried the pressurization on with your ram-air vent open?"

"Wait one." Pax opened the vent knob again, ran his seat full-down, and flicked the pressurization switch ON. Blowtorch! Switch back to OFF. "Fuck that! It's like a flamethrower and it spews oil on the canopy."

"Hold on, Ahab. On your left console, there's a safety-wired switch . . . behind your wing-lock handle. See it? Feel it?"

"Yeah. . . . And?"

"If you break that safety-wire and move the switch aft, to COOL, and turn your pressurization back on, you should be able to transfer wing fuel without getting heat into the cockpit."

"Break the safety-wire. Switch to COOL. Okay, I've done that. Here goes the pressurization . . . no heat; that's good."

"Any transfer?" Weaver asked.

"Not yet. I'm a tad under 1,400-pounds."

"We better head back, Ahab."

"Wait one, Needle. There—it kicked. I'm back to 1,500 pounds and it's climbing. Good on you, mister maintenance man."

"Ahab, switch back to Red Crown; you've got the lead."

Pax switched frequencies and checked back in. "Red Crown, Lobos back your freq; Four Zero Three has the lead."

"Roger, Lobo Four Zero Three. Red Crown holds you on station."

Pax engaged auto-pilot. By unhooking his shoulder harness fittings, he reached forward enough to remove the gun sight glass. He almost started cleaning it with his spare handkerchief, but he didn't. Instead, he removed his glasses and wiped them clean. He put the gun-sight glass in a leg pocket of his anti-g suit. He doubted he'd be firing at anything. And by releasing his lap belt buckles, he inched forward and wiped as far down the windscreen as he could—about halfway. It was the best he could do. He buckled himself back to the ejection seat and his parachute.

As soon as their relief, a Sea Bat section, checked in, Red Crown vectored the Lobos back toward *Gettysburg*. As briefed, Pax retained the lead headed back toward the ship. He and Needle Weaver would stay together through their descent until the controller separated them for individual approaches.

But about 60-miles from the ship, Pax's TACAN lost the ship's signal. "Needle, how's your TACAN?" Pax asked.

"Solid," Weaver said.

"Roger, you've got the lead."

"I've got it."

"Lobo Four Zero Nine, Trojan Approach, understand you have the lead."

"Affirmative, Trojan," Weaver called.

"Trojan holds the Lobos three-five-five at fifty."

"Four Zero Nine, concur."

"Lobo Four Zero Nine, your signal is Charlie on arrival."

"Roger, Trojan. Lobos are out of angels twenty for two point five." Weaver called and lowered his tailhook.

Pax lowered his as well. They checked each other's hook and exchanged double mike clicks (a nighttime thumbs up).

Good. The other planes will be on deck by the time we get there. Should I open the ram-air vent again? Probably. Else the inside of the canopy might fog over.

He twisted it open.

"Lobos, continue descent to angels one point two. Altimeter setting: two niner niner six. Come starboard, heading two-six-five. Report passing angels three point zero. Over." The controller's rapid directions painted a vivid picture: Trojan had a ready deck; where the hell were the fighters?

"Roger, Trojan. Lobos coming starboard to two-six-five, altimeter two niner niner six. Passing angels three for one point two." Weaver's transmissions came short and crisp.

They descended clear of clouds. "Trojan, Lobos level at one point two." Weaver called.

Pax felt like they were in a bank, but a quick peek at the attitude-gyro showed wings-level. And so far his canopy hadn't fogged.

"Lobo Four Zero Three, radar contact at ten miles, slow to landing speed. Over."

Pax extended his speed brake and retarded the throttle. "Trojan, Four Zero Three slowing," he called. At 200-knots, he lowered the landing gear and raised the wing. He knew that Weaver had continued inbound at 250-knots, gaining separation before the controller would slow him, also. But that was outside Pax's cockpit. For now—the next few minutes—his entire world consisted of a few instruments that fed him survival plasma: heading, altitude, and airspeed. He trimmed level at 1,200-feet, an on-speed indexer donut at 139-knots, engaged the auto-throttle, and followed the controller's heading commands.

Pax thought he recognized the voice, and after a couple of heading corrections he was sure. Good. The blacker the night, the more important a confident controller. And given an experienced one and good instruments,

Pax knew the final dance down an approach corridor could rival any Olympic event.

"Lobo Four Zero Three, this is your final controller. I have you radar contact at three miles; do not acknowledge further transmissions. Come left heading two-six-four; maintain twelve hundred feet. You are on centerline and approaching glidepath from below. Lobo Four Zero Three, commence normal rate of descent."

Pax eased the stick forward a smidge and waited to see the vertical speed needle settle. The controller had reported two and a half miles of visibility, so Pax began adding quick, forward glances through-the-windscreen, to his instrument scan. At two miles, he began to see a blur on the oily windscreen's bottom half. At one and a half miles, the blur had climbed halfway up the oily section.

C'mon lights. Move it!

"Lobo Four Zero Three, you are drifting slightly left of centerline and dropping slightly below glidepath. Come right two degrees, heading two-six-six."

Pax eased the stick back a couple of inches, sinking the blur half an inch lower into the oily section.

"Lobo Four Zero Three, you are back on centerline, but still below glidepath approaching three-quarters of a mile. Come left heading two-six-five. Call the ball."

The blur remained under the top edge of the windscreen's oily section. "Four Zero Three," Pax said, "Crusader—Clara (I can't see the ball)—two point eight—auto."

"Roger, Clara, Four Zero Three. You're drifting a little left and going a little low. Get it back up on glidepath," the LSO called.

At one-half mile, Trojan's runway deck-lighting and Fresnel lens eased above the smear line of Pax's windscreen. The glide slope "meatball" was turning cherry-red. He was indeed low.

"Gimme some power, Four Zero Three. You're low. Power . . . Power! Power!" the LSO shouted.

Pax jammed on too much power and climbed through the glide slope.

"Don't climb through it," the LSO called . . . after the fact.

Pax landed long, beyond the last arresting cable.

"Bolter! Bolter! Bolter!" the LSO called.

Pax added full power, gritted his teeth, and hurtled off the angled deck, back into the black, velvety nothingness. He would have transitioned to instruments for his missed approach, but when he glanced down for old faithful—the attitude-gyro—his lights flicked off and his radio died.

Chapter 20—ALL IN A NIGHT'S WORK

Low overcast and drizzle obscured stars and the sliver of waning moon as USS *Gettysburg* (CVA-35) plowed through the Tonkin Gulf. Plane captains chaining their aircraft to pad-eyes in the flight deck shied clear of deck-edge scuppers, beyond which, absolute blackness swallowed everything. Coming dawn would mark 10 October 1966.

One level below the flight deck, in the air operations spaces, nerves tightened . . . awaiting "the call." This seaborne air control center operated in perpetual dimness behind a heavy metal hatch. Galaxies of red and amber dial lights surrounded rows of individual radar-repeaters. Faintly-lit, wiper-like sweeps crossed greenish, phosphorescent screens illuminating damp, attentive faces. Other profiles formed and faded, from chain-smoked cigarette glows and ebbs. Terse questions begat brief, precise responses.

From a squawk-box, Captain "Corky" Conrad's rasping voice speared the silence. "Where the hell are the goddamned fighters?"

Slender, sandy-haired LCDR Bob Wright, the carrier air traffic control officer, stabbed the box transmit lever. "Eight miles out, Captain." He settled an expressionless stare on the air wing commander. But the blank look fooled few workers in the space. CAG Andrew Dengler knew that Wright's gaze gouged him with the same query: "Where the hell are *your* goddamned fighters, CAG?"

CDR Dengler's squinting eyes and nodding head promised that someone's ass would be had as soon as the recovery was over. The other planes had already landed; extra time into-the-wind for an aircraft carrier revealed sloppy airmanship. And that reflected poorly on the air wing commander. The tall, raw-boned CDR's Nomex flight suit had dark, sweat-soaked stains and white, salt-dried splotches from his completed flight. He had not earned the call sign "Thunder" by being timid. Yes, he would have someone's ass for this.

Again the squawk-box spoke: "Air-Ops, this is the captain. If CAG's down there, have him give me a call. Now!"

"Yessir, Captain," Wright said. His short-sleeved khaki shirt's underarms also bore growing damp patches, but his face remained mannequin-blank.

After dialing the bridge, CAG Dengler edged as far away from Wright's desk as the handset-cord would allow. "Captain, this is CAG. . . . Yes, sir. . . . I agree, sir. . . . I will, sir. . . . Yessir, Captain. . . . Yessir, I understand, sir. . . . Aye, aye, sir. . . . Thank you, Captain."

Dengler's ears turned red; he imagined sneering thoughts behind each dead pan in the room. By the time he regained his designated chair, CAG's entire face had darkened to full blush. Because he alone knew that his "Thank you, Captain," was spoken considerably after an irate Conrad had already slammed his handset into its cradle. Yes, by God, he was going to enjoy reaming some fighter squadron commanding officer's ass as soon as those unpunctual fighters trapped.

One of the air-ops sound-powered phone talkers covered his mouthpiece and relayed to LCDR Wright, "Commander, LSO says visibility is dog-shit; he can't see the plane-guard helo half the time."

"Roger, Airman Davis," Wright acknowledged. "CAG, your landing signal officer sounds unhappy with the weather. And Da Nang remains socked in."

Cutting through the smoky and dimly-lit nerve center for night operations, a final approach controller's litany fed through overhead speakers: "Lobo Four Zero Nine, radar contact at 4½ miles. Come left heading two-six-five; report gear down-and-locked."

"Lobo Four Zero Nine, 1,200-feet, steady two-six-five, gear down-and-locked, state two-point-nine," came the reply.

Petty Officer Smith, behind the lighted Plexiglas status-board, wiped away an earlier reported fuel figure and with a black grease pencil wrote two-point-nine backwards, next to the backward—from his view—four zero nine. He dipped his damp forehead for a quick wipe against a sleeve of his chambray uniform shirt.

From the speakers: "Lobo Four Zero Nine, this is your final controller. I have you radar contact at three and one-half miles; do not acknowledge further transmissions. Come left to heading two-six-three; maintain twelve hundred feet."

CDR "Banjo" Ballard, *Gettysburg*'s operations officer, appeared at CAG's elbow. "Holy shit, CAG, keep your fingers crossed for these fighter-jocks. The old man's running out of sea room; a bolter will set his hair on fire. He's been tearing the 'gator a new one."

Dengler envisioned the navigator wilting under CAPT Conrad's tirade, but there was little CAG could do about it. He sure as hell didn't feel like crossing his fingers. Somewhere on the ship, however, some fighter squadron CO had damned-well better be crossing his fingers.

Again from the speakers: "Lobo Four Zero Nine, you are on centerline and on glide slope at three-quarters of a mile. Call the ball."

"Lobo Four Zero Nine, Crusader, Clara, Paddles."

"Shit, CAG! He can't even see the ship," Banjo said, rubbing both hands over his hairless head.

From the speakers: "Tallyho, Four Zero Nine. This is paddles. Keep it coming; don't level off. Come a little right; that's it. Now, back left . . . ten-degrees."

"Lobo Four Zero Nine, ball, two-point-seven," reported the pilot.

"Whew," CAG said, blowing out a huge breath.

Petty Officer Smith replaced the backward two-point-nine with two-point-seven on his board.

From the speakers: "Roger, ball. Don't settle Four Zero Nine. Gimme a little power. Power . . . POWER! Don't climb through it. . . . Bolter! Bolter! Bolter!"

Roar from the Crusader's powerful Pratt and Whitney J57 and the metallic twang of the empty tailhook scraping down the angled deck filled the air-ops space.

"Shit," Banjo said. "We didn't need that."

Dengler reconsidered crossing his fingers.

The squawk-box blast surprised no one. "Air-Ops, tell CAG to talk to his LSO. I need those fighters aboard ASAP. I'm runnin' out of sea room. Do you hear me?"

LCDR Wright jabbed the transmit lever down without looking at it. "Aye, aye, Captain."

CAG lunged from his chair, pointed at Airman Davis, and asked LCDR Wright if he could borrow the talker's sound-powered phone. Davis handed CAG the mouthpiece and earphones.

From the speakers: "Lobo Four Zero Three, this is your final controller. I have you radar contact at three miles; do not acknowledge further transmissions. Come left heading two-six-four; maintain twelve hundred feet. You are on centerline and approaching glide path from below. Lobo Four Zero Three, commence normal rate of descent."

Dengler gave the talker back his equipment and regained his chair.

"CAG, are those fighter-jocks any good?" Banjo asked. "We gotta get 'em aboard."

The phone talker passed new information: "Commander Wright, LSO says we're out of the drizzle; visibility's better."

"Banjo, that was the squadron maintenance officer on the bolter. He's steady; I'll check on the wingman," CAG said and turned toward Hacksaw Grayson, the Lobo ops officer who stood talking to Bob Wright. CAG caught Grayson's attention, beckoned him over and asked, "Hacksaw, who—"

From the speakers: "Lobo Four Zero Three, you are drifting slightly left of centerline and dropping slightly below glidepath. Come right, heading two-six-six."

CAG put his hand on Hacksaw's shoulder and pointed at the status board. "What kind of pilot is Langford in Four Zero Three?"

"Good, CAG; he'll get aboard first pass."

Banjo heard, shrugged his shoulders at CAG, exaggerated crossing two fingers on each hand, and went eye-level with both pretzel-like offerings to the flight-gods.

From the speakers: "Lobo Four Zero Three, you are back on centerline, but still below glidepath approaching three-quarters of a mile. Come left heading two-six-five. Call the ball."

"Lobo Four Zero Three, Crusader, Clara, two-point-eight."

"Roger, Clara, Four Zero Three. You're drifting a little left and going a little low. Get it back up on glidepath . . . gimme some power, Four Zero Three. You're low. Power . . . Power! Power! Don't climb through it. . . . Bolter! Bolter! Bolter!"

Again, the engine roar and empty tailhook's scraping confirmed the bad news.

"Shit," Banjo said in a prolonged moan.

CAG, Banjo, and Bob Wright stared at the dreaded squawk-box. They knew what was coming—they thought.

The speakers boomed with a new voice: "Crusader off the angled deck . . . your lights are out. Lobo Four Zero Three, this is Trojan; turn your lights back on. Lobo Four Zero Three, if you read Trojan, turn on your external lights."

The insistent voice belonged to the air operations officer in primary flight control, the elevated control tower. That same voice startled LCDR Wright from the squawk-box: "Air-Ops, Pri-Fly, we've lost him; his lights went out as he left the deck. Do you have him on radar?"

"Not yet, Commander!" a controller shouted. "I've got no parrot on him;

he's too close for a skin-paint."

Bob Wright relayed the info: "No, Commander: no IFF; too close for radar contact. Sounds electrical. We'll tell you when we get him on radar."

Hacksaw arched his eyebrows and stabbed a finger toward Wright's phone; Wright nodded. The Mississippian dialed while he sucked his teeth. He painted a quick picture: "Skipper, Hacksaw in air-ops. Langford lost his electrical power on a bolter. Ship's not painting him yet. . . . Roger."

Clocks measure time, as do hourglasses and sundials, but some timespans defy measurement. Consider the "instant." A fleeting span, for sure . . . but measurable? And if not, why not? Because too many trustworthy people have reported having entire lives flash across a *memory-screen* during a life-or-death instant. They do not exaggerate. Extreme stress and associated adrenaline surges produce mental gymnastics that transcend mankind's limited understanding.

A normal night carrier landing puts a pretty good whipping on a pair of adrenal glands. Throw in abnormalities . . . say, a burned neck and less than a full windscreen to work with—contributing to a less than sterling approach—and those glands churn toward maximum production. Chunk a bolter into the cauldron and adrenaline flow nudges past its redline. But when the flight-gods are on a nasty roll . . . "Well, hell, shut off his lights and kill his radio!"

Pax didn't hear any flight-gods' dicta, but when the cockpit went black and silent—except for the engine's scream—his entire world went black and silent too. He had his *instant*. And as before, with his life on the line, an unexplained pounding filled his head, much as the bass drumbeat of poolside speakers had done, when—as a kid—he had swum underwater at municipal pools.

An indefinable, but demon-filled interval passed, during which, Pax's tortured mind fought with everything available to deny what had happened. And from unplumbed, visceral depths, his supercharged eloquence exploded with a close-snake-sighting scream: "A-a-a-a-r-r-r-g-g-g-h-h-h!"

The scream acknowledged grim reality in an unfair world, but it also spurred lightning-quick reactions. Pax's blind fingers sped to the master generator switch: OFF/RESET and back to ON. Nothing! He pulled it back OFF, yanked the emergency power handle, waited a lifetime—perhaps two heartbeats—and pulled the emergency generator switch aft to the LAND position. Nothing! He jammed and pulled the two electrical switches through every position combination, hoping somehow for a lucky mix.

Absolutely fucking nothing!

He grasped the goose-necked flashlight strapped to his chest and thumbed it ON. Eureka! But the flashlight beam illuminated OFF-flags grinning at him from useless instrument housings.

During these frantic attempts to restore a heartbeat in his electrical system, even swapping hands on the control stick while getting at switches and the emergency ram air turbine handle, Pax tried to maintain wings-level from memory of what the flight deck had looked like—a lifetime ago—when he had boltered from it.

Fuck it! How can you fly a Crusader with an airspeed indicator, altimeter, and needle-ball, below 500-feet over the ocean, at night, by flashlight? No way. I'm shuckin' outta here.

Pax reached up for the ejection-seat face-curtain.

Why didn't I do it right off the angled deck?

But a gnawing doubt delayed his ejection pull.

Where am I? Drifting right? I might be dead ahead of the ship.

Horror stories about pilots being run over by their own ship flashed through his mind. His flustered brain was at loggerheads.

Can a person's mind pop a circuit breaker?

A flicker. One speck of red to his left . . . in a canopy rim mirror. Jesus! He banked hard to the left and pressed his helmet and oxygen mask hard against the left side of the canopy. He released a bayonet clip on his oxygen mask and flipped the oxygen shut-off valve closed.

"Oh, God!" Pax screamed. "The ship! There's the fucking ship! I'm alive, and there's the fucking ship!" He was screaming at himself, but to his ears he sounded calm and rational.

The ship's lights were at his seven-thirty position—45-degrees aft of his left wing. Those precious and lovely lights proved that he was not upside down, or slow, or diving, or even already dead.

Try to keep the ship in sight, stay out of the water, and circle around abeam the ship's starboard side before ejecting.

It was a plan. But instead, he climbed into the nothingness of the overcast.

Whatever ragged smoothness Pax had retained deserted him. He jammed the control stick forward, trying to regain his limited view of *Gettysburg*'s lights. Those lights flashed back into view as he dropped below the overcast, while floating up against his shoulder harness. Leveling off, he slammed back down into his seat.

Fuck finesse! A blind-jammed stick's a well-jammed stick.

A crackle in his earphones, and emergency cockpit lighting started flickering on; OFF-flags began disappearing. An unbidden shudder tinkled like toppling dominoes.

Did I hear my own vertebrae chattering?

"Thank you, God," Pax said and snuffed a lung-full of humid night air.

"Lobo Four Zero Three, this is Trojan on Guard Frequency. If you plan to land this pass, you are high, and you are fast. Over."

The transmission had been rapid; Pax didn't know if it came from a controller or the LSO. Nor did he care. Whoever said it was correct. He had rammed his throttle forward to-the-hilt when he boltered, and nothing in the inkwell that followed had suggested retarding it. He had no idea how fast a Crusader could fly with its wing up and landing gear down, but he knew he'd nudged that number.

"This is Four Zero Three, Trojan. No sweat; I'll make it," he said, jerked the throttle back to idle, and started a couple of speed-killing S-turns approaching the ship's stern. The aggressive maneuvers came easy with so many revived flight instruments. And he saw the entire ship's lights plainly. His fast, nose-low attitude gave him an unobstructed view of the landing area lights, glide slope datum lights, and centerline drop-lights through the clean, upper half of his wind-screen.

But like the man said—he'd been high; he'd been fast. The approach, stillborn from inception, wasn't completely useless, though; it delayed his ejection plan. The top cell of the Fresnel lens appeared a couple of seconds before Pax made what might have been the first idle-throttle, nose-gear-only bolter in F-8 history.

Three things happened almost at the same time: Lobo Four Zero Three bounced back into the air; its lights and radio died again; and after spewing a string of acid-tongued oaths, Pax rammed the throttle forward once more.

Twelve sets of eyes strained toward the air ops TV glide slope monitor and watched the high and fast Lobo F-8 landing attempt. A muffled thump—without an accompanying tailhook scrape—and a delayed engine roar coincided with the air boss's squawk-box report: "He's lost his lights again!"

Banjo Ballard got another "Aw, shit, CAG!" on record before Captain Conrad issued a squawk-box invitation: "CAG to the bridge!"

CAG Dengler's stride left no doubt as to the ship's pecking order. LCDR Wright stabbed the box, "On his way, Captain."

CAG Dengler and CDR Coleman Dodd met in the hatch. "Did Langford land yet?" Dodd asked.

"No, Weaver did, but I can't talk about it now," CAG said and pursued his summons. He fished his fore and aft cap from a zippered flight suit pocket as he took the steps two-at-a-time up the ladders to the bridge.

Is the ship listing?

CAG entered an aft hatch onto the bridge. Captain Conrad's orderly, a marine corporal stationed inside the hatch, came to attention and saluted. "Good morning, Commander," the orderly said, did an about face and took four strides which placed him near the captain's elevated chair. "Captain, Commander Dengler's on the bridge."

Conrad nodded. "Very well."

The corporal glanced at CAG and nodded.

Dengler stopped near Conrad's chair and saluted. "Yes, sir, Captain."

Conrad continued scanning the flight deck and peering into the darkness. "CAG, your fighter pilot's already in deep shit; I'm about to make it deeper. We're damned near out of sea room: my fuck up. As luck would have it, we're making our own wind. Soon as the F-8 left the deck on that last bolter, we came port twenty degrees. We'll do that between each approach until he lands or runs out of fuel. Do you know what's wrong with the plane?"

"It has to be electrical, Captain, but what, we're not sure. The—"

"Who was his wingman?"

"The maintenance officer was leading the section. He'll come to air ops from the ready room; maybe he can tell us something."

"Is that pilot any good?"

"Their ops officer thinks so; Lieutenant Langford's second tour."

Conrad's unfocused gaze aimed past Dengler. "We better pray he's good. This is a shitty night for an electrical failure. I want a full rundown on the problem. Get back and get him aboard."

"Aye, aye, sir," CAG said as he saluted.

"Oh, no," Pax said. "You can fuck me once, but not twice in the same night."

He tried to climb to the left as soon as he cleared the angled deck. The ship's lights reappeared where they should have been.

Okay. A relative motion problem, pure and simple. I have to climb away from the ship to arrive about a mile and a quarter abeam, headed—what the hell was that final inbound heading?—downwind, and setup on airspeed and altitude. Can I do that? Why the hell not?

The pressure instruments, it looked like, would come into play. Pax contrived a ship versus cockpit scan pattern—mostly ship. His mongoose-quick glances into the cockpit focused his flashlight on a single instrument at a time. Ship, ship, and catch the altitude. Ship, ship, and catch the airspeed. Necessity infused a semblance of sanity to the process. But he kept feeling too close aboard and had to take sharp jogs away and right back.

His abeam position, when he got there, didn't look too bad. He arrived sort of on altitude and kind of on airspeed, but he'd yet to find a proper throttle position for maintaining altitude at approach airspeed. And he'd given up early on trying to read the standby magnetic compass by flashlight. Too hard.

While turning into the groove, however, the oily portion of Pax's windscreen came back into play. The devilish game of hide-and-seek resumed: an on-airspeed attitude kept the ship's guiding lights below the windscreen's clear portion; dropping the F-8's nose—for better peeks—got him low and fast. As Pax neared the ship and tried to figure his best move, the LSO's red wave-off lights began to flash.

That sonofabitch is waving me off!

Pax knew that the wave-off—for whatever reason—demanded compliance, but no red cape in bullfighting's long history ever made a bull as mad as those flashing red lights made Pax in his flashlight-lit cockpit. He added full military power and aimed at the ship.

I don't know how much fuel I've got left, but please give me enough to get to that LSO platform. Squeezing that wave-off pickle-switch won't be a freebie; I'll send that quick-triggered sonofabitch a little love note.

Pax's full-powered wave-off passed over the LSO platform's canvas windbreak screen. Even grinding his teeth in raging frustration, a certain satisfaction washed over him. He thumbed the remaining oxygen mask clip loose, let the mask hang to his lap, and shouted, "Reveille, you asshole!"

But as he climbed left again, to regain the ship's lights, he was more-than-a-little-bit sure the electrical failure was shielding his ears from some strong, harsh words.

LCDR Bob Wright's "Holy shit!" pretty well preempted the other slack-jawed observers in air ops. "Davis," he ordered, "ask how close that was to the platform."

Airman Davis had to repeat the question twice into his sound-powered phone, but he looked up grinning. "The platform talker says all the LSOs is in the net."

"Who could doubt it?" Banjo said. "He came close; I mean double-damned, straight razor close."

The squawk-box roared CAPT Conrad's query. "Why the wave-off?"

Bob Wright shrugged at CAG Dengler then answered, "We're checking, Captain."

Airman Davis shed his phone equipment and handed it to Dengler, who relayed the captain's question. After a pause he asked if everyone was okay back there. A lengthier pause and CAG ended the conversation: "Be careful back there, but we do need him aboard."

Banjo Ballard and Bob Wright watched Dengler return the phone apparatus to Airman Davis, and stared him back to his CAG chair. Dengler shook his head and snorted. "Broussard was monitoring the controller's final approach instructions. In his opinion, the approach had gotten dangerous, and Langford had no radio. So Broussard hit the wave-off lights. A few seconds later, Langford chased Broussard, his writer, and two LSO trainees into the safety net. Broussard doesn't think it was accidental; he is one pissed-off LSO."

Wright passed the first part of that information, by squawk-box, to CAPT Conrad.

A soft voice came from behind CAG Dengler: "If that F-8 *can* be landed aboard, Langford will get it done."

Dengler glanced around and recognized Tom Cain, the VA-136 lieutenant who'd turned in his wings. "What makes you say that, Tom?" Dengler asked.

"I've seen him get away with near-impossible things in the air. It's way beyond luck; he's uncanny."

"See me in my office after the recovery," Dengler said. As he swung back toward the glide slope monitor, CAG noticed Hacksaw Grayson frowning after the departing lieutenant.

Pax regained the ship's lights and began angling away again, toward yet another abeam position. His jury-rigged instrument scan almost felt normal. Almost. Ship, ship, and check the airspeed; he decided on 140-knots. Ship, ship, and check the altitude. A loud, self-directed pep talk focused his efforts: "Okay, Pax, you're not scared! You can do this. You're a great instrument pilot. Settle down! Get a perfect starting point, and fly your best approach."

He shouted at himself and flew flashlight-lit, partial-panel instruments. His starting point—abeam the ship—looked about right. But how long had he been flying? How much fuel remained? He knew both answers: too fucking long, and not fucking much. He'd descend slower this time, see the lights without lowering his nose . . . without dropping below the glide slope.

Five hundred feet. I'll maintain five hundred feet until I see the meatball.

Pax turned toward the ship while cross-checking the altimeter and airspeed by flashlight. The unfolding scene—that familiar arcing path into the groove—gave him hope. When he had 90-degrees of turn to go, the ship's guiding lights beckoned him aboard. With 45-degrees to go, he saw the amber meatball and fought a strong urge to start descending. "A ball high," he said. "I'll keep the ball a tad above the datum lights till touchdown."

As Pax watched the red drop-lights near alignment with the flight-deck runway centerline, showing him that he was almost on the final approach bearing, the entire montage—once again—slid behind the oily lower section of his windscreen. "Shit!" he screamed.

He tried to maintain the blurred lights on the same oily spot of the windscreen, but he knew that guaranteed nothing. He stood it as long as he could, and dipped the F-8's nose for a quick peek.

"Oh, shit!"

He'd drifted left and was going low; he was closer to the ship than he'd thought. And the ball had turned red: confirmation that he'd sagged well below glide slope. Again!

Pax added full throttle, pulled the F-8's nose up, and banked to the right—trying to leap back to the landing area's extended centerline. "Don't wave me off, you sonofabitch! Don't wave me off, you sonofabitch!" he screamed at the unhearing LSO.

After a short-lived, but instinctive delay, he banked back left and saw—out the left quarter-panel—an amber meatball climbing through green datum lights. His rough correction had placed him near the extended centerline, yet his F-8's nose pointed 15-degrees right. But that view was his best of the night by a damned sight.

Pax knew that LSOs lived in mortal dread of a pilot doing something stupid after he'd gotten too close to be waved-off. When Pax had added full power and raised the F8's nose, he knew that the LSO—by monitoring the final controller's commentary—had assumed that Pax had taken his own wave-off from a low and left-of-centerline position. But the LSO was mistaken. Pax had only added full power to keep from being waved-off again. He was mortally spring-loaded in a land-this-airplane frame of mind.

He banked left, kicked full left rudder, and reduced some throttle. He could not imagine what transpired on the LSO platform. After half-a-potato, he leveled his wings to conform to the looming flight deck and jammed the throttle fully forward. As LSOs were wont to say, he taxied to the number one cross-deck pendant. But he'd landed his airplane.

Pax pulled the throttle around-the-horn and felt his pulse slowing as engine rpm decayed. When he could, he raised the canopy—but caught himself, leaned forward and removed his glasses. He descended Lobo Four Zero Three's side with much care: step by step, handhold to handhold.

Gator Broussard stood waiting on the flight deck as Pax dropped from the F-8's extended last step. Broussard jabbed a stiff finger into Pax's chest in rhythm with his words. "You cocksucker!" he shouted. "That was the most God-awful, unprofessional approach that I've ever seen on an aircraft carrier. You're lucky you didn't kill yourself and a whole bunch of sailors."

From the instant he had known he was aboard, the adrenalin in Pax's system had been ebbing to wherever well-used body-chemicals go. He neither needed nor wanted more excitement. Besides, he knew Broussard had a point.

"Okay, Commander, it *was* a lousy landing," Pax said. "If I could've done better, I would've."

Aircraft handlers and high-revving tow-tractor drivers forced the conversation off the flight deck, but Pax felt Broussard at his heels on the way to the Lobo ready room.

Skipper Dodd, Hacksaw Grayson, Tom Weaver, and the squadron maintenance chief turned from their conversation by the SDO's desk as Pax swung the ready room door open.

"Welcome aboard, Ahab," Dodd said and grasped Pax's sweat-soaked shoulder. "We thought you were waitin' for a *daylight* landing."

"Bet you were skosh on fuel," Weaver said.

Pax shrugged, took Lobo 403's aircraft discrepancy log from Master Chief Franklin, and handed it back. "Let me shuck out of this flight gear first, Master Chief; I'll be right back."

He hung his wet stuff in the squadron flight gear locker, ducked across a passageway to a head, took a quick leak, and checked the blister on the right side of his neck. With a full coffee mug, he rejoined the front-of-the-ready-room conclave, which now included CAG Dengler, and retrieved the discrepancy log.

"Before you do that, Ahab," Dodd said, "tell us what happened."

He told them, after a fashion. Numerous ready room exclamations from the listeners slowed the process.

The SDO's squawk box interrupted: "Ready One, Air Ops, is CAG there?"

CAG Dengler nodded at the SDO, Windmill Newman, who transmitted, "Listening."

"CAG, this is Bob Wright. When you've got the dope on that last recovery, Captain Conrad would like to see you in his at-sea cabin."

Dengler shot Windmill a thumbs-up.

"Roger Air OPS; Ready One out."

"Before I leave," Dengler said, and looked straight at Pax, "I need to know something. Did you make that stupid-ass, low pass over the LSO platform on purpose?"

Pax felt every set of eyes boring into his own. He looked toward the front chalkboard, where Broussard stood with his arms folded over his chest. Pax nodded at the LSO, and looked back at CAG Dengler.

"Yes, sir, CAG, I sure did."

Dengler nodded, sneered, and turned on his heel.

Newman called, "Attention on deck!" And CAG was out the door with Broussard right behind. Skipper Dodd shook his head at Pax, and hustled out the same door.

Newman's repeated "Attention on deck!" sounded like an echo.

Chapter 21—PAYING THE FIDDLER, OR NOT

CAG Dengler maintained a determined stride through the dimly-lighted passageway, clearing bulkhead knee-knockers without breaking an unsung cadence. At the GAG office door he realized that Gator Broussard had been dogging his footsteps.

"You hear him admit that low pass was on purpose?" CAG asked.

Framed in the light from the open office door, Broussard clenched a fist and shook his head. "I shoulda jerked his ass out of that chair and clobbered him."

CAG nodded. "Don't worry; he won't get a chance to pull that crap again."

CDR Dodd emerged through the last knee-knocker and puffed toward the two officers, stopping next to Broussard. "CAG, gimme a minute before you see the captain."

"Can't, skipper; he's waiting," CAG said.

"Let us have a minute, Gator," Dodd said and flicked the back of his hand down the empty passageway.

Broussard arched his eyebrows at Dengler. CAG blinked, nodded, and exhaled with a groan. "Okay, Coleman, come in." CAG settled in the chair behind his desk and raised his chin toward an empty chair. Dodd ignored the gesture and remained standing—both fists balled.

"This isn't a visit. I came to see how the hell you could justify that 'stupid-ass, low pass' comment?"

"Whoa! You're out of line, skipper."

"Outta line bullshit! Did you even listen to what went wrong on that flight?"

"So he *says*."

"Kiss my ass, Andy! Where the fuck you coming from?"

Dengler sprang to his feet, launching his chair into the bulkhead behind him, and jerked his thumb toward the door. "That's it. Out!"

"With pleasure!" Dodd shouted back. "But before you shit on Langford, consider this: That's an F-8 on the flight deck that *you* sure as hell couldn't have saved. And neither could I."

Dengler remained silent, but jabbed his thumb toward the door again. He guessed Dodd could have slammed the door harder—but not much. As the door recoiled open again, Dengler saw the terrified Tom Cain in the outer office spring to attention.

"Come in, Lieutenant," Dengler said, "and shut the door—*gently*, please."

Pax finished listing Lobo 403's discrepancies on the aircraft's yellow-sheet, handed the metal-jacketed discrepancy log to Master Chief Franklin, and struggled formulating meaningful answers for the chief's queries. Satisfied at last that he knew the order of the failures, Franklin headed for the ready room door, which at that instant flew open to admit an agitated CDR Dodd. Windmill Newman didn't need to say a word; survival instinct popped the officers to their feet.

"Master Chief," Dodd, obviously cooling now from unexplained rage to rational thought, said in a measured tone, "I want to see every failed component of each inoperative system from four-zero-three . . . before you turn them in for replacements. I want to see them all together. Any problem, Master Chief?"

The chief disappeared before his "no, sir" had faded from the standing-at-attention officers' hearing.

"Pax," Dodd said, "soon as you've had the quack look at your neck—I mean no later than this evening—write down the sequence of events on that flight. Hacksaw, get it from Weaver, too—at least as he can remember them."

The two officers nodded to their "yes, sirs" and departed, lest additional assignments splatter their way.

Pax took a quick shower and stopped by the dispensary, where LCDR Jed Potts, the "friendly quack" flight surgeon, salved and bandaged the blisters on the right side of Pax's neck. Potts furrowed his brow. "Hmm, maybe you shouldn't fly for a couple of days, Pax."

"I'll see how it feels."

Potts shrugged. "It's your neck . . . so to speak."

Pax took his bandaged neck through the dirty-neck wardroom breakfast-line, and sat by Guy Lawrence, the Lobo LSO.

"Hey, Ahab, how's the neck?"

"Good. . . . Does the bandage show that much?"

"Not really. The skipper called, talked a little about the flight, and told me to quiz folks on the platform—except for Gator—to find out what happened."

Pax looked down and shook his head. "Well, . . . I'm sure as hell glad I wasn't back there tonight—not much fun, I guess."

"Not nearly like you were having, huh?"

Pax didn't know whether Lawrence's remark was a dig about his low pass or a comment on his aircraft's failures. So what? He didn't care. His eggs started tasting like rubber. He swallowed a sip of coffee and left the wardroom.

When Pax entered their stateroom, Hacksaw looked up from his F-8 NATOPS manual. "Hey, roomie, neck okay?"

Pax shrugged. "What? You cramming for a test?"

"Boning up on the A-C system. Weaver's sweatin' bullets; he thinks Dodd may have his ass for tellin' you to break the safety-wire on that pressure-suit cooling switch."

"Why? It got me the wing fuel."

"Yeah, and blowtorched your electric bundle . . . under the Buick hood."

Pax wrinkled his brow and tried to concentrate, but nothing meshed. "Screw it; I'm bushed," he said, shedding his uniform. Worming his way between the top rack's sheets, he squinted down at Hacksaw. "If you don't see me for a couple days . . . I'll be right here."

Hacksaw flicked off the light, stepped into the passageway, and stuck his head back inside. "Don't forget the flight write-up Dodd wants." He got no answer, so he shut the door.

CAG rapped twice on Captain Conrad's at-sea cabin door. From within, a muffled rasp responded, "Come in."

As Dengler pushed the door open, he watched the uniformed captain roll himself into a sitting position on the single rack's edge. Yawning, Conrad stuffed his stockinged feet into slippers as he pointed Dengler at the single chair. "Damn," Conrad said, glancing at his watch. "Ship captains don't sleep; you die. And in a second, too, while you can. Okay, what happened to the Lobo bird?"

"Two things: pressurization failure off the catapult and a complete electrical failure off the first bolter. More importantly, Langford admitted flying as low as he could over the LSO platform. He's been a loose cannon before tonight, and I listened to a list of horror stories from another officer who knew him in his last command. Langford's a crash waiting to happen."

Conrad had moved to a small stainless steel sink in the corner and was splashing water on his face. As he dried he asked, "What's his skipper think of him?"

Dengler sneered and shook his head. "Ah, you know skippers; they vouch for their own. Gator Broussard wanted to kill him."

"Andy, why the low pass?"

"Because he's a fucking idiot, and I'm convening an evaluation board on him day after tomorrow."

Conrad said nothing; his face remained blank for ten seconds. "He's your aviator and that F-8 he landed is your aircraft. They're both your responsibility, and I won't burden you with my opinion. But I'll see Lieutenant Langford *and* his skipper—you as well, if you wish—after dinner this evening."

"Aye, aye, Captain." Dengler left to the sound of a longer and deeper Conrad yawn.

Gettysburg's hangar deck throbbed with maintenance activity. CDR Dodd ducked under wings and snaked between horizontal stabilizers looking for Lobo 403. When he found it, Hacksaw Grayson and Master Chief Franklin stood at the foot of a jacked-up maintenance platform beside the plane's forward starboard fuselage. Above them two electricians bent under a fuselage access panel referred to as the "Buick hood" (for its resemblance to a former automobile's engine cover).

Dodd nodded to his operations officer and maintenance chief. "Hacksaw, Master Chief."

"They're fishing the main wire bundle out, skipper," Franklin said. "The fuckin' thing's burnt plumb through. And the goddamned A-C turbine's tore to shit."

From behind the master chief's back, Hacksaw motioned for Dodd to follow him and cupped a hand toward the CDR's ear, "Climb in and look out the windscreen."

Dodd climbed the foot steps, checked the ejection seat pins, and lowered himself into the cockpit. Hacksaw watched Dodd's head bob up and down a couple of times, and Dodd looked down at him. "Gimme a flashlight."

Hacksaw found one, climbed the steps, and handed it over. Dodd flicked the light forward from several angles then handed it back. "I want photos of this windscreen, inside and out; get some shots of the canopy as well."

Hacksaw smiled and shook his head. "Ain't that somethin'?"

Dodd emerged from the cockpit, dropped to the deck, and walked back to Franklin. "Master Chief, fix this airplane, but *do not* allow anyone to clean this windscreen or cockpit until I tell you to. Understand?"

"You got it, skipper. You said you wanted these fucked up parts. Where? In the ready room?"

"You bet," Dodd said and shot his maintenance chief a thumbs-up.

At 1900, on *Gettysburg's* navigation bridge, CAG Dengler, CDR Dodd, and Pax stood beside CAPT Conrad, who was sitting in his elevated chair. The silence weighed on the standing, apprehensive officers. Pax had answered Conrad's pointed questions, but neither CDR had uttered anything beyond their "good evenings"—some thirty minutes earlier.

The captain hitched around toward Pax and—from beneath his dark, bushy, and protruding eyebrows—glared at him. "Tell me, Lieutenant, what were you thinking when you made that low wave-off?"

Pax glanced down, took a deep breath, and met Conrad's stare. "Captain, I was trying to tell the LSO that I knew the rule—that wave-offs were mandatory. But that, by God, I had a cockpit full of shit he didn't know about, and if that wave-off was for *technique* . . . well, don't give me another one."

CAG Dengler almost growled. "That's the most irresponsible statement I've ever heard, Lieutenant."

Ignoring Dengler's comment, Pax maintained eye contact with the captain.

Captain Conrad didn't acknowledge CAG's opinion, either. "How's your neck, son?"

"Much better, sir," Pax said.

"Good. Go on down to your ready room."

"Yes, sir," Pax said and left.

Conrad waited a moment, and spoke to Dodd. "Any problems with the kid's flying?"

"None, Captain. Maybe in *your* prime you could have handled that flight; I doubt that I—"

"He never should have gotten airborne!" Dengler interjected. "He should've said, 'Suspend cat one!'"

Again, the captain seemed to ignore Dengler. "Thanks, Commander Dodd.

Why don't you join your young tiger."

Dengler waited until Dodd was beyond earshot then shook his head. "With all due respect—"

"It's your CAG, Andy; I'll not dictate how you run it. But I'll be damned disappointed if you convene an evaluation board on Lieutenant Langford."

"Captain, you haven't *heard* the things he's pulled."

The edges of Captain Conrad's mouth curled, but his eyes didn't follow suit. "No, but someone mentioned that your source is a little suspect. Isn't he the A-4 jock who won't fly over the beach?"

"How'd you know that?"

"This is *my* ship, Andy. She's big, but she ain't that big."

Dengler bit his lip and slapped his fore-and-aft cap against a leg. "I'd like to think about it."

"Think about it as long as you want to, but know this: I didn't maneuver this ship near shoaly water, trying to catch that crippled bird, to see its pilot's wings clipped. I'll attach a negative endorsement—a heavy negative—to *any* adverse recommendations from the board. And I *won't* forget I had to do it."

Captain Conrad glanced beyond Dengler's shoulder. "Commander South," he called.

Gettysburg's navigator came to a stop beside Dengler. "Yes, sir, Captain."

"Commander, please tell CAG Dengler—as best you can remember— my exact words to you when the F-8 without lights made that low wave-off last night."

CDR South closed his eyes and rubbed his chin. When he looked up his upper body rocked forward slightly and he nodded. "That kid's got no radio, no lights, and probably no instruments. That low pass, that might've put the LSOs in the net, was telling them he didn't appreciate their wave-off. And that's exactly what I'd've done." The navigator shrugged. "Maybe not verbatim, but it's close."

"Thank you, Commander," Conrad said nodding once. "That's all."

As the navigator returned to his duties, Conrad glared at Dengler from beneath those same bushy eyebrows. "I don't give a good Goddamn what anyone says, Langford's next approach was at least as shitty—maybe worse, compared to normal—and the LSO sure as hell didn't wave him off. Message sent; message received. End of story."

Dengler hadn't advanced to CAG by tilting windmills; he knew when the slope had become too steep and too slippery. Obvious chagrin transformed into a broad and gracious smile. "There will be no evaluation board, Captain."

"Good decision, CAG; get on back to your real work."

"Aye, aye, Captain."

Conrad watched Dengler leave the bridge, and scrunched down into his chair and closed his eyes. A small grin played at the corners of his mouth.

Sitting in his first-row, ready room chair, CDR Dodd finished reading Pax's flight summary from the previous night. In their own chairs, LCDR Weaver and Pax anxiously waited. Hacksaw stood at the front of the ready room, studying the squadron's LSO "greenie" board—which displayed color-coded grades for every shipboard landing approach by each VF-39 pilot.

"Sonofabitch!" Hacksaw said. "Who the hell put this cut-pass down for Ahab last night?"

"Gator Broussard, himself," Motel Bates said from the SDO desk. "Mumbled how dangerous a pass it was as he colored the square. Said he'd never seen a worse pass."

"Maybe he never heard a worse pass," Needle Weaver said, "but no one on the ship *saw* the fucking pass—including him."

Pax glanced at the board and saw his string of mostly yellow/fair, a few green/ okay, a couple of brown/no-grade, and the final red/cut pass—which meant extremely dangerous. He touched the dressing on his neck.

In a perfect world, Gator's ass would've been flying 403.

CDR Dodd stood and took a step toward the greenie board. He tapped Pax's flight summary against his leg and stared at 403's failed parts—lying on the deck by the ready room's front bulkhead. He motioned dialing a phone to Motel. "See if CAG's in his office."

Motel dialed a number and looked up. "Do you want to talk to him?"

Dodd shook his head.

"He's there," Motel said.

"Thanks," Dodd said and strode from the room.

CDR Dodd looked into CAG's office and caught Dengler's eye. "Got a second?"

"Guess so," Dengler said and pointed at the door. "Careful of the door; its hinges are bent."

Dodd smiled and shrugged. "Sorry about that, I apologize."

"Good enough. Have a seat."

"CAG, I've read both pilots' statements from last night's flights. They jibe, and I have all of 403's failed parts in the ready room if you'd care to see them. But I'm here trying to change your mind about Langford, if I can."

Dengler looked at his desktop, chewed his lip, and shook his head. Then his head snapped up. "I've already told Captain Conrad that I'd convene an evaluation board on Langford."

"Andy, that doesn't make sense."

"So you said; so you say again. He endangered the LSOs and the flight deck personnel. He's pulled stunts that you probably aren't even aware of in previous commands, any of which could have killed him. And yet, you take up for him."

"I do."

Dengler checked his fingernails and shook his head a couple of times with his eyes shut. When he looked up, he clamped both hands on the desk edge and shoved himself erect. "Coleman, I think you're wrong; Langford's a loose cannon. But I also value your opinion, both as a commanding officer and as a friend." CAG came around the desk, stuck out his right hand, then continued as they shook, "I'll respect your judgment *this* time and tell Captain Conrad I've changed my mind. Let's hope we both don't regret it."

The same pilots were in the ready room when Dodd returned. Their eyes asked the same unspoken question.

"Needle," Dodd said, "tomorrow's a no-fly day. At the APM I want you to explain the danger of breaking safety-wires in the cockpit. I'm not saying doing it's wrong, but be sure everyone realizes the responsibilities involved, how well they need to know their systems to justify breaking safety wires. Got it?"

"Aye, aye, Commander," Weaver said and left.

"Ahab, give that neck a couple of days vacation from the cockpit. Hacksaw, tell Irish Blaine to schedule Ahab as Pri-fly observer day after tomorrow—for the whole day. And, Motel, tell maintenance to pick up these broke-dick parts."

Dodd moved to the duty desk and tapped its surface. When Motel finished his call, Dodd said, "Call Gypsy Lawrence; tell him I'd like to see him."

Motel pointed at the front wall chalkboard. "Gypsy's on the flight deck . . . in the alert-five bird, sir. He gets relieved in twenty minutes."

"Okay, I'll wait."

While Motel worked the squawk-box and telephone, CDR Dodd leaned back in his chair and stared at the LSO greenie board.

The APM (all pilots meeting) had droned for over two hours. Needle Weaver was expounding on the F-8's air-conditioning system, the full pressure suit's interface with it, and the dangers of breaking safety-wires in the cockpit. Pax listened with a serious scowl.

I sure as hell wish I'd known this much a couple of nights ago.

CDR Dodd stood and faced his pilots. "Thanks, Needle. I probably don't need to mention how important our NATOPS manual is. I'm fairly sure that you aviators spend a great deal of time . . . scouring those pages for information that you'll need. Because, as Pax's flight proved, there'll be times you won't have a chance to leaf through an Emergency Procedures Flip-Pad. You'll have to sing the songs you already know.

"As best we can reconstruct events, that superheated air—that Pax diverted through the pressure suit's plumbing system—dumped directly onto his main wire bundle . . . under the Buick access panel. Over time, maybe forty-five minutes, that hot air started burning through the wire's insulation. Pax's first indication might have been when his TACAN needle started searching and he lost his distance measuring equipment. Anyway, the first bolter jarred the melting wires—displaced them—so nothing electrical got juice. The RAT worked, but without wires. . . ." Dodd shrugged.

"Then Pax flew into the overcast. His reaction to going blind again was to jam the stick forward; I think we can say, with some degree of desperation. We think this push might have undone the bolter's displacement, and swung the wire bundle back into alignment. For whatever reason, the RAT emergency system electrons flowed, and Pax had emergency bus instruments . . . until his second bolter, which plunged him back into darkness."

Dodd walked from behind the lectern to even with the first row of seats. "Pax brought the plane back, so we can pretty well backtrack his equipment failures, which put him in extremis. Had that failure been mine, and my RAT hadn't worked, I probably would have ejected. Remember, there was absolutely no horizon. None. Sometimes, gents, fate just shits in your hard hat. Know your limitations. And know this: I'd rather have you here, telling me what went wrong, than having to wonder. We can always get another airplane."

The officers snapped to attention—again, without command—as Dodd left the ready room.

Chapter 22—PRI-FLY

With no CAP alert-15, in flight gear in the ready room, or CAP alert-5, strapped in the airplane, or an oh-dark-thirty morning briefing, Pax should have squirreled away some serious "Z"s. But it didn't happen. Instead, he jerked back from near sleep—time and again. The sheets became clammy, and in his restless flouncing he scrunched the top sheet and coverlet against the bulkhead or kicked them toward his feet.

But he discovered these inconveniencies after a jarring consciousness confirmed he wasn't in some cockpit, captive to that "blind" bolter. With each dry-mouthed-gasp into wakefulness, Pax's right hand clawed at the mattress—trying to reset some gremlin-screwed electrical system. As his breathing slowed, he twisted, raised on an elbow, and yawned.

I could get more rest skipping rope . . . and a hell of a lot less nerve-jangling. I don't want to wake up Hacksaw; he's got a 0630 brief. Since I can't sleep, I ought to write Sally. Tonight. I'll do that tonight.

After thrashing himself into an exhausted, near-comatose sense of nothingness, Pax heard something—talking.

Hacksaw's words came from a great distance, but whoever yanked his arm had to be much closer. One in the same, it turned out. Hacksaw's voice and smile seemed poised on the rim of an unconsciousness sludge-pit. Pax levitated toward the light . . . and wakefulness.

"Okay, roomie, okay. I'm awake. What's goin' on?" Pax asked, shaking himself into awareness.

"Headin' to my briefing; that's what. Want any breakfast you'd better hoist your dead ass up. Hey! Outta that sack! Get your butt movin'."

"Right," Pax said, yawning. "I'm awake; I'm movin'. Thanks, pal." With that, he dropped to the deck and Hacksaw departed. More yawns and stretches later, he'd shaved, dressed, and made his way to the wardroom. Coffee and pancakes looked good, but few pilots remained eating—none that he knew. A second cup of coffee got his heart pumping.

This'll be a day in hell—tower duty, for the entire flight schedule. Rat's ass!

By the time Pax climbed the ladders to pri-fly, CDR Noble, the air boss, had already directed 0800 launch pilots to start engines. Pri-fly's bullet-proof glass and abundant insulation muffled the flight deck's teeth-rattling cacophony. Protected from searing jet exhausts, and with its excellent look-down visibility, pri-fly presented choice real estate for selling naval aviation to visiting dignitaries. VIPs could absorb the spectacle from on high without suffering its rough edges. And although Pax would rather have been in a cockpit, any opportunity to watch the unfolding flight deck ballet always fascinated him.

But squadron reps weren't dignitaries, nor were they on holiday. During launch and recovery periods at least one rep from each aircraft type manned pri-fly, available to the air boss for his queries during emergencies. They were also the phone contact between pri-fly and the rep's own ready room if airborne situations got dicey or when deck-spot *go/no-go* decisions were needed. At least somewhere in his past, Pax had heard that bullshit job description. Most pri-fly reps, however, only needed a couple of scars from finger-pointing "heavies" to feel like they were standby whipping boys for things gone awry.

Once initiated, most reps became adept at skirting the nudged-for, easy answers that would satisfy an aircraft handler's problem, or an airborne tanker's low give-away fuel numbers, or agreeing to could-be harmless head-nod queries from the air boss or his assistant. During a Mediterranean deployment, Pax—by trial and error—had earned his pri-fly stripes, by learning which decisions were his and on which ones his skipper or ops officer might desire an input.

The air boss raised his chin at him. "Hey, Lieutenant, how's the neck?"

"Much better, thank you," Pax said.

How does he know who I am? Ah, yeah . . . the gauze.

The LCDR assistant air boss (Pax knew this from reading the block, black letters stenciled on his yellow jersey) chuckled and said, "I bet you can't wait for your next night hop."

Ignoring the remark, Pax moved to a forward-facing window, to better see the bow catapults.

How will I feel for that next night flight? Who knows? Ask me then.

Pax watched Angel Nine One, the plane-guard helo forward of Hacksaw's

F-8 on the port bow catapult, as its rotor blades commenced to turn. He shook his head considering how boring it would be to hover on the ship's starboard side during every launch and recovery on the slim chance that either a pilot might have to eject, or a flight deck worker might get blown overboard and need to be fished from the drink.

"Trojan, Angel Nine One ready to lift," came the helo pilot's call.

The assistant air ops officer had the mike. "Angel Nine One, you're cleared to lift and take station."

Pax's thoughts drifted until both Lobo F-8s on the bow cats spun their engines up for launch.

Cat one fired first, slinging Irish Blaine down the track. A slight pause later, cat two thrust Hacksaw Grayson airborne behind Irish, but offset a tad to the left. Pax moved back away from the window, letting other reps move up to watch their guys.

A matter-of-fact radio transmission sliced through extraneous chatter. "Trojan, Lobo Four-Zero-Two, airborne off cat two with an oil pressure failure. I'm turning downwind."

CDR Noble flashed a look at Pax with a quick open-handed shrug—a "feed me info" look.

"His engine could seize in as few as twenty-eight seconds, or it might run for several minutes, Commander. But he's *got* to land, and damned soon." Pax reached for a phone to alert the ready room. He relayed the situation to the XO.

Pax watched Hacksaw's plane start dumping fuel as it started to turn downwind. The air boss glanced at Pax, then spoke into his hand-mike, "Make a long, deep pattern, Lobo; we have an emergency pull forward in progress. How long till you get dumped down enough to land?"

"Can't say, Trojan. Maybe five minutes—I'm dumpin' fast as I can."

The air boss glared at Pax. "Does he have both a gauge *and* a light?"

"The plane does," Pax said. "I'm sure he's checked them both."

CDR Dodd huffed in through the external hatch. "Has he got both indications, Pax?"

"Don't know, sir, he hasn't said. But I'm sure that he does."

"You wanna ask him, Coleman?" Noble said, offering Dodd the mike.

Dodd took it. "Lobo Four Zero Two, Dodd here. Is the light on?"

"That's affirmative, Commander. The light's on; the gauge reads zip. How's my ready deck coming?"

Noble took the mike back. "Four minutes, Lobo."

"Roger, Trojan, I'll be turning inbound in about a minute."

Noble blasted the deck hands with the flight deck speakers. "Keep it moving, people. We've got a wounded duck, and it's gotta land."

"If he doesn't move the throttle till he's on final, he's got a chance," Dodd said.

Flight deck personnel had the birds on the fantail hooked to tractors and their conga line was snaking forward. The highly animated flight deck officer, air bos'n, flight deck chief, and flight deck leading petty officer had command of the situation. The deck would be ready.

"He's started his turn," Noble said. "He's coming around . . . dumping big-time."

"Yeah, getting rid of enough fuel for this approach will be iffy," Dodd said.

Pax saw Weaver and Anderson scooting into the back of pri-fly, also known—in such situations—as "vulture's row."

The last of the towed planes had moved up near the foul-deck line. Pax saw the LSO platform windbreak come erect, and the LSOs moved to their work station. Hacksaw's wings leveled in a long straightaway.

Dodd tapped Noble's shoulder. "Ask him his fuel state."

"Lobo, Trojan, say your state."

"Six point five, Trojan. Looks like she's quit dumpin'."

"No way, not this pass," Pax said and lowered a set of binoculars. "He hasn't jettisoned his sidewinders yet, either."

Noble jerked around toward Dodd. "We can't have him jettison the bastards toward the ship."

"Trojan, Lobo, I can't make it this time; she's too heavy. Fuck me!" Hacksaw called.

"More'n likely," Dodd said to Pax. "Boss, when he clears the ship, please tell him to jettison those sidewinders."

Noble nodded as pri-fly and flight deck personnel watched Hacksaw's lubricant-bleeding F-8 wish-and-hope its way along *Gettysburg*'s port side.

"Lobo, Trojan, jettison your sidewinders," Noble said.

"Roger, Trojan."

Both missiles fired and fell into the sea, as Hacksaw—at his velvet-handed best—coaxed and yearned for another gentle circle from his hexed J57 engine, before its dry-running vitals fused.

"He stopped dumping," Dodd said. "How long since he launched?"

Noble glanced up at the clock. "Nine minutes."

Pri-fly observers remained focused on the gently turning bird. Pax couldn't remember when he'd taken his last breath.

Nine minutes . . . already?

Hacksaw's turn would give him minimum straightaway. No one could have brought it around any tighter.

"Trojan, Lobo, I'm set; keep your fingers crossed."

An unexpected transmission—a loud, new voice—cut through: "Trojan, Angel Nine One, I've got a chip light and serious vibration. I gotta land!"

"Shit!" Noble screamed, and with the flight deck speakers asked, "Have we got a spot forward for Angel Nine One?"

The flight deck officer shook his head at the tower and shrugged. Looks switched from the flight deck back to Hacksaw.

"Bring it close aboard, Nine One," Noble said. "Your landing traffic's on short final."

Hacksaw's down-home voice reported, "She quit, boys!"

"This is Nine-One; I'm vibrating bad, boss."

CDR Noble had sucked in a quick breath to answer the dying helo, when several fingers pointed toward the F-8. Hacksaw had ejected, and Lobo Four Zero Two's descending left turn sealed its fate.

Noble's release from the dilemma came through in his transmission. "Bring it on in, Nine One; you got the whole landing area."

"Hacksaw's got a good chute," Dodd said.

Noble growled into the mike. "On the flight deck! Angel Nine One will be landing aft. Break Nine Two out of the pack—ASAP, people; there's a pilot in the water."

Dodd had binoculars on Hacksaw when the troubled Angel Nine One lurched into the landing area and flopped down hard enough to rock back and forth a few times.

"He's in the water," Dodd said.

Pax estimated 1½-2 miles aft of the ship, but actual distance counted for little. Getting Angel Nine Two airborne did.

"Between swells and these piss-poor binoculars, I can't see how he's doing," Dodd said. "But I can see his vest; it's inflated. He's cutting the chute cords."

Pax watched the crew break Angel Nine Two out of the packed, forward deck. Two A-4s had already been cleared.

Noble turned to Dodd. "Five minutes till helo liftoff."

The underfoot thrumming lessened; *Gettysburg* was slowing. Pax wormed between Weaver and Anderson at a rear window, but he couldn't see Hacksaw. Dodd had passed Weaver the binoculars. "He comes and goes," Weaver said. "Three foot swells, I guess; when I see him, he's splashing around."

"Okay, gents," Noble called out, "way too many people in pri-fly. Give us a break. If you're not a helo rep or a Lobo rep, I'd appreciate it if you'd go on about your business. Thank you much." The accused *vultures* eased toward the hatch—their departure neither rapid nor happy.

Angel Nine Two's rotor blades began to spin. Pax nodded silent approval. Hacksaw had been in the water seven minutes.

"Trojan, Angel Nine Two's ready to lift."

"Roger, Angel," Noble said. "You're cleared. Vector zero-eight-five . . . about six miles. Report pilot in sight."

"Nine Two, wilco." The helo lifted, dropped its nose, and accelerated toward the downed pilot. Its flight path almost followed the sun's reflected slash across the water. Everyone squinted toward the rescue action.

"Nine Two, pilot in sight."

"Roger, Nine Two, report when pilot's aboard."

Two mike clicks came back: OK—and by the way, I'm busy.

"They're streaming the collar," Weaver said. "It's down to the water."

Pax couldn't see what was happening beneath the helo, and squinting into the sun's reflection made his eyes water. After ninety seconds, the boss took the binoculars from Weaver.

"Shouldn't be taking this long," Noble said. "There! He's going up. *What* the hell? He's got *one arm* hooked through the goddamned collar. He let go and dropped back down. Shit!"

"Angel, Trojan, what's going on?" Noble asked.

"We got a problem, Trojan. I'm putting a swimmer in."

"Boss, how high did he get before he fell?" Dodd asked.

"Ten or fifteen feet, not high." Noble said.

The clock's second hand was running downhill—devouring minutes in heartbeats. The air boss's phone rang. Many "yessirs" and a crimson face left no doubt as to whom he was listening. He hung up.

"Angel, where's your swimmer?" Noble asked.

"Going in now, boss."

Noble had the binoculars steadied on the helo. "At last," he said. But the second hand seemed to accelerate. Two minutes later the pri-fly observers saw a form raised into the helo.

"Angel, what kinda shape's he in . . . ?" Noble asked. No response. "Angel,

Trojan, how do you read? Over."

"Trojan, Angel, we're working a problem. That was my swimmer in the sling. I'm putting another swimmer in."

The boss's phone again. He took a deep breath and answered it. "Yes, sir. . . . I don't know, sir. . . . Yes, sir, a second swimmer's going in. . . . As soon as I know, sir."

"Angel, Trojan, how's the pilot?" Noble asked. Pax saw a bead of sweat run down Noble's cheek and noticed—for the first time—a fair amount of gray in Noble's dark brown hair.

"We're on the gauges in this hover, boss—can't see him. The second swimmer's going in now."

"Confirmed," Dodd said, lowering the binoculars. "Another swimmer's in the water."

Noble moved nearer his forward window and looked down at the flight deck. He looked at Dodd. "A flight surgeon has two corpsmen and a gurney standing by, Coleman."

Dodd nodded. "Thanks, but this is dragging out too long; something's fucked up."

Almost three minutes later, looking through the binoculars, Dodd said, "*Somebody* is being hoisted up; let's hope to hell it's Hacksaw."

The boss's phone again. He lifted it, but paused to listen to the radio report coming in.

"Boss, Angel Nine Two inbound. I'll return for my swimmer. Copilot says it doesn't look good."

The assistant air boss answered, "Roger, Angel, you're cleared to land abeam the island."

The air boss listened a few seconds to the phone and hung up.

Dodd, Weaver, Anderson, and Pax pressed against pri-fly's forward side-windows awaiting Angel Nine Two.

Weaver asked Dodd the question Pax had been wondering, "What the hell was the story with that *first* swimmer?"

Dodd only shook his head, but Noble answered, "Good question, and I'm eager to find that out. Soon as they retrieve that second swimmer, we'll know."

The helo sidled into position and plopped down. Three white-jerseyed medics scurried beneath the rotors, shoved the gurney aboard, and one (Pax guessed the flight surgeon) clambered aboard.

Pax clasped Anderson's shoulder. "Commander, can you relieve me? I want to go to sick bay."

"Go ahead," Dodd said, "we've got this covered."

"Appreciate it, sir," Pax said and ducked out the rear hatch. Directly after exiting the tower, he heard the helo lift.

Godspeed.

Pax walked into sick bay before Hacksaw's gurney arrived. He glanced around the empty ward and wondered if they'd taken Hacksaw to the island's flight deck, emergency-treatment station. A rising clamor in the passageway negated that notion.

"Gangway! Gangway!" voices shouted. "Gangway! Medical emergency!"

Amid the shouts, heavy and rapid footfalls prodded Pax—now back in the passageway—to stand clear of sick bay's entrance. Two white-jerseyed corpsmen and two brown-jerseyed plane captains, sweating rivulets, huffed the gurney around a 90-degree turn through the double doors. Ashen-faced Hacksaw's eyes were closed; a short, plastic tube curved from his mouth down along his cheek. Jed Potts, the flight surgeon, followed a few yards behind the gurney as he removed his flight deck helmet. Pax arched his eyebrows and shrugged. Potts, with lips drawn tight, gave him two abbreviated head shakes before disappearing into sick bay.

Holy shit.

Pax backed against a bench along the corridor and slid down the bulkhead taking a seat. He lowered his head toward his knees and let his arms hang by his legs. The plane captains, whom he now recognized, saw him and came over.

"Commander looked bad," one said. "Think he'll be okay?"

Pax shook his head. "I don't know."

"I sure hope so," the other said and raised a thumbs-up before they left.

Pax started leaning forward again, when CAPT Conrad came striding down the passageway. He nodded briefly at Pax and turned through the double doors. Less than a minute later both corpsmen raced from sick bay, and around a corner.

Maybe they kindled a spark in Hacksaw.

Almost as fast as they left, the corpsmen returned, trotting alongside a rolling cabinet. It and they disappeared through the double doors. Pax felt someone sit beside him.

"What's the word?" the XO asked.

Pax shrugged. "The flight surgeon made me think Hacksaw wouldn't make it, but there's a lot of scrambling around in there."

From sick bay came a loud shout: "Clear!" And another: "Clear!"

"Maybe they haven't given up," the XO said.

"Seems like."

Flight Surgeon Jed Potts charged from the double doors and skidded around the same popular corner. But Pax and the XO's questioning looks died unanswered as Potts came back five seconds later with a short, heavy-set, khaki-clad CDR. Both disappeared into sick bay.

"That's Bob Yanks, the senior medical officer," the XO said. "Maybe a good sign."

"Let's hope," Pax said.

Bud Banks appeared. "How's he doing?"

The XO glanced at Pax and back to Bud. "Don't know yet. Lots of hustle and bustle in there, but nobody's talking."

CDR Yanks exited sick bay as fast as he'd entered it and disappeared around the well-traveled corner. A moment later, their friendly quack—tall, lanky Jed Potts—emerged and trudged toward them. "Jesus!" he said.

"How's Hacksaw?" the XO asked.

Potts glanced from the XO to Pax and back to the XO. He shook his head, frowning. "Sorry, I thought I indicated to Pax that Grayson didn't make it; he drowned."

The XO put a hand on Pax's shoulder. "I'm sorry, Pax. Gotta tell the skipper. See you in the ready room."

Pax raised his open hands level with his waist and gaped at Potts. "Well what in hell was the scurrying around about?"

Potts's head shook back and forth, and his stare focused beyond Pax and Bud. "This is the worst fucking day in my whole life."

Potts had taken a deep breath to explain when the ship-wide 1-MC loudspeaker system crackled to life with the bos'n pipe's loud, shrill whistle. The voice came loud and deep: "Officers and men of *Gettysburg*, this is Admiral Jensen. I didn't say good morning, because it's not been a good morning. Most of you know we lost a pilot: Lieutenant Commander Cecil F. Grayson of Fighter Squadron Thirty-nine. What I also have to tell you is that fifteen minutes ago Captain Frederick C. Conrad, *Gettysburg*'s commanding officer, died of a heart attack. *Gettysburg*'s executive officer Commander Roy Clark will be *Gettysburg*'s acting CO until further notice. That is all."

Potts whispered, "*That* was the scurrying."

As Pax entered the ready room, the SDO's squawk box delivered an update from air ops: "I repeat, we'll pick up today's flight schedule with the third launch."

CDR Dodd flashed the SDO, Buckshot Walker, a thumbs up and the ready rooms—in order—acknowledged the info. The phone rang; Walker answered it, listened and said, "Roger that."

"Skipper," Walker said, "that was CAG's office; CAG wants to see you."

CAG didn't invite Dodd to sit, but turned his head aside and grimaced. "Coleman, I'm sorry about Hacksaw; he was a good man."

Dodd nodded. "Thank you."

"And I'm even sorrier for what I'm about to say. After twelve solid hours of internal debate, I've had to change my mind about Langford. I'm—"

"In what regard?" Dodd asked. "How—"

Dengler raised his hand between them to stop the queries. "I'm convening an aviator evaluation board for Lieutenant Langford. VA-136's commanding officer, Commander Tom Goodwin will preside."

"A *fucking evaluation board*?" Dodd shouted.

Dengler nodded. "The paperwork's being finished. You and Langford will get your copies later today. He will be relieved of duties involving aviation until the board reports out."

Dodd turned and shut the door. As he came back around, facing CAG, his enunciation came crisp and clear. "Andy, my ops officer drowned . . . and now *this*? Why don't you blindfold me and kick me in the nuts? I'd think more of you. *Changing your mind*? That's pure bullshit! You've flat-out lied to me, Commander, and I'll *never* forget it."

Chapter 23—HEADS OR TAILS?

CDR Dodd's face remained flushed as he entered the ready room after striding back from CAG's office. He beckoned to Weaver and Pax and flopped down next to the XO, who awaited the word. Dodd looked at each of them, in turn. "Gents, we're short-handed for a few days. No job changes until we find out how bad we're hurt. XO, tell Motel he's acting ops officer for a few days; his first job: have Blaine schedule replacements for Ahab in pri-fly for the rest of the day. Better get going on that."

The XO moved to the duty desk.

Dodd looked at Weaver. "Needle, you and Motel get me everything you've got so far on 403—including those windscreen and canopy photos. ASAP."

Pax figured he was involved, but he didn't know how. His curiosity must have shown when Dodd looked up at him. Dodd stood and said, "Sit here, Pax. I want you between me and the XO, so I don't have to say this more than once."

The XO returned to his chair; both he and Pax focused on their leader. Dodd spoke directly to the XO. "CAG's ordered an evaluation board on Langford."

The XO's face scrunched up. "Wha—"

Dodd raised both palms at them. "Wait till I'm through. Commander Goodwin will chair the board. Camp Brogan and three lieutenant commanders—one each from VA-135, VA-51, and VAH-4—will be members. It convenes 1000 tomorrow morning in wardroom II annex. Pax, you and I get copies of the convening order later today. Gents, that's it; that's everything I know."

Both commanders waited for Pax's reaction. He glanced at each of them and shrugged. "Am I supposed to say something?"

Dodd rubbed his hands together. "I doubt you can say anything to us that I haven't already said to CAG. He's hellbent on this board, but I don't understand why."

217

The XO's subdued query didn't carry past his listeners. "Skipper, could you take this to the admiral?"

"I don't think so. Not yet, anyway. And if the board does what I *hope* they'll do, there'll be no need."

Pax said, "I'll be there in the morning. Commander Anderson said I should start inventorying Hacksaw's belongings. I'll try to do that tonight."

Motel Bates entered the ready room carrying a damp survival vest and its inflated floatation devices. He shook his head at the CO, XO, and Pax. "This is what killed him."

Pax's ears throbbed red as he glared at the air force water wings. "Those fucking things aren't authorized."

"Where'd he get them?" Dodd asked.

Pax stood. "Give me five minutes and I'll tell you." Grabbing the green mesh vest he left the room.

While he lugged Hacksaw's wet vest and water wings aft toward the parachute loft, Pax's disposition bubbled up to near righteous rage. As he entered the loft he saw Silky Chandler bending over a sewing machine, talking to two other riggers. It was all Pax could do to keep from throwing the soaked vest at them. Instead, he cleared his throat. "Excuse me, men; I need to talk to Petty Officer Chandler . . . *alone.*"

The two riggers not named Chandler hauled ass.

Chandler watched as Pax approached and spread the soggy, maleficent evidence on the parachute packing table.

"We were talking about that, Lieutenant," Chandler said.

"Oh? What were you saying?"

"I was tellin' 'em how goddamned glad I was that I wouldn't sew that air force shit on Commander Grayson's vest."

Pax faced the table, stretched his upper torso across it, and blew out a long exhalation. "Thank God! I should have known."

"Jeez, I guess," Chandler said and snorted. "You're one fierce-lookin' sonofabitch when you're pissed."

"I didn't mean for it to show."

"*Show*? Fuck me. Bet I don't find those two strikers 'fore we get back to Cubi."

Pax jerked his thumb toward the vest. "Who did this?"

In a loud, stage voice Chandler said, "Lieutenant, I don't know." But he leaned closer to Pax: "VA-136."

"You sure?"

"Uh-huh, Commander Grayson went from me to our sister squadron, but Commander Milano had put his kibosh on that modification: 'No fucking air force water wings.'"

"So how do you know who modified Grayson's gear?"

Chandler's voice dropped again. "No names, Lieutenant, but the rigger's a friend; he told me. Half their pilots are wearing 'em."

Pax nodded and extended his hand to the tall petty officer. "Thank you, friend . . . for *not* helping kill a friend."

Chandler grasped Pax's hand, and his eyes welled.

Pax squeezed Chandler's shoulder, picked up the vest, and retraced his steps to the ready room—albeit at a much slower pace.

Dodd, the XO, and Motel interrupted their conversation to watch Pax drop the suspect floatation gear on the deck. "Our guys didn't replace Hacksaw's Mark-III Charlie," Pax said.

"Somebody did," Dodd said.

"A VA-136 rigger—Hacksaw asked him to."

"Who says?" asked the XO.

"A friend," Pax said.

"Motel, tell Pax what you told us," Dodd said as he and the XO left. But Dodd stuck his head back through the door. "You two keep that info to yourselves, for now, okay?"

They nodded. Motel picked up the vest and moved back a row, to their regular seats. "I heard the helo crew debrief Hacksaw's *rescue*."

"Angel Nine-Two?"

"Uh-huh. Hacksaw was thrashing around in the water when they got to him, but both of these water wings had moved to the middle of his back. It'd be like someone holding you up by the back of your belt, but with his fist about a foot under the water. Anyway, he paddled both arms pretty hard keeping his head above water. Guess he'd had to do that the whole time he was getting clear of his chute."

"How about his helmet?" Pax asked.

"They never saw his helmet; he must have shucked it. When they drug the sling close to him—within a couple of feet—he almost couldn't get to it. When he did grab it, he couldn't get into it. The crewmen motioned for him to get it on, but he shook his head at them and motioned for them to reel him in anyway. They tried, but he let go and fell. He must have been completely exhausted.

"The first swimmer they put in . . . never had *any* water rescue training. Never. As soon as the swimmer got close, Hacksaw said, 'Help me! I'm drowning.'"

Pax leaned close to Motel. "So what the hell did he do?"

"The kid was crying and slobbering in the debrief. He panicked, told Hacksaw, 'Me, too,' and got into the sling himself—signaled to be reeled up."

Pax stared open-mouthed at Motel. "No shit?"

"The next couple of minutes passed with the winch guy signaling the swimmer to do his damned job. But he wouldn't. He even quit looking up at the helo."

Pax leaned hard into the high-backed chair and ran his hands over his head. "That explains that dead time, when nothing was happening."

"Hey, I'm sorry about Hacksaw, but how'd you like to be that kid . . . living with that the rest of his life? Heads are gonna roll in the helo community."

"Was the winch guy the second swimmer?"

"Right," Motel said, nodding, "by the time he got to Hacksaw it was too late. Grayson's whole head was underwater."

Pax picked up the vest and water wings and placed one of the inflated devices under an arm. "Hell, you'd think these things would keep you afloat. Is our gear that heavy?"

"Don't know; it'd be easy to test. The main problem, I think, is that the navy guys have them sewed on their vests wherever they're most comfortable—out of the way of shoulder holsters, flares, radios . . . you name it."

Pax rested his head on the seatback and closed his eyes. "Think I'll start sleeping in my Mark-III Charlie."

Motel gave him a sideways glance. "Want me to help you inventory Hacksaw's stuff, get it in some foot lockers?"

"No, thanks, but I appreciate the offer."

"Well, that wasn't purely a good-guy offer. Some of us don't have air-conditioned staterooms. And I'm next senior to move into one."

Pax turned on the stateroom lights—every one of them—before he sat down at his desk, facing the door. Even having his back against a wall didn't remove an eerie feeling. It took a while before he felt like facing away from Hacksaw's rack. It was his now.

I better strip the lower bunk and move my sheets down. Be like Hacksaw to walk in on me while I'm doing it. . . . Ah, shit.

Hacksaw's safe combination dial hadn't been spun; the T-handle twisted the lugs free, and Pax pulled it open. A thick rubber band squeezed a stack of Wilma's letters.

Yeah. First things first.

Pax wrote Mrs. Cecil F. Grayson a single page letter—not many words, but his best ones, with no description of the accident.

I'll give her as much of that as she might ask for, when I see her again—if I see her again.

And in what he feared could be their last communication, he wrote Sally how the day had gone, except for his next day's evaluation board.

It won't be hard for her to recall Wilma's vulnerable moment at the XO's party. Who knows? Maybe Sally had been right: marrying naval aviators was a chump's bet.

Screw the inventory. He put a clean, short-sleeved khaki uniform together, shined his brass, spit-shined his shoes, changed his bedding to the lower rack, showered, and sacked out—not that it did him much good. Sleep had forsaken Pax. Hope for sleep fled before racing thoughts of shitty air-conditioning systems, shitty electrical systems, shitty LSOs, shitty CAGs, and shitty swimmers.

Pax passed through the ready room on the way to wardroom II annex. Dodd patted the seat next to his own. "Get any sleep, Ahab?"

"No, sir," he said and eased into the XO's chair.

"Let me tell you a few things before your meeting," Dodd said. "Foremost, keep your cool; don't get mad. Be honest answering their questions, but *do not volunteer* anything. Okay?"

"I guess so, Commander; I feel sorta adrift, but thanks."

As Pax stood, Dodd motioned for him to lean his head close. "When you're done for the day, let me know what happened."

With a quick nod, Pax raised a thumbs-up and began the trek toward what he hoped wouldn't turn into an inquisition.

Passing through the dining area of wardroom II, Pax saw Gator Broussard and Tom Cain drinking coffee at one of the rear tables. He opened the annex door at 0955. A tinge of apprehension gripped him.

I should have gotten here earlier.

Five officers sat on one side of a long, green-felt covered table.
Holy shit. I thought "in front of a green-covered table" was an expression.

CDR Goodwin, seated halfway down the long table, swept an arm toward a straight-backed, armless chair, opposite and facing himself from five feet away across the table. "Have a seat, Lieutenant Langford."

The CDR introduced himself—even though he and Pax had served together in a previous squadron for six months—and the other unsmiling board members, amongst whom Pax knew only Camp Brogan, who managed a covert wink. The other names meant no more to him than when he'd read them in the convening order. But their uniforms reflected considerable attention; spiffing up his own had been a good idea.

The CDR tilted an open folder toward himself, and with deliberate cadence and pronunciation began to read, "Lieutenant Langford, you've no doubt read the convening order and understand that in the early hours of 10 October, your deliberate maneuver during an obligatory wave-off was deemed dangerous and placed other personnel at high risk." The CDR paused and glanced at Pax, who remained motionless and mute. "The purpose of this board is to determine—as best we can—your future value to naval aviation." Again the glance to no response. "Any questions?" the CDR asked.

"No, sir."

"We have a couple of witnesses to interview. During these interviews, you will remain available in the wardroom. We will call you back after the interviews, so you can answer questions from the board. . . . Understand?"

"Yes, sir."

"Good. As you go into the wardroom, please ask Commander Broussard to come in."

When he opened the wardroom door, Pax had to fight himself to keep from flashing Gator Broussard a big grin. He wanted to, to piss him off—that fuzzy whisker's width this side of insubordination. But providing additional fuel—"he thinks this is a big joke"—for his own immolation didn't seem prudent.

"Commander Broussard," Pax said, "I believe they're ready for you."

Gator's eyes never met his as they brushed by one another, and Pax headed for the coffee urns. "Tom, you want some more coffee?"

"No, thanks."

Pax carried his cup and saucer to the table and sat opposite Tom. "Any word on *your* orders, Tom?"

The wingless lieutenant—like the first witness—found items of interest around the wardroom to look at, but Pax was not among them. "Not yet, but CAG thinks I might get back to a recruiting spot in Salt Lake City."

"That's home, isn't it?"

"Uh-huh."

Pax shuddered inside contemplating what kind of "testimony" earned such cushy orders for a confessed noncombatant.

Not to worry, though. Whatever tales were told could've been much worse. At least Tom never knew about Sally being on that dumb-ass snow flight into the grass strip at Olathe. And with Hacksaw gone, I alone know about my glasses.

But the wild card . . . the driver behind this bullshit board has abso-fucking-lutely nothing to do with aviation—and everything to do with my indiscreet zipper and CAG's wife, Robin.

"What?" Tom asked.

"Huh?"

"You were mumbling," Tom said. "I wondered about what."

"I need another coffee," Pax said and stood. "Want one?"

Tom shook his head. "I've had too much already; I need to hit the head. If they come looking, will you tell them I'll be right back?"

"Sure."

Maybe he'll flush himself off the ship.

That thought made Pax smile.

No sense being too serious in a ludicrous skit.

Broussard came out at 1130 to tell Tom—he wasn't looking at Pax yet—there would be a lunch break, but the board would see him at 1300.

Pax didn't eat; he went to his stateroom and stretched out. The phone rang a couple of times, but he let it ring.

From 1300 until 1500, Pax sat alone at the wardroom back table. By the time Tom Cain came out and said, "Five minutes—they're on a head break," Pax had about decided he didn't care anymore what happened. After a couple of minutes, Pax entered the annex and stood behind the *hot* seat, awaiting his appointed evaluators. CDR Goodwin came in last, sat, and pointed at Pax's chair. Pax eased into the chair and squirmed through several postures, trying to find a comfortable one that didn't show him reared back with his arms crossed. At last, he placed both hands between the small of his back and the chair—sort of a seated Parade Rest.

"Lieutenant," Goodwin said, "we have heard many disturbing reports today—if they're true—about your carefree, at best, attitude toward rules, regulations, and safety requirements in naval aviation. In fairness to you, we thought we'd get your perspective on these particular events."

This ought to be fun. I wonder if I've forgotten any of them.

"Lieutenant, are you listening?" Goodwin asked.

"Excuse me, Commander . . . was there a question in there somewhere—I mean other than the listening bit?" Pax knew his wide-eyed deadpan could infuriate a saint.

Goodwin's ears reddened and his face registered a faint, tight-lipped sneer. When the sneer softened to a smile, Pax's interior alarms raised the hair on his arms and the back of his neck.

"After hearing some of these stories today," Goodwin said, "I remembered the time you insisted on flying an FJ-3M in our squadron after the maintenance chief told you the plane was down. Fact is, you went ahead and flew that plane. The chief went to the skipper, who ordered you back to the field. As I recall, the skipper started to chew you out in the ready room . . . but you spun around and walked out. We thought you'd be grounded; you should've been grounded for that."

After several silent beats, Pax said, "Are you asking me to confirm that?"

"No, Lieutenant. I don't need your corroboration. I didn't want to have told the board something that you were unaware of.

"Lieutenant Cain, who said the two of you served at Navy Olathe together, told of three separate flying incidents that we'd like your version of. The first concerned an unprepared field landing in a snowstorm."

Pax leaned forward and scratched an ear. "Well, . . . for starters, it was not an *unprepared* field. It was a grass runway next to a Quonset hut hangar. We were authorized to land at grass strips; I'd been flying NavCad applicants for a week out of a grass strip near Doane College at Crete, Nebraska, before flying back to Olathe. Navy Olathe tower wasn't answering my calls, so I decided to use the non-radio field there that I'd used before."

Goodwin's lips were set in a near snarl. "Lieutenant Cain said the blowing snowstorm was below weather minimums."

"I don't remember it being that bad," Pax said. "The grass runway was practically clear. . . . But then I don't mind flying over the beach, either."

Goodwin raised his voice. "That's uncalled for! We're not discussing anyone's flying *here* but yours."

"That's fair, Commander," Pax said, "but Lieutenant Cain is senior to me, and in view of today's *disclosures*, don't you think the good lieutenant would have reported me for breaking any rules?"

Camp Brogan leaned backward and covered his mouth. The three LCDRs stared at Goodwin, gauging any storm.

"Moving on," the CDR said, "what about your failure to secure the rear cockpit in that T-34, which nearly caused you to crash at Olathe?"

"Guilty as charged. I learned a serious lesson there."

"Not so fast. You can't gloss over almost crashing a navy aircraft," Goodwin said.

"I didn't scratch the paint; I didn't even blow a tire. I made a dumb mistake. I admit it. What else can I say?"

Goodwin pointed a finger at Pax and fired imaginary bullets in rhythm with his words. "Your attitude hasn't changed one iota since you were an ensign, has it?"

Pax replaced his hands between his back and the chair.

"Okay, Lieutenant, suppose you explain to us why you decided to ignore Lieutenant Cain as he tried to wave you off during an 80 knot, 90-degree crosswind landing attempt at Fort Collins, Colorado."

"I didn't notice his wave-off signal. But I'm surprised he mentioned that, since he agreed—after the fact—that given the same conditions he might well have done exactly as I did . . . and landed himself. And as before, no scratched paint, no blown tire." Pax looked at each board member, pausing a second on each face. "Given the same conditions, I'd do the same thing over again, but with much more confidence . . . unless, of course, I saw a wave-off signal."

CDR Goodwin looked at the other board members and asked, "Any other questions?" They shook their heads.

"Okay," Goodwin said and smiled, "I happen to remember something else from our Fury squadron. Didn't you flame-out on the runway once, right after landing—with no fuel remaining?"

Pax took a deep breath and nodded. "Yes, sir, that's almost a true statement."

"You came as close as anyone could have come to losing that airplane. Besides being dumb, it should have embarrassed you to death," Goodwin said, leaned back, and crossed his arms.

Pax couldn't help smiling.

Goodwin reached across the table and fired some more finger-blanks at Pax. "Does reviewing your near misses seem humorous, Lieutenant?"

"No, sir, Commander. Near misses are never humorous," Pax said. "But your selection of evidence does amuse me. Flame out on the runway? Yes. My available fuel used up? Yes, but I had a wing drop-tank full of fuel. I was an ensign; it was my third flight in a Fury, and in the squadron. My section leader was a lieutenant with one or two deployments under his belt. As fuel-check totals began to diverge—with me on the low end, I started getting nervous. At 1000-pounds difference, I mentioned it to my leader. He said we took off together; we'd done the same things, so *my* gauge had to be bad.

"A little later, my gauge read low enough that I told him I thought we ought to go back and land. He said not to worry, that we'd shoot an instrument approach. I told him I'd see him on deck, left him, made an idle descent back to NAS JAX, declared a deferred emergency, and still had to make one 360-degree turn while a Sea Air Rescue bird took off. I made a high, fast approach, going to idle about the 45-degree position. The engine quit during the landing roll. I don't deny there was embarrassment after that flight, but it wasn't mine."

"Sheeit!" Camp Brogan said. The other board members frowned in Camp's direction.

Goodwin cleared his throat. "Let's move on to your most recent flight, Lieutenant, when even with a runaway air-conditioning system on deck, you chose *not* to abort."

"Excuse me, Commander," Pax said, bringing his hands close to his stomach, and rubbing them together, "but that's a pretty casual and misleading description of what happened."

"You had time to transmit 'Suspend cat one,' but you didn't do it," Goodwin said.

Pax overrode a sudden urge to stand. "With a great deal more respect than your statement deserves," Pax waited a couple of beats, "Commander, you haven't the remotest idea . . . of how much time I had . . . to make that decision. As an incident report on that flight has not been released, I don't understand how you've reached such an *opinion*."

Goodwin's face reddened, but he smiled that benevolent godfather's forbearance. "Perhaps I misspoke, Lieutenant, but we're here to find the truth. Please tell us when you discovered your air-conditioning failure?"

Pax rubbed his eyes and took a deep breath. "I've reconstructed that sequence . . . dozens of times since the flight. My best estimate is between a potato and a-half and two potatoes after the cat officer's wand touched the deck. By my count, the cat-stroke usually hits me at two and a-half potatoes.

There might have been a second to guess what had gone wrong, make an abort decision, and get the transmission out.

"Believe me, as bad as that super-heated air was burning my neck, if I thought there had been a chance in hell of staying on deck and shutting that pressurization switch off . . . that's damned well what I would've done. I'd never seen that failure before, so maybe I wasted *half* a second figuring what was wrong. . . . I'd like a glass of water now, if that's okay, Commander."

"Anyone else thirsty?" Goodwin asked.

"Yes, sir," Camp said.

"Let's take a five minute break," Goodwin said.

After the break, Goodwin asked Pax to recount the rest of the flight. Pax related the entire incident—without interruption.

One of the LCDRs asked him if he'd been reluctant to break the safety-wire on the pressure suit cooling switch.

"No, sir," Pax said. "I was flying with the maintenance officer; he was confident with the suggestion, and I had to have the fuel."

"Would you do the same thing again?" the LCDR asked.

"Yes, sir. Next time, though, after I got the fuel, I'd turn that pressure suit cooling switch back off. Maybe then it wouldn't burn through my electrical bundle."

"Is that what the NATOPS manual recommends?" the LCDR asked.

"Yes, sir."

Goodwin sat straight up. "You didn't know that?"

"No, sir, I didn't," Pax said. "I knew the switch was safety-wired. I never thought I'd have to break it."

"But you did," Goodwin said.

Pax pursed his lips and nodded.

"Lieutenant Langford," Goodwin said, glancing at the other board members, "I think any fair board would give you the benefit of the doubt on getting airborne that night. But not knowing your air-conditioning system came back to bite you. Had you turned that switch back off, after you got your fuel, you *might* not have burned up your electrical system. That's hindsight, I admit. However, beyond any mechanical failures, this board is faced with your decision to drive the LSOs from the platform in a personal attempt to intimidate them from doing their assigned job. Their duty is to not only protect pilots, but to safeguard the ship and flight deck personnel *from* pilots.

"I know you've reviewed your decision that night. Given time to consider your actions, if you were placed in the same circumstances again—and waved-off—would you make the same decision?"

Pax crossed his arms, uncrossed them, and rubbed both hands together. And he took a deep breath and blew it out. "Commander Goodwin, I know there are a lot of things more important to the navy—and to me—than landing an airplane back on its ship. But in an airplane, with the ship's landing lights on—meaning they're open for business—I'll keep trying to land until I'm out of fuel. If an LSO can see me, and gives me a wave-off, I'll take it in a heartbeat; I'll keep taking wave-offs till I'm out of fuel.

"However, when I know an LSO cannot see me, and I've got a whole shit-pot of problems he doesn't know about—including no radio—I think I owe it to him, to me, and the navy . . . to at *least* give him a hint that I'd appreciate a little more elbowroom than the norm. . . . But I don't think I'd fly over an LSO platform *that* low again."

Goodwin shook his cocked head and harrumphed out a short breath. "You haven't changed any, have you?"

Pax didn't respond.

"Any more questions for Lieutenant Langford?" Goodwin asked and eyed the other board members.

"Yes, sir," Camp Brogan said. "Pax, how many unsatisfactory flights did you have in the training command—how many *downs*?"

Pax looked at Goodwin as he said, "None."

"That it?" Goodwin asked as he picked up his folder. The other board members nodded.

"Lieutenant Langford," Goodwin said, "The board will discuss these proceedings then make its recommendation to CAG Dengler. His office will notify your commanding officer of his decision. You're excused."

Pax didn't care to see any of his squadron mates after leaving the board members at their green-felt-covered table. For if anyone were to ask him how it had gone, he wouldn't know what to say.

Do I have a prayer? Did I ever have one?

"Hell, yes!" he said and realized how loud he'd said it when two oncoming sailors braced the bulkheads on either side of the passageway. "Carry on, men," he said with a straight face. He ducked into the library and hid his face behind an opened magazine while he tried to conjure up some options to the fighter pilot life. Few came to mind, and none that did carried any appeal. He'd returned to the life he loved, but his grip on it was loosening. Staring without focus at a *National Geographic Magazine* solved no problems, so he strolled back to his stateroom.

Chapter 24—INNOCENT, NOT EXACTLY

Having skipped lunch, Pax ate dinner before trudging up to the ready room.

Did I piss off CDR Goodwin? Probably. Could I have been smoother, more contrite?

Pax mumbled to himself thinking about that.

Yeah, maybe so, but could I live with myself after doin' it? That's the kicker. I should've paid more attention when Dodd told me to watch my temper? Crud! I lost my cool as soon as that smug prick, Goodwin, opened his yap. Rat's ass!

Dodd stared at him in the ready room. Pax tried not to smile, but eventually he had to cock his head and shrug. The commander crooked a finger at him. "Brogan voted for you, even after you wire-brushed Goodwin. He also said it wouldn't have made any difference if you'd kissed his ass instead; their minds were already made up. Broussard played the crucified warrior role like he'd been practicing for a month."

"I hate to ask," Pax said, "but what's gonna happen now?"

"Knowing CAG . . ." Dodd said and put a hand on Pax's shoulder, "I'd say you're on the way home."

Whew! I wasn't ready for that.

Pax's knees gave warning: they'd be turning to jelly. He flopped into the nearest chair. Dodd sat beside him. "Pax, I'll have another go at CAG tonight; maybe I can change his mind. I doubt it, but I'll fire my best shot."

Pax didn't trust his voice to reply. So he closed his eyes and nodded. He felt Dodd stand, but when he looked, the skipper was striding from the room. No one else had heard their exchange, but the word wouldn't tarry. He headed for his stateroom. After passing a few knee-knockers, he picked up an echo to his steps. He looked and found Motel trailing him.

"The carpenter shop brought two cruise boxes," Motel said. "We stacked 'em inside your stateroom while you were eating. If you'd like, I thought we could inventory Hacksaw's stuff."

"Don't know, pal, this hasn't been my best day."

"Yeah, I heard Camp telling Bud Banks about the board. I wanted to say something about that."

The two cruise boxes filled the extra space in the stateroom. Motel quickly flipped a lid open on the top one. "I've done this a lot," he said. "We'll be through inside an hour."

The phone rang. "Lieutenant Langford."

"Pax this is the XO. I talked to the skipper. He's writing a letter of resignation. If he can't change CAG's mind about your board, he's going to hand it to him. I don't want that to happen."

"Well, me neither. Maybe I can change his mind."

"Better hurry!"

"I'm on my way, XO. Thanks."

Motel's questioning look shouted a string of questions.

"Sorry, pal, go ahead and start. I'll get back ASAP."

Pax rapped three times on CDR Dodd's door. Dodd opened it with a paper in his hand. "Oh, thought you were the yeoman. Need something?"

"Sir, I need to talk to you . . . before your yeoman does any typing."

"The XO call you?"

"Sir, may I come in?"

"Sure," Dodd said, stepped aside, and looked both ways down the passageway before closing the door. "Have a seat."

"Skipper, I want to ask a favor. I need to tell you something, but I'm going to ask you to promise you'll never repeat it. Ever."

"Why should I make a promise like that?"

"You'll under—"

Two rapid knocks shook the door.

Pax raised both open hands. "Please. No typing till you hear me out."

Dodd hesitated before peeking around the door. "Sorry, Ski, I found some mistakes. I'll bring it to the office later, but thank you."

When Dodd regained his seat, Pax said, "Thank you."

"No need to thank me; I won't make a blind promise."

"Okay, but I'll tell you what I need to. Maybe you'll decide not to submit a useless letter."

"I can't imagine where you're coming from, but I'm listening. Fire away."

Pax scooted his chair closer to Dodd and whispered, "Robin Dengler and

I spent a night together in a motel."

Dodd's mouth gaped, both his arms fell straight down, and he shuddered. "You did *wha-a-a-t?*" Dodd tilted his face toward the ceiling, and gazed with disbelief at Pax. "No! Don't say it again. Are you fucking crazy? *Suicidal?*"

"Skipper, I didn't know who she was. It happened my first night in San Diego; I never expected to see her again. Honest, I'd forgotten about her . . . till that night on your deck."

"Holy shit! How'd *CAG* find out?"

Pax shrugged. "She must have told him."

Another gape, arms slack again, another shudder. "W*ha-a-a-t?* No! Don't say it again. Why the hell would she do that?"

Pax shook his head and told Dodd about the brief Mex Village encounter with Robin Dengler the night before *Gettysburg* deployed.

Dodd massaged his temples before giving Pax the fisheye. "Ahab, do you have any fucking idea who Robin Dengler *is?*"

"Well, yeah . . . *now.*"

"Who is she?"

"She's CAG's wife."

"Humph! Let me explain something. If CAG gives you walking papers— say, tomorrow—you've got two chances to appeal the Goodwin board's decision: Commander Naval Air Force, U.S. Pacific Fleet in San Diego, VADM John Kimbrough, and Chief of Naval Operations in Washington, D.C., ADM Bob Hughes.

"Kimbrough flew F-8s; he *might* appreciate that flight of yours the other night."

Pax nodded.

"One small hitch, though," Dodd deadpanned. "The fellow giving you your walking papers is John Kimbrough's son-in-law . . . *and,* oh-by-the-way, Robin's daddy." Dodd cocked his head and eyed Pax. "Makes you think about taking a meat cleaver to your crank, huh?"

When Pax returned to his stateroom, Motel glanced up from his writing. "We'll be done here in a couple of minutes, Ahab."

Hacksaw's wardrobe locker stood open and empty, as were the drawers in his chest. Motel had scribbled two full pages of a yellow legal pad that now lay on the desk. One cruise box sat filled, a second, almost filled.

"Wow!" Pax said. "You ought to be admin officer."

"I looked in his safe, but it'd be better if we inventoried that together. I'll add the safe's contents to the list and have admin type it with places for us both to sign. Tomorrow I'll get the supply officer to put locks on both boxes and mail them to Wilma."

"Like a diet Pepsi?" Pax asked and opened the mini-fridge under the sink.

"Yeah, thanks."

Pax handed Motel the cold can, opened Hacksaw's safe, and pulled out a worn leather wallet. "I checked this last night: eighty-two bucks, American Express card, ID, and a Trojan rubber." Pax went back to the fridge and this time fished out a Coors Light.

"I saw those in there. Aren't you afraid someone'll find 'em and turn you in?"

"I asked Hacksaw the same thing. His answer: 'Who the fuck wants hot beer?' Besides, did you look in those drawers under his rack?"

Motel nodded. "Uh-huh. I felt like locking the door. No telling what Coors Light will be worth after another line period."

"You want to buy that mini-fridge? We paid eighty-four bucks for it; you can have it for seventy-five."

"Deal," Motel said and reached for his wallet.

"I'll write Wilma a check for $157, shit-can the rubber, and send the credit card with the check."

Motel handed him the $75 and asked, "What's your status?"

Pax took a long pull of Coors—enough to make his eyes water. "This could be my last night. If you delay moving till tomorrow, you could probably move right into the bottom rack."

"None of us—I mean nobody in either fighter squadron—can figure this. Camp said Gator bled over the board members telling his tale, but so what? Anyway, the main reason I came down was to tell you not to give up. Lots of folks get new life from COMNAVAIRPAC. Kimbrough flew F-8s; he knows bullshit when he sees it."

Sure enough, an image of a meat cleaver flitted through Pax's brain. "Hope you're right, pal."

Motel left and Pax continued sitting at his desk, wondering what to do next. He decided to get Wilma's letter done first, with the enclosures. After that the load got heavier. How to tell Sally? He thought about it from every angle. At last, he picked up his pen.

14 October, 1966

Dearest Sally,

Last night I wrote that Hacksaw had been killed and Captain Conrad had died. What I neglected to mention, was that CAG convened a FNAEB to determine whether or not I would continue flying. That board was held today, and I got a down. I may head home as early as tomorrow. Believe me, there was nothing—not a thing—wrong with my flying. That evokes the obvious question: Why did CAG haul me before a board? Spite or revenge, I guess. And perhaps with reason; it's hard to know. Remember the night at CDR Dodd's house, when we met CAG and his wife? Well, I lied to you when you asked me if I knew her. Hell, I was in shock. The first day I got to San Diego, she and I spent that night in a motel. I had no idea who she was, but she did say she was married. She also wouldn't fool around with naval personnel. I lied to her, too . . . told her I was a doctor. That last night at Mex Village, she passed me back near the restrooms and told me he knew . . . and to be careful. Evidently, I wasn't. You may not have read past my two lies; I wouldn't blame you. But as bleak as not flying might be, I consider a rift between us a greater loss. My future is too hazy to even compose a complete sentence, now. I pray we can talk when my compass settles. With hope,

Pax wasn't satisfied with the words, but he knew the sweetest poetry couldn't improve what he had to tell her. In frustration, he smashed the Coors can flat and threw it in the below-bunk drawer with some of its brothers.

He'd turned out the light and put his head on the pillow when the phone rang. "Langford."

"Pax, Ollie Anderson. CAG's office called and told us CAG agreed with the evaluation board. He wants you off the ship tomorrow. CDR Dodd knows. You've got a seat on the 0800 COD flight to Cubi. Your orders and records will be in the ready room at 0600."

"Thanks, Viking."

He had a parachute bag packed and was stuffing a carry-on bag. Loud knocks on the door startled him. When he opened it, Camp Brogan and Bud Banks stood framed in its light. "Come on in," he said, "if you don't mind standing. There's a whole lotta packing going on in here."

"We heard," Camp said. "You got screwed, pal; I'm sorry . . . we both are."

Bud said nothing, but nodded along with Camp.

Pax zipped the small bag shut. "Whoever said, 'the military's hurry up and wait,' never got kicked out of a fighter squadron."

"Skipper Milano said Kimbrough knows F-8s," Camp said, "and that he's a good guy—says he'll be fair with you."

"Dad worked for him twice," Bud said, "and I think he likes him, too."

Pax envisioned a few more meat cleavers. "Yeah, maybe it'll work out. Not much chance of getting back here, though, even if I *get* lucky."

Camp extended his hand. "We've got three Alpha strikes tomorrow; wish us luck."

Pax shook both their hands. "You guys don't need luck. It's MiGs that'll need it."

Bud started to say something, but didn't. He raised a thumbs-up, winked, and turned away.

The SDO's call came at 0500, as he'd requested. Pax had a quick shave, a quicker breakfast, stuffed his flight gear in a second parachute bag, and sat in the ready room signing inventory sheets for Hacksaw's belongings. Ollie Anderson passed him a large envelope. "Here's your pay record, medical record, personal record, and orders. You're space 'A' the whole trip, Pax. Meander over God's entire creation going back, if you want to."

Tom Weaver sat beside Pax. "Ahab, if you don't mind, I'd like you to stop by the shore det at Cubi and see what the hell Roller Rinc's doing. They owe us a plane out of corrosion control, but being two pilots short, we can't afford to send anyone in till it's ready."

Pax nodded. "Be glad to."

Skipper Dodd and the XO came in. "Keep your seats," Dodd said and sat on Pax's other side—opposite Weaver—but talked directly at Pax. "We haven't got much time, Pax, so listen up. Take at *least* two weeks getting back to San Diego. When you get there, call Lieutenant Fred Harrington; he's John Kimbrough's flag lieutenant. Set up your appointment to see Kimbrough through Harrington. Got it?"

Pax nodded. "Yes, sir."

Petty Officer Chandler and a helper scampered into the ready room and handed Pax a Mae West and cranial helmet. "Where are your bags, Lieutenant?" he asked. Pax pointed; Chandler and his striker grabbed them up. "They'll be in the COD, sir; I'll see you on deck."

The skipper stood. "Listen up, gents. Some of you have to brief in a few minutes, so I'll be quick. Pax, your departure is premature. We expect you back in the fleet, but fact-of-life . . . it won't be with us." As he talked, Dodd slid the LSO's greenie board into view. Pax's last red "cut" pass was covered with a green square. To the right of that square, in bold letters: OK (VSH, T-1).

"In the end, gents, when we add up the pluses and minuses in a naval career, the thing that means the most to us is how our peers rated us. Would they be comfortable going into combat with us? Have no doubt in your military mind, Pax; you're top drawer with us. Keep your chin up." He turned to CDR Connor. "XO."

CDR Connor stepped to the lectern. "Pax, the last two days Gypsy Lawrence has been down in the carpenter shop. He made a little doodad for your *I-love-me* wall." Connor raised a 10-inch square plaque that was painted green and had an OK on the top half. The bottom half showed (VSH, T-I)— in LSO parlance, Gypsy Lawrence had graded Pax's last pass as almost perfect, with a little Very Shit Hot, Taxi to the 1-wire.

The Lobo pilots stood and clapped. Pax could do nothing but shake his lowered head. Tears flowed . . . tears he couldn't stop. He got to his feet, accepted the plaque, saluted the blurred room and stumbled out.

A white-jerseyed ensign, wearing a cranial helmet, had Pax and Tom Cain wait on a flight-deck-level ladder-landing—inside the island structure—aft of flight deck control while the first Alpha strike planes launched. The Grumman C-1A, Carrier Onboard Delivery (COD), flight would launch after the strike birds were airborne. But even dogged shut, the heavy steel hatch didn't muffle enough noise to allow easy conversation. Nor did Pax feel he needed to say anything to the elephant-memoried, loquacious, and wingless lieutenant.

But it was after Tom cocked his cranial-helmeted head trying to read the plaque, and Pax held it up for him, that Pax saw the wood-burned words on its back: One black-assed night—10-10-66. And that did it. An uninvited— yet overpowering—weight, albeit unreal, lifted from his shoulders.

At least someone else understood.

The COD's deck-run takeoff reaffirmed Pax's appreciation of steam catapults, but it was a fleeting thought—followed by the realization that he'd be lucky to continue making any type of navy takeoffs. They refueled at Da Nang, South Vietnam, and chugged across the South China Sea to Cubi Point in the Philippines. The two lieutenants had much to think about. Nothing to talk about. The COD's final 100-miles was spent dodging thunderstorms, while its pilots tried to make the TACAN work.

Pax felt relieved when Tom Cain caught a helo ride on over to Clark AFB. Otherwise they might have been sharing a too quiet room. The Roller Rinc maintenance queries could wait until morning. Truth be told, Pax hoped a good night's sleep might garner some enthusiasm for the task. He tried to stay under the BOQ full-force shower until he forgot what "navy shower" even meant, but his conscience took hold . . . about the same time his rumbling gut invited him to dinner.

Since no carrier had been pier-side, the Cubi Club sounded livelier than Pax expected. Most of the noise came from the bar, so he investigated, but didn't recognize anyone there. He ordered a San Miguel and sat at the bar's end—apart from the rowdies. After a few minutes, though, one of the dice-rolling drinkers brought his glass down a few stools from Pax—an A-4 driver, it turned out, off *Intrepid*. They expected her in Cubi the nineteenth, when they'd head home, combat deployment completed.

"Any fighters aboard?" Pax asked.

"Don't need fighters," the A-4 jock said. "We got a *Skyraider* guy who bagged a MiG-17. Who the hell needs a buncha prima donna fighter pukes?"

Pax raised his bottle. "You got a point. Have a good trip home." He left most of the flat-tasting beer at the bar, but dinner proved tasteless, as well. He hadn't yet decided where to kill two weeks prior to seeing VADM Kimbrough, but Cubi Point—for sure—would fill little of the itinerary.

Early next morning, Sunday, the 16th, at the corrosion control hangar, Pax found two VF-39 men who were helping apply masking tape on a VF-37 "Sea Bat" fighter. A short, stocky AMH, Petty Officer Second Class Fritz Braun, saw Pax, waved, and put down a roll of tape. "Hey, Lieutenant Langford, what brings you to Cubi?"

"Petty Officer Braun," Pax said and nodded, "I came from your real home. Where's Lieutenant Rinc?"

"Haven't seen him yet, sir."

"How about the rest of our crew?"

A voice came from behind Pax. "They're dickin' off in town." Pax looked around at VF-37's Lieutenant Tom Shaw, both thumbs hooked into his belt. "Braun and Gaffney earn their keep; the rest don't."

While Pax chewed on Shaw's declaration, the portly LDO beckoned to him, "Let's take a walk." When they'd cleared the hangar, Shaw continued, "I'm surprised it took this long to get someone in here checking on Rinc."

"There's a problem?" Pax asked.

"You mean other than him being a shit-heel souse?"

"Yeah," Pax said, "other than that."

"He's set up in town, lives with some local, and stays shit-faced about half the time. He shows up here about every third day for maybe an hour—for a booze run, I expect."

"When's the next COD flight to the ship?"

"Tuesday, but an A-3 may be going out tomorrow. You got something to send?"

"Not something," Pax said. "Rinc will need a seat. You made out your daily sitrep yet?"

Shaw nodded. "But I ain't sent it."

Pax patted both shirt pockets. "I'd like to add a paragraph."

Shaw tore a page from his wheel book and handed it and a pen to Pax. "They usually get transmitted about 1800. Is that soon enough?"

Pax nodded.

Pax recognized the *Gettysburg* A-3 pilot at lunch in the Cubi Club and secured a spot for LT Rinc to the ship the next day. He had Petty Officer Braun deliver the message to Rinc that he was scheduled to fly to the ship—takeoff time noon Monday, showtime 1030 at base ops.

In the bar, prior to dinner, Pax watched the same *Intrepid* crowd rolling the same dice for the same tepid San Miguels. And before long, the same *Intrepid* A-4 pilot from the evening before came over. "You hear about the MiGs yet?" he asked.

Pax shook his head. "What MiGs?"

"One of our A-4 drivers flew in about noon. He said some fighter weenies got some MiGs yesterday during an Alpha strike."

"Whose fighters? Which ship?"

"He didn't know. *We* don't have any; they had to be from *Oriskany*, *Gettysburg*, or *Coral Sea*."

"Did he know F-4s or F-8s; where is this guy?"

The A-4 jock craned his neck around, but looked back with a shrug as he walked away. "Don't see him; if he comes in I'll send him over."

Pax finished dinner and was leaving the club, when a gray navy pickup pulled up curbside in front of him. Tom Shaw opened the driver's door and got out—waved at Pax across the hood. "Hoped I could catch you. Petty Officer Braun said Rinc was one pissed off navy lieutenant after he got your message."

Pax smiled. "I don't care how happy he is, so long as he shows up tomorrow."

"What I needed to tell you: Commander Weaver acknowledged your note; another det leader will be on the next COD. Now, you ready for this? Commander Milano, Brogan, and Banks got three MiG-17s yesterday."

Pax's immediate "Shit hot!" and double thumbs-up were genuine. But so was the stab to his heart.

Pax saw Rinc off Monday in *Gettysburg*'s A-3, before stopping by the shore-det hangar. Tom Shaw's wide grin was reflected in most of the crew's faces. "Rinc still pissed?" Tom asked.

"If he was, it never came up," Pax said and handed Shaw two envelopes. "Please see that Brogan and Banks get these. No hurry. You can wait till the ship comes in. I've got a helo ride over to Clark AFB this afternoon. I'll get a space-A MAC flight from there back home."

"Stateside? I hope nothing's wrong."

"Me, too," Pax said, shook Shaw's hand, and walked away.

Chapter 25—GOOD NEWS, BAD . . .

Sally spotted Becky's car in the driveway, back near the garage, and hoped the front door wouldn't be locked—but it was. The harsh, clattering half-buzz, half-bell phone's ringing threatened her balancing act with purse and overnight bag while she keyed the lock. As always, a jangling phone put her teeth on edge. She strode to the kitchen and snatched the receiver. "Hello."

"Western Union," a sing-song female voice said. "We have a telegram for Mrs. Turner Banks, Junior. Are you Mrs. Banks?"

Sally's throat tightened. Jumbled fears for Bud raced behind her eyes. She had trouble catching her breath, let alone trying to talk. Becky rounded a corner, wrapped in one towel, drying her hair with another. Sally thrust the phone at her. Becky read Sally's face and, with a look of distaste, accepted the instrument as one might a container of soured milk. "Hello. . . . Yes, I'm Mrs. Banks. . . . Please, go ahead."

Sally sensed Becky relaxing and wondered what the telegram was about, when her sister-in-law jumped right out of the wraparound towel. "What?" Becky screamed and landed with her mouth and both eyes wide open. Sally thought the hair-drying towel, now catawampus and hooding the top half of Becky's excited face, lent an R-rated, slapstick aura to whatever was happening. "Read it again, please," Becky said and beckoned for Sally to share the handset. Sally leaned near the upturned receiver.

"I don't blame you," the female said. "'My Becky girl, Please join me in Hong Kong from four November to nine November to celebrate MiG-17 kill. Tell Mom and Dad. Much love. Your Bud.'"

Sally spun around a couple times, and scooped up Becky's towel.

"Okay," Becky told the phone, "a MiG-17; I got that. Repeat the Hong Kong dates. . . . Four to nine November—next month. . . . And I'll get a copy of the telegram tomorrow. . .? Thank you; oh, thank you so much."

Becky blushed a purplish-red as she rewrapped herself in the elusive towel. "Sorry about that," she said, but little shame restrained the half-smile that played around her mouth or the sparkle in her eyes.

"Dad'll be home in an hour; can you wait that long to call them?"

Becky's brow wrinkled. "Don't you want to do that?"

"No, he asked you to. Besides, anyone who tells my folks that Bud shot down a MiG will get on Dad's best side forever."

"I hope Pax got one," Becky said.

Sally shook her head. "He didn't. Bud would've mentioned it if he had."

"We need a map," Becky said. "Where the hell *is* Hong Kong?"

"Who cares! You lucky dog, you're gonna love it."

Next day Sally received two letters from Pax. She checked the numbers on the envelopes' back flaps—their code system—to know which one to open first. "Oh, *no!*" she wailed.

Becky peered from the kitchen doorjamb. "What? What's happened?"

"It's Hacksaw; Hacksaw Grayson got killed."

"How?"

Sally read more. "Engine problem. He ejected and drowned. . . . Oh, *poor* Wilma."

Becky sat next to Sally on the sofa. "Pax and Hacksaw were roomies, huh?"

"There's more!" Sally looked up from the letter. "*Gettysburg*'s captain, too—a *heart attack*. Pax saw him seconds before it happened."

"Who the hell's drivin' the boat?"

Sally cast a blank-eyed stare toward Becky. "Don't know."

"Did he mention Bud getting the MiG?"

"No, maybe it's in this one," Sally said, inching her index fingernail beneath the second envelope's flap. As she scanned the first two paragraphs, she stopped breathing. Her lips remained parted. She sensed, rather than heard, the question from Becky and looked up. "What?"

"Did he mention Bud's MiG?"

"Not yet." She finished the letter, and reread it. When she folded it and looked up, Becky's questioning gaze changed to concern. Sally shook her head. "No, he didn't mention it—must've happened later."

"Are you okay?"

"Uh-huh, a little tired maybe." Sally traced fingertips across her brow. "Think I'll lie down a few minutes."

A day passed before Sally called her mom; she wanted to be alone for the call. And she'd not mentioned Pax's predicament to Becky. She didn't want to throw a damper on Becky's enthusiasm for Bud's aerial victory and their upcoming Hong Kong trip. After she dialed, the pulsing buzz in Sally's ear sounded weak, as if energizing the distant ringer bled strength.

Five rings are enough.

Her mother's breathless "Hello" stopped Sally's hanging up.

"Hi, Mom. Where were you?"

"Dragging groceries in. If Bud gets *another* MiG, we'll have had everyone in Olathe to dinner. How's it with you?"

"Okay, I guess. There's no way Dad can be any happier than Becky is. Sometimes I want to strangle her—jealous, I guess."

"We're sorry about Pax . . . *and* his roommate. Coleman Dodd wrote Turner a long letter explaining everything. He asked your dad to go to bat for Pax with John Kimbrough."

"Who's he?"

"COMNAVAIRPAC at North Island. Dad worked for—"

The front door swung open and Becky lugged her garment bag through the living room. "Equipment broke," she said. "I'm outta this uniform and into the shower."

"I'm sorry, Mom. Becky came back. Who'd you say Kimbrough was?"

"He's COMNAVAIRPAC at North Island. Dad worked for him a couple of times."

"Will Dad do it?"

"Says he won't. Says Kimbrough's a good friend who's feeding planes and pilots to an air war on the other side of the world. Turner thinks it'd be imposing. He said friends don't do that. Besides, it might come down to *why*, and Turner says no way is he going to tell John Kimbrough his daughter's sleeping around."

"*Whose* daughter?"

"Kimbrough's daughter. Pax's CAG is married to her."

"Is that fair; won't Kimbrough rubber-stamp anything CAG Dengler sends his way?"

"You'd have to think so."

"And Dad won't help?"

"Maybe it'll work out. Besides, how much do we know about Pax? Not having a family may've left marks we can't see."

Sally looked at the ceiling. "Whatever that means. I keep thinking if I'd slept with him in Olathe, this might not have happened."

"You can't *know* that, so don't waste time worrying about it. In fact, we don't even know if what Pax *told* Dodd happened took place. Your dad hasn't one hundred percent bought off on what Dodd told him happened on Pax's last flight."

"Mom, . . . Pax as much as asked me to marry him before the ship left."

"He had a job when the ship deployed. You didn't say yes, did you?"

"If I fly home, can I change Dad's mind?"

"You know your father."

"Got to go, Mom. Love you."

"And we love you; don't get too upset."

As she hung up, Sally heard mail falling through the slot. She picked up three letters addressed to Becky, two from Bud. She wanted to know what Bud had to say. For a brief moment, steaming them open crossed her mind. She tried to calm herself with a glass of wine, but it disappeared long before shower noises ceased. After some serious conservation, a second glass contained a mere sip by the time Becky, in a terry cloth robe, made it to the kitchen.

"You've got mail," Sally said, trying to seem casual as she lifted her chin toward the living room.

Becky looked into the refrigerator. "More wine?"

Yep, I should've steamed the bastards open.

"Uh-uh, I'm okay. Did Bud get another MiG?"

"Why? Did you hear something?"

Sally killed glass number two. "Not *yet*. You've got to be the cleanest person in San Diego."

"Oh, . . . the letters," Becky said, grinned, and moved into the living room.

Sally filled another glass, shook her head, and poured it back into the bottle. Becky returned to the kitchen, reading as she walked. As she placed one page face down on the table, she threw a quick, questioning glance at Sally, and hurried through the rest of the letter. Becky's shoulders sagged as she looked up. "Did you know about Pax—him coming home?"

Sally nodded once. Becky cocked her head and opened the next letter.

Quiet. God this kitchen is quiet. Is that faint hum from the refrigerator, or from gears grinding in Becky's head?

"Have you seen him?" Becky asked, slipping the pages back in their envelopes.

Sally shook her head. "No."

"Heard from him?"

242

Another shake. "Not since his last letter."

"Bud says Pax lost his lights one night and put the LSOs—*in the net?*—but nobody except CAG and the LSOs made that much of it. Bud's skipper and Camp thought Pax got a royal screwing. What did Pax say?"

"Not much; I doubt I'll hear from him till he finds out what's going to happen."

"Huh? What the hell's going on with you two? Have a fight or something?"

Another shake. "Hey, may I see what Bud said about it?"

"Read them both—the whole things," Becky said and chuckled. "Bud'll never be a Lord Byron . . . but at least he writes, which is more than *you* led me to believe."

Sally skimmed the pages looking for the least hint that Bud thought Pax deserved to be sent home. No such hint appeared. Bud's comments backed Pax across the board. She pushed the letters across the table. "Thanks, Becky. I shouldn't have asked."

"When's he supposed to get here?"

"I don't know. He may have to see an admiral at North Island. Maybe I'll hear from him after that."

"*Maybe?* Hey, gal, I'm married to your brother; I've got sister-in-law privileges! Did that asshole dump you? *Talk* to me."

After dinner, Sally called Ann Dodd, who picked up after the first ring. "That's amazing," Ann said. "I was reaching for the phone to call you when it rang."

"I couldn't reach Wilma Grayson yesterday," Sally said, "but I wanted to find out how she's doing and if there's anything I could do to help out."

"That's one reason I was going to call. We had one hell of a time getting word to Wilma about Hacksaw. She and the boys had gone with friends to Yosemite after school Thursday, and we didn't know anything about where they were staying or how they got there. Lois Weaver and I took turns sitting in their driveway till they got home Sunday."

"That's *awful*. Is she okay?"

"Everything considered, she's fine. There's a ten o'clock memorial service tomorrow morning at the Miramar chapel."

"I'll be there."

"Good. Sally, I'm sorry about Pax. Coleman's beside himself; he even wrote your dad a letter."

"That's what Mom said."

"Will he help?"

"I don't know; the situation's tricky."

"Amen to that understatement."

"Ann, I've got something boiling over—see you tomorrow."

That little lie shouldn't be considered hanging up on Pax's skipper's wife, but I didn't want to get into a conversation on alley cat morals. Damn! How many people know?

Next morning, Sally and Becky felt lucky to snag two last-row seats in the overflowing Miramar Chapel. Aviators in service dress blue uniforms, and many wives and girlfriends, lent a greater aura of respect to the proceedings than Sally remembered from her last such ceremony.

When they filed from the chapel, many attendees were pointing upward and eastward, toward a small smudge, barely above the horizon, that grew larger until four separate pieces became discernable—Crusaders in a diamond formation. Abeam the chapel, the formation's southern offset allowed a single plane to pull up and disappear directly into the sun, one navy version of the "missing man" formation.

Sally and Becky approached Wilma Grayson who knelt with an arm around each of her two oldest sons. "Look, boys," Wilma said and pointed. "That's how your daddy flew up into heaven."

Sally turned away and squeezed her eyes shut. When she opened them, she recognized Robin Dengler walking away. Sally touched Becky's arm. "Wait here for me."

No scheme. No plan. A quick shot from the hip.

She overtook CAG's wife at the latter's Oldsmobile sedan and stopped across the hood from her. "Mrs. Dengler, I'm Pax Langford's fiancée; may we talk?"

Robin Dengler gasped a quick breath, canted her head, while striking a contemplative pose. When she straightened up, her chin rose a few degrees. "We have nothing to discuss." And breaking eye contact, she got into the car and maneuvered from the chapel's parking lot, leaving Sally standing curbside.

Sally's lips compressed into a hard, straight line. The clipped words came low-pitched and venom-filled. "Not too smart, Robin."

Becky's voice surprised her. "Was that who I think it was?"

Sally nodded. "But I'm not who you think *I* am; I'm an imposter. I told CAG's wife that Pax and I were engaged."

Becky grinned. "Made her jealous, didn't it. . .? I know, you asked me to wait. But standing alone over here, well, you looked like a mailbox. Besides, everyone left. Wilma wanted us to join the squadron wives for lunch, but I told her we had afternoon flights . . . that you'd call her."

After fuming for two days over Robin Dengler's rebuff, Sally dialed Wilma Grayson's number Sunday afternoon. One of the boys answered. "Grayson residence."

"Hi, I'm Sally Banks. Is your mother there?"

"Yes, ma'am . . . I'll get her."

"Sally, I hoped you'd call. Have you heard from Pax yet?"

Ouch! That hurts.

"Not yet, Wilma. Have you?"

"He wrote me a sweet letter after the accident—nothing more. He'll call you when he gets back. Ann Dodd doesn't expect him before this weekend; Coleman told him to kill a couple of weeks coming home. She mentioned Coleman had written your dad for some help. . . ."

Sally knew the long pause called for a response. "That's what I understand."

What else had Ann told Wilma?

"Anyway, I'm taking the boys to a movie this afternoon. May I have your number? I'll let you know if I hear from him. Ann Dodd said she has some contacts on the lookout, too. Okay?"

Sally thanked Wilma and told her the number.

Kill two weeks . . . from when?

She scanned Pax's last letter again, written on the fourteenth.

He probably left the ship the fifteenth. Two more weeks would put him here in six more days—Saturday, the twenty-ninth. We'll see, won't we.

Two more days passed without word from Pax. Sally paced the house until Becky started counting cadence aloud. At work Sally caught herself a few seconds from being rude to an obnoxious, borderline-drunk passenger.

This isn't my life! I reject being a spectator, watching chips fall—some of which are mine—without so much as a peep. I'll call that snooty bitch. How deep a moat can a sleeping-around CAG's wife have? Besides, what can it hurt?

Sally plowed through the hurdles: an unlisted telephone number; a reluctant Ann Dodd, who only gave up the number and address after receiving a blood-oath of anonymity. And an hour of busy signals, but persistence paid. "Hello."

"Robin?"

"Yes, who is this?"

"Sally Banks. Maybe Commander Grayson's memorial service *was* an inappropriate setting, but we *do* need to talk."

A click, and the dial tone—although not unexpected—raised the hair on Sally's neck and curled the corners of her mouth into a predator's grin.

Two San Francisco flights claimed most of Sally's Wednesday. But when she got home, a sleepy-eyed Becky sat up from a sofa-nap to say Ann Dodd had called and asked that Sally call her as soon as she could.

Oh, hell. Did Robin guess who'd given out her phone number?

"Did she sound aggravated?" Sally asked.

Becky shook her head. "No, but she's hot to talk to you. She called back in less than thirty minutes."

Sally slipped into shorts and a sweater before dialing Ann's number. The "Hello" came before she'd even heard a ringing signal.

"Ann?"

"Yes, Sally? I'd picked up to call you again."

"Am I in trouble?"

"Huh? I've got word on Pax. Fred Harrington, Kimbrough's flag lieutenant, called. Fred was in VF-39 last year, so I'd put a bug in his ear. Pax called Fred this morning for an appointment with Kimbrough. Fred said he set it up for ten o'clock on Monday—the thirty-first."

"Where's Pax *now*?"

"Fred didn't know."

"Okay, that's more than we did know. Thanks, Ann."

The hesitant question eased from the phone. "Did you call her?"

"Uh-huh, but we didn't talk."

"She *hung* up."

"That she did."

"She's some broad! What'll you do now?"

"I don't know."

"Whatever you decide, good luck . . . and keep me posted."

When Sally hung up, Becky—with raised eyebrows—asked, "Is *she* helping you?"

"I think so. Pax sees the admiral Monday morning."

"Is he here?"

"Nobody knows."

"Men are so damned dumb. Why should Pax *assume* that you're pissed off? You're not, are you?"

Sally pondered the question a couple of beats, and shook her head. "Not too much, I guess. Some at him; some at her; maybe even some at me."

The phone jangled. "Maybe it's Pax," Becky said.

"Uh-uh," Sally said and picked it up. "Hello."

"It's me, Wilma. Pax called this morning—said he'd fly in from San Francisco tomorrow. He wanted to know how it was going with the boys."

"That was nice of him."

Becky's right-on—too damned dumb to be turned loose.

"I guess he'll need his car."

"Says he doesn't; said he'd call you after taking care of his business with the admiral on Monday."

"He told *you* to tell me that?"

"No, he didn't. But he said there was no point in talking to you until he knew where he stood with the navy."

Sally fought hard to keep her voice even. "In other words, I can't stand by him until he doesn't *need* me to. That must come from being an orphan."

"Maybe. I hadn't thought of that. Anyway, we know where he is, and he knows where we are. I have to run now; see you sometime. Bye."

Next morning at nine-thirty, Sally parked Pax's Corvette in front of a white stucco house two blocks east of La Jolla Boulevard—not far from The Cove. She'd driven by the house twice already, checking out the address Ann Dodd had given her. Sally recognized the Olds in the driveway; seeing it again accelerated her heart beat.

She marched up the sidewalk, using a sheathed umbrella as a walking stick, and pushed the doorbell. She jabbed it four more times before hearing movement from inside. The door opened a crack. Robin's canted gaze peeped out. "You again! I want you outta here. Now! If you *don't* leave, I'm calling the police."

The door would have slammed, except for the umbrella thrust into the jamb. Sally struggled to keep it there. "Robin, if I do leave, I'm driving to the ferry and going straight to your dad's office. I'll tell him *why* Pax is on the way home."

"Go away!" Robin screamed.

"You got it," Sally said. A calm detachment replaced her anger as she dropped the umbrella and retraced her steps down the sidewalk. She'd played the scene over and over, the night before.

She won't let me leave; she can't!

Yet, Sally arrived curbside . . . stepped down to the street.

"Wait!" Robin called from behind the door's peekaboo crack. "Please wait." The door opened wide, and Robin—wearing a pink jumpsuit—picked up the umbrella. "I'm sorry; believe me, I couldn't be sorrier. Won't you please come inside?"

Chapter 26—LOOKING OVER THE EDGE

Pax parked his rented Plymouth behind Hacksaw's—what *used* to be Hacksaw's, he reminded himself—red VW bug in front of the small house in La Jolla's Bird Rock section. Wilma waved from the front door; two Grayson boys tumbled from the front porch and ran to him. "Mister Langford! Swing us around! Swing us around!" both boys yelled.

"Not in his uniform, boys," Wilma called.

"When we get back," Pax said. "I promise."

"Ah shoot!" the older boy said.

"Ah shoot!" little brother echoed as both trailed Pax back to the porch. Pax hugged Wilma and tried not to think of the tears in her eyes. It didn't work.

"Things happen fast, don't they?" she said.

He held her by both shoulders. "How are you holding up?"

"I've no regrets, and the boys are strong . . . like their daddy. Boys, go inside with Grammy and help her with Todd. Mister Langford and I will be back in a couple of hours."

Without explanation, Wilma insisted on driving Pax in her car. The first few blocks passed quietly. Pax didn't know why Wilma had urged that he be there, insisted almost, as a *favor* she'd said.

"Thanks for coming, Pax," she said. "I want your advice on a personal matter. There's a house in Point Loma I want you to see, because I'm thinking about moving into it."

"Wilma, I don't know beans about real estate."

"Maybe not, but you certainly know math."

The empty house, overlooking San Diego Bay and the North Island Naval Air Station from a Point Loma hilltop, had Pax's full attention. "Would you buy or rent?" he asked.

"I might rent it, but I couldn't afford *to* rent it."

Pax furrowed his brow at her, but Wilma kept her gaze on the bay. When she did look at him, her mouth rounded into a small smile. "I own it, Pax; I inherited it."

"*When?*"

"A couple of weeks ago. Cecil's uncle left it to him, . . . but to *me* if Cecil had already died, which he had. And some insurance money came with it."

Pax loosed a long, low whistle. "That's great, Wilma . . . wonderful for you *and* the boys. Wow!"

"I know; that's how I feel. I love this house—always have. The navy will pay for the move, but jerking the boys from one school to another might not be the smartest thing."

Pax shrugged and pursed his lips. "On the other hand, it might help get 'em through the next couple of months. Children come tough—tougher than we think, sometimes."

"That's what I wanted to hear . . . from you," Wilma said and tapped Pax's shoulder with a soft fist.

"Okay, go for it. But seeing this house—pretty as it is—didn't require a uniform."

"We've got a quick delivery to make—won't take long."

Pax's mind shifted into high gear as Wilma drove through the gate at Fort Rosecrans Military Reservation.

A delivery? Here?

"Cecil's uncle loved San Diego, and he loved this cemetery. He talked us into becoming long-term neighbors. When Cecil's aunt died—two years ago— Uncle Fred had her cremated. He asked us to see them interred together here. Cecil and I will be in the next niche. I wanted you to be here with me to wish the three of them farewell. Your uniform's so you can salute when the bugler plays taps."

"Cecil's uncle served in the military?"

"Sorta. You ever hear of a navy captain by the name of Corky Conrad?"

Pax's head snapped around.

"Yeah, *that* one," she said and smiled. "They didn't want anyone to know, so it wouldn't look fishy when Uncle Fred signed Cecil's officer of the deck underway quals."

Pax saluted the clear, plaintive notes of taps and realized how glad he was not to be living in the Gettysburg stateroom without his Mississippi friend. Wilma drove them the length of the burial grounds. Row upon geometric row of vertical, white gravestones stood at tireless attention—some overlooking San Diego Bay and North Island, others facing the near-limitless Pacific.

"We're lucky in one regard," she said. "In a week or two it'll be hard to schedule an interment . . . when *Oriskany*'s bodies start arriving. Did you know any of the pilots who got killed?"

"I haven't seen any names, but I don't think so."

"If there is any silver lining to that tragedy, and from Cecil's death, I'd hope Crusader pilots are too scarce to be getting rid of a good one."

Pax smiled at her and patted her hand on the steering wheel. "Me, too, and thank you."

Conversation lagged as they exited Fort Rosecrans, but at the first red-light Wilma faced him. "You *know* that there are no secrets amongst navy wives, Pax. Ann Dodd told me why you're here."

He deemed it a perfect opportunity to stay quiet, so he did.

"I'm *sure* you'd never sniff around a senior officer's wife on purpose. I know that. But Cecil and Uncle Fred had *no way* to know where CAG Dengler was coming from. They both thought he'd gone over the edge. So you'll *know* that's true, I want you to have my last letter from Cecil. He told me that Uncle Fred promised that you wouldn't have a pilot board—whatever they call those things. Maybe it'll come in handy; it can't hurt." At the next stop sign, she snapped her purse open and fished the letter out for Pax.

He read while she drove. "Huh! CAG reneged on his word to Captain Conrad."

"Yeah, after he died. What a *spineless* bastard."

"Hacksaw was something else. He never said one word about carrying my side to Captain Conrad. Did Commander Dodd know about Hacksaw and Conrad?"

"I don't think so. Besides, if he did he'd have told you."

"Wilma, I was outside sick bay when they brought Hacksaw in. Captain Conrad came huffing down the passageway right after him; he must have run clear from the bridge. Now I know why. The shock must've killed him."

"Maybe. I wondered if there could've been a connection."

As they stopped in Wilma's driveway, she asked the question looking straight ahead. "What about Sally? Don't you want to see her?"

"After I see the admiral. Till then I've got both feet in the air . . . no traction."

"It'll be a long weekend. Will you come to dinner tomorrow or Sunday?"

"Thanks, gal, but I've got a lot of thinking to do; I need solo time. If things work out, though, I'd sure like a rain check."

"You've got it, no matter how things go. But before you leave, did you send me *everything* from Cecil's wallet?"

Did I hear her right?

She smiled at his confusion, but her eyes never left his.

"I don't—"

She cackled a short laugh. "I'm not questioning your honesty, Pax, but I always put a little flat package in Cecil's wallet before a deployment. I'd always tell him I didn't expect him to use it . . . but if some irresistible thing held a gun on him."

He nodded. "Yep, it was still there."

"Brand?"

"You're not a trusting soul, are you. . .? Trojan."

The smile stayed, but it hardened as tears traced her cheeks. She fished a tissue from her purse. "Sorry."

Becky's knitted brow and slack jaw lent weight to the question. "You said you'd tell her daddy she'd been sleeping with junior officers?"

Sally nodded. "At least one that I know of."

"And she *believed* you?"

"Wouldn't you?"

"I don't count. What would you have done if she hadn't called you back?"

"That wasn't an option for her; she *had* to call me back."

"I almost wish she hadn't. We'd see how far you'd really go with this *fiancée* bit."

"What do you mean bit? Pax did ask me to marry him . . . sorta."

"Okay . . . sorta. I can't understand anyone bitchy enough to tell her husband she'd been screwing someone who worked for him."

"Me neither, but we haven't been slapped around by a jealous husband, have we?"

"Did you believe that?"

"Sounded reasonable to me—almost understandable—the way she told it. Anyway, she promised she'd tell her dad what happened . . . before he talks to Pax."

"Right!" Becky said. "What makes you trust her? Did she cross her heart?"

"Yes! Because I'll be driving her to her daddy's headquarters an hour before Pax sees him Monday morning."

By Sunday evening Pax had changed his mind.

Had I known how this weekend would drag . . . well, I'd've jumped at Wilma's dinner invitation.

The solitary thinking about Monday's meeting with VADM Kimbrough had fizzled.

How the hell can I downplay the rage that drove me to scatter LSOs into the net?

Thinking about it, even walking North Island's sidewalks in broad daylight, torqued his jaws till his teeth hurt. And even as he turned the corner next to AIRPAC headquarters and stared down the street toward Kimbrough's residence—for the third time that day—he couldn't say why he was there.

Hoping for a miracle? Maybe.

He reversed course and backtracked to the BOQ.

What the hell will they do with me? I don't know squat about ships—don't wanna learn about 'em. Nor do I want to go back to the oil fields. Well . . . well, nothing. I'm not drivin' this boat. If they kick me out, they kick me out. Goodbye navy, goodbye flying, and goodbye Sally.

But this time, he couldn't even pretend "and good riddance."

Pax left a 0600 wake-up call at the desk and spent a solid hour preparing his service dress blue uniform, achieving a glass-like sheen on his black Corfam shoes. A hot shower and eight hours sleep, he thought. Didn't work out. He stared, unseeing, toward the ceiling; he stacked and shuffled excuses; he weighed—and discarded—any possible benefit of dragging in Robin's name; he tried to figure how Hacksaw's letter might be mentioned. He even counted sheep.

Sally parked her own coupe curbside at CAG Dengler's stucco house 0700 Monday morning. She hoped Robin would make good on her promise.

Telling her dad about Pax won't be easy. I sure as hell don't envy her—at least about the telling part.

The front door opened; Robin waved, threw the newspaper inside, and strode down the sidewalk. "You're damned punctual," she said and slipped into the passenger seat. "We'll be way too early."

"Maybe, but I don't trust the ferries. In Coronado, if we're ahead of schedule, I'll buy the coffee."

Robin bit her lower lip and shook her head. "I don't know how you got me to do this. I almost backed out."

It's called blackmail, but you're too nervous—and therefore unpredictable—for me to say so.

"We both want a fair shake for Pax. If his flying isn't good enough . . . so be it. But this way, neither of us will have a guilty conscience. Believe me; you're doing the right thing."

"Easy for *you* to say."

"Would it be easier if I went in with you?"

"No, it wouldn't. Not a bit easier."

A short line for the ferry assured Sally that Robin could make her 0900 appointment, so she pulled into a Coronado café parking lot. "C'mon, coffee'll do you good."

Pax shaved, donned his uniform, and decided—at 0645—to stroll around a block or two. But thirty minutes later he marched up the NAVAIRPAC headquarters front steps. He peeked into VADM Kimbrough's outer office and spied who he hoped was the flag lieutenant. "Excuse me, are you Lieutenant Harrington?"

"That's me," said the slender, black-haired lieutenant in his short-sleeved khakis with an aiguillette.

"I'm Pax Langford. Am I out of uniform?"

The flag lieutenant checked his watch. "Uniform's okay; we're in a transition period. Admiral Kimbrough'll probably be in blues, but *damn,* you're way early."

"I know, but I have nothing more important on my plate. Thought I'd . . . be available in case the admiral catches a lull in *his* schedule. Would I be in the way, sitting in that corner?"

"Not in the way, but your ass'll be numb by 1000. Go ahead; take a seat."

Pax picked through several Approach magazines on a coffee table until he found the October issue, but it lay unopened on his lap. A wall opposite the corner chair absorbed his unfocused gaze. So much at stake, so many explanations to catalog, so many cogent reasons to keep flying. His thoughts ricocheted between Fort Worth's Masonic Home Orphanage and the double funeral for Brandy and little Pax. But his mental armor began cloaking any remaining vulnerabilities. He'd long since embraced any survivor's mantra: "Nothing can hurt if nothing matters."

"Lieutenant Langford!" Harrington's sharp voice made Pax aware of the previous "Lieutenant" call he'd ignored. He stood, shook his head, and checked his watch: 0750. Thirty-five minutes gone by.

"Yes?" he said.

"Admiral Kimbrough will see you now." Harrington turned and preceded Pax into the large, wood-paneled office of the West Coast's naval aviation commander.

"Admiral, Lieutenant Paxton Langford, from VF-39," Harrington said and pulled the door closed as he left the room.

Pax stopped three feet in front of the admiral's desk and stood at attention. The admiral sat without a blouse, in his white shirt—sleeve cuffs rolled back twice—and black tie. He wore black-framed reading glasses that matched wiry black and gray hair. Muscled, tanned forearms said athlete. Kimbrough glanced up and resumed scanning what Pax guessed was his evaluation board summary.

Is he keeping me at attention to get my mind right?

A vision of a blindfold and last cigarette flitted behind Pax's eyes, but the firing squad props faded . . . to be replaced by a giant meat clever.

Kimbrough stood and ambled to a window, scratching at his hairy forearms. Talking to the window he said, "Son, why the hell are you here? Chasing my LSOs off their platforms won't earn you any brownie points, but hell's fire—*an evaluation board?*" He abandoned the window and stared at Pax. "What am I missing here?"

"Admiral, I needed to land. I couldn't get it done being waved off."

"I can read, Lieutenant. What did your skipper think about that low pass?"

"I don't know for sure, Admiral, but he never seemed upset at me."

"I sure as hell can't imagine Captain Conrad forcing this thing. Was he?"

Pax could feel Hacksaw's letter to Wilma in his right pant's pocket—pressed flat against his thigh by his thumb.

Now. . .? No, not yet.

"No, sir."

"That leaves CAG Dengler and that LSO . . . Broussard. How'd you piss them off?"

The big meat clever flicked behind his eyes again; a shiver tried to get started. "I know I flew pretty low over that platform, Admiral."

The admiral returned to the desk, picked the folder up to eye-level, and dropped it. "That's in this evaluation, son; like I said, I *can* read." Kimbrough's deep baritone vibrated against Pax's throat. "I asked how you pissed off your CAG."

Shit-oh-dear! Does he know? Oh, Christ!

"Admiral, one day my skipper and I knocked a panel off Broussard's A-4, going by him supersonic."

Kimbrough shook his head. "Maybe I'm whipping a dead horse. Son, do you want to keep flying F-8s . . . in combat?"

Pax nodded. "Yes, sir, more than anything."

Kimbrough leaned onto the desk, resting on his fists, his eyes boring into Pax's. "Lieutenant, you better make me understand why the hell you're here."

"Admiral, I pissed CAG Dengler off the night it happened. He asked me if I intentionally flew that low over the platform. I leaned heavy on the truth and told him I sure as hell did. His face got red and he stomped out of our ready room, with Gator Broussard right behind. That must have *something* to do with my being here."

Kimbrough's frozen glare eased into a slight smile. His eyes sparkled. He stabbed the intercom box: "Fred, get me Commander Rankin at VF-124 on the horn." Two clicks sounded.

Kimbrough went back to the window. "We can't send you back to Gettysburg, son. Too uncomfortable for too many people. . . ."

Nothing can hurt if nothing matters. Fuck it!

The flag lieutenant's metallic voice came from the intercom: "Admiral, Commander Rankin on line two."

Kimbrough jerked his glasses off and picked up the phone. "Ted, I've got Lieutenant Langford over here in a bind. He got cross-threaded with CAG Dengler and their solution was a fuckin' evaluation board. . . ." The admiral looked closely at Pax's nametag. "That's right, Pax Langford. . . . Uh-huh. . . . No foolin'. . . ? Okay, I'm sending him over there right now, but you can't fly him until I get it ironed out with Washington. . . . Thanks, Ted." He replaced the phone and looked up. "Stand at ease, Lieutenant, and take that frown off your face. You'll be okay. We'll send a message to OP-05 today and tell 'em this evaluation was bullshit—paperwork to follow. They'll probably call us, authorizing you back into a cockpit. *Oriskany's* fire on the twenty-sixth didn't *hurt* your case. It killed three F-8 pilots and hurt a couple more."

Pax's furrowed brow relaxed. He took a bottomless breath—almost a gasp. "I'm flying, . . . sir?"

Kimbrough nodded; a small smile creased that weathered face. "Attack guys don't always understand us fighter jocks. Does CAG fly the F-8?"

"Not with us, sir. He may fly some with VF-37."

"I imagine Commander Rankin will put you in with the next carrier qualification class, get you some refresher traps, and send you the first place you're needed . . . except *Gettysburg*, of course. Now, quit wasting my time." Kimbrough half-stood and extended his hand across the desk. "Go make us proud, son."

Pax shook the admiral's hand, nodded, and headed for the door, squeezing his welling eyes shut. It almost worked. Fred Harrington looked blurry as Pax marched past—giving a firm thumbs-up to the flag lieutenant's questioning shrug.

Clear of the office and around a corner, Pax had finished blowing his nose when he saw Robin Dengler top the last step from the first floor stairwell. She saw him. "Pax?"

"Mrs. Dengler."

She stopped beside him and raised a hand to the corner of her mouth. "Did you see Dad?"

"Yes."

Her mouth hung open for an instant, her eyes wide. "What happened?"

"It's okay; Admiral Kimbrough's a great guy."

"You're going back?"

He nodded. "But not to *Gettysburg*."

"Oh, thank God. Pax, I'm so sorry this happened."

"Me, too, but it's over." He raised a casual salute toward his forehead. "Take care," he said and left the building.

Three hours later, Pax had checked into VF-124 at Miramar Naval Air Station and put his clothes away in a BOQ room.

I'll have lunch at the club, and call Sally. And I'll keep calling till I get her, invite her to dinner, and buy some flowers. Before the night's done, I'm gonna know if and when she'll marry me—the sooner the better. 'Cause by the grace of God, I'm a naval officer, flying F-8s, and my war's waiting on me.

Chapter 27—MAGNETICS

She picked up after the first ring. "Hello, this is Becky."

"Hi, Becky, . . . Pax. Is Sally there?"

"Not yet . . . probably a little after four—no later than five. How *are* you, Pax? What's happened? Have you seen the admiral? Talk to me!"

"How 'bout Bud's *MiG*? Are you as proud of him as I am? 'Course you are."

"*Answer* me, Pax. We've been going crazy. What's happened?"

"I saw Admiral Kimbrough; I'm flying F-8s and he's sending me back to sea. I called to ask Sally to dinner. Think she'll go?"

"Maybe. If you'd been in town several days without calling me, I'd say yes . . . so I could meet you at the door with a fire ax. But that's me. . . . We've worried about you. And I'm sick about Hacksaw; that must've hurt you a lot."

"I appreciate that, Becky. I'll call later . . . and thanks."

Sally's question preceded her through the doorframe: "Did he call?"

Becky glanced up from an opened magazine, her brow wrinkled. "Who?"

"Don't mess with me!"

"Wow! Give him *that* look, and he'll be *glad* to get back to war."

Sally's glare and stance brooked no nonsense. "What . . . did . . . he . . . say?"

"Said he'd call back to invite you to dinner."

"That's it?"

"He mentioned Bud's MiG."

Sally looked back and shut the front door. "Anything about talking to the admiral?"

"Yes, the admiral's sending him back to fly F-8s at sea. But we *knew* that."

Sally raised a hand to her brow. "You didn't let *on* that we knew . . . did you?"

"After your *extensive* instructions? No, Miss Banks. . . . Mrs. Banks did not spotlight your fraudulent blackmail."

"I'm sorry. I've been running nonstop, and I'm exhausted. Thanks. Maybe a quick shower will help." Sally headed for her bedroom.

Becky followed. "My mom called. She and Dad are paying for a *suite* in the Hong Kong Hilton . . . *and* my full airfare, in case I can't connect on standby. She called it their belated wedding present."

"Wow!" Sally's smile matched Becky's. "*That* makes me jealous. What a thoughtful gift."

What's the problem? She'll either say yes, or she'll say no. . . . Yeah, that's the problem. Christ! Talking to the admiral was easier.

He counted three long ring signals before she picked up. "Hello."

" . . . I've heard a lot worse hellos in my life."

"Becky said you threatened me with dinner. Is that true?"

"I'd like your company for dinner. Yes."

"Becky also said you remain employed."

"Looks like. . . . Are you hungry?"

"Yes."

"Twenty minutes."

"Okay."

Becky looked at the ceiling. "That lovey-dovey talk's making me sick to my stomach. Should I introduce you two when he gets here?"

"We'll do fine, thank you."

"Why don't we have a big glass of wine while you're waiting?"

Sally cocked her head, considering, and started for the kitchen. "Great idea. Red or white?"

They heard the car door slam, but neither one moved. "My God," Becky said and put a hand on Sally's, "Your face blushed tomato-red."

"You let him in," Sally said and rushed from the room. But before Becky had taken two steps, Sally came back. "Never mind; I'll do it." She got to the door and pulled it open as soon as he knocked.

Pax stood rooted in a blue sweater and matching cords, not breathing.

"You've lost weight," she said and reached for his hand—which she missed. Because he closed their separation and wrapped her in hungry arms, letting loose a near-sob at her neck . . . and another.

Becky had come from the kitchen, but reversed course at Pax's first guttural tribute and returned to the breakfast table.

After the initial shock, Sally relaxed and hugged him back, but it didn't count in the overall squeeze. He had her pressed flat against him, and he wasn't letting up any.

"I can't breathe," she said.

"Sorry." Pax glanced away, swiping at his eyes with a handkerchief, as Sally straightened a green sweater over her dark slacks and led him toward the kitchen.

"Damn!" Becky said. "If I'd known you two were gonna wrestle, I'd've gone to a movie."

"Hi, Becky," Pax said. "Sorry 'bout that. Don't know what came over me."

"Sorry, *hell*, I hope Bud knows that move. At least I do—now. And I'll put it on him in *Hong Kong* . . . in four more days."

"You're meeting him?" Pax asked.

Becky nodded. "Yep."

Sally hefted car keys on her palm. "White Knight or what you came in?"

"Let the Knight rest; they don't charge me mileage. Good for you, Becky. Give Bud my best, and tell him to get another one."

At the car he remembered the flowers and reached into the back seat. "I brought these for you . . . and forgot 'em."

She opened the box of long-stemmed red roses. "Thank you. I should get them into some water."

"No. Please don't. Not now. I don't want you where I can't touch you."

Sally said nothing, but put the flowers in the back seat and slid next to him. She leaned her head on his shoulder and rested a hand on his thigh. That loosed the stored lightning. Sally twisted around, ending up in both his arms. They kissed hello; they kissed they'd missed each other. They kissed as blood-drained brains demanded they must. Then his elbow . . . her shoulder . . . his knee . . . her head—some damned thing—honked the horn. And startled, they both broke into what became hysterical laughter.

"I think I've worked up an appetite," she said.

"Amen to that, but are you *hungry*?" They both chortled again and took several deep breaths. The house front door opened, and Becky took a couple of steps out onto the porch. Sally rolled down her steamed-up window.

"Were you all wanting curb service?" Becky called.

"No, Pax was showing me how all the gadgets work."

"Ri-i-i-ight . . . gadget . . . got it," Becky said and went back into the house.

From close by his side, Sally directed him to a neighborhood Italian restaurant in Point Loma. Each time she traced his neck with a fingernail or rested a hand on his thigh, Pax felt the small hairs under her touch flow with the motions of her hand. And he heard crackles of static electricity discharging behind that touch. A near-full moon smiled down, warming the sky. "What was the evaluation board about?" she asked.

"Not tonight. I'll tell you everything, sometime, but not tonight."

They both ordered Chianti and held hands across the small, round table. He moved the lighted candle aside. "On the way to your place tonight I kept telling myself that whatever happened would be okay—I'd handle it. But when you opened the door I knew I'd been lying. I've been in love with you longer than I've known. I need you; I want you to be my wife . . . for always. Will you marry me?"

"When?"

"Is that a *yes*?"

"That's a *when*."

"Yesterday . . . now . . . soon as we can get to Vegas, or whenever *you* say. You know I've been married before. The details belong to you. But know I've gotta go back, and it could be soon."

The waiter came with menus and wine.

Pax tilted his head and squeezed her hands.

"What would you think if I wanted to keep working?"

"As a stew?"

"Yes, like Becky's been doing. I don't fancy being in the officer's wives club or even being in the O-club when you're not here."

"Is *that* a yes?"

"That was a question and a statement. How do you feel about my working until you're through with these deployments?"

"Even when I'm here . . . between deployments?"

"Yes, unless I get pregnant or something and have to quit."

"If that's what you want to do. Is *that* a yes?"

Sally pulled a hand free and drank some wine. "Will you call my dad? I don't want to pull another *Bud and Becky* on my folks."

"I'll call the president and the pope, if it'll earn me a *yes*."

"It *could* work out. Becky leaves Wednesday for nine days. There are a lot worse honeymoons than a week in San Diego."

The waiter returned and stood waiting.

Pax looked up. "Sir, would you please ask this beautiful lady if she will marry me?"

The waiter gave Pax a questioning look, glanced at Sally, and back to Pax.

"But of course," he said. He faced Sally and dropped to one knee.

"Enough!" she said. "The answer's *yes*."

They laughed, they ordered, they ate, and their eyes danced. He raised one of Sally's hands to his mouth and kissed her fingertips. "I'll call your dad tomorrow."

"After that, I'll call Mom."

"I'm sure I can get a few days off before jumping into a cockpit again. We *could* take Becky to the airport on Wednesday, and drive straight to Vegas? At least that's an option."

"Let's see how the calls go."

CDR Rankin approved three day's leave for Pax, but told him to make sure to leave phone numbers where he could be reached. "We don't know when or where the first gap will come, but as soon as OP-05 gives us a green light . . . you're first in line to fill it. So stay on a short leash. Understand?"

Pax waited until 1500 to call Olathe, hoping to catch Banks before he left the office. The captain answered his own phone. "Captain Banks."

"Hello, Captain, this is Pax Langford."

"Hi, Pax, what's happened out there?"

"Well, you know about Bud's MiG. And Admiral Kimbrough decided to give *me* another chance."

"That's good news; I'm glad to hear it. Bud'll be glad . . . and Sally, too, I'd imagine."

Pax swallowed. "That's why I'm calling. I'm in love with Sally and I want to marry her."

The silence spanned several long beats, but Pax had nothing to add.

The captain cleared his throat. "Pax, . . . I expect that'd be up to Sally."

"Sally wouldn't give me a firm yes until I talked to you. So we're talking."

"*When* are we talking about?"

"I'm thinking Vegas, maybe tomorrow, because I'm first in line as a ready replacement. If you don't have any objections, Sally'll be calling her mom this evening."

"Pax, *I* don't know you well enough to trust you with my daughter's future. . . . But I do know my daughter well enough to trust her judgment. If she says okay, we'll welcome you into the family. And I speak for her mom, as well."

"Thank you, Captain. My best to Mrs. Banks. Goodbye."

Sally's incredulous query ended on a high note. "He said *what?*"

"What I said. But he did add that he knew you well enough to rely on your judgment."

"That's nice."

"Good enough for me. Are you going to call your mom?"

"I called earlier . . . couldn't wait. Don't you know *their* conversation would be fun to hear?"

"What'd your mom say?"

"She thought the admiral made a smart decision, but only time could tell about mine."

"Fair enough. Have you told Becky yet?"

"This is Becky's last night; may I invite her to come to dinner with us?"

"Sure. Twenty minutes."

"Okay."

The sky-blue Plymouth had its nose pointed toward Las Vegas. Two smiles in the front seat stretched wide, while two hands—sometimes three—intertwined, squeezed, and caressed. "What are you thinking?" she asked.

"To tell you the truth, I'm a little worried."

"About what?"

"What if I find out you're a blonde?"

She grunted and dug a thumb into his ribs.

"Whoa!" he said and laughed. "That'd be a serious shock."

"You shouldn't have teased Becky like you did."

"What makes you think I was teasing? I didn't want her to be disappointed or too demanding. History shows that MiG-killers—without exception—have been impotent for over a month. They taught us those things . . . so we wouldn't panic."

Sally twisted around to face him. "In a case like that, I hope you never get a MiG."

"Not to worry. I'll get mine early in the deployment; you'll never know the difference."

"Are you disappointed that my folks aren't coming?"

"The one member of your family that I need there will be there."

She held his right hand in both of hers. "Pax, I'll make a deal with you."

"Sorry, I'm not interested in platonic relationships."

"Be serious. I know you were married. . . . You don't know much about me. If you have any questions you'd like to ask me . . . about anything . . . ask them now. I'll answer them truthfully, from now till we get to Vegas. After that, don't ask."

"Sweet girl, you checked our baggage with that statement, and I'll never be back to claim any. I couldn't love you any more, and I'll never love you any less."

She nestled into his side and leaned her head on his shoulder. "Why won't you tell me where we're staying?"

"Because I don't know."

She straightened to look at him. "Aren't you worried that we'll need reservations?"

"Nope. We'll have reservations, and I'm sure we'll like them."

"How do you *know*?"

"Trust me."

"Okay, but we have to get the license before midnight; that's when the courthouse closes. We can get married anywhere in town . . . at any time."

They stopped for gas on the edge of town, where Pax made a phone call. He frowned and shook his head walking back to the car. "Damn!" he said and slammed the steering wheel.

"What? No rooms?"

"That's not it."

"W*hat*?"

"You'll see. We're close."

"We've *got* a room?"

"Sorta. Where's the court house; we'll get the license first."

She showed him, and the two couples waiting ahead of them didn't waste any time. Fifteen minutes later they were pulling up in front of the Dunes.

"We're staying here?" she asked and leaned forward looking toward the top of the hotel.

He nodded and smiled at her. "If it's okay with you."

Pax handed the keys to a valet. "We're checking in; name's Langford. Please bring everything."

Holding hands, they stopped at the front desk. "We have reservations," Pax said. "Lieutenant and Mrs. Langford."

"Is that Paxton Langford?" the clerk asked.

Pax nodded and Sally squeezed his hand.

"We have you and Mrs. Langford in a honeymoon suite for three nights, sir. Your room and meals are complimentary, Lieutenant." The clerk raised a hand, snapped his fingers at the waiting bellboy and handed him two keys. "David, please show Lieutenant and Mrs. Langford to their suite."

Sally's pull slowed Pax a few yards behind the bellboy and their luggage. "Honeymoon suite? Complimentary? What's going on here?"

"I didn't know it would be for three nights, and I didn't know it would be free. But it doesn't surprise me. Remind me to tell you the story sometime."

"Humph! You can count on it."

Bellboy David opened their 8th floor door and motioned them through. Both their mouths dropped open, even as they looked from a large window overlooking downtown and back at each other. The sitting room (with flowers and a fruit-bowl), a huge bedroom, and two large bathrooms earned David his customary honeymooners' sawbuck tip.

"Nice," she said and kissed him.

"How does this sound?" he said. "I'll call for the next opening in the chapel here, and make dinner reservations for right after. Okay?"

"You sound like you've done this before."

"Not too many times, but if you kiss me again—like that—well, things might get out of order."

Sally laughed and left the room. "While you're arranging our life," she called over a shoulder, "I'm taking a shower."

Pax's arranging took little time. The check-in clerk floored him. "Yes, sir, Lieutenant. We have two fifteen minute blocks set aside for you in the chapel and two dinner reservation times immediately after. The first chapel time is 7:45, the second at 8:45 . . . your choice. Do you have your license? And will you have any witnesses?"

Pax looked at his watch: 7:03. "We need witnesses; we have the license; and give us the 7:45 slot with an 8:00 o'clock dinner reservation. Do you have the preacher *and* the witnesses, and what does it cost?"

The clerk told him, and he told Sally to shake a leg . . . that they were getting married in forty minutes. He placed one more quick call before shaking his own legs.

The Sultan's Table maître d seated them near the parquet dance floor, and an instant later the sommelier placed an iced champagne cooler by their table. In response to Pax's questioning look: "Compliments of the Sultan's Table . . . for the newlyweds."

Pax raised his glass. "To my beautiful bride. Do you feel married?"

"I feel *legal* . . . and happy. Ask me about *married* in the morning. Now tell me: how are we *getting* this treatment? Who do you know?"

Their waiter interrupted, but at least they didn't have to read anything. The proffered evening's special—hot seafood cocktail, butterflied filets, and early peas in an artichoke heart—sounded good to them both.

He reached across the small table and held both her hands. "You've made my life, Sally. I'm so proud that you're my wife. You've no idea."

"Remind me, please. As soon as we get to the room I want to call my folks."

"Good idea. I'll try to remember."

"*Now*. Who do you know that's responsible for this?"

The waiter returned with their appetizers. Aroma and curiosity, followed by appetite, delayed further conversation. About mid-main-course, lights dimmed, and an amplified voice announced, "Ladies and gentlemen, the Dunes and the Sultan's Table are proud to present from Mexico City, the Magic Violins of Villa Fontana."

From each quadrant, electrifying violin notes filled the two-level dining room, while a dozen spotlights zoomed their beams rapidly in zigzag patterns across opposite walls. In unison, however, each powerful, concentrated beam settled on one of twelve tuxedoed violinists and stayed on its particular slick-back-haired musician as he promenaded between tables serving up his enticing notes. Sally's eyes matched the moment as she traced the back of Pax's hand with a fingernail. Near show's end, three of the violinists gathered at Pax and Sally's table and delivered a spellbinding rendition of "The Wedding Waltz." Their last note and deep bow received explosive applause from the capacity crowd of diners. He and Sally both wiped their eyes. If Pax knew any one thing, he knew that the image of Sally's face, as she watched those musicians, would remain etched in his memory forever.

They chose to skip dessert. Pax signed the check and left a ten-spot on the table. Along with their key, the clerk handed Pax a telephone message. He glanced at it, slipped it into a pocket, and joined Sally at the elevators. At their door, Pax said, "Shh. Stand back." He put an ear to the door, listened, nodded, unlocked and opened it.

Sally's brow furrowed. "What?"

"Sounds like mice," he said. "I'd better carry you in . . . in case." He swept her off her feet and over the threshold. When he put her down they kissed, but he broke it off. His voice came husky. "If you want to call home, you'd better do it now."

"Do you mind?"

"Of course not."

Sally smiled throughout the call, but tears traced her cheeks. She handed the phone to Pax.

"Hello," he said.

"Congratulations, Pax," Banks said, "and welcome to the family. Sounds like everything's going well. Babs says welcome, too, but she can't talk right now."

"I understand, sir. Don't worry about anything. I'll take good care of your daughter . . . even when I'm not here."

"Have you heard something?"

"Yes, sir."

"Soon?"

"Very."

"*You* be careful, and don't *you* worry, because we'll be here for her."

"I know that, and it makes it easier . . . some."

"Does she know?"

"No."

"Oh-h-h, shit. Good luck, son."

The dial tone told Pax he should hang up.

Sally emerged from a bathroom with a hand towel over her eyes. "Isn't that awful? I don't know what makes me tear up like that. I couldn't be happier," she said and put the towel back to her eyes and sobbed.

"Well, for goodness' sakes, hon," he said and led her to a chair, where he pulled her down onto his lap and wrapped his arms around her.

She straightened, looked into his eyes. "You know, I had no idea we were going to do this until yesterday," she shook her head, "and I don't have a diaphragm."

Pax fought all the evil gods of darkness to keep from smiling at her wide eyes and trembling lips, but he successfully did so. "Don't worry; it's okay."

She deadpanned, "I should have known a *doctor* would be prepared."

"You wouldn't be reclaiming any of that desert baggage we checked, would you, Mrs. Langford?"

"Ooh, say that again; I like the way it sounds."

"You wouldn't be—"

"Not the *whole* thing. Mrs. Langford. Call me Mrs. Langford again. . . . Okay, that slipped out; I couldn't help it. I won't do it again."

"I'm going to brush my teeth, turn out the lights, and pull those drapes wide open. We might not get a better chance to watch Vegas at night."

And he did that, and waited in bed for her while trying to decide when to tell her that this was their last night. Message orders were being processed in San Diego at that very moment, directing his MAC flight departure from March AFB, Thursday midnight—in 25-hours. CDR Rankin wanted him at the squadron with his gear no later than noon.

The shaft of bathroom light silhouetted his nude bride, before she flicked it off. She took tentative steps, hands extended in front of herself, feeling for the bed. "Those downtown lights must burn a lot of juice."

"They're worth every penny it takes. You can't *imagine* how beautiful you are in their glow."

"Brr, I'm cold," she said.

He fixed that.

A while later, she whispered, "I may be getting cold again."

Doctor Langford administered a stronger formula, but a similar remedy.

He'd shaved, showered, and started to get dressed . . . but after donning his boxer shorts he stopped. And took a deep breath. He padded bedside and watched the rhythmic rise and fall of the chin-tucked sheet, which covered—but couldn't conceal—her siren's lure. He lifted the sheet enough to kiss her neck. "Good morning, hon. We'd better grab some breakfast, because—"

"Ooh!" She covered her mouth and asked, "What time is it?"

"Five o'clock."

"In the morning? Five o'clock in the *morning?*"

"Uh-huh. We're headed back to San Diego."

"Why? And who says so?"

He turned on the bedside lamp and handed her the bad-news-laden telephone slip. She sat up . . . sheet be damned . . . and read the vile notification.

She looked up. "You have *got* to be shitting me."

"Nope. I wish it were a joke, but if so, it would be in damned poor taste."

"Sit yourself down right here, while I brush my teeth. I feel a cold front passing through."

It was a bad one and took half an hour to remedy.

"We may have missed breakfast," Pax said.

"Good enough. I can eat tomorrow . . . and so can you. It'll take me five minutes to pack. Go ahead and call for the bellboy if you want."

Chapter 28—AN EAR FOR BUGLES

They drove through Barstow as the sun yawned clear of the horizon. Sally lifted her head from his shoulder. "You want an apple?"

"Okay."

They alternated bites until the concave core remained.

"An orange?"

"Okay."

She peeled it and pulled apart sections to hold in front of his mouth. She ate each third piece. Without asking, she peeled and fed him alternating bites of a banana. "We make a pretty good team," she said, "me peeling, you eating. What? Why are you smiling?"

"I'm smiling because you make me happy, Mrs. Langford."

She wiped around his mouth with a tissue and dabbed at her own. "You said you'd tell me; I'm ready to listen."

He looked sideways at her. "About what?"

"Who paid for our room and dinner, and why'd they treat us like we were special?"

"We're honeymooners. That's their gig . . . treating people *special*."

She slid close to him and put a knuckle against his ribs. Her calm, deliberate voice promised violence. "Bud's not here to confirm this, but believe me . . . I can dig into your rib hard enough to make you scream and kick your shoes off. I ask you again: who paid?"

"I'm not sure—"

She increased the pressure.

He twisted away from the knuckle. "Wait! Dammit! I know who got the reservation, but I don't know *for sure* who paid."

She twisted the knuckle in front of his face, and her Peter Lorre imitation—which must have taken lots of practice—couldn't have surprised him more. "Tell me everything. Don't make me ask again."

"A big, black bodyguard arranged for that room. He *might* have paid for it, but I suspect his boss did. . . ." Pax glanced at her questioning face. She faked spitting on that twisting knuckle.

"His boss was—and is—*big* in Vegas. The boss, his sons, and the bodyguard showed up at a ranch I was working on in Arizona one summer. They and a few other hands from a ranch in Montana came to collect a herd of 3,700 near-yearlings for a gambling debt. It was late spring roundup in . . . let's see . . . 1950; I was 16-years-old.

"Long story short, none of the cowboys—who were white—wanted to work with this black bodyguard. We were branding in a corral, where ropers would catch and have their horses drag a calf up near the fires where two-man teams would flank 'em, so more seasoned hands could brand, cut, dehorn, dope, and inoculate them. Anyway, the white guys were in one corner . . . fixin' to quit. I walked over to the black guy, shook his hand, and hollered at the ropers to bring us a calf. They did, and that broke the deadlock."

"And he remembered you for that?"

"That wasn't everything. It's hot dusty work, and fellows trade off, so everyone gets a few minutes' blow. Nobody came our way that afternoon. We kept on working, and the ropers kept bringing us the biggest calves. The foreman's daughters kept carrying water bags to the other groups, but they wouldn't come near us.

"When that day's catch was branded, I walked over and filled a water bag and offered it to my working day's partner first. He looked at me, took it and drank his fill, and so did I. A few days later, after we'd loaded the herd on a train, the boss, his sons, and the bodyguard were loading their car for Vegas. The big man sidled up to me and shook hands; I could feel something in his big palm. 'Mister Pax,' he said, 'I stays with the boss in Vegas. If you ever need anything—I mean anything—call me at this number.' He'd given me a card with his name and number on it. I'd always kept it, but till now . . . well, I'd never even considered using it."

"Did he remember you?"

"I guess he did, but I didn't talk to him. I left a message with a woman. When we got to Vegas, she told me where we'd be staying."

Sally kissed his cheek. "He sounds like a nice man."

"Uh-uh. He's a dependable man, but a dangerous one."

"Couldn't the same thing be said of you?"

"Not by you, sweet thing . . . not by you."

She stretched and yawned . . . which made him yawn. "I'm feeling a little chilly again," she said.

He patted her leg but kept his eyes on the road. "Turn on the heater."

"Humph. Does that mean the honeymoon's over?"

"No, it means I'll be damned lucky to have my stuff at the squadron by noon."

She snuggled close again, rested her head against his shoulder. "Tell me why CAG wanted you gone—I mean how he justified it."

He gave her a short, sterile recap of his last flight. As he talked, she inched the collar of his golf-shirt down and circled the still-pink skin with a finger.

"*Did* you fly too low over the LSOs?"

"*They* thought so; that's what counted."

"What would they have said had you ejected as soon as things went black?"

"They would have asked me if I tried the RAT—ram air turbine." Her face remained blank. "The emergency generator," he added.

"But you *did* that."

"Yeah, but they would've asked."

"Could that happen again?"

"God, I hope not."

"Me, too."

The timing looked too close to chance making it. He drove straight to the squadron and jogged up to the duty office.

The JOOD pointed down the passageway. "Stick your head in the skipper's office, Lieutenant. He asked about you a couple of minutes ago."

As soon as CDR Rankin saw Pax, he waved him into his office. "Come in and shut the door. I'm glad you got here. This is as late as we could have gotten you to March AFB using commercial airlines and the shuttle. As it worked out, we got our T-39 up. Commander Bastrop will fly you direct to March whenever you're ready."

Pax, standing in front of Rankin's desk, asked, "Do we know where I'm going?"

Rankin threw back his head and let loose a couple of big guffaws. "Things movin' a bit rapid for you, kid? You're going to VF-10, in CVW-10, in USS *Grant* (CVA-40). By getting you right back in-theater, they can bounce you a couple of periods at Cubi Point, give you a couple of day traps, and a night one, which'll get you current and legal—without waitin' here for the next CARQUAL period. What do you think?"

"I need two hours to pack and turn in a rental car. I have a brand new wife who'll need to get an ID card . . . sometime after I'm gone."

"Done! I'll tell Bastrop to be ready by 1500. You tell your wife how to get up to our admin office; they'll be expecting her. One other thing, and I'm telling you this because it happened. Commander Austin, your new CO, sent me a message saying he didn't want you, that he'd been talking to CAG Dengler in Cubi. I sent him a zinger back and said you were coming anyway . . . that if he wanted to take Dengler's evaluation over Admiral Kimbrough's, to please send his next message to the admiral. You won't have any problem with him. He's fair; he got bum dope. Your orders and records are waiting for you in admin." Rankin stood and offered his hand. "Tear 'em a new ass out there."

Sally watched in the BOQ, as he packed his stuff and put on a short-sleeved khaki uniform. He checked out, and they dropped his gear at the squadron. From her place, she followed him in their Corvette to Lindbergh Field, where he turned in the Plymouth. She stayed behind the wheel when he emerged from the terminal. And he wasn't too surprised when she veered from the freeway toward her place again. "The navy can spare you for another thirty minutes," she said. "I can't . . . or at least I won't."

"Well, stop by a drug store."

Damn it's good to be married again.

He stopped next to the hangar at 1500—straight up. Her grip on his hand tightened. "When'll you be back?"

His brow furrowed. "I don't know; I didn't ask. You can park here when you come for an ID card. They'll give you my mailing address in admin. I'll write you the particulars as soon as I know them. I love you, Mrs. Paxton Langford."

They hugged and kissed in front of the car. She looked up into his eyes. "In case you're interested, I feel well married and couldn't be happier."

"Me, too," he said, stroked her cheek with the back of a hand, and walked toward the hangar.

A petty officer first class yeoman handed Pax a thick Manila envelope. "Lieutenant, the dispensary didn't have your health record; same with dental. Your orders, pay record, personal record, flight voucher, and a VF-10 officer roster and lineal list are in the packet. We put a red arrow where you fit; you're the senior lieutenant."

Pax flipped the locks on his briefcase and pointed inside. "I have my health and dental records. Thank you for the roster; that was thoughtful. I appreciate it."

A flight-suited CDR leaned in the admin door. "Might you be the package for March Air Force Base, Lieutenant?"

"Yes, sir, Commander. I've got some bags in the JOOD office to pick up."

"No you don't. They're in the plane, and I've already filed. What say we get airborne?"

Pax was alone in the passenger compartment. His two parachute bags, an overstuffed hang-up bag, and a beat-up briefcase seemed paltry enough warchest to make him wonder if he had everything. Upon reflection, he guessed he did. But more to the point, a warm feeling settled in . . . knowing he had a damned good reason to make it back home.

Which kinda offsets knowin' MiGs are a small part of Vietnam's challenges.

The first Gettysburg officers' boat departed for the Kowloon pier at 1330. CAG Dengler beckoned for CDR Dodd to join him between the fore and aft cabin, alongside the coxswain. "You'll be glad to hear," CAG said, "that Langford got an up in San Diego. He's ordered to VF-10 in Grant." Dodd said not a word. "You don't have any comment?"

"None that you'd care to hear."

CAG Dengler looked away, staring toward the towering buildings of Victoria. Skipper Dodd resumed his seat in the aft cabin, where he leaned toward Camp Brogan. "CAG said Pax got an up from Admiral Kimbrough. He's headed for VF-10."

"In Grant ?"

Dodd raised a thumb.

"That's good news," Brogan said.

"Is Bud Banks aboard?" Dodd asked and pointed toward the forward cabin. "He'd like to know."

"Yeah, he's up front, but you don't want to get between him and the Hilton Hotel. Becky's waiting on him there, and he's wearing track shoes."

"Not a bad way to start your first combat deployment, huh? Bag a MiG and meet your wife in Hong Kong."

"I guess," Brogan said and shrugged, "but tell me . . . what the hell can he do for an encore?"

"I *suppose* they'd both settle for him being in the fly-off when we get back home. That's my goal for everyone." Dodd's jaw muscles tightened as he looked away, but he continued, in a whisper, "I imagine Hacksaw and Wilma would've settled for that."

EPILOGUE

A popular turn of events seldom escapes claims from several quarters. Pax's good fortune differed little from the norm. Skipper Dodd knew in his heart that Turner Banks—at Dodd's behest—pulled some strings with VADM Kimbrough. Wilma Grayson knew in her heart that Hacksaw's last letter tilted the decision. While Sally Banks, in her heart, felt that her bluff with Robin Dengler made the difference.

Truth be told, *Oriskany*'s fire, which killed three and injured two more F-8 pilots, counted some. Even Fred Harrington's passing of Dodd's opinions to Kimbrough contributed . . . some. But human nature, that old reliable linchpin, might have played its part as well. As VADM John Kimbrough would tell his daughter, soon after her downstream divorce: "I *never* knew what you ever saw in that fella."

The single questioning niggle in Kimbrough's mind that 10-31-66 Monday morning, after he'd talked to that Lieutenant Langford: Why in the world would Robin drive clear to North Island, even ride the ferry, to invite him and his wife to dinner?

Printed in the United States
33308LVS00004B/55-306